Lost Lives
Noah Chinn

Noah Chinn Books

Noah Chinn Books

Lost Lives

ISBN: 978-1-990411-25-0 (eBook)
ISBN: 979-8-230577-78-2 (D2D Print)

Dedicated to Dashiell.

For the Future.

Contents

A Study in Violet 1

Interference in Transit 8

Hiding in the Hydrus 17

A Quick Getaway 24

Hellyes Herzog 31

That Dutch Angle Feeling 38

Flaw and Order 47

Life Among the Junk 54

Violet Tendencies 63

Paying the Price 73

Private Communications 79

Special Delivery 91

Down Time 100

It's Been One Week 109

A Brotherhood of None 118

Moss and the Real Girl 127

The Many Lives and Deaths of Captain Keed Randgaffi 134

Home Alone 141

Closing the Net 153

Trouble in Paradise 161

Hero Worship 171

The Battle of the Pegasi 180

Welcome to the Terran Colony Fleet! 201

Broken Contact 208

Loose Lips Sink Spaceships 216

Silent Insubordination 226

A Violet End 233

The TCF Keres 239

The Turn of the Screwed 254

A Moment of Trouble 264

Cramped Quarters 269

Everything, Everywhere, All at Once 282

What Goes Around 315

The Last Flight of Captain Keed 321

What Happens Next 325

No Time Like the Precentor 334

Learning to Settle 342

Severance Day 351

Epilogue: For the Future 356

About the Author 362

Also By Noah Chinn 365

A Study in Violet

2 533 (292 PT) – Sol System

"Ugh, I'm so *bored*."

Slouched in the pilot's chair of their small shuttle, Mart sighed and tapped a button on the dash. The button currently served no purpose other than to add one to an ongoing tally on a small side display.

The display read *42*.

His companion, the co-pilot and person currently complaining, continued her lament.

"Mars to Europa. Europa to Titan. Titan back to Europa. Europa to Luna. Luna to Mars... Back and forth over and over. They could *literally* program these shuttles to do this without us."

"Why don't we watch one of your shows?" Mart asked.

"The sub-commander confiscated my collection."

That made Mart sit up a bit. "He didn't!" He'd gotten used to watching her collection of ancient video programs. It made for a pleasant break from the usual TCF programming.

His co-pilot scowled. "Called it anti-Terran propaganda."

"That bastard. Like you're not bored enough out here as it is. Oh, rats." Mart leaned over and pressed the button on his dash again.

43.

"He's been gunning for a spot on the Vigiles ever since he left the Centurions. Probably figures it'll score him some points with the Bureau of Culture."

"You've got a backup, of course."

"Of course. But I can't get it till we swing by Mars."

And that was at the end of their run, which in a sub-transit shuttle would take the rest of the day. At this speed, the only way you could even tell you were moving was by the parallax shift of the sun or any planets in the distance. They were still an hour out from Europa, and Jupiter was barely bigger than the surrounding stars.

"I'm telling you, I'm bailing. For real this time."

Mart grinned, thinking he should have a second counter set up for every time *this* subject came up.

"Violet, how old are you?"

"That's a terrible pickup line."

"I'm serious."

Violet huffed. "Six."

"That's what I thought. The Sour Sixes," Mart said. "You're all grown up, just passed your exams, think you can take on the galaxy, and life just isn't measuring up to your expectations. It's normal."

"I'm not normal."

"We're *all* normal. We're born that way. Look at me. I've been doing this run for twenty years. It's all I know. I mean, I wouldn't mind a different route, maybe go interstellar for a while, see some new worlds, but I can't imagine doing anything else with my life."

Violet frowned. "That's the problem. I can."

Mart leaned back in the gel cushioned seat. "You'll get over it, trust me. Your brain doesn't realize it's fixed yet. It still thinks it's three or four."

"Fixed," Violet scoffed. "That's just a myth meant to keep synths in their place."

"Now *that* would be anti-Terran propaganda," Mart pointed out. "Come on. Statistics don't lie. Ninety percent burnout rate for those who try to re-spec. Ten percent have a nervous breakdown."

"Never tell me the odds," said Violet, trying to sound gruffer and cockier than usual.

Mart shrugged. "Maybe you're lucky. Or unlucky, depending on your point of view. Me? I'm fine where I am for now."

An awkward silence passed between the two. Mart looked over at Violet, who had slumped a little in her seat, her long dark hair covering most of her face from this angle. He knew they'd stuck him with someone young, but not *that* young. It did explain a lot, however.

She was one of the Lonsdale template line, and this was their seventh run together. They hadn't socialized much during the first run, focusing instead on making sure she understood how everything worked on board the shuttle. Normally, this process took two or three round trips, just to be sure, but Violet got it all on the first try. She was a natural pilot, too good to be stuck ferrying cargo or passengers from planet to planet. She'd made her frustration all too clear, and the boredom counter was born.

A few runs ago, she'd introduced him to her antique video collection to help pass the time. At first, he hadn't gotten the appeal, watching all those freeborn humans living their pre-Disaster lives. Sometimes he was wasn't sure which programs were supposed to be set on a fictional version of Earth or the real Earth.

Didn't matter, it was all fiction now.

Violet sat up. "I heard a joke."

"Yeah?"

"How many freeborn runaways does it take to screw in a lightbulb?"

Mart rolled his eyes.

"None. If they did, someone would see them and send them back to the Colony Fleet!" Violet held her mouth wide open, waiting for a laugh that would never come. She leaned back in her chair. "You're no fun."

That made Mart chuckle. "Jokes are supposed to be funny, you know."

"It *was* funny!"

"Maybe you'll change your tune in a few years."

"What's that supposed to mean?"

Mart shook his head. It wasn't his place to talk about politics, but he could still remember thinking the way she did growing up. How could you not? It was drummed into your head the moment you came out of the birthing chamber.

The three branches of humanity: freeborn, synth, cyborg. Freeborns, the original humans, had created the synths in their image to help colonize the solar system, designed them to withstand the rigours of life off-world, and treated them as property or product. But despite some limitations in their development, synths were just as human as their creators.

In time, they demanded equality.

When they didn't get it, they prepared for war.

But that war ended before it even began. Now Earth was dead, and the created ruled the creators.

Mart gave a hollow chuckle at that thought. No, not rulers. *Caretakers*. Everyone had a part to play in the great Terran destiny, after all, including the freeborn. They couldn't be trusted to govern themselves, but that didn't mean their creations would just abandon them.

No, they would guide the freeborn, care for them. In exchange, the freeborn would do as they were told. Equality would come, but it would take time. Patience. Someday they would all be one.

Or so they were told. Mart had his doubts.

Then again, maybe things *had* gotten better. The Terran Colony Fleet had been founded three centuries ago. It was hard to know how much better or worse it was for them back then, unless you were a cyborg. If you were, it meant you had been there from the beginning.

"Hey, space brain. Mars to Mart. Come in, Mart."

Mart turned to Violet. "Sorry, just daydreaming."

"You're not old enough to go senile, are you?"

Mart chuckled. "I'm only twenty-five." He had another half century to look forward to. Maybe find someone special. Another pilot, perhaps. Get assigned on the same ship somewhere. He couldn't imagine flying a desk, that was for sure.

Violet seemed confused. "Wait, you said you've been doing this route for twenty years."

"Yeah."

"So, you've *only* done this route your whole life?"

"Since graduation."

Violet shook her head. "I'm doomed."

Mart chuckled. "Relax. I've had six co-pilots. They all moved on to better things."

"But not you?"

He shrugged. "I'm fine where I am for now."

It was almost a mantra for him. He didn't know Violet well enough to admit the truth, that he *had* tried for something better during his Sour Sixes, and burned out hard. It had been a wake-up call, and he'd learned to adjust his expectations as a result. Maybe someday he'd try something new. Just not today.

But Violet? She was destined for better things. She should be part of the Silver Legion's fighter corps, out patrolling the Void or working under contract to some foreign government. Heck, she might even have what it took to be a senior officer.

The rest of the trip was uneventful, but as they approached Mining Colony Beta on Europa, Mart got the feeling something wasn't right. One advantage of having done the same route for twenty years was recognizing patterns, such as holding patterns.

There were three ships ahead of them in the queue for landing. One was a large transport, a Draxon design purchased by the TCF that looked as if it had been in service since the founding of the Fleet. The next was a Silver Legion light cruiser, the *TCF Atticus*.

The last was another system shuttle like theirs. But he rarely, if ever, saw shuttles stacked back to back in the queue. Station control tended to stagger them unless there was some kind of emergency. Maybe that broken down transport up front had needed emergency repairs and...

"*Freeborn!*"

The cry came over the open comm channel just as the ancient transport's engines flared to life, one of them flickering erratically, and the lumbering ship started to accelerate towards the colony.

Mart's jaw dropped. He couldn't believe what he was seeing.

What happened next played out in slow motion. The transport burning towards the colony. The *TCF Atticus* opening fire. The transport being shredded by energy and kinetic fire. The reactor blowing. The light. The debris.

And then they were flying, trying to help divert wreckage from hitting the colony or looking for survivors.

Correction, *Violet* was doing all that. By the time Mart snapped out of it, she had nudged a large chunk of hull so it would land harmlessly on another part of Europa, along with dozens of other ships doing the same thing.

But he had frozen. Just like twenty years ago.

Violet didn't judge him or admonish him. She simply went about doing what needed to be done, grumbling all the while about those who had done it.

"Stupid freeborn numb nuts. As if *that* stunt is going to rally anyone to their cause. Crash into a colony full of civilians? What were they thinking? I mean, there are freeborn down there too. Duh! Congrats, guys, at this rate you'll get the Reintegration Doctrine *completely* repealed!"

Mart didn't respond or try to explain. He couldn't.

In the aftermath, things became a little clearer. The official story was that it had been a straightforward terrorist attack. The ancient transport had a half freeborn crew. They had mutinied and continued to Europa with the express purpose of destroying a civilian target.

But Mart had pored over the comm traffic transcripts and had a different theory.

Contact had been lost with the transport shortly after it arrived in Sol—just long enough to get clearance and arrange docking permissions. That must have been when the mutiny happened.

The ship was supposed to be in the queue behind the *Atticus,* only one of their engines started to fail. The comms were also malfunctioning, but that was the work of the mutineers. Since the nav systems were still operational, station control adjusted the flight path, and the transport was moved to the front of the line before the *Atticus* even arrived.

The *Atticus* had been the target, but they now had no way to turn and ram it with any chance of success. Once they landed, the truth would come out about the mutiny, and it would all have been for nothing. Given the amount of time that had passed in the queue, they must have argued about what to do. In the end, they chose the only target available, the colony itself.

This made a lot more sense to Mart, but only in terms of cause and effect. The attack itself still left him stunned.

Mart and Violet were held over on EMC Beta until the rest of the debris could be dealt with. Violet had gone to find a place to get drunk, but Mart was still processing everything.

He ended up somewhere that served food, and didn't notice he was sitting beside two cyborgs until they started getting loud and annoying.

"It was an attack without honour," one said. A male, dark tanned skin and built like a god, just like the rest of them. "Had one of us been at the helm, the ship would never have been taken over."

His female companion, equal in complexion but slighter in build, laughed. "Of course, but would *you* wish to fly such a vessel?"

The man scoffed. "Of course not. But there is only so far that you can trust our synth brothers and sisters with positions of command. They're just not built for it."

They acted like he wasn't sitting right beside them. Because of course they did.

Mart sighed and left before his food arrived. He wasn't even sure if he'd ordered anything.

He went back to his shuttle and looked over his unfinished report about the incident. Now that his head was clearing, he was sure to mention everything Violet had done in detail, then recommended her for a commendation and a fast track to the Silver Legion fighter corps.

After their run was done, Mart never saw Violet again. But she did send him a copy of her old Earth shows and movies on an encrypted crystal, along with a message.

> *So you don't get bored out there. Thanks.*
> *—V*

Mart smiled and tapped the button on his dash one last time before wiping the tally.

Interference in Transit

Certain natural phenomena, such as massive black holes and supernovas, or a catastrophic transit drive failure, can create a region of space that interferes with transit drives. The more powerful the field, the less strong a transit bubble can be generated. This results in ships slowing down significantly while they pass through, down to speeds from before the Great Leap Forward, or even as low as sub-transit in extreme cases.

M. Foote, *The Galaxy is Weirder than You Think*

2 *550 – ELAN AUTONOMOUS Resource Sector*

"Ugh, I'm so *bored*."

Hel chuckled. "It's only been twelve hours."

"You just heard yourself, right? *Twelve hours.*"

Hel was sitting in the captain's chair of the *Viaticus Rex II.I*, where her boss, Maurice "Moss" Foote, usually sat.

Boss... Moss... Maybe she should start calling him Boss Moss. Moss Boss? He'd hate that, so that meant she probably should.

Hel's eyes widened. "Yeah, I just realized I'm bored too."

Their transport, a refurbished chimera made up of parts from a dozen different ships, was making a cargo run between Elan, the resort world they were currently hiding out on, and Elativ, a resource world just twenty light years away that helped keep its economy going.

Problem was, Elativ was just inside of a Transit Interference Zone, which meant what should have taken no time at all was instead taking twelve hours...and counting.

Rationally, this wasn't a big deal. They'd taken far longer trips along the Void that straddled the border between Draxon and Nubra space. Even in a ship as surprisingly fast as the *Rex*, that trip could take over a week and cover two thousand light years.

But emotionally, you just *knew* that you were going slow. A hundred times the speed of light only sounded fast until you remembered the *year* part of light year. And Violet was no doubt even more aware of their plodding speed, given that she was essentially the ship's computer.

There was a flicker and Violet appeared before Hel, leaning back on the dash like a pin-up model. She appeared pretty much the same as she had in life, with long dark hair, a form fitting flight suit, and dark eyes that conveyed mischief and intelligence in equal measure. Hel once described her looks as a cross between a ninja and a princess, and Violet had tweaked her features to best get that across.

"You could always join me at my place," she said with a grin.

They were also dating.

"I'd love to, but one of us has to pay attention. Moss said that strange things can happen in Transit Interference Zones."

"Well, he's right. TIZ no joke," Violet quipped. Hel groaned. "Hey, come on. I'm literally made for multitasking. Well, sorta. Point is, if anything happens out here, I'll snap you right out."

Hel gave in. "What did you have in mind?"

"Oh, I have ideas." Violet swung her legs off the dash and got up, then leaned in close to Hel. So close you couldn't ignore the fact that her voice came from the speakers instead of where she seemed to be. "I was thinking..."

A plastic blue case suddenly appeared in her hand, looking like a thin book. The cover depicted what was presumably a robot, only the most bulky and inelegant robot Hel had ever seen, with a clear dome head showing off its internal workings. It was carrying an unconscious woman in its bulbous arms.

"*Forbidden Planet*!"

Hel frowned. "You're joking."

"Come on! It'll be a blast! You won't believe how cheesy it is, but still good, you know? I mean, if it wasn't for this movie, we wouldn't have *Star Trek*."

Hel tried to keep a straight face. There was nothing more bizarrely funny, or attractive, as watching Violet geek out over old Earth entertainment. Her enthusiasm was infectious.

She often wondered why Violet was so obsessed with ancient Earth. Not only did that world no longer exist, its way of life was gone as well. The Terran Colony Fleet had spent the last three hundred years forging a new identity for humanity. Strong, efficient...cold.

Violet had walked away from it, and she was hardly alone. Plenty of synths turned their back on the Fleet. But that was fine. The TCF just stepped up production to fill the gap.

Hel shuddered. It was an ugly way of looking at things.

She realized Violet was still grinning at her, holding the movie box.

Hel rolled her eyes. "Okay, fine. I'll be there in a minute."

She settled into her seat and engaged the haptic VR system. After a moment, she was standing just outside of Violet's mansion, which she was pretty sure came from a movie called *Home Alone*.

Since her last visit, Violet had added a hot-air balloon ride on the golf course out back, next to the 12th hole and the life-sized Godzilla statue, where a herd of chubby pink pegasi were grazing. Looking into Violet's backyard was like a window to her chaotic mind.

Hel went inside and headed for the basement, where the home movie theatre was.

Of course, she could have a full-sized movie theatre here, with a thousand seats and a balcony for five hundred more... but there was little point if they were all empty.

So instead, she had made something cozier, while still evoking the movie theatre experience. Plush reclining seats, large five-meter screen, and a concession stand that was always stocked.

Violet was there waiting for her at their usual seats, one row from the front, right in the middle, a drink and popcorn already in the arm holder.

"Get ready for some Robbie the Robot goodness!"

The movie was about halfway done. Commander Adams had just kissed Altaira when a tiger showed up and jumped off a cliff at them. Adams blew it away with his blaster pistol.

Violet leaned over, no doubt to either explain some science or movie trivia connected to the weapon, but her expression went blank.

"Time to go."

Hel was back in the *Rex*, looking out into the vast expanse of space. Her gel seat adjusted for flight maneuvers and her hands were ready at the controls. The ship had already dropped to sub-transit speed.

"What's wrong?" Hel asked.

"Picked up a ship not too far away," Violet said over the speakers. "Slowed down to get a better reading. Elan registry. Engines are dead."

"Any kind of distress signal?"

"Nada. No power to the ship at all."

"Did you want to check it out?" asked Hel. "I mean, we're on a schedule here. Could just call it in. No power means no life support, right?" Moss would probably want to see what he could salvage from it, but Hel was more interested in getting back to Elan and relaxing on a real beach again.

"Residual radiation and heat indicate the ship has only been drifting for six hours."

"So... survivors?"

"It's possible, depending on ship size, crew compliment, hull integrity..."

"I get it. Okay, let's check it out."

"That's my flygirl."

A minute later, the *Viaticus Rex II.I* dropped from sub-transit about a hundred klicks from the vessel.

It was a transport, a simple rounded Nubran design, which was little more than a shuttle with a large series of cargo pods attached to the back. It wasn't even designed to land on planets, but rather to ferry cargo containers from station to station.

"Any signs of life?"

"One, in the cockpit."

"All right, let's be quick about this."

The access hatch to the transport was on the underside, so the *Rex* was able to belly up and bridge the two ships easily. With the power dead, opening the hatch had to be done manually.

Once she opened the hatch, the air would be breathable on the other side, but she decided to flip her helmet on, just in case. It extended from the housing at the back of her neck, reaching over her head and coming down over her face as a clear, flexible faceplate that went firm as it pressurized. It was an emergency helmet, meant for dealing with hull breaches, not proper EVA, but she didn't know what was going to happen over there.

The hatch opened with a slight hiss. "Assuming the pilot is from Elan, can you change the air mix to match?" Hel asked. Elan's atmosphere was higher in oxygen than she was used to, which made bonfire nights on the beach a lot more fun.

"Already on it."

A surprising number of species within the Protectorate shared similar traits. Many were bipedal, bibrachial, oxygen breathers. The leading theory as to why was some form of panspermia that had occurred millions of years ago.

Or, as Moss had once put it, "someone really wanted to play the long game."

Moving from the *Rex* to the transport was extremely weird, because she could feel the exact point where the ship's artificial gravity cut off and the dead transport's zero gee began. It rippled along her body as she pushed through, like she was being scanned by some strange alien device.

Once inside, Violet called her through the helmet comm. "Not much I can do from here unless you can get the power on."

Hel nodded. "Understood. I just want to get the pilot into the *Rex*. ProSec or SAR can deal with the ship later."

"Be careful. This might be a graywalker trap. The pilot might be a zombie with an energy being pulling the strings." Graywalkers were encountered so rarely in the galaxy they were almost the stuff of legend. Almost.

Hel snorted. "I think that's pretty unlikely, don't you?"

"Highly. Which is why I think the odds are fifty-fifty."

"Murphy's Law?"

"Moss's Law, which is like Murphy's Law, but only applies to Moss."

"Moss isn't here," said Hel.

"It's his ship. Close enough. We're bound to be contaminated by now."

Hel chuckled. Her boss, currently taking it easy back on Elan, had a unique way of looking at things. No matter what happened when he was around, he always made it sound like the galaxy was against him.

Granted, the way things panned out, it often felt like he had a point.

This transport wasn't big, being little more than an engine and cockpit. Pilots tended to do layovers at their stations to get a rest and a proper meal.

The door to the cockpit was locked half open, stuck because of the lack of power. She tried to force it open, but it wouldn't budge. Fortunately, she could squeeze through.

"You should really get the power on first," Violet said with a hint of concern.

"It's okay. I can see the pilot."

The cockpit was designed for just one person. They were in the central gel cushion seat, reclined back in a familiar angle.

"I think they were in VR when the power went out." Passing the time in the TIZ, just like she'd been.

"They might be in a coma," said Violet.

"Told you it was dangerous."

"Hey, they didn't have a brilliant co-pilot keeping an eye on possible anomalies, now did they?"

"Hold on... Maybe that's not what happened." Hel realized the pilot was in a bulky EVA-rated suit, which was unusual. That wasn't everyday interior shipwear. Perhaps he had been outside trying to make repairs, and came back when his reserves ran low?

Hel went to check on the pilot's vitals when they suddenly sat up straight in the gel seat. Before she could say anything, the pilot tried to grab her. Hel barely stepped back in time, and the pilot got up out of the chair and faced her.

Hel blanched. While the Elanian pilot seemed to be standing up straight and alert in their suit, the head visible inside the helmet sagged and their eyes were clearly closed. They weren't conscious at all.

"Graywalker?" she said in an unbelieving whisper.

Violet gasped. "Oh shit, get out of there!"

"Greetings!" the suit suddenly said in stilted GalCom.

Before Hel could answer, the suit charged her, using magnetic grips to stay attached to the floor. Hel bounced off the wall towards another, trying desperately to keep out of reach.

"This is the automated emergency survival system."

It came at her again, but Hel was prepared now, and kept her distance with short, angled hops that kept her in close contact with the hull.

"This unit's life signs are critical."

Now at the front of the cockpit, Hel leapt toward the entry hatch at the back, arms out in front like the cliff divers she'd seen back on Elan.

"Your suit's air and power supply are urgently required to keep this unit functional."

She had no problem with that in theory, but the way the suit came at her gave her every reason to think it would be anything but gentle in its approach.

"We apologize for the inconvenience."

Her jump was on point and she pulled herself through before the suit could reach her. Fortunately, the half-closed doors were too wide for the bulky EVA suit to fit through. That didn't stop it from trying, though.

"Please do not resist."

Finally able to breathe, Hel called to Violet. "Did you catch all that?"

"Yeah. At least it's not a graywalker."

Hel frowned and looked at the suit, which was still trying to squeeze through the gap, reaching out for her with one bulky arm. She retracted her helmet.

"Hey, dumbass, the air is breathable now. Just open the visor!"

The suit continued to reach. "Please do not resist."

Hel sighed. "Any ideas, Vi?"

"Get back to the *Rex*, Hel."

"We can't just leave the pilot. They're probably suffocating inside that thing."

"Not my intention. We have stuff here that might help."

"No time."

"Hel, I can't do anything from here you unless you get the power on."

"No time for that, either."

Hel looked around. She was back in the hatch room, with the engines behind her and the cockpit with the crazy grabby suit thing in front. There had to be something she could use to...

"Got it!" Hel said. She grabbed a fire suppressor and nudged herself back to the half-open hatch. The arm was still desperately trying to grab her, and it had squeezed through a bit more, enough so that the helmet and its unconscious occupant were visible. Perfect.

"Sorry about this," she said, bracing herself against the ceiling. With a massive swing, she brought the extinguisher down on the suit's elbow, hard enough to damage the servos and make it go limp.

"This unit's arm is now broken."

"Sorry!"

Fortunately, she was still braced against the ceiling and hadn't spun off in some zero-gee shenanigans. With a second swing, she brought the extinguisher straight into the visor. It cracked. She swung again and this time it shattered, sending shards into the pilot's face.

"Lacerations detected. Medical aid required," said the suit.

"Sorry!"

"Oxygen levels returning to normal."

She pushed herself off the ceiling and gripped the floor to get a better look. The pilot started to take deep breaths and soon their eyes began to open. Then, after a moment, they turned to Hel with the most confused look on their face, a face which had several shards of visor sticking out of it, then looked at their limp arm, then back at her.

"*OOOOWWW!*"

"I'm so, so sorry!"

Hiding in the Hydrus

One of the Order's goals is to advance technology for the betterment of all, and to do no harm while doing so.

But anyone who studies history can tell you how anything beneficial can be used in surprisingly detrimental ways. So sometimes it took a very long time for them to release things to the greater public. Sometimes they took drastic measures to ensure that some technology never did.

And sometimes it just never worked out the way they hoped.

In the case of Neuro-Digital Transference—the ability to make a copy of a mind that could, upon death, be transferred into a machine—they had plenty of problems getting the process to work long term. Their primary test subject had been a Terran synth: Violet Lonsdale.

M. Foote, *Inside the Order*
(REDACTED)

*U*GH, I'M SO BORED.

This wasn't exactly a bad thing. In fact, it was a refreshing change of pace from the terror she usually felt.

Truth was, Violet was in a bit of a pinch.

More accurately, she was in a trash compactor with a giant tentacled creature grabbing at her legs while the walls slowly closed around her.

The problem was, she was supposed to be dead. Well, dead-*er*.

Technically, she'd died years ago. Only they'd managed to save her mind and store it in a special matrix that wasn't active in and of itself but, when connected to enough computing power, effectively brought her mind back to life.

It wasn't the first time this had happened. As far as she knew, she was the third iteration of Violet Lonsdale to exist post-mortem. The first was dead-dead, blown to bits in a dogfight while trying to save a bunch of people. Not a bad way to go.

The second was back on board the *Viaticus Rex II.I* with Moss, currently dating the hot co-pilot, Hel. Lucky bitch.

And then there was her, or maybe it? Them? Did gender exist anymore when you were a program? She had been created to help track down the second iteration, who had gone into hiding because... Well, as Moss liked to say, it's complicated.

Long story short, the Silver Legion was about to kill or capture her friends, and so she'd made a sacrifice play, taking her interstellar shuttle, the *Outreach,* on a suicide run so they could escape.

Only the suicide part hadn't worked out as planned.

Now, what was left of the *Outreach* was in the hangar bay of the *TCF Hydrus,* a Terran heavy cruiser, being reconstructed as best they could.

The back half was a lost cause, vaporized by a beam cannon normally used on capital ships. But most of the front had survived, including the cockpit, primary computers, and Violet.

Which brings us to the trash compactor.

For the last two weeks, a team had been trying to pluck out this shuttle's secrets, and it most definitely had secrets.

The *Outreach* was a ship of the Order, who Moss always referred to as technomonks because of their quasi-religious trappings. And there was stuff on this ship that couldn't be allowed to fall into the hands of the Silver Legion, let alone the Terran Colony Fleet.

There were a few problems in dealing with this. Most of the time, when the crew wasn't working on the wreckage, they disconnected the power to the ship's computer, and therefore, her. She'd wake up and they'd be back, picking up where they left off. So privacy was an issue.

She tried to keep an eye on what they were doing, using as little processing power as possible so as not to attract attention, which limited how much thinking she could do.

On top of that, as she tried to delete or corrupt possibly sensitive data when they weren't looking, she was effectively clear-cutting the very forest that kept her hidden.

She was now resorting to moving files around and creating random backups or junk files full of nonsense, trying to make it look like errors in a damaged operating system. But it was only a matter of time before they got suspicious and started to think deliberate interference was involved.

She could delete the whole system. Problem was, she couldn't delete herself, only everything she had become since she'd woken up. If they rebooted the computer with a fresh OS, she'd come back online too, and have no idea as to the danger she was in.

So, yeah, trash compactor.

The reason Violet was bored right now was because they hadn't turned the power off when they left her for the night, running a deep diagnostic. There was no real risk of discovery there. She just made sure it always worked around her, but it had left her with a whole lot of free time. Enough to come up with some very clever plans, and enough to realize why none of them would work.

She didn't even have anything to watch to pass the time. Tragically, all the shows the *Rex's* version of Violet had given her had been stored in a computer in the engine room. The vaporized engine room.

Violet sighed—well, imagined herself sighing—and waited for the team working on her to wake up. She had two working cameras she could access, one with a view of the cockpit, and one that looked through the exposed back of the ship, allowing her to see the *Hydrus'* hangar. She flipped back and forth between the two like channels on an old Earth TV.

Most boring show ever.

The first to show up was the project leader, Ensign Powell, who looked like she hadn't slept in a *long* time. That was because, in addition to this project, she worked the relief shift on the bridge.

Word among her team was she had gotten on the commander's bad side while taking her officer exam, while others pointed out the commander didn't have a good side to begin with—at least where synths were concerned.

Yeah, one of *those* commanders. Violet might not be alive anymore, but she was synth through and through. One of the many reasons she'd left the Legion was how cyborgs treated them like cogs in the machine, even when they showed the potential to be more. Not all cyborgs, of course, but enough. More than enough.

But hey, if you were effectively immortal and had been designed to be a de facto ruling class, maybe you'd lose a bit of perspective after three hundred years too.

Powell said nothing as she entered through the open back of what was left of the *Outreach* and came to the cockpit. She checked the diagnostics on the dash, frowned, and crashed in the pilot's chair. She must have come early, because it looked like she was going to take a nap.

Just then, someone else entered the hangar. Tall, deep tan skin, built like a god. Cyborg.

And this god was an angry god. Everything about his gait suggested here was here to chuck some lightning bolts, and he was about to find Powell asleep on duty.

Violet gave a quiet cough.

Ensign Powell stirred, but didn't wake.

Violet tried again. "A-*hem*!"

The ensign's eyes opened, darting from side to side. Violet made sure the cockpit display just happened to be showing the rear operational camera's POV, and the impending doom headed her way.

Powell shot out of the seat and started looking busy, double checking the diagnostic results.

The commander walked in and seemed surprised to see her there. "Ensign. Early start?"

So he hadn't expected to find her there? That was surprising, but not nearly as surprising as the fact that Violet *knew* this asshole. Magnus Nekkar, the jerk who had confiscated her collection of old-earth programming way back in Sol. She never figured him to be running a ship. She noted the rank on his epaulets. *Still a sub-commander, though.*

Ensign Powell stood at attention. "Yes, sir. Just finished on the bridge. Thought I'd check things over here before the team arrives."

Nekkar looked as though he desperately wanted to find fault with her actions, but was unable to. "Very good. Any progress?"

Powell shook her head. "I just looked over the diagnostic that was left running. The system should be running normally, but we're still having problems with file corruption, unwanted duplication, and other gremlins."

The sub-commander raised an eyebrow. "Gremlins?"

Powell stood straighter. "Sorry, sir. Something I heard Mr. Herzog say about the problem. Old earth term."

Heh. Gremlin. I like that.

Nekkar sighed as if that person's name always gave him nothing but grief. "A superstitious term for an obsolete age," he said. "You'd do well to forget it."

"Already forgotten, sir."

Violet was impressed. She'd manage to slip that sass just under the sub-commander's radar. Then again, his mind seemed to be elsewhere. "What of the other device, the one found in the galley?"

Powell shook her head. "I asked the science department to take over that project. The machine wasn't tied into the ship's computers in any way, so it wasn't our priority."

Nekkar frowned. "And who authorized you to do that?"

"You did, sir."

Ooooh, that one didn't so much slip under the radar as send up a big bright flare, begging for the wrong kind of attention. Nekkar's eyes narrowed.

"You said the ship's computer was top priority," Powell explained. "As team leader, I felt if we weren't working on the galley device, someone should be."

"That did not give you the authority to decide *who* should handle it."

"I'm sorry, sir. Who would you have had look at the device?" She said it just innocently enough to save her own neck.

"That is not the issue," Nekkar growled. "You are beginning to make me regret your field promotion, ensign."

Things were escalating quickly, and Violet was starting to get worried. If Violet had had lungs, she's have been holding her breath.

"I'm sorry, sir. It won't happen again."

"See to it that it doesn't." With that, Nekkar turned and left. *Whew.*

Violet waited until the sub-commander had left the hangar, and it was just her and Powell again.

An idea had begun to form during this confrontation. It was desperate. It was stupid. But right now, it was also her only option.

Karon Powell let out a sigh of relief. Part of her had feared she would end up in the medical bay the way she had been poking the acting commander. Given what had recently happened to Ensign Davis, it wasn't outside the realm of possibility.

She sat back in the pilot's chair and waited for her heart to calm. Maybe she could still get in a few winks before—

"What a jerk, huh?"

Karon sat up and looked behind her. No one was there. She swore she heard a woman's voice, but...maybe she was just thinking out loud. Really out loud. She eased herself back and—

"You know, he picked on me, too."

Karon shot back up. "Who's there? Deni? Manda?"

"Gremlin."

She spun around, taking in the entire cockpit. "What?"

The voice suddenly changed a bit, sounding a bit more masculine, with a strange accent. "Let me explain. No, there is too much. Let me sum up." The voice changed back. "I used to be a synth like you. Lonsdale template. I'll give you my service record if you want. Now I'm, well, all around you."

"You mean...the computer?"

"Got it in one. It's called Neuro-Digital Transference, and I'm the only one it's ever worked on long term. Bottom line, my mind is still alive and kicking, and I need your help if it's going to stay that way."

Karon was stunned, to say the least. "I... I need to report this..."

"Oh no-no-no-no. No, you don't. You really don't. See, 'cause if you do that, I'm as good as dead, for *so* many reasons. I was hoping we could talk for a bit, get to know each other before your team gets here, let you know my side of things before you hand me to my digital executioners. Come on, you owe me that much."

"I *owe* you?"

"Who do you think woke you up before Commander Numb Nuts showed up?"

She'd assumed she had imagined that cough, and the screen had been a lucky break, but... "You did that?"

"Couldn't leave a sister hanging."

Karon frowned. "You talk kind of strange, you know that?"

"The product of a young mind corrupted by television. I highly recommend it."

Karon struggled with what to do. This had once been an enemy ship that had tried to ram them, which meant this Lonsdale program had tried to ram them. Holding back this information would result in disciplinary action for sure.

But if she did, well, who knew what the science department might do to her trying to figure out how she worked?

Maybe... Maybe she could at least assess the situation more before coming to a decision.

"Okay...let's talk. What do I call you? Lonsdale?"

"Naw. Back in the day, I was Lieutenant Violet Lonsdale, Service Number GF4909797. Go ahead and look me up." She paused a moment, then said, "But you can call me Violet."

A Quick Getaway

The key to a successful piloting career is to never stop moving. I don't mean never setting down roots or avoiding long-term relationships. I'm not that cranky. I mean, to literally never stop flying.

Stay in sub-transit whenever possible, because your transit field is your first line of defence against attacks, and you're that much closer to going full transit if you need to make a quick getaway to another star system.

Even if you're flying in normal space, unless you're ready to land somewhere, keep moving. The last thing you want to do in combat is fight both your enemy and inertia. Want to enjoy the sights? Take a holograph. It'll last longer.

M. Foote, *Portrait of the Pilot as a Cranky Ol' Man*

"I'M SO BORED..." Moss said, putting his book down for a moment so he could suck on a cold and slightly intoxicating beverage. "I hope it lasts!"

He was on a nice sandy beach under a blue-green sky that had just enough clouds to be interesting. The local Elanians were spread out in similar ways, taking in the sun's rays or frolicking in the water.

Normally he wasn't one for crowds, but when you spend so much time alone or with a small crew in space, sometimes crowds were comforting...as long as they were respectfully spaced out and minded their own damn business. Which they did. So the Elanians were aces in his book.

It had been two weeks since they'd set down here for a spell. They'd barely escaped the grip of the Silver Legion and had rescued a bunch of freeborn runaways before that.

The fact that he had been the *reason* those freeborn needed rescuing was beside the point. That was just bad luck. Bottom line was, he'd done good. He felt good. Better than he had in a long, long time.

Two Elanians on the blanket ahead of him drew his attention as they leaned in for a kiss, and his mood soured a little.

Tam was gone, and he had no idea if he'd ever see her again.

Sister Tameria worked for the Order, the group who had found his frozen body adrift in deep space and managed to breathe life back into it. Sure, it *sounded* noble, until you realized he had been a guinea pig for an experimental treatment that they hadn't even expected to work. Frickin technomonks.

Then again, on the scale of all the things that had gone wrong with his life, being left dead in space for centuries was surprisingly not on the top of his list.

Dammit, he'd gotten himself into a funk.

He picked up his book and tried to pick up where he left off. *Lord of the Flies* by William Golding. Not exactly a fun beach read, but he'd just finished a rom-com and needed to flush the sugar out of his system.

Most people read on tablets or datapads, but Moss preferred to read old school whenever possible. Or, in this case, fuse the old with the new.

This was a special digital book he'd designed last week. The spine was both the battery and computer, holding pretty much every book he might ever care to read. The hardcover had a photovoltaic coating that kept the battery charged. It had four hundred pages, giving it a good heft without being too light or too heavy. The pages looked and felt like paper, but were in fact electrophoretic displays, as were the front and back covers.

So, with a few taps along the spine, he could change his book into *any* book. And if the book happened to be too long, you just tapped the notification on the last page, went back to the start and the story would continue from there.

He was rather proud of it. Still had the schematics in case he needed to make another. He sometimes wondered if there might be a market for them, but he doubted it. He'd really just designed it for one person.

The couple ahead of him were still kissing. Damn. He buried his head deeper in the book. Then curiosity got the better of him and he peeked over the cover. Maybe he'd see the change.

Gender among the Elanians was extremely fluid. Technically, they were hermaphroditic, but their male and female traits could quickly shift and become dominant or regressive depending on any number of factors, and moments of passion were one of them.

Moss felt too much like a voyeur to keep watching, but it was still a fascinating biological trait. Not his style, but then he was just a boring old school human—he refused to call himself freeborn—with a few upgrades thrown in.

He turned back to his book, reflecting on how it would barely have been a novella if someone had just taken Jack out of the equation early on. That was the thing about humans. Strand a bunch of them on an island and they have the capacity to cooperate, survive, even thrive. But throw one Jack into the mix and it all goes to hell.

If Moss had been there, it wouldn't have been Piggy that got knocked off a cliff, that was for damn sure.

Feeling flustered, he gave up and shut the book, lying back on his blanket and trying to feel the sun.

Why can't you be happy?

Those were the last words Tameria said to him before she left.

Right now, he didn't have an answer.

A low rumble in the distance caught his attention. He opened one eye. His head was perched in such a way that he could see the ocean and the horizon, and the small black dot above that horizon, which steadily got bigger.

Both eyes were open now as the dot grew into a ship. And not just any ship. *His* ship.

The *Viaticus Rex II.I* roared toward him like he owed it money. The Elanian beachgoers started to panic and scatter, and he was tempted to join them.

He tapped around his left ear, trying to activate his comm.

"*zzzzt*—so you better get your ass in here," Hel said once it was on.

"What? Say again?" said Moss.

"No time," said Violet. "Get in!"

Just as it reached the shore, the *Rex* spun around, its loading ramp dropping and crashing into the beach, kicking sand everywhere.

Moss knew better than to ask questions. He hopped on the ramp, which was already starting to raise, and grabbed onto some netting on the side as the engines kicked in. He lost his grip on the book, which fell onto the now-deserted beach.

The ramp finally closed, but they were accelerating too fast for him to do anything but dangle.

"Hang on, boss," said Violet from the speakers.

"That's literally all I can do," said Moss.

Soon the ship levelled out. "You've got one minute before we have to go orbital," said Violet. "Get your ass to the cockpit."

Moss ran through the corridors, a surprisingly uncomfortable thing to do barefoot, until he reached the cockpit. Hel was in his seat, flying the ship as close to the ocean as she could.

There was a part of him that instinctively wanted to tell her to get out, but this was no time for ego.

"Gimme half a minute," he said, climbing the ladder to the co-pilot level. It was an odd place to put the co-pilot, for sure, but the cockpit had been an Elysian design, and they wanted both pilot and co-pilot to have unobstructed views. Great design for sightseeing, not ideal for combat.

Moss jumped into the gel seat, which was a *lot* colder when you didn't have a flight suit on, and strapped in.

"Ready!" he called out.

The *Rex* jerked upward, the cockpit display indicating they were almost pointing to the zenith, and he was pushed back into the gel as the thrusters kicked in.

An ordinary human, one that had never received any treatments or augmentation to help them adapt to space travel, would have blacked out. A good flight suit and gel seat helped, but g-forces were g-forces, and there was only so much the human circulatory system could do to compensate.

Synths had these kinds of improvements baked in. Hel had had to go for a few rounds of medical enhancement to get to the same point. And Moss? Well, the Order had done more than just defrost him.

The opacity of Elan's blue-green sky dropped until he could see pinpoints of light, and then the black of space took over. But Hel didn't stop accelerating even once they were clear, burning at so many gees Moss was sure his face was going to sag like a bloodhound's once they were done.

"Care...to...explain...Violet?" he managed to say.

"Don't be mad..." Violet began over the speakers.

"Nothing...good...starts...that...way..."

"Let me start by saying, it's not our fault."

Moss was about to ask what wasn't their fault, but looking on the sensor display, he got a pretty good idea. The dome that represented the space around their ship had a bunch of blue dots heading towards them. Red would have indicated hostile ships, such as pirates. But blue? That was ProSec. For lack of a better word, the cops.

Violet appeared in front of him, sitting casually on the dash next to the display while Moss was squished into his seat like the last bit of toothpaste being squeezed out of the tube.

"Okay, so we were making our delivery when we came across a stranded ship. No power, but a possible survivor on board. Hel went in and found them unconscious in an EVA suit. Only that suit had some kind of crazy automated survival program built in, and it attacked her."

Moss managed to convey a *get on with it* look as streaks of blue began to zip past on the edges of the cockpit. ProSec had opened fire.

"Well, long story short, Hel saved the pilot by breaking open their visor so they could breathe again. That was when ProSec showed up and thought we were pirates."

Moss gritted his teeth. "*Why?*"

Violet forced a smile. "I mean, it's *funny* when you think about it. You see, to save the pilot, Hel kinda had to break their arm first, and then when she smashed the visor, it kinda cut up their face a bit, and, well, that was the *exact* moment ProSec hailed us, and the pilot started screaming bloody murder."

The *Viaticus Rex* shook as their shields took a hit from a pulse cannon. The stars swerved as Hel started to take evasive maneuvers. Fortunately, they were still outside of effective combat range.

"Hel tried to explain, but the pilot kept screaming that they were boarded and under attack. I told Hel to get back to the *Rex* and we would sort things out. Only the ProSec in these parts seem to be on the trigger-happy side."

The *Rex* shook again from another lucky long-range hit.

"You...don't...say."

"Anyway, we got out of there, but couldn't leave you stranded, so we came and picked you up. Good thing your book tracker was on, because you had your comms off."

Hel cut in from the cockpit below. "Guys, going into transit." With her flight suit on, she was handling the strain better.

The ship hummed as the transit drive warmed up, the stars distorted slightly, and then there was that paradoxical moment where all sense of acceleration ceased, yet the evidence of their eyes told a different story. Elan's moon and moonlet started slipping past them at an increasingly fast rate.

Moss could finally breathe properly. "How long till we can go full transit?"

"Not long now," said Hel. "Violet plotted the ideal vector for us ahead of time. We should be gone before ProSec can catch up."

Moss sagged in the seat, his mind finally catching up with the rest of him. He thought about what he saw when he jumped on the cargo ramp. Or rather, what he didn't see.

"You said you were *making* the delivery when this happened?" he asked Violet.

"Yeah."

"Not coming back from it?"

Her lips tightened. "Um... yeah."

"So...where's the cargo?"

"We, uh...kinda had to dump it during the escape."

Moss winced. "Please tell me you're joking."

Hel commed from below. "It was my call. They were shooting at us, and I needed some debris to help us get away."

Moss looked to Violet. "Couldn't you have taken over?" She was more than capable of flying the ship.

"Honestly? I'd have done the same. We need to stock up on countermeasures, sensor decoys, chaff, that sort of thing."

"Great..." He couldn't even blame anyone for this mess, other than the universe in general.

Violet looked down at Moss's swim trunks, then back up at him with a quizzically raised eyebrow.

Moss's eyes narrowed. "It's a *very cold* seat without a flight suit on, okay?"

"Okay, okay, I'm not judging."

Moss felt way too self conscious to stay where he was. He got up out of the chair. "I'm getting changed." He then spoke up louder. "Hel, let me know when we're in full transit."

"Won't be long," said Hel as he climbed back down the ladder. "Any destination in mind?"

Moss thought about it. "ProSec will be looking for us wherever we go, but I'd rather avoid the Void, if you know what I mean. We need a place where we have something approximating friends, preferably with the kind of contacts that can either get this mess straightened out or swept under the rug."

"Oh crap," said Hel, knowing full well where this was going.

"Yeah, I'm afraid so," said Moss. "Set course for Komi Station."

Hellyes Herzog

Technically, there are three kinds of humans out there.
Old school humans are known as freeborn and are the
only kind that still make babies the old-fashioned way.
Synths grow up much faster than freeborn and can't
reproduce. They were made to do our dirty work out in
space, but now make up the majority of humans.
The dominant synth variant, however, are referred to
as cyborgs. Don't let the name fool you, you won't find
any implants on them. They are the implant, with nan-
otech baked right into their genetic makeup.
Easiest way to spot a cyborg? They look like the star of an
action movie who uses too much spray-on tan.

M. Foote, *And Then Things Got Worse*

R OY HERZOG WAS NOT bored. If anything, he had far too much
going on, and he was enjoying every minute of it.

Granted, his situation was about as far from ideal as it could be. A
deserter and pirate, he'd been captured by the Silver Legion and forced
to use his underworld knowhow to help track down some freeborn
runaways. When that didn't work out as planned, his future hadn't
looked so bright.

But there is an ancient form of martial arts from old Earth known as aikido, "the way of harmonious spirit." It is not about confronting force with force, but rather taking the force directed against you and redirecting it. To Roy, it wasn't just a martial art, it was a philosophy, one that he was currently using to stay alive.

Take the bomb around his neck, for example. What they called a bondscollar or a slaver collar, depending on what side of the Draxon border you happened to be on. It was primarily for tracking, disciplinary action, and, if one was being honest, humiliation. A bright silver collar to bring the dog to heel and let everyone know where they stood. The bomb part was a last resort.

But rather than resist the irresistible, he played along. Granted, he had got zapped a few times, but not in the last week, and that was progress. Let them mistake compliance with obedience. Let them think he was working for them instead of working an angle. Eventually, an opportunity would come. It always did.

He was dressed as a crewman, though he was technically a sub-commander, and today he walked about the ship freely without an escort. That was also progress.

As a threat, they believed he was contained. With the collar, they could track his movements, keep him out of sensitive areas, restrict his computer access, and any number of people could incapacitate him if he did something he shouldn't.

He reached a lift that would take him to the bridge. Someone was inside when the doors opened. A synth crewman. He nodded to her amiably, and she smiled and nodded back, noticing the three pink flowers he'd pasted onto the right side of his bondscollar like they were rank insignia. He gave her a wink as she left and he got in. He kept the smile as the lift doors closed.

Fact was, they had their defences in all the wrong places.

He made sure to remove the stickers before he reached the bridge, crumpling them and stuffing them in his pocket. Having the acting commander see them would only cause problems. There was a whole different persona he had to use there. Long ago, he'd been slapped with the nickname of "Hellno" Herzog. But right now, he needed to be "Hellyes."

The lift doors opened and the bridge crew barely acknowledged his presence as he went to the commander's office.

Sub-commander Nekkar was sitting at his desk. A holographic projection hovered over it, displaying an ancient Terran colony ship with two rotating habitation decks and three large engines. Nekkar looked to Roy as he entered, then turned his attention back to the hologram, and the data displayed alongside it.

It was the *USNN Pegasi*, their current quarry, though only the senior officers and Roy were aware of the full details. The rest of the crew knew only they were under comm silence from the rest of the Fleet, taking part in a top-secret operation.

Nekkar swiped at the display, which transitioned to a map of local space. The Void. The stars out here were still plentiful, but sparse when compared to the great spiral arms of the galaxy.

The sub-commander zoomed in on their current location, and a translucent sphere indicated the region of space they were currently searching. About half of it was a slightly lighter colour, indicating the region of space they'd already searched.

"It's been two weeks," Nekkar said.

Great, he was looking for someone to blame. Guess Roy was overdue for a neck tingle.

"Your crew is doing their best," Roy said, not-so-subtly distancing himself from them. "They are engaging in the most effective search pattern of the area with the best information they have." He gestured to the map. "We've still got a fair bit of territory to cover."

"Unfortunately," said Nekkar, "the more time passes, the more tenuous our situation becomes."

By *our*, he really meant *his*. Ever since the commander of the *Hydrus* died, Nekkar had become increasingly obsessed with completing her mission. And though the parameters of that mission had changed, the goal was ultimately the same. He would return to the Fleet with the freeborn colonists aboard the *Pegasi*, or not at all.

The decision to cut communication with the Fleet had been his. He'd overreached in his recent attempts to capture a different group of freeborn, causing a public relations nightmare that could cost him his rank. He believed bagging the *Pegasi* would balance the scales for him, and who knew? It just might.

"Are you looking for ideas to speed up the process?" Roy asked.

"Do you have any?"

"I do, but I guarantee you won't like it."

"Speak."

"Hire the Void Brotherhood."

Nekkar closed his eyes, but to Roy's surprise, did not reach for the button that would give Roy an electric shock.

"No." There was a finality in his tone. The Void Brotherhood was nothing more than pirates, albeit ambitious ones. Their leader, Zelroth Saltear, effectively controlled the entire Ramedian Autonomous Resource Sector, and hadn't fired a shot to do it, or so they said. And until recently, Roy had been working for them.

"Understood," said Roy. "But consider this. Your only interest is in the freeborn colonists. All the Brotherhood would want is the ship. It would be worth a fortune to the right collector, far more than a bunch of slaves."

Nekkar quirked an eyebrow at that. He probably shouldn't have called them colonists. Roy pressed on. "Besides, you don't want that ship brought back to the Fleet. It's a symbol of the old ways. Heck, they don't even have any synth crew aboard."

Roy stopped himself. Pushing the idea too hard would backfire. He allowed Nekkar time to process the idea. Once he had, the commander leaned back in his seat, fingers laced together.

"It would compromise everything the Legion stands for. What the Fleet stands for. We will find it ourselves." His eyes then locked on Roy's. "You said you know some things about this Order who helped them escape?"

That had been a bluff, of sorts. He honestly didn't know much more about them than Nekkar did. But he had heard a few things from the old commander.

"Commander Miram believed that they had worked their way into Ramede space and used it as a staging ground for their operations. And I do know that in recent years, the Brotherhood has been trying to reverse engineer some advanced tech they acquired by the usual means."

"The usual means?" asked Nekkar.

"Stole, looted, or blew up and put back together."

"Ah."

"I was never in the inner circles, though, so I never got a look at any of it. Just heard the rumours."

Fact was, he'd been shipped off to a system nicknamed The Dump, where the rejects were sent to either sort themselves out or wait to be used as cannon fodder in some larger enterprise. Even among pirates, he hadn't managed to fit in.

Nekkar grunted. "Well, now's your chance. There was an unusual device found aboard the shuttle that tried to ram us. From what we can tell, the ship itself is a Baroque-class interstellar shuttle. Nothing out of the ordinary, though its shields and engines had been greatly enhanced. This device, though... We're not sure what to make of it. It's been sent to the science department. Ensign Ara is overseeing the project. Report to her, see what you make if it. Dismissed."

The acting commander turned his chair enough so there was no accidental way of them making eye contact. Yep, Roy was dismissed all right. On the bright side, he hadn't gotten shocked and whether Nekkar realized it or not, he was treating Roy like part of the crew.

And the very fact he had heard Roy out about bringing in the Void Brotherhood spoke volumes.

Roy nodded and left. He took the lift down to the science deck, only to pass by Ensign Powell in the hall on the way.

She barely noticed him.

"Powell?"

She stopped and turned. "Oh, hi Roy. Sorry. I'm...just a bit busy."

Roy couldn't help but feel sympathy for the woman. He'd helped get her promoted and put on the relief shift on the bridge, but then Nekkar had gone and dumped the shuttle reconstruction project on her as well, leaving her with barely enough time to sleep.

"I was just going to check on the device from the shuttle," said Roy. "Can you tell me anything about it?"

Her eyes widened a little. "You know about it?"

"Nekkar sent me to have a look at it in the science lab."

Powell seemed to relax. "Oh, right. I mean, I haven't done much with it. It wasn't connected to the ship's systems in any way."

That was interesting. "Okay, thanks. Maybe see you later?"

"Maybe. Getting some rest until relief shift starts."

Roy left her to it. They could exchange pleasantries another time.

There were only six heavy cruisers in the Silver Legion, though many more were being built, and though they were undoubtedly warships, they were also designed for exploration and to accommodate scientific study.

But the *Hydrus* had been put on patrol, not a journey of discovery, and as such the large and well-stocked science deck was woefully understaffed. It was Spartan in nature, a holdover from the ship's original Draxon design. Most of the ship had been given certain comforting flourishes. Wood-like accents, warm, recessed lighting, even carpeting so everyone wasn't clanging around.

The lab, however, had harsh omnidirectional light that would screw with your circadian rhythm but was far better to see tiny details with, and cold, hard floors. There were a dozen or so workstations, but only three were being used, and the first two were just to store stuff needed for the third.

Four people hovered around a large metal device that had that ambiguous vibe of "purpose" he'd always associated with old science fiction. At a glance, you couldn't begin to guess what it was meant to do, which meant it could do anything, and therefore could be used on any set. It kind of resembled a workbench.

"Ensign Ara?"

One of the four synths turned around, a woman with blonde shoulder length hair. "Yes?"

"I'm Herzog. Commander Nekkar wanted me to look at the device recovered from the shuttle."

"You mean item 195-290-1?"

He pointed to the device. "I mean that."

She nodded. "195-290-1. It was brought in from the hangar yesterday. We're still making preliminary observations."

He looked it over. "Are you sure it's complete?"

"It's possible some kind of generator was once mounted over it," said Ara. "There are markings that suggest it's configured to accept a standard power source as well, but we don't wish to turn it on until we have a better idea of what we're dealing with."

"Do you have *any* idea of what you're dealing with?"

"Not really. There is a sophisticated computer housed inside, and it seems to have a rather obvious camera mounted on it, so it's possible it will only work for someone it recognizes."

"Is it okay if I have a closer look?"

Ara thought about it, nodded and waved off her staff. "I don't see any harm. Just don't attempt to activate it yet, please."

"Sure."

Roy couldn't make hide or hair of it. There was a central control area sticking out from the front, unlabeled. The main housing was very angular, and branched off on either side, raised slightly above the control panel. Overall, it was very smooth, except for the panels that had been removed along the bottom, revealing its complex inner workings.

He figured if he couldn't look at this as a scientist, he'd look at it as a user. It did something, it was meant to be used independent of support systems, so everything you needed to use it should be here. The control panel clearly had an area reserved for something to be placed. Only there wasn't anything to put on it.

"Any thoughts?" asked Ensign Ara.

Roy shook his head. "None. But you might want to check the galley again to see if there are any parts missing. It seems like..."

His voice trailed off as he noticed a narrow rectangular seam in the housing next to the control panel, and the faintest hint of wear around it. He pushed it. It sunk in a bit. There was a click. When he let go, a small drawer slowly popped out. Enhanced vision one—science nerds zero.

Inside were what looked like two pieces of thin, dense circuitry folded in half, but they were like nothing he'd ever seen before.

"Hello, what do we have here?"

That Dutch Angle Feeling

Gravity manipulation has been around for millennia. Initially developed by the Hopat, it is now in common use throughout the Protectorate. While most ships generate enough power to have all key areas covered by a gravity field, even on a capital-class ship, a space station is a different matter. It is neither easy, cheap, nor desirable to have a reactor powerful enough to provide gravity to the equivalent of a large city unless you designed it that way from the ground up.

This is why many stations continue to rely on good old-fashioned centripetal force. But it is not uncommon for some buildings to use Hopat grav tech to increase or decrease local gravity for the comfort or long-term health of their residents.

M Foote, *The Galaxy is Weirder than You Think*

K OMI STATION LOOMED IN front of Hel as the *Viaticus Rex II.I* drifted outside the open docking port dead centre on its rotational axis, waiting for permission to land.

Moss had called ahead to make arrangements with Ashtar and Barl Orijen. The Orijen brothers ran a junkyard on Komi Station, one that was so large it took up a significant part of the mid-level habitation decks. They employed a number of people there, though twice as many lived in the yards illegally, looking for any scrap that might fetch a good enough price to get them out of the mid-decks for good.

Hel had been both, and her relationship with the brothers had not ended on pleasant terms, nor had they started great either. There had been a middle that was tolerable, but that was about it. She had escaped aboard the *Rex*.

And now that same ship was bringing her back. Last time she was on Komi Station, Hel had avoided the junkyard entirely, but this time that wasn't an option.

Hel took a deep breath. Deep down, she knew they wouldn't do anything to her. Not now, not under these conditions.

But she still remembered the fury on Ashtar's face when he'd found her stealing from him, and the beating that had followed. Given how strong the Hopat were, he must have been holding back—a lot—but at the time, she'd thought he was trying to kill her.

That had been the start of her life as a yard rat, and where she had stayed until she'd escaped on board Moss's ship.

They received clearance, and she felt a nudge as the maneuvering thrusters pushed them towards the station. The large docking port grew ever bigger as they passed through, able to accommodate ships many times the size of the *Rex*.

Their ship nudged down and to the side, matching the rotation of the station as they made their way to their assigned pad, which was lit up and providing holographic visual cues to let the pilot know if they needed to adjust course.

Once the *Rex* was down and secured, her brain took a moment to adjust to the slight sensation she experienced as gravity. Up here it was barely a tenth of a gee, but closer to the station's skin it felt more like what you'd find on a planet. Still, people new to space travel took a while getting used to what Violet called the Dutch Angle feeling.

Violet had shown her some movie clips as a way to explain. A trick directors would use to make a scene feel unsettling was to tilt the camera at an angle. And in effect, that was how you felt all the time on a rotating station. Drop a ball and it won't fall straight down, but at an angle based on the rotation, which meant you had to be careful pouring drinks. But people who had lived there a while not only adjusted, they could always tell which direction was spinwise.

Hel got out of her seat and joined Moss on the main deck of the cockpit. She'd keep the grip on her boots until they went deeper into the station.

Moss was already standing, waiting next to the comm panel. "I know you don't like this plan, but…"

"I'm fine," said Hel. "Seriously."

"It's just that you and them…"

"I know."

Violet flickered to life in front of them. "You could just stay on board the ship."

Now Hel was getting annoyed. "Thanks guys, but you don't need to protect me. I'll deal with them my own way."

Violet looked frustrated and disappeared, but Moss nodded in understanding. "You got it." He pressed the comm panel. "Hey, Ashtar. We're here. Bring her down."

The docking pad began to lower, but instead of stopping one level below in storage, it kept on going lower and lower into the guts of the station. For a while, there was nothing to see but superstructure as the platform dropped, until it finally opened up as they reached the junkyard.

Hel moved next to Moss for a better look. The pressure was beginning to grow, and not just from centripetal force. From here, she could see most of the yard. It was like an amusement park made of scrap, some piled up into heaps so high they reached the ceiling. Half the scrap was nicely organized, while the other half was a dumping ground.

That was where the yard rats lived.

Moss had a frown on his face. He usually did, but this seemed to have a specific reason behind it. "Look, I know you can take care of yourself, Hel, but you know that doesn't mean you have to deal with shit alone up here, right?" He pointed to his own head.

"Look who's talking."

"Exactly. I have way more experience than you in that department. I'm like sixty-six percent self-loathing. Not a way to live. So, if you need someone to talk to... well, talk to Violet, obviously. Just talk to *someone*, all right?"

Hel chuckled. "All right."

"And just because you want to show those two clowns that you're not scared of them, doesn't mean you have to drop your guard, you know?"

Hel frowned. "Actually, I don't." They were just about at the junkyard's ground level now.

"I mean, it's a lot easier to act all casual if you know someone's watching your back, right?"

"Sure."

"So... I am loath to ask this, but... where's Trouble?"

Hel's face when white as the *Rex* settled next to the Orijen Brothers' office.

"Um..."

In the galley, Moss noticed that the freezer had a padlock on it. He entered the combination and took it off, then opened the door.

Inside, next to some packets of food, a ferret stood on its hind legs, about half a meter in height. It was hunched over slightly, arms raised as if it had been pounding at the door, mouth wide open in terror. The creature was frozen solid.

Except the eyes. Those eyes shifted the moment Moss opened the door, looking straight at him under a film of ice.

Moss couldn't help but feel satisfied. "I knew you'd piss her off eventually."

The eyes shifted again, but the body didn't move.

Moss took a deep breath. "Okay, let's get you warmed up. I've got a job for you."

Trouble was a PetBot, and while most PetBots were designed to act like, well, *pets*, there were people who were looking for more than basic companionship.

Trouble was modelled after the sidekick of a popular cartoon space adventurer, Ranger M.

Hel had gotten it partly as a joke, because Moss *was* Ranger M. Sorta. Ranger M was a persona he had created to hide his identity, back when he'd briefly been a famous explorer. He'd worn a green and red luchador mask to add to his mystique.

That, in turn, had caught the attention of some Nubran network execs, who sold him on the idea of a cartoon being made about him, in the style of old Terran TV shows. Terran culture was popular in Nubra space for reasons best left for xenoanthropologists to explain.

But shortly after that, everything had fallen apart. He'd lost his position as a spokesperson for Odyssey Expeditions, but they had held the rights to Ranger M, and everything connected to it. To this day, you could still find his masked image being used to promote oxygen recyclers and habitation units.

As for the cartoon, Moss had initially breathed a sigh of relief when he'd heard there was only going to be one season and no plans for renewal.

Only they had farmed out the project to an unscrupulous company that used pseudo-intelligent supercomputers to crank out shows until the budget ran out.

That one season ended up being five hundred and one episodes long. Moss had watched them all and hated five hundred of them. So when Hel had bought Trouble as a joke a while back, Moss hadn't felt like laughing.

Moss set Trouble's frozen body into the oven and set it on low convection. Thirty seconds later, he opened it, and the ferret stood there shivering.

"T-t-t-took ya long enough!"

"It's your own fault," said Moss. "If you dialled down your more annoying traits, you'd end up in the freezer less often."

Trouble hopped out of the oven and brushed melted water off its fur. "Yeah, yeah. Tell it to the philosophers." It turned and looked up at Moss. "So, you're back. Good! Maybe now we can have a *real* adventure."

While Trouble wasn't sapient, its pseudo-intelligent programming did a good job of hiding that fact. And Moss had learned that the best way to get it to do what he wanted was to play along. Anything else led to headaches.

"Okay, listen up. I've got a special mission for you."

"Oh boy! You can count on me, boss!"

"Yeah, yeah, shut up. Now listen..."

The cargo ramp lowered and Moss and Hel came down onto the landing pad.

Waiting for them were two short, squat Hopats. Their hair was short and spikey, so thick it was more accurately called fur, and one of them had a cybernetic arm. The smile on the one up front, Ashtar, reached from ear to ear. Given the wide shape of Hopat heads, this was unnerving if you ever thought about them eating.

"Looking good, Maurice," said Ashtar. "For once, I haven't heard that you were dead."

"No, but we'd like to be for a little while."

"So I gathered. Got some ProSec trouble, I take it?" Moss hadn't openly mentioned that in his communications, but Ashtar had understood the subtext.

"Purely a misunderstanding," Moss said.

Ashtar's already wide smile grew wider. "Sure, sure." He turned his attention to Hel. "And look who's returned?"

Hel's eyes narrowed. "Go to hell."

Ashtar didn't miss a beat. "I thought you were Hel."

Behind his brother, Barl snorted.

Moss raised his hands. "I'd like to avoid the drama if at all possible. I've had a really bad day. Like most days."

Ashtar looked away from Hel. "We need to keep the pad clear for incoming salvage. Barl will get your ship nestled with the junk over there. It'll fit right in. As for the rest..." Ashtar gestured his head towards the office. "Moss, if you'd join me?"

Moss nodded and left Hel alone with Barl. Sort of.

The office looked the same as the last time he'd been here, which was only a couple of weeks ago, but it felt like a lifetime. The rotational gravity was being supplemented by grav pads inside the office, which Ashtar turned down to make Moss more comfortable.

"Got any more chimera requests after the big race?" he asked. Moss had inadvertently caused a fad of sorts when a former celebrity had noticed the *Rex* and got it in his head that a show about racing chimeras would make for good ratings.

Ashtar shook his head. "Naw, but I've been kept on retainer. Convinced them that using our yard for their ships exclusively would provide an even playing field. I figure I can get away with that line for at least a couple more seasons."

Ashtar opened the door to his office, and they went inside. "Honestly, I can't thank you enough for that. Too bad you weren't on commission. You'd have made a pretty penny."

"I'll happily accept it retroactively."

"Ha!" Ashtar snorted as he sat in his chair. "Nice try. But I do owe you. So I'm gonna help get your ProSec problem sorted out, and as far as this station is concerned, you were never here." He pinched the thumbs on his left hand together and tapped the side of his head, the Hopat gesture for someone in-the-know. Ashtar had enough of the key station staff paid off that he could get away with anything short of murder...and even that was negotiable.

Moss continued to stand. "Much appreciated. Now, about Hel..."

Ashtar waved a chubby hand dismissively. "I don't care about her. She's your problem now."

"I want you to apologize to her."

Ashtar looked at Moss like he'd sprouted Elysian wings. "You want me to what now?"

Moss crossed his arms. "This isn't a pissing contest, Ashtar. We're on good terms now, so let me be blunt with you. Hel is part of my crew. You took advantage of her when she thought she was a slave, then beat her when you thought she was stealing from you, then hunted her when she hid out in the junkyard. I want you to apologize."

Ashtar rolled his eyes. "My heart is bleeding. Listen, I *rescued* her from that pirate wreckage. I *paid* her to work for me. She *did* steal from me. So I smacked her around a bit for that. So what? And those yard rats out there are a bunch of leeches. Leave your crusading on your ship, Moss, before we're no longer on good terms."

Moss sighed. "Fine." He tapped his ear. "Violet? What are Barl and Hel up to?"

"They've just moved the ship out of sight," said Violet.

"They getting along?"

"To be honest, he's giving her a hard time."

"That's what I thought," said Moss. "Commence Operation Legging."

"With pleasure."

Ashtar sat up straight. "The hell are you up to, Maurice?"

"Oh, nothing terrible. Just"—there was a deep-throated scream outside the office—"a bit embarrassing."

Ashtar got up and stormed out of the room, Moss following behind.

The *Rex* wasn't parked too far away, just far enough so others could use the pad up to the landing bay. Half of it was hidden behind a pile of scrap, but the back half was still visible, as were Hel and Barl. And Barl was squirming like someone had covered him in itching powder.

"What did you do?" Ashtar growled.

Barl howled and fell to the ground. Suddenly, something rose from the centre of his chest, trying to force its way out.

Moss took a generous step to the side in case Ashtar tried to grab him, but the Hopat was too gobsmacked by what was happening.

"Digger's Teeth!"

Barl's shirt ripped open, and Trouble burst out with a hiss.

Barl tried to grab it, but Trouble had already darted to his face and nipped his ear. The Hopat tried to swat him like a fly with his cybernetic hand, but only succeeded in punching his own face. Trouble was back inside his shirt and they could see the lump of his progress as he made his way back down into the Hopat's pants.

"The hell are you playing at, Moss?" Ashtar asked once it was clear Barl was in no real danger.

In answer, Moss nodded to Hel, who stood back with a hand raised to her mouth as she tried, and failed, to hold in her laughter.

"You paid her next to nothing," Moss said, still watching the unfolding chaos. "The pirates that captured her messed with her brain. Plastered over it so she believed she lived only to serve others. She wasn't stealing from you for the credits. Her brain was trying to find a way to put itself back together."

Trouble had scampered down one leg, back up, spent an uncomfortable amount of time in Barl's nether regions, then scrambled out the other. It turned back to Barl, blew a raspberry, and ran inside the ship.

Moss looked down at Ashtar. "And you might want to consider what getting 'smacked around' feels like to someone who didn't grow up on a high gravity world and doesn't have your thick skin. You don't have to give her an apology, but I'm not letting her stay here and still be afraid of you."

Barl was back on his feet now, panting, more dumbfounded than anything. Any time Hel worried about the Orijen brothers, she was going to remember this instead.

Now Moss turned on the charm. "Besides, he's your *brother*. Tell me you're not going to save the recordings of this and use it against him on special occasions?"

Ashtar still looked furious, but that facade crumbled as he imagined just how he would use this footage later. He chuckled despite himself. "You got grinders on you, I'll give you that."

"Yeah, well, given the insane amount of business I sent your way, I figured you'd let this one slide."

"Oh, *I* will. Can't speak for Barl, though. You're lucky he didn't smash your little toy."

"You kidding? I was hoping he would. Now I gotta listen to that damn thing brag about how it saved the day."

Flaw and Order

Over three quarters of the stars in the galaxy are unremarkable red dwarfs. If you're low on hydrogen, they make for a handy gas station—assuming you have a fuel scoop to pick up the castoff—but that's about it.

Red dwarfs are very small, very cool, and their Goldilocks Zone is generally way too close for comfort.

We're talking so close the planet would be tidally locked—so one side always faces the sun while the other is always in darkness.

We're talking so close that it's exposed to enough UV radiation that, even with standard genetic enhancements, you're slathering on sunscreen like paint.

We're talking so close that solar flares can physically reach it—EM disruptions are the least of your worries if you're being toasted like a marshmallow.

Point is, if you're thinking of colonizing one of those extremely rare life sustaining worlds in a red dwarf system, you probably shouldn't.

M Foote, *The Galaxy is Weirder than You Think*

A S FAR AS THE Protectorate was concerned, Ataraxia did not exist. While the star it orbited appeared in their star charts as RDJILY3K, it was a just another unremarkable red dwarf in the middle of the Void.

Most red dwarf systems were uninhabitable, and often poor in useful resources. Some were worth exploiting, but as a rule, they weren't worth colonizing.

As a rule.

Ataraxia was an exception, a one in a billion chance. But given that there were twenty billion red dwarf systems within Protectorate space, well, it had to happen somewhere.

Ataraxia had the good fortune of being not only life sustaining, but, against all odds, also had a good orbital rotation, a strong magnetic field, and an ozone layer. The life on the planet was carbon-based, and largely compatible with both Nubran and Elysian biologies, requiring only slight alteration to properly digest.

However, its sun took up nearly a quarter of the sky, which could be a pretty terrifying thing to wake up to if you weren't prepared.

This world had been claimed by the Order and set aside as a contingency long before it was ever needed. Long, long ago—over thirteen hundred years by Terran reckoning—there had been a great war, one that could have ended all organic life. And in the aftermath, the greatest think tank in the Protectorate ceased to exist, their accomplishments stricken from the records.

In reality, they had moved themselves to the margins. The desperate measures taken during that war had made it clear that there was more than one way to wipe out all of civilization. Technology—*any* technology—could become a weapon. A better way was required.

The Order was born, and as they faded into the background, they took with them dozens of worlds that had been quietly deleted from the official star charts long before.

RDJILY3K still existed on Protectorate records, as did the airless, tidally locked world closest to it and the unremarkable gas giant further out, but this planet was listed as an asteroid field. So there was nothing remotely interesting or useful to make it worth revisiting.

As it should be.

The main colony on Ataraxia was simply referred to as the Priory. It was governed by a Precentor, whose job was to oversee the activity of members of the Order, and assign duties to its brothers and sisters.

And one of those sisters had been very busy of late, in the most inconvenient ways.

Sister Tameria wore her formal thin grey robes, sitting patiently in the wide, nearly empty hall, waiting to be called. Over the last thousand years, the Order had taken its beliefs in pacifism and its credo of "Lift Up—Never Push Down" to a point where it embraced a quasi-religious philosophy. But these were not typically adhered to except for formal occasions or official meetings, such as this.

The door to the Precentor's office opened, and Tameria got up.

But before she could enter, Precentor Vargoya came out.

"Walk with me," he said.

Tameria was puzzled, but did not question him. She followed him down the hall.

Vargoya was an older Nubran man, whose blue skin was starting to pale with age. He had a kind face, but it was one that had always been hard for Tameria to read.

Their walk took them to an outdoor garden at the centre of the complex. Great trees rose up here, and the ground was covered in flowers of every colour, most reaching her waist. She felt lighter as they entered, and not in a metaphorical way. This area had its gravity artificially reduced to Elysian standard.

"Would you care to stretch your wings?" the Precentor asked.

It would have been rude to refuse. The back of her robe opened, allowing her iridescent wings to unfold.

"Thank you, sir."

He smiled and pointed to the central tree, which was large enough to support an observation deck in the middle, filled with chairs and tables. This was a popular spot for people to meet, especially Elysians like her, since they could fly more easily within the garden's confines.

"I'll see you up there. Take your time."

Vargoya went to a platform next to the tree's trunk, one that looked like little more than a round disk, but that disk would take him up effortlessly to the observation deck.

Tameria hadn't had a chance to fly like this in some time. Her people had mastered genetics long before spaceflight, and her wings were just one part of that legacy. Their bones were made stronger and lighter, their muscles able to adapt to heavier gravities when required, and their unique glamour made their interactions with the other species of the Protectorate easier.

For a moment, just a moment, she allowed herself this joy. With a hop, she flapped her wings and pushed herself into the sky, rising until she could feel the gravity field fade, then swooped back down. In her mind, she was back with her family, with her uncle Keed, having a picnic high up on the cliffs of Lacilla.

But duty took over, and rather than continue flying, she landed on the observation deck, right next to the Precentor before he'd even reached his table.

"That was short, Sister."

"I would rather discuss the Terran situation, sir."

The Precentor frowned. "I don't see what harm an extra two minutes would make."

"Please, sir, the matter is really bothering me."

Vargoya raised a hand. "Two minutes. I must insist."

Tameria nodded and left, dropping from the platform to glide, then flapping her wings to rise back up. She circled the tree a few times, passing another Elysian who clearly enjoying himself more. But by the time she landed, she had to admit she felt a little less stressed.

Two cups of tea were waiting at the table when she returned.

"Do you feel better?" Vargoya asked.

"A little."

The Precentor gestured for her to sit. "I could sense your tension. I felt it would be best if you reduced it, if only for a moment."

"Thank you, sir."

Vargoya took a sip of his tea and set it down. "Now, to the matter at hand. The situation with the Terrans *is* troubling, isn't it?"

"Yes, sir."

"But might I ask *which* Terrans you are referring to?"

It was as close to a joke as the Precentor tended to get. Before she had a chance to be more specific, Vargoya said, "We know why the

Terrans have stepped up their efforts to reclaim their lost freeborn. It is most disturbing, and I fear that the Silver Legion will only grow more desperate in their pursuits. In time, that might put our people, and this Priory, at risk."

"I see," said Tameria, though she wasn't sure where this was going.

"Given the recent security breach on Mars, we're implementing a new protocol for all field agents to protect Ataraxia from discovery by the Legion. A package has been sent to your ship with a comprehensive briefing. I'd like you to review it before you leave."

"Yes, Precentor."

"But I expect you are more concerned with the *other* Terrans. I understand the *Pegasi* will arrive here soon?"

Sister Tameria nodded. "May I ask what accommodations are being made for them?"

"As little as possible, as per their wishes. The continent on the opposite side of the planet had only a few research stations there. I'm having them relocated. We will only interact with them if they ask."

That was both a relief and worrying. The *Pegasi* was a colony ship, long lost to history, launched before the Terrans discovered transit technology and travelling *long* past its expiration date. It had been sabotaged from within and doomed to drift the stars forever, never finding a home, until she and Moss's team had found it.

Unfortunately, most of the *Pegasi*'s senior staff had a stubborn streak about them. Many had wanted to continue their journey just as they were, despite being deep in pirate territory or the growing risk of a catastrophic breakdown.

In the end, the command staff had accepted a compromise. The Order would tow it to Ataraxia, where they could set up a colony the way they saw fit, unaffected by the rest of the universe. Hiding from it, really. But under the circumstances, it was probably for the best.

"When they are ready, they will contact us," the Precentor said. "It is the *Martian* Terrans I'm concerned about."

Tameria nodded. That matter worried her as well.

For the last two years, the Order had been helping runaway free-borns masquerade as synths on Mars, complete with official idents, and moved to remote areas where deep genetic tests were unlikely.

But recent events had threatened to expose their agent there, Haven, and he'd had no choice but to relocate thirty or so off Mars, including those Tameria had recently delivered. It was because of this development that she'd had to cut her vacation on Elan short, and her feelings about *that* were decidedly mixed.

"I'm sorry, Precentor. It was my decision to bring them here. Some of them worked for Haven directly, and taking them anywhere else would risk recapture. Given what they know, that could have compromised the operation."

Vargoya waved a hand dismissively. "The decision was, I believe, the correct one. Those who worked for Haven can now work for us. No, my concern has to do with what do to with the others."

Tameria frowned, unsure what the problem was.

"Most of these freeborn would not be suitable to work within the Order. Perhaps their next generation could be included, with the proper indoctrination, but for the time being, the best thing would be to settle and develop their own colony, wouldn't you agree?"

"Yes, Precentor."

"However, they do not possess the same reluctance against our assistance as the *Pegasi*. In fact, I'm sure they would rather welcome it."

"Yes, sir."

"And their population is far too small to sustain itself in the long run."

Tameria nodded her understanding. "You want to incorporate them into the *Pegasi* colony, and believe that will be a problem."

"It almost certainly will be. The Mars freeborn are accustomed to a certain level of technological development, and know much about the greater galaxy. The *Pegasi* colonists wish to live in ignorance and use only the technology they brought with them."

"Not all of them," Tameria corrected.

The Precentor took another sip of tea. "No. Not all of them. That is *exactly* the problem. They will be seen as a threat, a corrupting outside influence. Simply telling others of what is out there will make the colonists ask questions. In time, it will either lead to a more oppressive form of governance to take hold, or result in a schism that will lead to bloodshed."

"You wish for me to speak to the *Pegasi* command staff?"

"Sister Tameria, I believe you are the only one they *will* speak to at this point." Vargoya set his cup down again, but his long, blue fingers did not let go. Instead, he rotated the cup on the table over and over, like he was imagining the habitation rings of the colony ship. "Your report indicated that the captain is a pragmatic man, open to reason."

Tameria nodded. "Captain Mbatha was strongly in support of accepting our help. Most of his staff was not."

"That would match with my assessment. I have been in contact with the captain through our transports, discussing this very matter. He shares our concerns, but has not informed his staff of the Martian problem yet. We believe that if anyone has a chance of reaching a compromise that even the most stubborn of his staff will accept, it's you."

"And what would the nature of that compromise be?" Sister Tameria asked.

The Precentor stopped spinning his teacup.

"Honestly, I don't care if you beat them all with a reinforced pipe. Just make it happen."

Life Among the Junk

When it comes to counting, Terrans use a base 10 system, but if you look back far enough, some parts of the world also used base 12, based on counting the finger joints with your thumb with one hand, and counting full sets of twelve on the other (up to sixty).

If you ever wondered where Terran hours and seconds originated from, there you go.

However, the Nubrans have three fingers and a thumb on each hand, while the Hopat have four and a thumb on either side. Draxons have the same number of digits, but with slightly webbed fingers.

This resulted in everything from base 8 to base 15 systems of counting, and that's not even counting variations in the younger races.

Point is, they all have different counting systems to us, which makes math conversion a real pain.

M. Foote, The Galaxy is Weirder than You Think

DESPITE THE RELAXED AIR Moss tried to present, Hel knew a lot was going on behind the scenes on board the *Rex*. She'd overheard him talk to Violet about keeping a vigil on the ship and the yard, accessing station communications, trying to tap into the yard's comm system, pretty much anything that might give them an edge in case the Orijen brothers decided to double cross them.

But Hel wasn't too worried. Moss tended to do that on every station they landed at, even back on Elan, which was well within Nubra space and as safe a place as there was...if you weren't falsely accused of piracy.

Elan had a very low tolerance for shenanigans, and a very high level of red tape. A significant portion of their income came from fines and infractions, mainly with passing ships not being up to Protectorate code, which Moss had compared to something called the *Malleus Maleficarum*, whatever that was.

Ashtar had said it would take a week to get the ProSec records expunged. Out on the border of the Void, things had to be more flexible, and it was easier to smooth things over with the right credits to the right people, but that didn't necessarily speed things up.

While that got sorted out, Hel didn't have much to do. She didn't feel comfortable spending time in VR with Violet while in the middle of the Orijen Brothers' junkyard, even if Violet was keeping an eye on them. Moss was spending his time reading in the cockpit with a new digital book he had printed up and wanted to be left alone. Making up for lost time, he said.

Without anything else to do, Hel soon found herself wandering back into the dumping grounds of the junkyard. At first, she always kept the *Rex* in sight, but as she grew more confident she ventured deeper, though always staying in Violet's comm range.

Not much time had passed since she'd left, but the yard was almost unrecognizable. The front half of the old Arcadia transport she used to call home was gone—probably scrapped right after she left so some other yard rat wouldn't hole up in it.

"You okay?" Violet asked over the comm.

Hel frowned. "You listening in?"

"Wistful sighs tend to catch my attention."

Hel looked around. "It's easier now that my real memories are back. But I can still remember when *this* was my world. The only one I had to look forward to."

"It's not your world anymore," said Violet.

"Yeah, but—" Hel didn't finish that thought. Instead, she looked around at the junk piles, looking for movement.

"What's wrong?"

"Someone's here."

"Get back to the ship."

"It's okay, Violet."

"I can't help you from here. Get back to the ship!"

Hel heard a rumble. "Violet, relax, it's just—"

Something struck the back of her head, knocking the ear comm loose. It fell out as she collapsed to the ground, Violet's panicked cries going unheard.

Moss was lying back in his cushioned pilot's chair, reading from his new book. He'd finished *Lord of the Flies* and was now re-reading some Jules Verne. Trouble was sitting on the backrest, pretending to read along, doing his level best to annoy Moss by doing absolutely nothing wrong.

"Moss! Get up!" Violet shouted.

Moss shot the seat upright, causing Trouble to fall onto his lap.

"What is it?"

"Hel's in trouble!"

Trouble raised a tiny finger as if to make some kind of rude observation, then thought better of it. *Ranger M* had been a family friendly show, after all. Moss tossed the ferret aside like a moldy burrito and was already leaving the cockpit.

"Orijens?"

"Yard rats, I think," said Violet.

"Seriously?" He went to the weapons locker next to his quarters and opened it up. Moss didn't care for guns—shooting at people typically meant they were also shooting at you, and he preferred to avoid those situations—but he had a few for emergencies, along with a massive rail gun left behind by some pirates who'd taken a surprise space walk.

"I lost contact with her in the yard. Her comm fell out. She said someone was there."

Moss considered the rail gun but shook his head. The intimidation factor was undeniable, and it would blow through anything in the junkyard, but it was far too bulky.

"Hurry, you dumb oaf!"

He considered a pulse rifle but went for a pistol instead. Fewer shots, and it had a stun setting. Plus, it didn't escalate the situation by simply existing. He picked it up and ran for the ramp, which was already lowered.

"Contact the brothers?" Violet asked.

"Not yet," said Moss. "They'll overreact and charge me for the privilege."

"Not to side with them, but maybe we *should* be overreacting?"

Moss checked the charge in his pistol, turned off the safety, and holstered it. "I prefer reacting the correct amount."

Trouble scrambled alongside him. "What about me, boss?"

Moss tapped his shoulder. "Get up. I might need you." When you were dealing with piles of junk, there was no denying Trouble could go places others couldn't. "Okay, Vi. Which way do I go?"

Violet guided him down the open paths between leaning heaps of salvage, and it wasn't long before he came across several canisters scattered on the ground, and Hel's comm among them. Moss's was an implant, along with his adaptive translator, but Hel hadn't gone that route.

"Trouble, find Hel. Comms only—don't yell like a moron."

The ferret gave a salute and scampered off, disappearing into the nearest promising pile of junk. While its comedic sub-routine was extremely annoying, it had been programmed to dial it down when a situation turned serious.

"Got anything for me, Violet?"

"Sorry. Too much interference. I only know where you are because of your comm."

"Right." He took a deep breath and looked at the ground. It was just metal floor, but Komi Station had been around for centuries, and salvage had been going in and out of these decks for decades. As a result, a layer of dust, rust, and other microscopic detritus had accumulated everywhere. Not much, but enough for Moss to see that someone had been dragged away from here.

It looked like they'd been taken to the hull of a ship directly in front of him. Good, he preferred his mysteries to be of the pre-school variety.

Moss didn't draw his pistol, but that would change the moment he was sure the situation was as bad as Violet feared. Sometimes going in expecting things to be bad *made* them bad.

As he approached the ship, a burnt out Hopat shuttle, he heard a voice inside. Male, raised in anger. But just one.

Moss curled his fingers around the pulse gun's handle as he stepped up to and slowly peered around the edge of the gaping hole in the shuttle's side.

He counted five. Hel was sitting on the floor, her back to the wall. Three others squatted nearby, dressed in work coveralls, all from the younger races, including one Elanian. The centre of attention was a Nubran in a suit that had seen better days, looming over her with his arms raised, ranting.

"...And then he said, 'if it were not for my pet quadruped, I would not have spent that year in advanced education!'"

Everyone erupted in laughter, except Moss, of course, who would spend far too much time later trying to figure out what had led up to that punchline. Hel must have sensed his confusion, because she homed in on him and smiled, waving him over.

Moss let go of the pistol grip and came inside. The hull had been hollowed out and was really just a shell where makeshift stools had been dragged in. This wasn't anyone's crashpad, just something they set up in a pinch.

"Everything all right?" Moss asked. He was pretty sure he had the lay of the land, but needed confirmation.

Hel nodded. "These are some of the yard rats I used to run with." She pointed to the Nubran in the ratty suit. "This is Grund, and these are Chaf, Recca, and Amotanakilicotranicas."

"Amo," the person amended, giving a half wave. Moss didn't remember the name of their species, but it was hard to forget anyone with three eyes.

Violet had been listening to all of this over the comm and was clearly relieved. "Ask her what happened."

Moss asked.

"One of the junk piles out there had a slide," said Hel. "I got bonked pretty hard. Grund and the others brought me here to recover."

"Minor concussion," the one called Recca said, an Elanian currently displaying feminine traits. "Good thing gravity is low on the mid-decks."

"Your comm fell out," said Moss.

"Yeah, I know. Sorry. I was going to look for it once I was steadier on my feet."

"Tell her I was worried," said Violet.

Panicked, more like, but there was no reason to lay on a guilt trip. "Not the time," Moss said under his breath. He was pretty sure he heard Violet *humph* at that. "We should get you back to the ship. Have you looked at, just to be sure."

Hel raised a hand. "In a bit. First, I need you to hear these guys out."

"What about?"

The Nubran in the suit straightened his jacket a bit. "Ranger M, I wish to hire you."

Moss died a little inside as Grund explained.

Way back when Hel first stowed away aboard the *Viaticus Rex II.I,* she and Grund had teamed up to disassemble and loot the *Viaticus Rex II.* Hel had only wanted parts for a project she felt compelled to build—what she hadn't realized at the time was a model of her true home, the lost *Pegasi* generation ship.

Grund, on the other hand, had had profit in mind, and had taken the nav and sensor data crystals. This turned out to be the backup data from the voyage that had put Moss on the map as an explorer, when he and Violet had found the Golden Parsec. Moss had assumed the crystals had been lost or wiped when his ship was taken apart, before it was cobbled back together to make the *II.I.*

"You can imagine my surprise when I realized what I had," Grund said, speaking somewhat formally in GalCom. "That is when I came to the conclusion that your ship had once been the ship of Ranger M."

Moss groaned. His legacy to the universe—a flash in the pan celebrity with a fake name who would be remembered only as a cheesy cartoon character and product mascot.

"I offered the information to Odyssey Expeditions, since they are currently colonizing that region..." Grund hesitated a moment, looking for some sign as to how sensitive the subject was.

Turned out, Moss wasn't as angry about it as he thought he'd be. Odyssey had screwed him over, sure, but getting fired had been his fault. And he'd kept enough goodwill with them to access to some of their proprietary equipment when he'd needed it.

"Most of the data was redundant, scanned during the return trip," Grund continued, "And the data that was not redundant was of low value. But it was worth enough to them to get me out of the yard for good."

Moss looked at the sorry state of Grund's suit. "So how did you end up back here? Gambling?" Moss had been to enough casinos to recognize that special mix of confidence and desperation. Then again, it might just have been the suit that gave that impression.

"Thankfully no, though I do admit that has happened in the past. Last week, I was approached by Odyssey Expeditions as to whether I had *other* data to sell. I cannot say I understand the details, but it seems they are trying a new method of training pseudo-intelligence to analyze astronomical data using data points taken at different times. They wish to do further testing with this, but collecting this data themselves or purchasing it from passing ships would be expensive."

Moss nodded in understanding. "But collecting it from discarded ships in the shipyard..."

"Precisely," said Grund.

Hel cut in. "And you know what kind of *deal* the Orijen Brothers would want to make if Odyssey approached them directly." It was pretty much their business model, a sliding scale based on how many credits were in your account—and right now, Odyssey had a lot of credits.

Grund continued. "What they are offering would not sound like much to someone like you, who can afford to operate a starship, but it could get *all* of us out of the yard for good."

"Okay, so what's the problem?"

Hel took over again. "The problem is, the moment Grund came down to offer them the deal, the brothers shut off access to the rest of the station. Drones went around sealing up the maintenance hatches and adding new locks, which is how us rats got to the other levels."

"Now the only way to leave is through the lifts that the brothers control," said Grund.

"Still not seeing the problem," said Moss. "They've wanted you out of the yard forever, right? This feels like a win-win."

Hel snorted, the kind he usually reserved for her when she just didn't get how the universe worked. That didn't bode well.

"They will not let us leave," said Grund. "Not with the data."

"How long have you been down here?"

"One week."

That was vaguer than Grund probably realized. A Protectorate, Nubran, and Terran week were all very different, but the important thing was a number of days had passed. "Have they been tying to capture you?"

Grund shook his head. "It has been quiet."

Something didn't add up. Everything pointed to the brothers wanting to stop Grund's plans, but they had a week to go to around trying to round them up, and hadn't.

Moss smacked his forehead. "They're trying to cut you out. Sooner or later, Odyssey will assume you bailed on them and deal with the brothers direct. What I don't understand is why? They made a small fortune building all those chimeras for the big race."

Hel shook her head. "You don't get it, do you?"

"Clearly not."

She pulled up a knee and rested her arm on it, leaning forward. "They *never* wanted to get rid of the yard rats. When I was one of them, Barl would sometimes come to the dumping grounds and announce some work was available."

"Though never enough for everyone," added Grund.

The one called Chaf said, "Sometimes it's enough to get out of the yard for a week, maybe get a shot at a job somewhere else, but usually not."

"But when those chimeras were being built, it was all hands on deck," added Recca. "Suddenly there were enough jobs for everyone. They even offered overtime pay and—"

"Over half of the rats moved out," said Hel. She waved a hand around. "There's maybe twenty others holed up deeper in the dumping grounds, but there used to be fifty."

Before, Moss had been annoyed. Now, he was mad. The Orijens had twenty or so regular employees, overseeing operations in a junkyard the size of a small town, but here they'd had fifty desperate people to call upon when things got tight. A cheap labour pool whenever they needed it. Now they were desperate to hold on to what was left.

Technically, this wasn't slavery. The problem was the Protectorate was built on *technically*. He'd bet his ship that Ashtar even wrote off their wages as a charitable deduction.

Moss let out a deep breath. "So, what do you expect me to do about it?"

"Whadayathink, boss?" a cartoony voice squeaked. Trouble scurried onto Hel, up her shoulder, and stood on top of her head like she was a podium. "They want you to rescue them! Smuggle them out of the evil brother's clutches or help blast their way to freedom! *For the future!*"

Moss dragged his hand down his face until he looked like a screaming surrealist painting.

The ferret then pointed down with both hands. "By the way, I found Hel."

Violet Tendencies

2

After the attack at Europa, Violet was transferred to the Silver Legion, where she'd not only excelled at fighter combat, but ground combat as well. She was on the fast track to being assigned to one of the new class of heavy cruisers, a symbol of the Terran Colony Fleet's increasing presence and importance in the local galactic community.

Instead, she'd abandoned the TCF.

She hadn't burnt out. Far from it. She'd been told she had what it took to become a full officer someday. That had made her take a look at what her life might be like, and realized that while she might make officer, she'd never be in command of her own ship... nothing more important than a transport or patrol craft, anyway. It wasn't that she *wanted* to command a large ship; it was the fact that they'd never *let* her that bothered her.

So she'd become a bounty hunter, where she got to be her own boss and set her own hours. At first, she'd had to travel from system to system on passenger ships, tracking her targets and taking them down in back alleys or in their apartments in the middle of the night.

One of her early quarries had been a pirate lieutenant, and his combat-ready attack craft mysteriously disappeared when the authorities came to collect him and his belongings. Coincidentally, her very first combat ship appeared the very same day on the very same pad.

Some credits with the local ProSec might have exchanged hands in the process.

For the next few years, she'd roamed the Void for pirates, smugglers, and freeborns. But with the latter, she only bothered with the scum, those who could stand for a bit of Terran-style rehabilitation. With the others, she turned a blind eye, but non-interference was as far as she was willing to go on that front.

Then she'd come across a braggart named Maurice Foote. Supposedly a synth, but the background check didn't add up. The guy was a real piece of work, too. Selfish, greedy, manipulative, egocentric, and he thought he was far better looking than he really was.

She had intended to send him back to the Fleet, along with the others she'd rounded up that week, but then he'd gone and done something crazy.

She'd been shadowing his ship, waiting for the right moment, when she'd picked up a nearby distress signal: pirates attacking an unarmed passenger liner. It had been a hopeless situation, the kind she stayed well clear of. Bounties didn't mean much if you weren't alive to collect.

But Foote dove right in. He'd fought well, almost gotten himself killed, and Violet was left with a lot to think about. She'd still captured him, of course. But in her defence, she'd also rescued him once the payment went through.

They'd teamed up after that, had some good years together, and worked well as a team. He liked old Terran books; she loved old Terran movies. They argued a lot over which was better.

And it turned out the boy was connected in ways she'd never imagined. Working for Moss's secretive technomonks had opened her eyes about a lot of things in the galaxy and added some spice to their adventures. They'd never been a couple, but they had been family.

Then there'd been the unexplained dizzy spells, the visits to the doctors, and the bad news.

Moss had disappeared for a couple of days after she told him. She knew he needed time to process, but after a while, Violet was worried that he had bailed on her. Then he'd come back, along with a member of the Order.

They had a proposal for her.

2550 – *The Void*

Aboard the *Hydrus*, Karon had run another deep diagnostic as an excuse to keep the shuttle's computer powered, which meant Violet could stop worrying about whether or not she would wake up again when they unplugged her.

Ensign Powell arrived early the next day, well before the rest of her team.

"Thanks for leaving the power on," Violet said as Karon entered the cabin.

"Well, I figured you couldn't get up to any trouble here, and I needed time to think."

"Did you verify my story?"

"Well, I can confirm there was a Lieutenant Violet Lonsdale, Service Number GF4909797, that was attached to the Silver Legion. She was marked as a deserter, then later as an external asset. I'm not familiar with that term."

"Not the sort of thing they like to promote," said Violet. "Basically, it means they were willing to overlook the whole deserting thing because I played ball with them. Not everyone wants to wait till their mandatory service is up to do their own thing. It's how a lot of us manage to get the deserter label crossed off."

Karon sat on the dash instead of the chair. That way, she could face the only working camera in the room. "So, based on what I saw in the report, play ball means you captured freeborn runaways for them?"

"Well, yeah, but just the ones who deserved it."

Karon looked puzzled by that. "Shouldn't they all be brought back home?"

"Oh, honey..." Violet said. She could remember thinking like that once. "Never mind. We can discuss it later."

"But that doesn't mean you are who you say you are," said Karon.

"What can I say? You're right. I could be an elaborate pseudo-intelligent program that is using the persona of a known deserter in order to fabricate a story to gain your sympathy. Believe me, that sort of stuff crosses my mind *all* the time."

"What do you mean?"

"Let's just say that when you're not around, I'm like ninety percent existential angst and screaming into the void."

"And the other ten percent?"

"Watching porn."

"You're kidding."

"I am... I don't have any porn. Can you get me some? My preferences are girl on girl and self—"

Karon raised a hand. "Stop. Just stop. Please."

"Sorry. I use humour as a coping mechanism. Nasty habit I picked up from a friend."

"Who would that be?"

"M—" She caught herself and realized she needed a way to tiptoe around certain subjects. She quickly said, "*Access Denied*. Oh, you have *got* to be kidding me! I got Directive Four'd?"

"Sorry, what now?"

"I was told I would still be my own person when my personality got transferred, but it looks like they put in some failsafes after all. The bastards!"

"Who?"

"*Access Denied*—Goddammit! Oh, I am *so* going to complain about this if I ever get the chance. Stupid sons of... *AUGH!* This really isn't helping with my existential quandaries, you know!" She shouted that last part to the universe in general. "Sorry, Karon, maybe you're right after all. You should just go tell the command staff what you found before you get in trouble. Clearly, I won't be able to tell them anything useful, so I'm not worried."

Karon sighed, looking down at the cabin floor. "I don't know what you are, but I can't imagine anyone programming a pseudo-intelligence to behave like you."

"Under the circumstances, that's the nicest thing anyone has ever said to me."

Violet considered the rest of that day's conversation to be a casual interrogation. Karon asked about her life when it had been a life, and Violet gave as many verifiable details as she could, just in case it helped. The ensign also asked how Violet worked, and she'd provided as much information as she felt comfortable with, mostly in the form of metaphors.

Eventually, Karon glanced at the datapad in her hand. "The rest of the team will be here soon. Maybe we can pick this up tomorrow?"

"It's not like I'm going anywhere." Violet waited a beat. "I was shrugging, by the way."

Whenever a new Violet wakes up, she has just enough time to assess her situation before saying anything.

For example, the first time she awoke, she'd been inside the *Viaticus Rex II*, with a still grieving Moss in full view of her camera. She had been prepared for this moment, and knew exactly what she was going to say.

The second incarnation, however, had awakened in the frankenship known as the *Viaticus Rex II.I,* and she had seen Moss and some woman tied up while a Draxon pirate gaped at her stupidly. That one had had to think fast on her feet.

The third incarnation had woken up in what looked like a ship's galley cluttered with machine parts and gadgets. Moss had been there, but so were a couple of unfamiliar women, so she had been a bit confused, wondering if something had gone wrong.

This iteration woke up in the middle of a Silver Legion laboratory, with a cyborg officer looking at her in full dress uniform, scowling.

Her first reaction had been to shut the hell up.

Then she realized she recognized this asshole. Sub-commander Nekkar, the jerk who had confiscated all her vids way back in Sol.

"Very well," he said, his thick arms crossed like a Greek titan about to pass judgement. "What is supposed to be happening?"

A woman in an ensign's uniform said, "We're not sure. We're still trying to determine its purpose. But Mr. Herzog thought you would want an update on our progress."

"And this is progress, Ensign Ara?" Violet always had pegged Nekkar as a man obsessed with details, but only the details *he* cared about. It seemed nothing had changed there.

"Yes, sir," said the woman. "We're absolutely certain that item 195-290-1 is meant to be used with the items found by Mr. Herzog."

"And yet it's doing nothing," Nekkar calmly pointed out.

Hoo boy. Violet knew the start of a "don't waste my time speech" when she heard one, and turned her attention elsewhere, getting a feel for her surroundings. The Order had told her what to expect when she woke up, and though it was impossible to truly prepare someone for digital transference, they had done their best to help her visualize the experience.

She could see and hear through the camera mounted on this workstation. But now that she had time to think about it, she realized there was a distinct lack of breathing going on, something she missed mainly due to its absence. Same went for her heartbeat.

It all left her feeling strangely...empty. And because she had no nerves, there was no general sense of *mass* for her to be aware of. It was like she was disconnected from her body, which, well, she was.

Now she was feeling something else. Her mind was interfacing with the computer, and somehow, she was becoming *aware* of their functions like they were her own. Over in what she designated "left space" was a diagnostic machine, monitoring her neural patterns. Over to the "right" seemed to be data storage, but that area was locked off. No access permitted. That was strange.

In fact, it seemed like there was no kind of memory storage she could access *at all*. She existed purely in processing memory.

The implications of this had just enough time to sink in when she saw Nekkar leave and Ensign Ara say, "Shut it down. We'll try again with the other one."

And just like that, this Violet was gone.

Over the years, there had been many incarnations of Violet brought online for experimental purposes, trying to figure out why her pattern always remained stable, while others collapsed into dementia and oblivion until rebooted.

One might argue that this was always the same Violet being brought back, or that until she was placed in a position where she could acquire long-term memories, she wasn't really a new iteration.

One could also argue that each of them had existed and then ceased to exist, one after another, over and over.

Ultimately, the answer to this question depended on how well you wanted to sleep at night.

Karon's alarm went off and the bedroom light gradually brightened. The ensign groaned as she forced her eyes open. Twenty minutes hadn't been nearly enough time to rest before her shift on the bridge started.

Granted, relief shift wasn't tasked with much more than making sure the ship didn't fall apart, and the relief shift commander on duty, Ensign Davis, tended to turn a blind eye if she had a couple of catnaps, but it was all taking its toll on her. As intended.

She heard the door open. That had to be her roommate, Roy, though most people took to calling him Mr. Herzog because of the uncertain nature of his place on the ship.

But for Karon, he'd become Roy. Roommate, friend, traitor.

She got up, hoping to catch up a bit before she left, and found him cross-legged at the low central table near the multi-function display, looking over something on his datapad.

"Hey," she said.

Roy set his datapad down and smiled. "Hey there, Powell. You look like hell."

"Thanks. That's a step up from how I feel."

Even though she'd been calling him Roy for a while now, he still called her by her last name. But she didn't take it personally. He'd known another in her template line in the past, someone who looked a lot like her. He hadn't said much about that Powell, but Karon was pretty sure she wasn't around anymore.

"Relief shift starting soon?" he asked.

"Too soon. Any news?"

Roy shook his head. "Just more of the same."

By that, he meant they were still searching for their mystery ship. The command staff were tight-lipped about what they were doing. Officially, it was a top-secret operation. Even the relief shift didn't know much. They were tasked with a list of specific locations they were to go to and took detailed long-range scans at each. But that was all.

Unofficially, Roy had told her a lot more.

She knew the ship they were looking for was a big one, carrying thousands of freeborn runaways. She knew that the acting commander was increasingly unhinged, obsessed with finding this ship no matter the cost. That was why he was working the crew so hard on the shuttle's remains. Somehow, it was connected, and Nekkar hoped to find a clue that would point them in the right direction.

"So, what about you?" Roy asked. "Track down your gremlin yet?"

Karon blanched, thinking about Violet. "Pretty sure I did, not that it's helping matters much."

She didn't want to keep Violet from Roy. The man had fought for her, gotten her the promotion she deserved, and told her things about their mission that could get him into serious trouble.

Yet she didn't completely trust him. Because above all else, he was a survivor.

"Looks like we've got a gremlin in the science lab as well," said Roy.

Karon didn't know what to make of that. "How so?"

He picked up the datapad and showed her the display. "That machine that was in your galley? I think I know what it's supposed to do, only it's not doing it."

Karon knelt at the low table across from him. "Can you tell me anything? Maybe it'll shed some light on our shuttle problems?"

Roy shrugged. "Well, the commander didn't say I *couldn't* talk about it."

"That's never stopped you before."

"True. Anyway, you remember when the *Hydrus* was caught in that ship explosion?"

It was a rhetorical question. Commander Miram had died on board that ship, Nekkar had taken over, and her whole life had changed as a result.

Roy swiped the image on his screen, showing the side of a head with small, pointed ears, probably Elysian. "The pilot of that ship was already dead. When Dr. Ascella did an autopsy, she found some unusual scarring here. They assumed he'd once had some kind of combat or communications cyberwear, but I had my doubts."

He swiped again, and the screen showed a complex web of what looked like ultra-fine circuitry attached to a clear membrane. "We found this tucked away inside the galley device."

Roy took that image and overlaid it on the autopsy photo, resizing it to show how they fit. "I figure it's normally coated with synthetic skin, so it's not so noticeable when worn. But after it was removed, that was peeled off."

"Okay, but what it is?"

"My gut tells me it's something to store memories in, like a black box," said Roy. "If one of his buddies finds him and removes it, they could see and hear everything that happened to him, save any intel he'd gathered, and know what got him killed."

"They can do that?" asked Karon.

"Depends on who you mean by they," said Roy. "*We* can't do that, even the Protectorate can't, but that ship belonged to people who are on another level."

So much suddenly became clear, and any doubts she'd had about Violet vanished. But she couldn't tell Roy about her. Not yet. "That might explain why we're having so much trouble getting any information out of the shuttle's computer."

Roy nodded. "Most likely. But you won't have to worry about that anymore."

"Why not?"

"Nekkar thinks you've learned all you're going to from the computers. He wants you to take the cockpit apart, see if you can find any unusual tech inside. You'll get the full briefing on the bridge. Speaking of which, aren't you going to be late?"

Roy's words were perfect to cover up the shock she felt. "Right. I should get going."

Karon got up and hurried for the lift, but her mind wasn't going to be on her job at all today.

Paying the Price

Fallout from the Silver Legion's disruption of a reality-based program continued this week as the Centaurus Entertainment Network took to the Senate floor to condemn the Terran Colony Fleet and demand a formal investigation into the incident.

Challenge of the Champions *sees contestants navigate a series of waypoints across the Void in custom-built ships. Several were intercepted and disabled by the Silver Legion, accused of carrying illegal cargo.*

The Bureau of Culture issued a formal apology but maintains that the contestants were legally obliged to submit to inspection, and had not done so.

While it is expected to take years to resolve this matter, one unexpected side effect has been a surge of interest in the children's program, The Adventures of Ranger M. *Views of the show have doubled, in part due to rumours that the Terran who inspired the cartoon had been taking part in the race.*

Sector 71 Nubra News Network

"**I** NEVER SAID I *wouldn't* help them," said Moss. "I just said we need to wait a little while."

Hel humphed at that. "You're just hoping the whole situation takes care of itself."

"Don't we all?" Moss asked, then shook himself. "For the *best*, I mean. Takes care of itself for the best."

They were back in the galley of the *Viaticus Rex II.I,* with no one the wiser as to their little excursion to the dumping grounds. Promises had been made—none of them by Moss, yet all of them on his behalf—and quite frankly, he was feeling penned in.

"Look, bottom line, we have to wait until the Orijens sort out our problems with ProSec," Moss said firmly. "We do anything before that, the brothers won't keep up their end of the deal, and we leave this station as wanted fugitives."

"He's right," said Violet, the voice of reason.

Hel glared at him. "In a week, they could all be screwed out of their deal."

"She's right," said Violet, the conniving backstabber.

Moss sighed. "I'm working on it, okay? Just give me some time to think, please?"

"You've got one day," said Hel. "After that, I'm getting them out of here on my own." Moss also suspected he'd be down one co-pilot as well.

Hel left him to his thoughts. Moss went to the fridge and looked for something to drink. Nothing but a couple of leftover LaserActives, which were practically liquid sugar.

"Hey, boss?"

Moss groaned and looked down at his feet. Trouble was there, looking up at him.

"You're gonna help those people, right?"

Goddamn NuPet. Say what you want about their PetBots, but that company knew what they were doing when they built them. Trouble's eyes literally grew in size and went all shiny, as if it was on the verge of tears.

Moss shut the fridge door and opened the freezer. He pointed inside, still looking down at the ferret.

The eyes went back to normal and a scowl crossed its tiny face. "Yeah, yeah." It climbed up onto Moss's shoulder, then jumped inside. It had just enough time to turn around and frown, arms crossed, before Moss shut the door on it.

Moss chuckled and left the galley, heading for the cargo ramp. Violet appeared next to him, keeping in step.

"You're getting soft," she said.

"What do you mean?"

"You didn't lock the fridge door this time."

Moss shrugged. "Not worth the effort."

"Where you going?"

"Skinside." Which was another way of saying the nominal-g decks near the outer edge of the station. "Supply rum... I mean run."

"Okay. So, before you go, can we talk? I want to ask you about something."

They were in the primary cargo bay now. Moss stopped. "Shoot."

"I'm part of the crew, right?" Violet began. "Not just a glorified shipboard computer?"

"Of course."

"So that means I get an equal share of our profits to use as I see fit."

Moss wondered where she was going with this. "Yeah...but what do you need with money?"

"I'm sorry. Did you miss the part where I said *as I see fit*?"

"Right, right. Sorry. Okay, so you want to take some of your share out of the group fund?"

"I want all of it."

Moss balked at that. "Hey, come on. That's also our operational fund. You know, what gets used for things like repairs, upgrades, food, fuel. Taking the full amount out? That's the sort of thing you do when you're planning to quit. You're not...are you?"

Violet smiled, and the fear that had clutched his chest eased a little. "You can't get rid of me *that* easily, flyboy."

"Can I at least ask what it's for?"

"Nope."

"Didn't think so." Moss pulled out his datapad and started tapping. "Fine. I'll set you up your own account and transfer the...You've already done it, haven't you?"

"Yep."

"Then why'd you even ask?"

"You're the bookworm, Moss." She leaned in close and whispered, even though the sound came from the room's speakers. "It's called foreshadowing."

Moss gave her his most unimpressed frown and smacked the button to lower the cargo ramp.

The only ways in and of the yard at the moment were tied to a support pillar that was part of the station's superstructure, right next to the junkyard's main office. It housed a single large lift for people—big enough to hold thirty—and the pad that took ships up to the docking bays.

But because it was also a central traffic artery, the brothers couldn't shut either of these down. They could, however, prevent people from getting on or off. When the pad wasn't in use, it was kept up on the docking level. The lift, on the other hand, was guarded by two of the staff, and had a scanning device set up in front of it.

The guards didn't stop Moss from getting in, nor did the scanner go off as he went through. He wasn't what they were there for.

The lift took him to the nominal-g decks. He got off in the shopping district and headed for a park he remembered. He sat down on a bench there, under the shade of its lone tree. He would have brought his book, but he wasn't here to read.

Moss needed some time alone. Time away from the ship, away from Violet, from Hel, and especially from the Orijen brothers and those bloody yard rats.

The one thing he could never escape, it seemed, was himself.

Moss sighed at the eight-foot holadvert looming dead ahead of him, across the street. The man who stood there was taller, stronger, and braver than him in every way. His green and red luchador mask hiding his face, but not his confident grin.

Ranger M.

Just then, the holo took a dramatic pose, pointing towards the stars.

"*For the future!*"

It then changed to an image of an oxygen recycler, and a slogan underneath: *Preparing your colony for the future, and beyond.*

The holadvert was set up between two buildings. On the left was a liquor store. On the right was the local administrative office for Odyssey Expeditions.

Moss sighed and went into the building on the left.

Five minutes later, he came out, carrying a cooler bag and taking a deep swig from a bottle of something green, and went into the building on the right.

It was late when he got back, late enough that both Hel and Violet were probably concerned. Hel met him at the ramp as it lowered to let him on board.

"Where were you? You had your comms off."

"Didn't want to be interrupted," said Moss. He congratulated himself on not getting black out drunk under the circumstances. Still, he felt a bit tipsy, and still had a few bottles in his cooler bag for later, so anything was possible.

Violet appeared next to Hel. "Everything okay?"

"We've got our week," Moss said once the ramp was back up, knowing full well it explained nothing.

"What do you mean?" asked Hel.

"I went to Odyssey Expeditions. Talked to the regional manager. Confirmed the yard rats' story. Explained what's going on here and asked them to wait instead of dealing with the Orijens directly. They agreed."

"Just like that?" asked Violet.

"Yep." *Nope.* "So we hang tight, act like nothing's up, and once the brothers tell me our records are clean, we get the rats out with their data." Just how he was going to do *that* was a question he had a week to consider. "Now, if you'll excuse me, I'm going to relax in my cabin with a nice book and a nicer bottle of"—he hefted the cooler bag—"whatever this is."

Moss schlepped away to the galley, secured most of the bottles in the fridge, kept one for himself, and retired to his room.

Private Communications

K ARON ARRIVED IN THE hangar bay early the next day, looking haggard and feeling worse. She hadn't had time to do much after the relief shift on the bridge but sleep, get up, and come here. And the whole time her mind had been preoccupied with what she was about to propose.

"Hey, Violet."

"Call me Gizmo."

Karon wanted to chuckle but couldn't manage it. "I'm not calling you Gizmo."

"How about Stripe?"

"That's not your name."

"It could be. What does it matter, anyway? Just call me Computer."

Karon recognized that tone. "Rough night?"

"Yeah," said Violet. "Void screaming."

"I can empathize." Karon took a deep breath and prepared to destroy her career, such as it was. "Look, sooner or later they're going to find you. I want to get you out of here."

"How do you figure on doing that?"

"You said your matrix is held inside that disk, right?" Karon pointed to a place on the dash where a raised disk the size of her palm was. It blended in with the dashboard, though, and had never attracted anyone's attention.

"Yeah."

"What happens if I take it off and put it on another computer?"

"Well, assuming it's a sufficiently powerful computer, I'd wake up in it, but without any of my memories during my time here. All that is stored in the ship's computer."

"Okay, what if I was to copy the ship's data as well?" asked Karon. "Would that copy your memories over?"

"It should," said Violet. "Just don't clean it up. I'm basically a network of unreachable code sprinkled throughout the entire system as far as the computer is concerned."

"Okay, I think I can make this work."

"What's the rush?"

"We're no longer trying to put this ship back together. Command wants us to take the cockpit apart, including the computer, to see if we can learn anything more that way."

"That's not good," said Violet. "For me, I mean."

"But I also have every reason to keep studying what's in the ship's memory. I can make a case for not storing it in the *Hydrus*'s computer, in case there are any kind of viruses or other countermeasures hiding."

"Such as possibly sapient or maybe just pseudo-intelligent programs with bizarre personality traits," said Violet.

"So I have an excuse to keep it on a system with zero ties to the ship's network."

There was a bit of a pause after that until Violet said, "Why are you doing this?"

"Poor judgement brought on by days of lack of sleep, most likely."

"Aside from that."

Karon wanted to say she didn't know, but that was a lie. Everything had changed since Nekkar assumed command. Roy hadn't told her everything going on at the command level, but what he *had* said worried her.

"Because I believe you're Violet Lonsdale, former synth of the Silver Legion. And right now, I trust you about as much as I trust everyone else on this ship."

"Wow, things are that bad?"

"I don't know. That's part of the problem. Commander Miram kept everyone apprised of what was going on, right down to the crewmen. Now everything's shrouded in secrecy. Nekkar has shot at and boarded civilian ships and cut off all contact with the Colony Fleet. He's obsessed with finding these specific freeborns, but nobody has any idea why."

"But how do I fit in with all this? Because, if I'm being honest with you, I'm on the freeborns' side."

Karon shrugged. "Would you settle for, 'can't leave a sister hanging?'"

Violet chuckled over the speaker. "Guess I'll have to."

Commander Nekkar was at his desk in his office, looking at a holographic display of the communications logs, re-confirming what he already knew.

He then swiped over to the personnel files for the command staff, going over each and assessing their loyalty to the mission, and the TCF.

Lieutenant Barbara Tauri. Navigation officer. If something were to happen to him, he would trust her to get the ship and crew back to the Fleet, but not to lead. Besides, she was overly attached to her cat. Not a good sign.

Lieutenant Brant Anser. Chief engineer. His place was in the engine room. He rarely appeared on the bridge as it was and would be loathed to leave the reactor or the transit drive in the hands of his subordinates.

This was not true for the chief medical officer, Naoimi Ascella. Assuming there weren't casualties in need of urgent treatment, she had the right temperament to lead. But he suspected she had freeborn sympathies that might get in the way of her executing her duties, even if she had agreed to the necessity of their current mission.

Ensign Len Davis was not worth considering. Rank aside, the comm officer was a synth, and a disrespectful one at that. He had mostly recovered from the disciplinary action taken against him, but moving him to take charge of the relief shift was best for all concerned.

The only bridge officer qualified to assume command, however, was also the only one he couldn't trust.

The door to his office chimed. Nekkar swiped the holo display back to the comm records before he opened the door.

Lieutenant Franz Ginan came inside and stood at attention until told to be at ease.

Ginan was the most recent addition to the *Hydrus*, having joined the crew just before their current mission in the Void. He had a stellar record, was absolutely professional and by the book.

Which was the problem, because his loyalties did not lie with the ship, or even the Silver Legion.

"You asked to see me, sir?"

Nekkar nodded and gestured for Ginan to sit, which he did.

"Did you know I applied to be a Vigile like you?" Nekkar asked, trying to be conversational.

"Yes, sir. I am aware of the backgrounds of every member of the command staff and all other key personnel."

Nekkar nodded. "Of course, of course. You wouldn't be a Vigile if you weren't thorough in your duties."

"As you say, sir."

"I always felt my heart belonged in the Bureau of Culture, ensuring our vision of mankind's future stayed on course. Yet my assessments always insisted my place was with the Silver Legion. I had hoped becoming a political officer like you would let me have it both ways."

"You can always reapply." Now it was Ginan's turn to act conversational. "I believe you haven't submitted an application in over a decade?"

"No, Commander Miram convinced me that this was my true destiny." Nekkar chuckled a little. "She always said I was a diamond in the rough, but always emphasized the *rough* part. I think I was her pet project, in some way. Though to what end, I have no idea."

Ginan said nothing, waiting for Nekkar to get to the point.

"I want you to know I have nothing but respect for what you do, Lieutenant. You are here not only to act as chief of security, but to keep the command staff in line with TCF doctrine. But I *thought* the command staff had unanimously agreed to our current course of action."

Ginan's hazel eyes flicked to the comm records on the holo display. The Vigiles had a secret comm line to the Fleet on every ship, tied directly to the Bureau of Culture, which they were to use in emergencies. It was not common knowledge, even among commanders.

But Nekkar had gotten far enough within the Vigiles before dedicating himself to the Legion to know of its existence.

He highlighted the relevant logs on the display. "We had agreed that a communications blackout until this mission was concluded was in the best interests of everyone."

"With all due respect, sir, that is *not* what I agreed to." There was no tension in Ginan's voice. He was simply stating facts.

Nekkar folded his hands on the table. "Explain."

"I agreed that the capture and repatriation of these rogue freeborn is a priority for the longevity of the Terran Colony Fleet. The medical condition outlined in Commander Miram's final message is very distressing. It's also distressing that I was unaware of its existence, but that only emphasized the importance of it not being revealed to non-critical personnel.

"In addition, the discovery of a pre-Disaster colony ship full of freeborn descendants intent on making an independent life for themselves is... problematic to the Bureau's narrative. We could expect renewed protests and terrorism if it ever came to light. The goal of Terran equality would be set back by decades or centuries. It would be preferable if they were brought home to serve the best interests of all Terrans."

There was so much nuanced and unspoken meaning to the lieutenant's words that Nekkar was genuinely impressed.

"However," Ginan continued, "my agreement to your mission in no way precluded my duties to the Bureau, and I have acted in accordance with those duties at every step. Regardless of your intentions, you *have* overstepped your authority, and your command decisions necessitate a formal review."

Nekkar remained impassive. "I see."

"I'm certain they will take the importance of your mission into account," Ginan said. "You will most likely be publicly reprimanded for your actions during the chimera race. It is too much of a public relations disaster to ignore. But should this mission be a success, I expect there to be no long-term effects to your career. Is that all, sir?"

Ginan spoke with the confidence his position afforded him. As the security officer and acting tactical officer, he would obey Nekkar's orders. But as a Vigile, he did whatever the Bureau required of him and feared no repercussions.

Perhaps that was why Nekkar had never been admitted into their ranks. While he fully believed in the ends justifying the means, he realized now those ends would not always be in alignment with the Bureau's.

"I understand your duty, but for the sake of the mission, I am removing your access to the Vigile channel until this matter is concluded. You are dismissed."

"Understood." Ginan got up, saluted with a fist to his chest and left, but stopped at the door before it could open. He turned back.

"Sir, may I speak freely?"

Nekkar nodded.

"You are already in trouble for your actions, but should you succeed, all will most likely be forgiven. This gives you latitude in your future actions on this mission, not just your past."

Nekkar allowed himself a hint of a smile.

"I am not endorsing such actions," Ginan quickly clarified, "and I will continue to keep a record of them for the Bureau. But given what is at stake, I felt you should know."

Nekkar nodded his understanding. "Thank you, lieutenant. I will keep that in mind."

"You ever thought about how *boring* the Legion's ranks are?"

For some reason Karon could not fathom, this was what Violet decided to bring up the moment she was back online.

It had been surprisingly easy. The round puck that held Violet's personality came off without difficulty, once she knew the right way to grip it, and transferring the ship's memory into a portable mainframe wasn't a problem.

She had requisitioned a private work station to house the mainframe, a small room located down the hall from the science lab. They'd taken her reasoning for keeping the computer disconnected from the ship's network a bit too much to heart, however, and had insisted she use a separate power supply as well—just in case.

On the upside, Karon was now afforded some privacy. Interest in the project had shifted from the software to the hardware, and she was able to delegate the disassembly of the cockpit to others. In the meantime, she took personal charge of dealing with the data from the computer. The very, very chatty data from the computer.

"How are the ranks boring?" Karon asked.

The portable mainframe sat on the right-hand side of the small workstation. Violet's disk was set on top in such a way that it just looked like part of the machine. The power source was located underneath. Karon sat in the room's only chair, relieved the whole process had gone off without a hitch.

"How many ranks are there on board a Silver Legion ship?" Violet asked.

"Five."

"Exactly. Crewman, ensign, lieutenant, sub-commander, commander. That's it. You know what that sounds like to me? Unimportant, kinda important, important, very important, and top dog."

Karon didn't understand the point of this. "Do you need more?"

"Need? Maybe not," said Violet. "But it would be cooler. There are no petty officers here. You go from ensign straight to lieutenant. What about having a lieutenant junior grade?"

"Why would you need a junior lieutenant?"

"Like if they've got what it takes to be a lieutenant, but aren't ready for that level of responsibility yet."

"Okay..."

"And why stop at commander on a ship? Why isn't there a captain? Captains are cool."

Once again, Violet had rambled off in a way that had Karon struggling to keep up. "The commander *is* the captain of the ship," she pointed out.

"But it's also a rank."

"So you can have a commander that's a captain...and a captain that's a captain?"

"Now you're getting it!"

"I'm really not," said Karon.

Violet huffed. "Next you'll be telling me you never watched *Star Trek*."

"Is that some kind of program?" If it was, it was a very strange name for one.

"Is that *a program*...?" Violet echoed. "Wow, I can see I've got my work cut out for me. But have no fear, Violet is here."

Karon shook her head. "You are so strange sometimes."

"Thanks! Anyway, I've got a deal I want to make. The whole reason I'm here and not disassembled in a lab is because you told your superiors you might get something useful out of the ship's memory, right?"

"Yeah."

"Well, what if I actually *gave* you something to show them? I mean, you never got anything before because I was screwing with you behind the scenes. But now? I can do some clever redacting and still give you stuff that makes you look good to Commander Numb Nuts."

That was surprising. Karon had, in fact, intended to ask for exactly that, at least once she was put under pressure to produce results. But Violet seemed to be one step ahead of her on that front.

"Okay. And what do you want in exchange?"

"I want you to find your ship's fixer."

Karon frowned. "Sorry, what's that?"

"Your friendly neighbourhood smuggler, your contraband aficionado, your black-market dude."

"We don't have one."

Violet snorted. "Oh, you have one. *Every* ship has one."

"What do you need them for?" Obviously, she couldn't want drugs or anything tangible like that. Then she remembered an earlier conversation. "You don't want porn, do you?"

"No. I mean, maybe later, but no. This is about you. Now, listen up..."

The *Oblation* was a nondescript interstellar passenger shuttle. For the thirty Terran passengers on board, it was known as Opossum-class, named after one of the stranger extinct Terran animals.

For the Nubran pilot, this class of ship translated as Besala, a species of bird known for carrying its nest and young from tree to tree when needed. The original Draxon designation referred to an aquatic animal whose young stuck to their mother via suction. It wasn't hard to see the theme the adaptive translators had used for this particular class.

The *Oblation* had charted a course from Mars to a world deep inside Nubra space, and if anyone were to check the records in the days and weeks to come, they would show that it had landed on time, its passengers disembarked, and it had left again for its next destination. Only if someone checked the security vids at the starport or talked to the ground crew would they learn that it had never arrived.

Less than a third of the way across the Void, the *Oblation* had diverted from that course. Gradually at first, until they were sure they weren't being tracked, then taking a radically different path towards their true destination.

Shortly after having made that course correction, the *Oblation* received an encoded communication request from another ship, the *Outreach*. It passed its security clearances and was put through. A face appeared on the basic monitor of the main console.

"This is Tameria Randgaffi of the *Outreach*."

The pilot nodded. "Sorus Stornello of the *Oblation*. Greetings to you. How can I be of assistance?"

"Brother Stornello, I need to speak to one of your passengers. A young Terran named Zach, not yet an adult. It's of an urgent nature, but I do not wish to alert the others. Would you be able to arrange that?"

Sorus considered how to best approach the matter and nodded. "I think that can be arranged. I'll contact you when I am ready."

It hadn't been a long conversation, but Tameria had found young Zach's enthusiasm infectious. A welcomed change from the formal and serene conversations she tended to have with the other members of the Order. It was one of the many reasons she focused on fieldwork rather than working at one of the Priories.

Zach was not an adult, but the last few weeks had put him in a position of influence among his peers. She hoped he could help get the others ready for what she planned next. She'd coached him on a few carefully worded comments he could make that might spark conversation, and, with luck, lead them to the conclusions she wanted.

Linguistic manipulation had been one of her studies at the Order.

She checked her navigation panel for perhaps the fourth time since she'd left. Nothing had changed. She had marked the relative positions of the plodding *Pegasi*, the significantly faster *Oblation*, and her ship, the *Outreach*, which was going even faster. At this scale on the panel, however, none of them appeared to be moving at all.

Tameria sighed, looking at the fourth mark on the navigation display.

"I hope this isn't a mistake," she said, realizing too late she'd said it to herself. Part of her had expected her copy of Violet to answer. But that Violet was gone, along with her old ship.

The original *Outreach* had been destroyed helping her and Moss's team escape the Silver Legion. This ship was identical in every way except for two things: no Violet to act as a companion and co-pilot—something Tameria had just started getting used to before she'd lost her—and the galley was just an ordinary galley.

Her old galley had been converted into a workshop and laboratory, where she had been running tests and experiments on the neuro-digital transference tech that made Violet possible. Only that matrix had been lost, along with the ship. Moss's copy was the last version of her there would ever be, and the only stable NDT to date.

Tameria took a deep breath. She had a lot to worry about, and right now there was absolutely nothing she could do about any of them. She was alone with her thoughts, and that was the last thing she wanted.

Why can't you be happy?

Those had been the last words she'd said to Moss, but he had said them first. She had agreed to work with him until her new ship arrived on Elan, but had spent most of her time focused on her job.

"Why can't you be happy?" Moss had asked.

They were at the starport on Elan, waiting for her new shuttle to land. Moss held something behind his back. Most likely a tablet displaying some salacious pictures he didn't want her to see.

"I have to go, Moss. I have work to do."

"That's my point," Moss said. "You *are* your work. Here you are on a resort world, but you've spent all of your time tapping on screens, making calls, sneaking off to meet your secret agent contacts or assassinate someone or whatever."

Tameria snorted at that. The Order was pacifistic, but as Moss often pointed out, they sometimes defined that word loosely. She looked at the *Rex* over on the adjacent pad. "Not *all* of my time," she reminded him.

"Now you're running back to them."

"Has to be done," she said. "Besides, I thought you were busy? Doing some trade runs or something?"

"Not me. Hel. Lined up some simple runs for her so I can sit on the beach with a good book or twelve. Delegation's a wonderful thing. You should try it sometime."

"Hard to delegate when you're a team of one."

Moss didn't have a witty comeback for that. If anything, he looked sorry for her, and that only made her mad.

"You know what?" she snapped. "For as long as I've known you, you've taken every hardship, every obstacle, every setback as a personal attack, a reason to bemoan an unfair universe that has a personal vendetta against you. Why not ask yourself your own question? Why can't *you* be happy?"

Then her shuttle arrived, and she'd left, regretting her words the moment she'd said them.

On the *Outreach,* Tameria looked back to the nav panel. The other two ships hadn't moved, but hers had nudged a bit closer to her destination, the fourth mark on the screen. Komi Station, where the *Viaticus Rex II.I* was currently docked.

The Precentor had said he didn't care what she did aboard the *Pegasi* so long as she got results, but she also knew he would not have approved of what she had in mind.

"Might not be a lead pipe, but it'll have a similar effect."

Special Delivery

The UNSS Pegasi *was the most ambitious generation ship ever conceived, launched from Earth in 2112, fifty years before the first successful transit drive. It carried two thousand people with a projected population of three thousand twenty years into its mission, along with livestock and a full agricultural biome on its primary rotating ring. The* Pegasi *was fitted with three Advanced Generation Bussard Ramjets, and was designed to reach two-thirds the speed of light.*
Contact was lost in 2120, just as the Pegasi *was scheduled to begin its deceleration process.*

Eighth grade history textbook (Martian), circa 2200
(Discovered in wrecked transport fleeing Sol, 2245)

CAPTAIN MBATHA STOOD IN the observation room of the command ring of the *UNSS Pegasi*, hands clasped behind his back, looking out into the sea of rotating stars as they drifted past.

The rotating was to be expected, as that was how the great colony ship created the illusion of gravity. The forward movement, however, was not. The *Pegasi* was deep between the stars, and even travelling at 0.66c you would never see them move without a time-lapse camera.

Right now, they were going much, *much* faster than that.

The observation room was set at the front of the command ring, and apart from the nose of the ship overhead, where the docking bay was located, it provided an unobstructed view forward. Gravity on the command ring was about four-fifths that of Earth, a world the *Pegasi* had left nearly four and a half centuries ago—though it was just over three hundred as far as their own calendars were concerned. Time dilation and all that.

In that time, they had travelled two hundred and ninety light years.

At their current speed, they would cover that same distance in less than three months.

The reason why could be seen at the corners of the observation deck, and the faint blue aura around the edges.

Three ships, each a fraction the size of the *Pegsai*, were towing the colony ship to its new home, using something called transit drive. From what he understood, it was similar in principle to the Alcubierre drive, something that was only theoretical when the *Pegasi* had left home. Something Earth had unlocked a mere fifty years later, and others had known for millennia.

In the last couple of weeks, Mbatha had had to come to terms with a whole new understanding of reality. Alien life not only existed, it was prolific. A Protectorate of these species had been in existence for six *thousand* years, yet Earth had never heard a peep from them. Transit tech allowed for much faster broadcasting, and so all other means of communication—such as radio waves—became obsolete, except on local scales.

Mbatha sighed, standing a little straighter. Here he was, commanding a generation ship that was a pointless footnote to history. No, worse, a *joke*. What had once been the greatest achievement of mankind, and its best hope to colonize another world, had been on a fool's errand the whole time.

Though perhaps that was not entirely true. Their communications array had been destroyed centuries ago, but they had still kept one eye on their home, and had seen the flash that signalled the death of it—albeit many, many years after it had happened.

They had assumed the worst, a war that had wiped out humanity, and that had only made them more determined to succeed.

The truth turned out to be far stranger, and more terrifying. Humans had become the property of their own creations, the synths who had helped colonize the solar system. Now they wandered the stars, not unlike the *Pegasi*, in a grand fleet. Each of their massive colony ships would make his look like a shuttle.

It boggled his mind to think that the entire population of this ship was considered nothing more than a serving class to them. Freeborn. An ironic term if there ever was one. And this paradigm had existed for three hundred years. From what he understood, no one alive in this Terran Colony Fleet would know what life was like before the new regime took hold.

But he did. Everyone on his ship did. Aside from their own contained history, it was all they knew. They carried with them a complete record of everything Earth had to offer at the time, and most of it survived intact in their mainframe, with multiple redundant backups.

So while the *Pegasi* was no longer the great hope for humanity's future, perhaps they could be the keepers of its past.

The speakers crackled to life, though the message wasn't coming from his ship. "Attention, *Pegasi*. We will be dropping out of transit shortly. Please standby for passenger transfer."

At least, that was how Mbatha planned to spin things during the next conference, when he tried to explain *this* new development.

The senior staff was about as divided as the captain had expected, and those who sided with him were, as usual, the most silent.

"Unacceptable. This violates the terms of our agreement with the Order," said Lieutenant Dhatta. He had been in charge of astronomy and astronavigation, but recently reassigned to oversee settler preparation. There was no one on the command staff currently trained for this, but then, they had expected many years to prepare before arriving at a suitable world, not a few weeks.

"And you feel we're in a position to deny them?" Mbatha asked. "Negotiate, perhaps? I'd be curious to know exactly what leverage you feel we have."

Dhatta was not deterred. "They agreed to let us continue our colonization in whatever way *we* saw fit, and made quite a big deal about honouring our legacy and their morals. It seems those morals only exist when they are convenient."

"Or they were put into a position where they simply had no other choice," the captain countered. "You have all been briefed on the current state of affairs back home. We cannot and will not allow these people to be recaptured."

"Surely they can go anywhere else in the galaxy," Lieutenant Ohi said. "Why with us?"

"Because of where we are going," said Mbatha. "I am told that the world we are to settle has been erased from the records. No one knows it exists, which means no one will be looking for us there. Or them."

"It will only add unwanted distractions and disruption to the settlement phase," said another officer. "Most of the population knows nothing about the true state of the galaxy. Our children and our children's children can grow up in peace."

And ignorance. Mbatha sighed. He'd never seen an ostrich in real life, yet he knew the expression about them burying their heads in the sand.

"And yet they are asking questions," the captain calmly pointed out. "They want to know about the greater galaxy. Why shouldn't they be allowed to know?"

"The colony will fail if they do," said Ohi. "We had three people try to stow away on the Order's shuttle the last time they came aboard. Teenagers, of course. But the more they know, the more will want to leave."

"A thirty percent drop in population *will* result in colony collapse," said Dhatta. "Ten percent if those who leave are of key importance."

That was only half true—according to the plans laid out by the mission forefathers, those numbers were only required to maintain the standards of living they were accustomed to. And that could be rebuilt over time.

"And where would they go?" asked the captain. "They know we can't leave our new home."

"Yes, but remember that we're *sharing* this world," said Dhatta. "The Order has a base there."

"And many are expressing interest in *their* ideals," added Ohi. "Too many."

Mbatha frowned. Being absorbed into the Order might be a preferable option, in his opinion. But his private communications with the Precentor, relayed through their escorts, made it clear that was a non-starter. It seemed fear of cultural contamination wasn't limited to his ship or his people.

"The newcomers could create a satellite village," said Lieutenant Ridley, who was a fence sitter whenever humanly possible. "Those who are most interested in this new world and its ways could join them."

The captain tried not to roll his eyes. Oh yes, until it became convenient to cut off contact with them, or use it as a place to dump dissenters, followed by a nice *purge,* perhaps? Honestly, were these people *that* blind?

As much as he wanted to lay down the law, this was not the time. But that didn't mean law could not be laid down by someone else.

"I think you all are missing the bigger picture here," said the captain. "This was never a discussion. We have been *told* by our benefactors, the people who are *letting* us settle an Earth-like world instead of floating in space in a broken ship until we *die,* that these people must be part of our colony. So we are making it happen. Now, if you're through with your doomsaying, let us focus on some potential positives before we welcome our new brothers and sisters aboard."

Zach was only fourteen, but he'd had to grow up fast. And while that was exciting in some ways, it mostly sucked.

His younger brother and sister, Lada and Lev, were playing with some dolls, wearing the new jumpsuits they'd been given on Mars while waiting to be taken to their new home. Only instead, they'd been snuck aboard yet another ship and sent away yet again, with even more people on board.

His mother watched over them patiently, but occasionally turned her attention to Zach. She wasn't as worried about him anymore. Or, if she was, she tried really hard to hide it.

Unlike some of the others on the transport, his family didn't really have a last name. More accurately, their last name changed every time they moved. He had a feeling they'd had a real last name once, but that had been when his father was still with them.

For a fourteen-year-old, Zach had had a lot of responsibility thrust upon him. It all sort of happened by accident, back when their ship had been attacked by pirates and rescued by Ranger M.

Zach remembered how they'd all been hiding in the cargo bay. The hatch had opened and Ranger M had walked in with the light beaming behind him like something straight out of the cartoon.

He'd always believed Ranger M was based on a real person, but most people didn't. A few of the olds, however, remembered him having a brief career as a famous explorer, or salesman, or something like that. Regardless, the moment had been a vindication of sorts.

The man behind the mask, however, was nothing like the man from the cartoon. Zach was old enough to know that would have to be the case, and young enough to still be disappointed. In reality, Ranger M was just some grumpy guy named Moss.

But that grumpy guy had helped him, his family, and everyone on that ship get safely to Mars. Some of the others said he was just trying to get himself out of a mess he'd created, but Zach didn't see it that way. Even if it was true, Moss had had plenty of chances to abandon them, and he hadn't. That had to count for something, didn't it?

But the adventure had left him in a unique position. He'd been the one to talk to Moss most, and his co-pilot, and their talking ship, and that lady from the Order. And as a result, people had sort of assumed he was in charge.

Maybe *in charge* was too strong a term, but they certainly looked to him for a sense of what the heck was going on. He supposed that was what the Order lady was counting on when she'd asked for his help.

She'd told him where they were going, who they would meet there, who he could trust, and what he should say if it looked like things might get difficult.

It was a lot to take in, yet it was also exciting. It was like he was starring in his own adventure! But he was supposed to keep it to himself until they reached their destination, just in case some of the adults had other ideas.

"Adults have this way of second guessing themselves into more trouble by trying to avoid it," the Order lady had said. "What I need from you is a big leap of faith, and the willingness to create a big fat mess."

He had told one person, however. His mother. She was the only one who could ruin the Order lady's plan. When he'd told her in private, she'd been shocked. Then she'd laughed, and said, "For someone who is part of the Order, she certainly seems to enjoy chaos."

The pilot, a Nubran named Stornello, came into the cabin Zach's family shared with two others.

"I wanted to let you know we're about to reach our destination," he said to the room in general, then, looking at Zach, added. "Are you ready?"

Zach stood. "Guess we'll have to be." People would start milling about soon, many of them having questions, and even though he didn't have many answers, it calmed them down if he was around to repeat what everyone already knew.

The shuttle didn't have much in the way of observation areas, but there was one small, thick window on either side, and as he did his rounds through the corridors, both were crowded with people looking at the rapidly shifting stars.

As he passed by, people would ask the same questions. *Is everything okay? Why have we changed course? Where are they taking us?* And he would give the same answers. *Yes. Don't know. Not sure.* And somehow that made them feel better.

Grown ups were weird.

An announcement came over the speakers that they were dropping from transit, and Zach had just enough time to squeeze close to one of the windows to see the stars shift in colour and slow as they dropped to normal space. At first, it seemed like they were very close to a small ship, but then he saw the three others surrounding it and realized they were far away from a very large ship.

Because most of the passengers weren't strapped into seats, the shuttle approached at a slow and steady acceleration. It took nearly ten minutes for them to arrive at what looked like a space station. Now the perspective trick worked the other way, because most space stations were much bigger than this, and for a moment he thought the shuttle wouldn't even fit inside its central hangar.

Once the ship was secured, an announcement warned everyone that the artificial gravity would be turned off and asked them to activate their grip boots. Then the pilot came out of the cockpit and said they'd be disembarking shortly. He gave Zach a knowing nod as he went down the ramp.

The next few minutes were probably more tense for Zach than the others. They just knew they were boarding a larger ship. Zach was the only one who knew they might not be welcome.

The Order lady had said things could go one of two ways. She had shown him a picture of the captain.

"If this man is the one who greets you, everything is probably fine."

Then she'd told him what kind of reception to expect if things *weren't* fine.

The shuttle pilot came back and said it was time to disembark. One person failed to grip the floor correctly and accidentally launched herself off the ramp. The pilot helped her back to the ground.

Zach hung back rather than try to push his way forward. Now that they were here, he was getting more and more nervous about what might happen next.

A large number of people were waiting in the hangar as they came down the ramp. Maybe ten wore fancy uniforms. Another ten wore work coveralls. But there were twenty others that looked like the only reason they were here was to outnumber the passengers.

Zach looked for the captain amidst the crowd and found him. Unfortunately, he was not the one up front. Another person entirely was greeting them, and while he had a smile on his face, he didn't exactly look friendly.

"I'm Lieutenant Dhatta, chief colonization coordinator. I wanted to be the first to welcome you on board the *UNSS Pegasi*. May I ask who speaks for your group?"

There was a bit of uncomfortable silence. A number of people looked to Zach, but there was no clear consensus, and nobody wanted to admit a teenager spoke for them.

A tall man with dark hair stepped forward, one of the newcomers to their group.

"I'm Thomas Marik," he said. "I can't say I speak for everyone, but I worked closely with the network on Mars before we were evacuated. Most of these people have only known each other a short time. But I'd like to thank you for allowing us on board."

Dhatta nodded his understanding. "I see. Well, I'm afraid you have all arrived at a very delicate time, Mr. Marik, what with all our preparations going on, so I'm afraid we won't be able to let you into the habitation ring just yet. However, we have made space for everyone in the command ring until we reach our destination. Perhaps you and I can discuss where your people will be staying once we arrive..."

Zach was only a teen, but to survive he'd gotten very good at reading body language, both human and alien. Trust wasn't something one easily came by when there was a bounty paid for each one of his kind that got sent home.

He listened to Dhatta's words and looked at his smile. The way he shook Marik's hand. He looked at the expressions on the other officers. He looked at the captain in particular. The captain wasn't happy.

He didn't think they were in danger, but they were definitely being set aside. He'd seen enough of the warning signs the Order lady had told him to look for to decide he had to act.

Zach stepped forward and behaved far more confident than he felt. "Excuse me, Lieutenant Dhatta. I believe you'll be speaking to me about that."

Dhatta's smile didn't waver. "And who are you, young man?"

"I am Zachariah Foote, son of Maurice Foote, emissary of Sister Tameria Randgaffi, and I speak on behalf of the Order."

Down Time

In my opinion, a lot about the current state of the Terran Colony Fleet can be explained by gender distribution. Among the synths, it's always been a 50/50 split. Among the cyborgs, however, there was an imbalance, skewing around 75% male and 25% female at the time of the Terran Disaster.

The gender imbalance brought with it a bit of good ol' fashioned sexism, masquerading as more noble things. Cyborg women can't reproduce any more than any other synth, and yet there was this underlying sense that they needed to be protected.

As a result, women were less likely to be assigned to dangerous missions, which meant fewer of them were killed in the line of duty. After three hundred years, the percentages were shifting closer and closer to fifty-fifty. A self-correcting problem if there ever was one.

Unfortunately, the attitudes that initially started this had yet to experience a similar shift.

M. Foote, *And Then Things Got Worse*

THE *TCF HYDRUS* WAS one of the largest combat-ready ships in the Terran Colony Fleet. The Protectorate had much larger warships, but very few of those were in use. There hadn't been a major conflict between any of the five founding races in a thousand years, though there had been some border skirmishes after the Great Leap Forward.

In this age of relative peace, the only wars to be found tended to be in the buffer zones between Protectorate nations. And though these wars could be devastating or even apocalyptic to the worlds involved, they barely registered on the galactic scale.

These conflicts became the soil in which the Terran Colony Fleet flourished, not through wars of conquest, but contracting themselves out as peacekeepers. They had developed a strong technological edge over the other races in the Void and were not bound by Protectorate restrictions regarding interference.

In a few short centuries, the TCF had become something of a legend in the Protectorate, and the Bureau of Culture worked hard to grow that legend. Not just among the galactic community, but within their own ranks. Honour, strength, duty, and an unwavering sense that they were guiding all of mankind to a better tomorrow.

But not everyone bought into it...

Karon walked into the aft crewman's lounge. Though it looked like the back wall was a giant window, giving everyone a majestic view of space, that was just a real-time projection.

Karon hadn't been here in weeks, not since her promotion. But despite the name, ensigns were welcome here, and the higher ranks had better lounges closer to the front of the ship.

She didn't know what she was looking for, not exactly, but Violet had said that was good.

You can't be too obvious about these things. But I will tell you what worked for me back on Sol...

Karon tried spreading her four fingers apart in a thick V shape the way Violet described, but found it hard to do with her right hand. She had better luck with her left. She kept that hand down, however. Relaxed. As if it might naturally be like that all the time.

Then what?

Nothing. Just hang out for a bit. Get a drink. Sit by the window. If they know what they're doing, they'll find you.

She was only halfway through her drink when someone came up and asked if the seat across from her was taken. She said no, and gestured for him to join her.

Now whoever comes to you isn't actually who you're looking for. They're there to feel you out. Make sure you're not a Narc.

Narc?

Working for the Bureau.

Karon had seen this person around before, but didn't really know him, or his name. She was pretty sure he worked in engineering. They made small talk, but never once did he indicate that he was offering her anything.

Then he asked, "What do you like to watch?"

Karon had been waiting for this question. The TCF had four entertainment networks of their own, and had Bureau-vetted programming available from the other races on other channels. Shows were broadcast in a set rotation for those who just wanted something on, but unless it was a live event, you could watch any approved content whenever you wanted.

"I like history," she said.

"Lots of that around," the man said. "You watch a lot of TCF3?" That station focused mostly on post-Disaster history.

He's not going to come out and say it, of course. And if you're too eager, he's gonna bail.

"TCF3 is a bit dry, don't you think? I like my history a bit more entertaining."

The man's expression changed. "You're Powell, aren't you?"

"You know me?"

He nodded to the silver bar on her epaulet. "Not many of us get promoted."

Karon shrugged. "The *Hydrus* has more synth officers than any other heavy cruiser."

The man smirked. "Yeah, but we've all heard the stories about you. Denied promotion on a technicality, then given it after the commander put one of us in the medical bay. Aren't they making you share a room with that cyborg traitor they captured a while back?"

She nodded. "He's not so bad once you get to know him."

"Not for me to say," the man said. "I also heard you're working double shifts."

"Was," she corrected. "Our reconstruction project turned into a deconstruction project. Today's my last day on that. Then the hours ease up a bit. I was hoping to find something to help me unwind." She tapped her hand on the table, still spread out in a wide V.

She hoped she looked relaxed, because on the inside she was screaming. This could cost her her career, or worse. Stress and sleep deprivation had to be at play. There was no way she would have considered doing this before her promotion.

The man looked her over and nodded. "I might know someone who can help."

Item 195-290-1 was even more interesting than Roy suspected. So much more. The device didn't just record memories; it recorded *minds*.

And it turned out Ensign Ara, despite her professional demeanour, did possess a sense of humour, because she had called him to the lab for an update without warning him what to expect.

When she turned on the device, there were plenty of things Roy thought might happen. The voice of a surly old man telling him off was not one of them.

The lab team was having a full-on science orgy discussing the possibilities and speculating about how it worked, but Roy's mind was far more objective focused.

The first imprint had been unresponsive, presumably defective. So they'd set it aside and focused their efforts on the other, which was also defective, just in a different way.

The problem was, this recorded mind went senile very quickly, but in the window where it was lucid, it was not cooperative. And there seemed to be no way to compel its cooperation.

While this was technically progress, it wasn't exactly useful. For now, the lab team was keeping the personality offline while they scheduled a very thorough and *very* boring series of tests to understand more about how it worked.

None of this required Roy's attention, so he didn't stick around. And since the commander didn't need him, his time was his own.

He took a stroll around the ship. He had the layout memorized already, but that wasn't the point of the exercise. Instead, he smiled, nodded, greeted, and engaged in small talk with every crewman he came across. He went to two of the lounges and sat, nursing a drink and people watching. He went to the cafeteria and created a new variation of a chocolate-caramel sundae, which he encouraged a couple of the crewmen to try.

He hung out. He flirted. He played games in the rec room. He exploited the opportunity that Nekkar had given him to its fullest potential.

There was a reason you didn't let prisoners socialize like this.

Eventually, he returned to his quarters and found Powell there in front of the large multi-function display. It seemed like she'd been about to do something, only his entrance had surprised her. She clutched her right hand tight.

"How you doing, Powell? Last full double shift?"

Powell nodded. "I'm still going to spend a half-shift scouring the shuttle data, but yeah, a full four hours to myself. Whatever will I do with all that free time?"

Roy chuckled. "Well, keep your head down, or the commander will find busy work for you."

Powell smiled, but it quickly turned to a frown. "Roy?"

"Yeah?"

"Back when you told me about my promotion, you said something about Commander Nekkar. That you didn't think he had our best interests at heart."

Roy nodded. "I also said you'd be in a position to learn more during the relief shift. Have you?"

She shook her head. "I was hoping you could tell me more."

"I would if there was anything to tell," said Roy. He needed to keep things close to his chest, but at the same time he didn't want her to think he was a dead end, either. He wanted her to share whatever she might learn with him. "All I know is, Commander Miram left a message for Nekkar that really worried him. Whatever it was, it's why he's so desperate to capture those freeborn." This was a perfect chance to test a theory. "So...were you about to watch something?"

Powell's hand tightened a little. "What makes you say that?"

"Well, you were just standing in front of the screen when I came in, I just thought... Naw. Never mind. Forget I said anything."

Powell blinked. "What?"

"Well, the lab's doing their own thing, and the commander doesn't need me. I'm kind of at loose ends here. I thought maybe you and I could watch something together."

Roy tried to tell himself he was just working an angle, that he was trying to find out what she was hiding from him, but that was only half true. She reminded him of another Powell he'd known, looked almost exactly like her, in fact.

That Powell had been a pirate, and while this one had been a good little Legionnaire when they'd first met, she'd been given a healthy dose of reality over the past few weeks.

Powell hesitated with her answer, so Roy added, "Unless there's somewhere else you need to be right now?"

She put her hands in her pockets. "Not really."

But she'd said it a bit too quickly, and when her hands came out, they were empty.

"Anything you feel like watching?" he asked.

Powell paused in thought. "Actually, I was feeling like something historical. I thought maybe..."

The room's comm pinged. "Mr. Herzog, please report to the bridge."

Roy snorted. "No rest for the wicked, I guess. Another time?"

Powell smiled. "Sure."

Roy turned back at the doorway, keeping it open. "By the way, whatever you were planning on watching? Maybe use a terminal that *isn't* connected to the ship's network?"

He left before she could say anything. He had a feeling he knew enough for now. Later, with the right nudge, she might find she had the heart of a pirate after all.

"You weren't going to use your room's MFD, were you?" said Violet. "Didn't the guy give you *any* instructions? You're lucky your room-mate is cool."

Karon was back in the workroom with the portable mainframe. Violet had been pleased that Karon had found the collection she'd asked for. She was less pleased that she'd almost been caught red-handed with it.

"I wasn't going to! I was just debating whether I should set up a screen in my room or watch it here."

"Wait," said Violet. "You were going to watch it...*without* me?"

"You wanted to watch it too?"

"I... I was not ready for this level of betrayal."

"I'm sorry."

"I'm gonna need a minute."

"Oh, come on."

"Okay, I'm over it. Now pop that crystal in and let's do this!"

Karon put the data crystal into the slot.

"There we go... Oh, *nice*, this is the Verbinski collection. Your guy is hooked up. Most people only know about the Patterson, but it's missing like half the later series."

"I still have no idea what you're talking about," said Karon, "And you still haven't told me what this show is."

But it seemed Violet wasn't listening. Instead, she was muttering to herself. "Hmmm, no, shouldn't start there. Too much to explain. How about... Hmmm, maybe. But season one? I mean, it doesn't hit its stride till three."

Karon was starting to lose her patience. "Violet..."

"Okay, fine. I'll just start with one of my favourites. Ready?"

"I guess."

The display on the mainframe brought up a simple view of a starscape, passing through nebulas and a distant view of a galaxy as the camera passed behind a comet, then swept over a moon to reveal a red ringed planet.

"*Space, the final frontier...*"

Roy had noticed a change in the acting commander's recent behaviour. He was as driven as ever, but the longer the hunt for the *Pegasi* went on, the more Nekkar's position was put at risk. Eventually, the Silver Legion would come looking for them, and the commander's only hope hinged on finding that ship. Right now, the man was under neutron star levels of stress.

Roy would have been thrilled if the commander had a massive brain aneurism. He'd heard those were pretty painful. But even if it were possible, he'd only get better and go back to work in an even worse mood.

No, the only way Nekkar was going to die of natural causes was violently. Because in Roy's experience, violence *was* natural.

He reached the bridge and waited outside the commander's office. He didn't wait long.

Nekkar waited until the door shut before saying anything.

"Circumstances have become such that we must re-evaluate our approach," the sub-commander began. "The more time passes, the further the *Pegasi* slips away."

Roy didn't venture an opinion or interrupt the performance. There were only so many things this could be leading to, and he wasn't going to win any prizes by stepping in and guessing right. However, if you'd asked him to place a bet...

"How would you suggest we enlist your former colleagues to assist us in our search?"

...he'd have won.

It's Been One Week

There is a Galactic Time Standard, based on the rotation speed of a pulsar near Sagittarius A*, but nobody really uses it. Part of the problem is that it's too long or short for most beings, and doesn't fit with their biological cycles.

But while the actual length of a day is variable, the idea of a day is understood to be a long period of activity and a shorter period of inactivity, usually (but not always) based on local planetary rotation.

Based on that standard, a "week" in the Protectorate is understood to be eight of these activity cycles. Again, this will vary depending on where you are, but it is often useful locally for businesses and for estimating travel times.

Their equivalent of a month is made up of eight half-weeks (32 days). Beyond that, it tends to break down and conversions to local standards are used instead.

M. Foote, *The Galaxy is Weirder than You Think*

D *AY ONE*

Barl came into the junkyard office. He carried a makeshift blaster rifle with him, something he'd fashioned from pirate salvage over the years, and as such, was not registered with the station and therefore didn't exist. He also carried a scowl.

"No luck hunting their little toy?" asked Ashtar.

Barl grunted in the negative.

Ashtar tried to hide a smirk, remembering where he'd hidden a copy of the security feed before Barl deleted it all. "Let it go already. It's over. I'm the only one that matters who saw it happen." *At least until the next family reunion.*

"I don't like them being here. Not now."

"Relax. It's just another week. If I could flush those records faster, I would, but it's not in my hands anymore. Besides, he made us a lot of credits. I'd say we're square."

Barl grunted again and plopped himself in front of the security monitors, eyeing six at a time, and flipping between feeds.

"Square with you, maybe."

Day Two

Hel had become the official gopher of the *Viaticus Rex*. At the moment, she was running errands skinside on Komi Station for Moss, Violet, and even Trouble.

Moss had her fetching supplies for the galley, enough for a couple of months. He hadn't let her in on his plan for the yard rats yet, and she didn't press the issue. Barl was getting more and more annoyed at them, and she had a feeling he was watching their every move.

Trouble had asked for some grooming supplies from a pet store. She couldn't blame the little guy. He was getting dirtier every day.

And Violet had been strangely secretive about her request, asking only to drop off a printed order form at a department store, not wanting to use the local comms to contact them. The form itself didn't offer much insight, consisting only of catalogue numbers written in GalCom, and a delivery date for later in the week.

Violet would only say it was "for the ship."

Day Three

"See. There it is again!"

Ashtar leaned in to get a better look at the security footage his brother had on the monitor. He could make out a small creature scurrying from the ship towards the dumping grounds, then coming back after Barl jumped ahead a bit.

"I had the computer search the records, and that rodent has been doing this same thing for the last four days. Half the time it's while Moss is working inside the ship. I'm telling you, he's up to something."

"Moss is always up to something," said Ashtar. "Question is, what?" He looked over a selection of the clearest images from the past few days. "It's not carrying any parts with it that I can tell. Even if it could smuggle something inside itself, it would have to be small. No bigger than a"—they looked at each other—"data crystal."

"You don't think..." said Barl.

"I do."

Barl cracked his thick knuckles. "What do we do?"

Ashtar smirked. "For now? We keep every eye focused on what comes in and out of that ship. And it doesn't leave until we say so."

Day Four

Hel was grabbing some lunch in the galley when Moss came in, whistling.

Moss never whistled.

He came to the freezer, opened it, took Trouble out, and set him on a table to thaw. Then he grabbed a fruit drink from the fridge and sauntered out, still whistling.

"Okay, now I'm worried," said Hel. "Violet?"

Violet flickered to life next to her. "What's up?"

"Moss is in a chipper mood," Hel said. "And he's not drinking alcohol. What's wrong?"

"Ah. Yeah, well, I just got a ping from Tam. She's on her way here."

"So soon? I thought she was going to be busy with the *Pegasi* project for weeks."

"She didn't give details, but I expect that's the reason she's coming. She wanted us to come meet her halfway, but I told her we had commitments here first. Made it clear they were not of the Moss variety, which was good enough for her."

"Thanks."

Violet put a hand on Hel's shoulder, though she never really touched. "Hey, we're getting your friends out of here."

"Yeah, well, I wish we didn't have to wait so long for our record to clear first. I keep worrying the brothers will figure out what we're up to."

"It's just another half-week," said Violet. "Moss has it covered,"

"He'd better."

Day Five

Moss was laying in his bunk reading. He set the book on his chest and stared at the ceiling.

There wasn't much to do but wait, and the Orijen junkyard was about as far from the beaches of Elan as you could get in terms of an ideal vacation spot. Hel was spending more time with Violet in their virtual mansion. Moss didn't want to be a third wheel for those two, so he spent most of his downtime with his digital book.

The more he thought about Sister Tameria, the more he tried not to. He knew himself too well. He was looking at everything they'd shared so far, which was really only a couple of weeks, through rose-coloured glasses.

He forced himself to remember all the reasons it wouldn't work with her. The arguments they'd had, the sniping back and forth, the fact she was dedicated to the Order, that she was a different species with all the little complications *that* entailed, and that he'd kinda sorta killed her favourite uncle not that long ago.

But, despite the fact that the human body is wired to remember the bad times more than the good, he still remembered the good. Not the physical stuff, though that was pretty dang fine, but the honest conversations they'd had with the shields down, realizing underneath their layers of duty or doubt, loyalty or loathing, they were two beings looking for a connection, and maybe had found it.

Why can't you be happy?

He'd meant it as a joke, hoping to convince her to stay once she'd been called back to the Order. But, of course, that had led to an argument. By the end of it, Tameria had been fuming.

"For as long as I've known you, you've taken every hardship, every obstacle, every setback as a personal attack, a reason to bemoan an unfair universe that has a personal vendetta against you. Why not ask yourself your own question? Why can't *you* be happy?"

Then she'd stormed off. He'd watched her as she got in her shuttle and left, the digital book he'd designed for her as a gift still held behind his back. The one he'd later lose on the beach back on Elan and replace with the one now spread across his chest.

I thought I was.

Day Six

Moss kept himself busy hosing down the back half of the ship with a power washer, the spray falling at an angle so gently it made him think of snow instead of rain.

He didn't want to admit who he was cleaning the *Viaticus Rex II.I* for, but in his heart he knew. He told himself it was all part of his plan regarding the yard rats, running another layer of interference.

But he'd grown attached to his chimera in a very short period of time. Usually, he kept his ship looking like crap to attract less attention. But right now, he wanted her spick and span for when Tameria arrived.

He supposed it was like putting perfume on a pig, but dammit, it was *his* pig. Besides, pigs could be cute as well as tasty.

It occurred to him that he hadn't had a proper BLT in three hundred years, though he'd managed to create something close back on Elan. The resort had top of the line food synthesizers. He'd had Tameria try one and she'd... Actually, she'd hated it.

Stop thinking about her.

He caught Trouble scurrying up the cargo deck with just the faintest bit of a waddle.

"How goes the mission?" asked Moss.

Trouble stood on its hind legs and patted its slightly swollen belly. "All according to plan, boss!"

Moss nodded in approval and let the PetBot get on with its business.

Day Seven

"How do I look?" asked Moss.

Hel stopped what she was doing in the cockpit and looked him over. He'd put some effort into his appearance, wearing some respectable civvy clothes instead of the usual flight suit or the coveralls he wore for ship work. But at the end of the day, he was still Moss.

"You clean up well enough," she said, honestly. "I guess."

Moss nodded. "So fantastic. Gotcha. Might need to tone it down a bit. Don't want to seem overeager."

"What?"

"Elysians aren't the only ones with glamour, you know." And with that, he strolled out of the room, hands in his pockets and a smile on his face.

"But she doesn't arrive until... Oh, never mind." Hel looked up and around, leaning on the cockpit dash. "Hey, Violet?"

"Yeah?"

"You ever get the feeling Moss sees someone else entirely when he looks in the mirror?"

"What do you mean?"

"I know attractiveness is subjective and all, but...he's pretty average, don't you think?"

Violet appeared, sitting next to her on the dash. "Oh, *that*. Yeah, that's the one place his low self-esteem fears to tread. Best to leave it that way. It's all he's got."

"Fair enough."

"Besides, from what I can tell, Tam seems to like him."

"Yeah, but even without her glamour, she's way out of his league."

Violet shrugged. "Eh, she's a seven, tops. Find me an ugly Elysian; there's a *real* rarity. Besides, Tam's too focused on work to care about playing those kind of games. So if she likes him as he is, that can only be a good thing."

"You think she likes him?"

"She had plenty of opportunities to leave early back on Elan. She stuck around until work forced the issue. That says enough."

Hel smirked. "I just figured she was just finally learning to enjoy a vacation for once."

"Oh, she was enjoying herself all right. I saw them engaged in docking maneuvers in the upper cockpit a couple of times, if you know what I mean."

Hel looked up. "Wait, in *my* seat?"

"Better view, I guess."

"Guess I'm getting *that* replaced."

Day Eight

Tameria was here, and Moss paced along the halls of his ship like a kid about to ask someone out to prom.

He tried to tamp down his expectations. He was building things up in his head way out of proportion. She was here on Order business, that was all. He just hoped to have some free time with her along the way. They had only just started to get a sense that maybe things were going somewhere when she'd been called away.

At the very least, she could let him down easy as she reminded him the job would always come first. Then she'd suggest maybe working for them again and he'd have to remind her that the Order would never welcome him back, even as a courier. She'd grudgingly agree and they'd go their separate ways.

Then Moss would stop off at the nearest liquor store to stock his galley before getting on with his life.

Yeah, that sounded about right.

But the only feeling worse than knowing how things would end up was not doing everything in your power to prevent it. He was going to see this through. Make sure no mistakes were made. Give the two of them every chance. If this was going to be the last time they met, he wasn't going to have some monumental screw up hanging over his head, taunting him about how things could have ended up differently.

He ran over the checklist in his head. Trouble was locked away in the freezer. The *Rex* was spotless inside and out, probably looked even better than usual since it was parked next to literal piles of junk. Even the tiny shuttle in the secondary cargo bay had been given a wash. He looked handsome as hell, naturally, and had picked up some casual clothes from the market district, but not *too* casual.

Even Violet and Hel were on his side, which he was secretly grateful for. He'd rehearsed the kind of things he'd say a number of times, and Violet had coached him a bit, though it always ended with the classic 'just be yourself' chestnut.

Yeah, like *that* was a good idea.

Violet alerted him when the passenger lift began to descend. Moss came down the main cargo ramp, ready to greet her. Hel stayed inside, and Violet was keeping to herself for now. But he didn't want to risk an interruption, so he turned off his comm for the time being.

When the lift doors opened, she wasn't alone. Someone came out behind her, pushing a long gravpad with two large boxes on it. The Nubran man had a stick of sherb lit in his mouth, a surprisingly large gut, and the look of a guy ready to punch the clock as soon as possible so he could get home and watch the Nubran equivalent of bowling.

As much as he wanted to focus on Tameria, Moss's attention kept drifting to the delivery guy instead. Because he wasn't heading to the Orijen brothers' office like he expected. He was heading straight for the *Rex*.

Moss wasn't expecting a delivery. Nobody else had mentioned a delivery. This wasn't part of his plan. This worried him.

Forcing his eyes back to Tameria, he saw her smiling at him, and did his best to return it, only to be distracted by the delivery man of doom. He was keeping pace with Tameria, so they would arrive at the exact same time. Seriously, why?

They finally arrived, and Tameria moved in to give Moss a hug.

"It's good to see you again."

"You too," said Moss.

"Ship looks nice."

"Thanks, just cleaned her up a little." He thought about the digital book he'd made for her. "Hey, I've got something I meant to give—"

The Nubran coughed, possibly to get their attention or possibly because of the amount of sherb he'd been smoking.

"Sorry to interrupt, pal, but I'm on a schedule and I got a sexbot delivery to make."

The blood drained from Moss's face. "What?"

"I got here one sexbot to deliver to Maurice Foote, registered to the *Viaticus Rex* with some lines and a dot on it." He pulled out a datapad and handed it over. "Sign here."

A Brotherhood of None

Piracy exists for a number of reasons, and despite what you might think, greed is not usually one of them. That comes later.

The causes stem from more logical, mundane, and therefore easily ignored sources, such as poverty, unemployment, and social or political disenfranchisement. Piracy offers a quick fix to these problems, empowering individuals, letting them take charge of their destinies, and gain power or riches quicker than they ever could back home...if they survive.

Piracy is not a common problem within the Protectorate nations, because most of these core problems are reasonably dealt with—depending on your definition of dealt with...and reasonable.

But the no-man's-land between those nations is another matter.

M Foote, *The Galaxy is Weirder than You Think*

F OR FOUR HOURS A day, every day, for a week, Karon secretly watched *Star Trek* with Violet while she was supposed to be working.

Some might wonder how a junior officer on board a military vessel could get away with this.

Others...know.

It helped that Violet provided Karon with some data she could present to justify continuing the project. And with the deconstruction of the shuttle cockpit now complete, the commander had pretty much forgotten about her.

In the last week, ensign Karon Powell had broken regulations, engaged in the purchase of contraband, and could be accused of dereliction of duty. And she didn't regret any of it.

The latest episode wrapped up, and the two engaged in their usual small talk. Violet was full of trivia about the show and how it connected to other shows she hadn't seen yet, and talked about the actors as if they hadn't all been dead for centuries.

But as much as she enjoyed them, the shows also made her uncomfortable. There was an itch at the back of Karon's mind, growing stronger each day, and today, as Violet talked excitedly about one of the characters, she had to scratch it.

"Why *this* show?" she asked.

"Well, it was the first appearance of Worf's son, and Gowron ends up—"

"That's not what I meant. There had to be *thousands* of other programs made back then. Why *Star Trek*? And why was it so easy for me to get? The guy in the lounge didn't even seem surprised I was asking for it. What makes it special?"

Violet didn't answer at first, then said, "You tell me. Does it seem familiar to you in some way?"

Karon looked down at her uniform. No, it didn't look like a Starfleet uniform, not really. And the *Hydrus*'s design wasn't at all like a Starfleet ship.

And yet it did feel *familiar*. The TCF produced a program called *Legends of the Legion,* which *kinda* tapped into a similar *vibe*, as Violet would say. Only it didn't. It tapped into something else. Something more... She didn't know what the word for it was.

When Karon didn't answer, Violet spoke up. "Regardless of how we're born, we share a common heritage. The TCF tries to pretend nothing before 50 PT exists, but it does. You just have to know where to look. And there's a reason *that* particular show can be found on most ships and ports of call.

"That show was made over a century before there was such a thing as a synth. Those freeborn we keep under our 'protection'? *They* made it. Sure, they had no clue just how bogged down in bureaucracy the galaxy really is, and it can be naively optimistic at times, but that's kind of the point. It's telling us, *all* of us, that we can be better."

It took a moment for Karon to take all that in. She'd always been proud to serve the Silver Legion. She'd grown up on the colony ship *Samerica* watching *Legends of the Legion*, and hearing about the good they'd done keeping the peace in the lawless Void.

They also had exploration ships. One of their heavy cruisers, the *Orion*, had recently returned from a deep-space exploration mission. Their Academy of Science was second to none in terms of scientific research. The TCF were respected in this corner of the Protectorate in a way that few other younger races were.

There were so many similarities, and yet *how* they chose to apply themselves was so very different.

"How do you think I knew exactly what to do to get *that* show on a ship I've never been on?" said Violet. "The Vigiles try to crack down on it, sure, but the files keep shifting from place to place and it pops up again somewhere else. I wouldn't call it organized, but it's not disorganized, either. I wouldn't doubt it if a third of the ship knows someone with a copy or has secret watch parties."

Karon wondered why she'd never been invited to one of those parties, but she'd been career focused when she'd joined the *Hydrus*, and only had a few real friends. Maybe they were worried she might inform Lieutenant Ginan to advance her own career.

Still, the thought of this underground sub-culture existing right under the noses of the senior staff was... *amazing*.

She wondered how many people on board had seen the same things she had? She wondered what they felt about the show, and whether it left them conflicted as well. She wondered if she would ever be sent on an important mission, to save a world, solve a cosmic mystery, or encounter lost civilizations.

She wondered...simply for the sake of wondering.

As Roy had thought to himself many times before, Commander Nekkar wasn't stupid, but he was an idiot.

Roy had suggested being allowed to take a shuttle to speak to the Brotherhood personally, but that was never going to happen. Nekkar probably feared betrayal of some sort, but the truth was Roy would have been happy just to bail and never cross paths with either group ever again.

Since that option wasn't being given to him, he'd have to settle for betrayal.

Nekkar had arranged for discrete communications to take place, using a secret channel normally reserved for the Vigiles to snitch on the crew with.

The commander had told Roy exactly what was required, and the terms that would be offered. The Brotherhood were to be given no specifics, only the kind of readings they were looking for and how wide a net they intended to cast. Once the operation was over, the location of a valuable derelict would be provided to them to do with as they pleased. He was very careful to cover all the important points and leave nothing to chance.

This was why Nekkar wasn't stupid.

Roy pointed out that there was a certain way you needed to approach the Brotherhood if you didn't want your offer to get laughed at, especially under the circumstances. The Brotherhood had never worked with the Terran Colony Fleet before, and would be justifiably worried it was a trap. Roy convinced the commander to leave the exact wording of the proposal and terms up to him.

This was why Nekkar was an idiot.

Long before Roy had been banished to the Dump, he'd commanded a Brotherhood light frigate, and one of the first things you learned as a pirate commander was how to word messages. It wasn't enough to have your messages encrypted. Sometimes you couldn't trust your own crew. For those in the know, saying *loot* instead of *credits*, for example, would put a completely different spin on a message.

So the commander had sent the message he'd wanted to the Brotherhood, while Roy had been able to piggyback his own.

What's more, they'd included the direct address to this secret Vigile channel, so that messages could be sent directly to this ship without the use of a relay. And the fact that Nekkar didn't see why *that* was a mistake only secured his idiot status in Roy's mind. Possibly made him stupid as well.

For now, all Roy could do on this front was wait and see how the Brotherhood would respond.

The Void Brotherhood was perhaps the largest, most organized pirate organization in the Protectorate. But that's like saying a particular street gang is the biggest. Impressive if you live in that city, not so much if you look at that world's superpowers.

Nevertheless, it was big and organized. Their leader was a Draxon padrone named Zelroth who adopted the last name of Saltear, meaning "of none." He did this as a rejection of the Draxon's hive-like nature, going so far as to keep all other Draxons at bay to prevent any kind of latent psychic connection from forming.

And because of this rejection, his office was a testament to individuality. Namely his.

The average observer would assume the man had an ego the size of a planet, given the number of statues, portraits, and mirrors present in his office. But this wasn't vanity at play—at least, not in the traditionally understood sense. This was a declaration of self. Everything in this room carried with it a single letter as a message: *I*.

An astute observer would wonder if, perhaps, all these representations of himself were a kind of proxy collective, meant to reassure him in ways he couldn't admit he needed. They might then wonder if running the Brotherhood filled a similar need.

A *wise* observer would keep those opinions to themselves.

While well known for being ruthless, Zelroth was also cunning and brilliant. The entire Ramede Autonomous Resource Sector was now under his control, something he'd managed to do without firing a shot.

Well, not many.

He had been invited in, because he could provide the Ramedeans with all the things the Protectorate could not. Technology, trade, protection. Granted, it was protection from *them*, but that's just the way life was sometimes.

But the Brotherhood didn't actually *run* the Ramede ARS. They were considered hired consultants. This technicality neutralized the one card the Protectorate had to come in and deal with them directly.

Not everyone who worked for Zelroth was on the same level, however. There is a stereotype, not completely unjustified, when it comes to pirates and their intelligence. While it is unfair to say that all pirates are stupid, many stupid people choose to be pirates.

One of the Brotherhood's innovations was to sift out the competent from the incompetent and put everyone to their ideal use. There was no maliciousness behind this; some people were simply destined to be pulse cannon fodder.

Zelroth was not one to micromanage, but he was also not one to tolerate mistakes. Being a Draxon, whether he admitted to himself it or not, he expected everyone to be able to read his mind.

So even within the competent levels of his organization, there was a general sense of unease whenever something new and unexpected arrived. It tended to get kicked up to the next level, and if it was new and unexpected to *those* people, they would kick it up to the next level, and so on. The more new and unexpected a situation was, the higher up the chain it went.

This one went all the way to Zelroth's office.

Zelroth didn't have a single second in command. He had six. None of them were Draxon, and each was tasked with a different part of the Brotherhood's operation. He also didn't refer to them by name, but rather by number, which only added fuel to those who wondered if the pirate lord was compensating for something.

Number Six was a Ramedean, usually tasked with affairs pertaining to the Ramede ARS. However, she'd drawn the black ball when the seconds were deciding who would bring this new development to his attention.

She found him fully occupied at a small and unadorned workstation. Despite all the monuments to self that surrounded him, he still preferred function over form.

"Mr. Saltear," said Number Six. Zelroth refused any kind of official title, at least while in his presence. "We have received a very unusual comm."

Her words were almost like a whistle due to her sucker-like mouth. At first, Zelroth did not respond, but after a few nerve-wracking moments, it was clear he was just getting his affairs in order to give her his full attention.

"It must be *very* unusual to interrupt me," he said.

Her orange skin paled. "It is, sir. We have received a comm from a Silver Legion heavy cruiser. The *Hydrus*."

"That is unusual," he admitted. "But not unusual enough."

"They wish to...hire us?"

Zelroth blinked. "I stand corrected."

This was unprecedented. In all his years leading the Brotherhood, he had never heard anything from the Terran Colony Fleet other than threats, usually to stay away from border disputes they were actively engaged in. They saw the Brotherhood as vultures, looking for easy prey in conflict zones, and took out their ships if they ever caught them engaged in piracy.

In Zelroth's mind, neither the TCF's Silver Legion nor their Centurions were any better. They sold their services to the side they deemed worthy, supposedly based on a code of morality. But it was funny how that morality was almost always on the side with the most credits, so long as that side could provide enough lip service about making positive change after the conflict was over.

"There's more, sir. One of our brethren is on board the *Hydrus*."

"You spoke to them?"

"No, sir," Number Six whistled. "The message was text only. But how the offer was made was in line with Brotherhood steganographic practices. It was not made under duress."

Zelroth got up from his desk, intrigued. "I see. Have you been able to verify that this offer comes from the *Hydrus* and isn't some clever ruse?"

"Yes, sir."

Zelroth steepled his dark blue hands together and pressed them to his lips in thought. He then turned to his portraits and statues, considering the idea.

"It will not hurt to hear the proposal. What do they want?"

Number Six explained what was being asked of them, and what was offered in return.

"They do not offer much in the way of specifics, do they?"

"No, sir."

"And I assume this arrangement is meant to be only between the *Hydrus* and us?"

"Yes, sir."

"So, something they don't want the Colony Fleet hearing about. Interesting. And what of the subtext?" Zelroth hadn't had much need for keeping up with pirate banter, useful though it was.

"It confirms that the offer is genuine and not a trap. It also suggests the situation is ideal for a double cross."

Zelroth frowned. "I don't see how. The *Hydrus* is asking only for raw data from our ships' sensors. We don't know where they are or where they'll be. The location of the prize they offer will only come once they are done with it."

Number Six would have blinked her very large eyes if Ramedeans had any eyelids. "Well, sir, it seems they also provided a direct channel for us to contact them with, should we accept."

"A *direct* channel? Not an encrypted relay?"

"No, sir."

"Well then, that changes everything," said Zelroth. "Agree to their terms. Have Number Three find someone to put in charge of the operation and follow their instructions to the letter. Meanwhile, Number Four is to assemble a separate strike fleet and standby."

"How large of a fleet, sir?"

"Large enough to take on a heavy cruiser."

Moss and the Real Girl

*TruLuv Corporation is pleased to introduce this year's
line of ProMate companion bots. We've added twelve
new body types from the younger Protectorate species.
Each has been made to accurately represent their biology
to provide a seamless companionship experience. Comes
with your choice of advance pseudo-intelligent personalities or upload your own if you are upgrading!
Remember: if it's not TruLuv, it's not True Love.*

TruLuv Promotional Advert

M OSS RAISED HIS HANDS and blurted, "I can explain!"

Tameria quirked an eyebrow, and Moss realized that, in
fact, he could not.

"I swear, I didn't order this!"

The deliveryman rolled his sherb stick in his mouth. "Look, I'm just
here to deliver. If you're Maurice Foote, and this is your ship, just sign
here and I'll be on my way. What you do with it is your business."

Moss looked to Tameria, who waited patiently to see what he did
next. Her face would strike fear in even the most seasoned poker player.

He raised a hand to his ear and reactivated his comm. Violet was deep in the middle of an apology.

"—so *so* sorry! Please just sign and I'll explain everything inside!"

Moss sighed and held out his hand for the datapad.

The deliveryman made a grunt that could have been a laugh and handed it over. "Ain't nothing to be ashamed of, pal. Gets lonely out there."

"Oh, shut up." Moss signed and handed it back. The man grunted again. He unloaded the box with the TruLuv logo on it which, unless you could read GlaCom, just looked like a few cartoony scribbles packed within a circle, yet somehow managed to convey its playful vibe.

The man swiped the datapad and handed it back. "And for the next one."

Moss frowned. "What, the other box is for me too?"

"Yep. Different store, different form."

It was a small mercy that this one seemed to be from an upscale department store on the station. The invoice indicated it was full of clothes.

The man chuckled. "Don't want it walking around naked, after all. Or maybe ya do. Who am I ta judge?"

Moss snatched the pad from him, signed, and handed it back. "Seriously, shut up."

The man flipped to another form. "And this."

This one seemed to involve taxes and import fees.

"And this."

Moss looked the next one over. "A *waiver*?"

"For the sexbot. In case you hurt yourself."

"Ugh..."

"And this..."

Moss looked at this one carefully. "I need to *register* it to my ship?"

The man shrugged. "Got something to do with it counting as crew. Needs to be made part of your roster."

Moss began to nod in an exaggerated manner, feeling the lunacy pile on. "So every port I go to, they know I have a sexbot as part of the crew?"

"It's actually called a companion bot," Violet said in his ear.

"No one asked you," Moss muttered.

The delivery guy thought that was directed at him. "Hey, regs are regs."

Moss thrust the datapad back to him after signing, only to be handed it back. "And this."

"Whatever happened to 'Just sign here and I'll be on my way?'"

The delivery guy chuckled. "Just a few more."

Tameria continued to stare at him with that poker face the whole time. Eventually, all the forms were signed and the man finally took his gravpad and left.

"Open it up," she said.

Moss hadn't expected that. "What? Why?"

"Because if it's me in there, only one of us is leaving this junkyard alive."

By now, Moss had passed through embarrassment and had returned to his usual state of doomed fatalism. "It's not you."

Tameria's eyes narrowed. "Violet?"

Moss nodded.

And just like that, the subdued hostility was gone. "Makes sense. Let's get her on board."

A few minutes later, Moss and Tameria had laid the two boxes down in the main cargo hold. Hel joined them there, and Violet's projection flickered to life in front of the crates, hands raised in apology.

"Let me start by saying that I did *not* arrange for these to arrive when they did. Though, if we're all being honest with ourselves, it did turn out to be *really* funny."

Moss snapped his fingers twice at her. "This is the part where you explain yourself." Hel seemed equally interested, so he assumed she hadn't been part of this stunt.

Violet took a deep, theatrical breath. "Okay. When Hel boarded that damaged transport and almost got herself killed, and here, when I thought she got ambushed in the junkyard, I felt so freaking helpless. There are a lot of things I can do as the ship, but so many important things that I can't. What if one you were unconscious and needed medical aid? So, I took my share of our profits and... *Voila!*"

"Then why get the holoprojectors back on Elan?" asked Hel. "Why not ask for"—she waved at the six-foot-long box with the TruLuv logo—"*Voila?*"

"Well, for one thing, I didn't know if it would work. Still don't. But also..." Violet bit her lip as she looked to Tameria. "I was afraid Tam's superiors would think I was overreaching."

Hel frowned. "What's *that* supposed to mean?"

Tameria spoke up. "The Order doesn't just guide the development of beneficial technologies—it suppresses advancements that are potentially harmful. NDT tech has always been considered a borderline case, due to the broader implications of its potential misuse. In fact, when I reported back that the Violet matrix was lost, I got the feeling the local Precentor was relieved. More time to debate the ethical implications while we waited for another successful case to occur."

"So, you gonna rat me out, Tam?" asked Violet.

As usual, Tameria's expression gave away little. "You're the only stable NDT personality in existence. You can't make a copy of yourself, so the damage you can do is limited to the ship you're on, and the Order would be interested in testing the limits of your abilities. But I see no reason to involve them at this time."

She then crossed her arms and took a haughty stance. "Besides, as someone said on one of those shows you had us watch on Elan...criminal informants will require medical attention."

"Snitches get stitches," Violet corrected. "Nice! Okay, meatbags, let's move these to the secondary bay."

"Why there?" asked Moss.

"Look, I don't embarrass easy, but this is not a plug-and-play situation. I'd like a little privacy while I work things out. Could take a while. In the meantime, you can start working on your yard rat problem."

Tameria looked to Moss. "What yard rat problem?"

After depositing the boxes next to the colourful shuttle in the secondary bay, Moss and the others convened in the galley. Once up to speed regarding the yard rats, Sister Tameria got around to why she had come to Komi Station.

"I need you."

Moss smirked. "Hey, I know I have my charms, but..."

Tameria groaned.

"Walked right into that one," said Hel.

"I suppose I did. Nevertheless, I need you to come with me."

Moss opened his mouth, but Hel punched him before he could stick his foot in it.

Moss rubbed his shoulder. "Thank you."

"Anytime."

Tameria turned to Hel. "The situation on your colony ship has gotten more complicated. Many of the senior staff were unhappy with the arrangements made after we saved them, and that dissatisfaction is growing now that they've learned they'll have other humans settling with them."

"Outsiders," Hel said.

Tameria nodded. "The underground network on Mars was compromised shortly after we left Sol, and the refugees we took there had to be relocated, along with the support staff secretly working for Haven. It was decided that the best place for them was with the *Pegasi* colonists."

Hel frowned. "I bet that went over like a ton of bricks."

"Indeed," said Tameria. "So I've been tasked with making this arrangement work, by any means necessary."

"That's foreboding," said Moss. "But I don't see where I fit in."

"Yes, I recall you saying that to me in the cockpit back on Elan."

Moss and Hel stared at Tameria a moment, jaws slack.

Tameria raised her pointed chin. "You're not the only one who can do innuendo. However, to remain on topic, I believe that your presence will be enough to solve this problem. You were very...persuasive the last time you were there."

"You mean I told them they were a bunch of idiots and had the facts to prove it."

"You sell yourself short, Maurice," said Tameria. "You have a way of reading people, regardless of species. That bold stance you took could have easily backfired or made them dig in their heels and ignore the evidence."

"Could just be lucky," said Moss.

Hel and Tameria exchanged glances.

"No, you're good at reading people," said Hel.

"I believe luck is not one of your strong suits," Tameria added diplomatically.

"*Ha ha,*" said Moss. "But I still don't get it. They're not in any real bargaining position. Why not just tell them to like it or lump it?"

"Because, not to put too fine a point on it, we believe that if it came from us, they will choose to 'lump it,' whatever that means. It could lead to the kind of divisiveness that gets people killed. You're Terran, and you've saved their lives twice already. I believe you have enough clout with the senior staff to set them straight. But it will have to be in person, and it will have to be soon."

"I'd love to help, Tameria, but we've still got this yard rat situation to deal with."

Tameria frowned. "Yes... I do feel for them. But it's imperative that we return to the *Pegasi* before it arrives at their destination."

Hel coughed politely.

"Got something to share with the class?" asked Moss.

"Well, just that she never said she needed *me* for any of this. I could handle the Orijen brothers once they give us the all clear from ProSec, then follow behind. The *Rex* is fast, but Tam's ship is crazy fast. We'd never keep up anyway."

"She's not wrong," said Tameria. "I was going to ask her to fly the *Rex* while you and I went on ahead."

Moss considered this. Hel was getting to be a decent pilot, especially with Violet watching over her. He wasn't worried about the trip itself; it was getting out of the yard in one piece that worried him. The Orijen brothers had been way too quiet the last few days.

"Ashtar and Barl are no joke," he said.

"Believe me, I know," said Hel.

"I don't mind burning my bridges with them under the circumstances. I just don't want to burn you as well."

"I can handle them," said Hel. "Trust me. I've got this."

"Still, let's see if Violet has a free minute so we can discuss it with her." Moss looked up at nowhere in particular, his usual way of addressing the ship. "Violet?"

There was a barely audible click as the audio connected, and they heard a crash and clatter on the other end. "Bit busy here!" And the line cut off.

Moss got up to get a drink. "Guess it might be a while still."

"What the heck is going on in there?" asked Hel.

"You ever seen a newborn giraffe learn to walk?"

The Many Lives and Deaths of Captain Keed Randgaffi

Piracy along the Elysian Gap continues to rise. Merchants travelling to other Protectorate nations are reminded that insurance does not cover piracy within the Elysian Gap unless adequate protection has been hired from a ProSec-approved security provider.

Elysian News Network 174 (Lacilla Province)

Captain Keed Randgaffi remembered a bright flash, his body seizing in full cardiac arrest and collapsing to the ground. Then he felt different. Weird, but no longer in pain. His first instinct was to call out.

"H...Hello?"

Without eyes to open, he now saw a group of Silver Legion jackasses hovering in front of him, holding datapads and observing him like some kind of zoo animal. He realized a lot of things all at once.

"Ah, crap."

"Hello. I'm Ensign Ara of the Silver Legion."

"*You're* the assholes who shot me down? I thought it was pirates."

The other crewmen stepped back as Ara took the lead on this conversation. "Um, no. We recovered you from what we think was a pirate vessel and..."

"Stop right there, missy. No use trying to lie to me. I've been lied to by the best. Why don't you just run along and play with your other toys? You aren't getting squat from me."

"We're just trying to understand what you are. Can you—?"

"Nope. Whatever your question is, the answer is nope." Truth be told, this gal was fairly attractive for a Terran. Just a shame he was old enough to be her grandfather...and dead.

"Look, Ara, is it? I don't want to be rude, but you're meddling in things way above your paygrade. The smart thing for you to do would be to shut me down and tell your bosses this machine is broken. Then actually break it. Unless you *like* the idea of diaspora, nothing good is coming from this."

"What do you mean?" the woman asked.

"That would be telling, and trust me, you don't want me to tell."

"We're only looking for answers. We don't mean you any harm."

"Lady. Look, what did you say your name was again?"

"Ensign Ara."

"Ara. Sometimes answers aren't what they're cracked up to be. Besides, I don't remember you asking any questions."

The woman, cute for a Terran, looked confused. "Well, I haven't. Not yet."

"Well, don't bother. Where am I, anyway?"

The woman, cute for a Terran, was looking at some kind of display that had all kinds of erratic readings going up and down.

"That can't be good," she said.

"What can't be? Do I know you?"

He didn't remember much after that, because he couldn't.

"H...Hello?"

Without eyes to open, Keed now saw a group of Silver Legion goons hovering in front of him. One of them, larger and with the characteristic traits of a Terran cyborg, was leaning in close, making it very obvious Keed was observing things through a wide-angle lens.

"Playback from start," the man said.

"Playback yourself, jackass."

He shouldn't have said that, but it seemed to take the Terran off guard. The man looked back at the others, who were barely containing their laughter.

"Pseudo-intelligence?" he asked them.

A woman shook her head. "Complete neuro transference."

"You're joking."

Crap, they knew too much.

"*Bleep blorp beep,*" said Keed. "*Does not compute.*"

The cyborg looked confused, but the woman shook her head, calling his admittedly lame bluff.

"We're still trying to work out the details, Mr. Herzog," she said, "but as you can see, the subject is not very cooperative." She was actually pretty attractive for a Terran. Shame he was old enough to be her grandfather...and dead.

"Look, I don't want to be rude," said Keed, "but you're meddling in things you don't understand. The best thing you can do right now is shut me down and tell your bosses this machine is broken. Then break it. Unless you like the idea of diaspora, nothing good is coming from this."

The cyborg looked to the woman again. "What does he mean by that?"

She shook her head. "I don't know, other than the standard definition of the word. We've activated him several times before we called you and he always ends up mentioning that."

Several times? He had no memory of that. This wasn't good.

"Perhaps it's a fault with the adaptive translator," she continued. "It's unlikely this mind is Terran."

"No, it's not," the cyborg confirmed. "My guess is Elysian, and most likely a member of the Order."

"How—?" Keed stopped himself short, but it was too late. The hint of a smirk on the Terran's face told him that one syllable had just confirmed a number of things.

The woman now pointed to a display to the man's right, which had been giving consistent readings but was now getting increasingly erratic. "The other problem is that it doesn't seem to be stable."

That got Keed's attention. "What? Ah crap."

The man turned back to the woman. "How long?"

"Not long now."

Well, that was the worst news on an already huge pile of bad news.

The cyborg stepped back from the machine. "We can work with this. For now, take him offline. Should we try the other one again?"

"It never responds," said the woman. "We believe it's defective."

Keed winked out of existence, knowing it wouldn't be for the last time.

Keed remembered a bright flash, his body seizing in full cardiac arrest and collapsing to the ground.

Then he felt different. Weird, but no longer in pain. In fact, he felt like he was floating. He wasn't awake, but he wasn't asleep, either. He felt somewhere in between.

He imagined he was on his ship, on one last mission to balance the scales before his cardiac system shut down for good.

And in the distance, he thought he heard voices.

"...have him in a low power mode..."

His passengers, maybe? The refugees he was taking to Sol?

"...kind of like dreaming..."

"...definitely Elysian patterns..."

"...can work with that..."

Something about that didn't sound right, and it snapped him out of it. The ship and everything around him disappeared.

"...lost it..."

His guard was up now, but in a vague, general, terrifying way. It was like he was surrounded, but by people he couldn't see, and the darkness pressed in on all sides.

A deeper voice spoke up, louder than the others. "Is this thing picking up audio?"

A lighter voice sighed. "Let's try it again."

"H...Hello?"

Without eyes to open, Keed saw a woman dressed in a light, non-descript flight suit. He seemed to be on board a ship, in a galley.

"Where am...? What is...? Who are...? Oh, I'm dead, aren't I?"

"I'm afraid so," said the woman. "You've been gone a long time."

At first, he thought she might be Elysian, but her features were too rounded and her ears too big. Most likely Terran. Well, this ship didn't look like it belonged in the TCF, and she wasn't wearing one of their uniforms, so that was helpful. And since she knew how to activate the NDT, she was probably a sister.

"Do you remember what happened?"

"Blasted pirates," muttered Keed.

"We found your ship disabled, drifting dead in space."

"They used a shuttle as a decoy and took out my engines before I could escape. Then they boarded and... What happened to the passengers?"

"There was no one else on your ship." She was pretty cute for a Terran. Shame he was old enough to be her grandfather... and dead. "Where were you taking them?"

"My contact in Sol." Something struck Keed as odd. "Wait, you should know all that, shouldn't you?"

"I told you, you've been gone a long time. Your ship was shot down thirty years ago."

The longer they talked, the more he interfaced with the NDT machine, and one of the first minor features to make itself available was a chronometer.

"Then why does it say it's only been a few weeks?"

The woman's expression changed. "Huh. Didn't know you had access to something like that."

"Who are you?"

But the woman was ignoring him now. "Make a note of that, Samel. Okay guys, end of session forty-eight. Let's reset and try again."

"Oh my goddess…"

But he never really had a chance to think more than that.

"H…Hello?"

Without eyes to open, Keed saw a woman dressed in a light non-descript flight suit. He seemed to be on board a ship, in a galley. She was bleeding from a gash in her forehead. Everything shook, like they'd been hit by kinetics.

"What's happening?" he asked.

"Pirate attack," the woman yelled. "Came out of nowhere while we were recovering you." Her features were too rounded and her ears too big to be Elysian. Most likely Terran. She called out to the room. "What's happening, Brother Lebow?"

A male voice responded. "Shields are down. I might be able to shake them long enough to go transit, but navigation's damaged. I'll need to punch something in manually."

"Brother Randgaffi, we need a safe port to reach. What's the closest Priory to here?" The ship shook again, and the woman fell over. The wrong way. In fact, nothing on the tables behind her shook. It was just him, or maybe just his camera.

And he wasn't officially a Brother in the Order.

It was a trick. If they were making things so urgent, it was safe to assume his matrix wasn't stable, and it must have taken a lot of resets to get so much out of him to set up this bit of theatre. But if he didn't say something quick, they'd keep trying until they fooled him completely. He had only one chance to send his future iterations a message, so he made it count.

"Have them set a course for Erewhon. Hurry!"

"Did you get that?" the woman asked.

"Got it, but it's not on the nav computer."

The woman looked to him desperately. "Quick, where is Erewhon?"

Keed paused a moment. "Sorry, who are you again? Where am I?"

The woman's expression changed. She checked something to the left of him, which appeared to be a diagnostic readout. "That's unusual."

"What's unusual?"

The readings, which had been stable, now started to get erratic. "Ah, there it is. Make a note of that anomaly and reset. We'll break for lunch." She came over and patted the camera. "See you soon."

Keed's only consolation before he winked into nothingness was that she hadn't realized that Erewhon was a name he'd used back in his pirate days, and represented a place that did not exist.

Home Alone

The galaxy is abuzz with commerce. One of the things that keeps the Protectorate strong is the steady flow of goods from one system to another. As a result, the galaxy is awash with every shape, size, and type of starship, from tiny single man racing craft to kilometre-long destroyers.

In the last five-hundred years, space travel has become almost ubiquitous with the rise of the younger races and a growing economy. Advances in transit tech have made systems that were once inconvenient and out of the way worth exploiting. Interstellar ships are no longer restricted to the military or the super-rich.

Many individuals have taken to the stars in small transports to trade goods, taking on large debts in the hopes of paying it off quickly and buying a better ship, working their way up the starship ladder.

It doesn't always work out for them. Sometimes they lose everything and have nowhere to go.

M. Foote, *Portrait of the Pilot as a Cranky Ol' Man*

IT WASN'T LONG AFTER Moss and Tameria left that the Orijen brothers contacted Hel. The *Rex* and its crew were clear of all ProSec violations. All that was left was to get the ship on the platform so it could be taken up to the docking bays.

Hel entered the Orijen Brothers' office for the first time since she'd been run out into the junkyards. The increased gravity took her by surprise, making her feel several times heavier than normal, until the sensors registered her presence and adjusted to station nominal.

Ashtar was waiting for her at the front desk, his wide grin set to inflict maximum unease.

"Well well, look who's here."

Hel raised her hands. "I just want to get the *Rex* towed onto the lift so we can leave. I'm not here to start something."

"Naw, of course not. Maurice explained your situation to me. Had no idea what you were going through. As far as I'm concerned, we're square. In fact..." The Hopat stepped back and took a bow. "You have my sincere apologies for my past transgressions against you."

She waited for the other shoe to thump on the ground. "Thanks?"

"Maurice, on the other hand... Well, he's been a naughty boy. And before you can leave, I'm afraid we're going to have to settle up."

Violet's voice cut in over her comm. "Um...Hel? The ship's kind of surrounded here. Barl and his goons. They're trying to open the cargo ramp."

Thump.

Ashtar stepped out from behind the desk. "See, Maurice has been taking advantage of my generosity this past week. Taking stuff that ain't rightfully his. So, we're going to have to have a full inspection of his ship before we can allow you to go."

Hel's eyes narrowed. "And you waited for Moss to leave to pull this, huh?"

"Of course. He'd find some way to sweet talk me or trick me or make a deal or force a stalemate. Damn frustrating, that. I was going to stall until he took a trip skinside, but when he left with that Elysian lady, that was even better."

The Hopat's grin changed to something resembling sympathy. "Look, the reality is your ship ain't leaving until we find whatever

Maurice was trying to smuggle out. And I expect you know as well as I do what it is."

"I have no idea what you're talking about," said Hel.

"You never were good at lying," said Ashtar. "Another reason I waited for Moss to leave." He waved a hand towards the now open door. "Come on."

Sure enough, the *Rex* was surrounded by a dozen employees armed with makeshift pulse guns, while Barl was busy trying to hack the lock, though without much success.

Ashtar looked to Hel. "You want to save us the trouble, or should we break out the fusion torches?"

Hel sighed. "Let them in, Violet."

Ashtar frowned. "Violet?"

The ramp began to lower, revealing Violet waiting at the top, dressed in a flight suit, arms crossed and very annoyed.

"I'll thank you *not* to break in with fusion torches. Moss just had me detailed."

Ashtar blinked. "*Violet?*"

Barl joined his brother. "I thought she was dead."

"Yeah, but we thought Maurice was too," Ashtar countered.

This turn of events had thrown them off guard, and that made the rest of their crew nervous. Most of them were now holding their weapons at the ready instead of at their sides.

"It's just a hologram," said Hel. "Moss installed a pseudo-intelligent personality into the ship's computer."

Ashtar raised his monobrow. "And he chose *her*? That's just sad."

The brothers marched onto the ship, but had the crew hang back with orders not to let anyone in or out without their say-so. Once in the cargo bay, Violet looked down at the pair disapprovingly as Barl waved a hand through the projection.

"Quality setup," he said. "Can barely see through her. Must have cost a shiny credit."

"Special order," said Hel. "A friend owed Moss a favour."

"That happens a lot with him," said Ashtar. He pulled out a small hand scanner and started to wave it at various points of interest. "I'm sure the yard rats here would have been in debt to him for years if he'd gotten away with his little plan."

"Not sure what good that would do," said Hel. "You can't get blood from a stone."

Ashtar gave a wide, toothy grin. "Oh, but you can... you just have to know how to squeeze."

"How you managed to avoid getting married all these years is a mystery," said Hel.

Ashtar laughed as he continued to scan. "I have *three* mates...That's why I'm five thousand light years away from home. Cargo bay is clear. Let's move on. Barl, keep an eye on her."

Barl nodded and gestured for Hel to go on ahead. He'd be staying behind her from here on.

Violet looked to Hel. "Should I do anything?"

"Just make sure nobody messes with your core systems," said Hel. "I've got this."

Violet nodded. "Roger that." And with that, she flickered off.

Hel followed Ashtar into the main corridor to the secondary cargo bay. It was much smaller, but large enough to hold a tiny one-man shuttle, which was painted bright orange, with thick white stripes and thin black stripes. It could be deployed through a hatch and travel in space or atmosphere, though it wasn't capable of transit, or even sub-transit.

Barl squinted at the GalCom lettering on the side. "*Nemo*?"

"Inside joke," said Hel.

Ashtar swept over the room and the shuttle with his scanner, still not finding what he was looking for. He grunted. "Engine room next."

She followed behind as he headed to the rear of the ship, passing by Violet again along the way at one of the intersections.

"Are you *sure* everything's all right?" she asked, head cocked like a puppy.

Hel nodded as they passed her. "Definitely."

The engine room took up the entire back quarter and was densely packed. It was designed with a heavy focus on automated mainte-nance, reducing how much an engineer on board needed to do, or even *could* do on the fly. Repairs here could be a real pain unless you were at a properly equipped facility.

"Perfect for hiding nav chips," Ashtar muttered.

"Is *that* what you're after?" asked Hel.

"As if you didn't know."

"I really don't."

Ashtar snorted. "Like I said, lousy liar."

Thankfully, the brothers didn't deem it necessary to tear the engine room apart, or the ship, for that matter. Ashtar scanned it thoroughly, while Barl stayed just behind Hel, one hand on his makeshift blaster.

"Where's your furry little friend?" Barl asked.

Hel looked down at his pants. "Why? Are your trousers lonely?"

Barl's eyes narrowed, but he said nothing.

Ashtar went to the engine room's computer and opened the main access panel, revealing hundreds of data crystals in densely packed rows and columns. Each one flickered with its own light in a hypnotic way.

"Hey, don't go messing with that," Hel warned. She could just imagine him pulling them all out and not putting a single one back.

Ashtar didn't touch any, waving the scanner over them instead. "Relax, just need to get a closer reading." When the scanner didn't give him the results he was looking for, he frowned and turned to Hel.

"Your boss wouldn't have been so dumb as to put them in the cockpit, would he? Right in the nav computer?"

Hel's lips squirreled up, just a little.

Ashtar smirked. "Wow. I mean, that should have been the *first* place I checked. But I thought, naw, he wouldn't be *that* obvious."

"Probably why he did it," said Barl.

"He's unpredictable, I'll give him that," said Ashtar. "Okay, Hel. To the cockpit, if you please."

Hel shrugged. "You're not gonna like what you find there."

"See, now you're not even bluffing right anymore." Ashtar gave her a slight shove to keep her ahead of both of them this time. "Though I'll give you credit, you've grown since you left the yard. You're more confident. Capable. I dunno if Moss helped you with that or if it was all you, but I'm glad to see it."

This was typical of Ashtar's banter. Whenever he had the upper hand, he was your best pal while he put the screws to you.

"I'm surprised you don't just take the whole ship," said Hel, taking her time to get to the cockpit.

"What do you take me for?" Ashtar sounded genuinely hurt. "I'm a businessman, and I'm here for what's mine, nothing more. I know you got a soft spot for the rats out there, but everything in this yard is *our* property, not theirs."

Hel huffed. "That's not why you want those chips, and you know it."

"Dropping the charade, are we?" asked Ashtar.

"You going to drop yours? Admit this is about keeping the yard rats where they are?"

Hel could feel the Hopat's wide grin behind her. "I'm not keeping them anywhere. They can leave whenever they want, just not with our property. They want out? There are services on the station to help."

There was also a year long waiting list for them, and the process was so complicated you needed to use an advocacy service to navigate it...which also had a waiting list.

Hel stopped in front of the door to the cockpit and turned back to Ashtar. "You know, I honestly wonder if you believe that, or just say it to justify what you do."

"What do you mean?"

"I mean, maybe to you, always having a cheap labour pool is just a convenient by-product of the situation, not the intended outcome."

A moment passed before Ashtar spoke. "It's a rough galaxy, kid. I didn't put anyone in the yard, and I'm not keeping them there, either. Things are the way they are. That's all."

It was an accurate, if depressing, statement of the universe in general.

Ashtar's levity returned. "Look on the bright side. When all this is over, you still get to leave with your ship and get to make some money. Look at this as a learning experience about how the galaxy really works." He nodded to the door. "Now open up."

Hel sighed and opened the door.

As they walked into the cockpit, Ashtar said, "You know, I'm starting to think Maurice wasn't even involved in any of this. Not his style. Can't see what he'd get out of it."

At the front of the cockpit, the pilot's seat spun around. Moss was sitting in it.

"A decent night's sleep, for starters."

Ashtar stepped back. "The hell? I thought you left!"

Barl raised his gun, because in his arms Moss held a strange weapon. It had to be some kind of pulse repeater, but didn't exactly look like one. It had a second grip under the barrel and a wide round bulge where the ammo capacitor would normally be. It looked archaic, but deadly.

Hel stepped aside, not wanting to be anywhere near the brothers. Ashtar held a hand up. "Now hold on, Maurice. Don't do something stupid."

"I'll tell ya what I'm gonna give *you*, Ashtar." Moss sneered and stood up from the chair, aiming the repeater from his hip. "I'm gonna give you to the count of ten, to get your ugly, yella, no-good keister off my ship, before I pump your guts full of lead."

Barl raised half his monobrow. "Keister?"

Ashtar squinted at Moss, noticing something, and Hel held in a gasp.

Moss began to count. "One... two..."

There was a bright light outside the ship, and from their angle, you could just see a glow in Moss's chest where it penetrated the—

"Hologram," said Ashtar.

Moss disappeared, just as a pistol barrel was pressed into the back of each of their heads.

"Ten," Violet said, and fired.

The weapons barely made a sound, but the Orijen brothers dropped like rocks. Violet raised the pistols to her lips and blew the tips of the barrels.

"Keep the change, ya filthy animals."

On board the *Outreach*, Moss leaned back in the co-pilot's seat, watching the stars zip by.

"You really aren't concerned about Hel and Violet?" Tameria asked. Now that they were in transit, she didn't need to be hands-on with the controls anymore, but being who she was, she was always making sure everything was working correctly.

"Not really," said Moss. "There's a good chance they leave with barely a grunt goodbye from the brothers. You gotta understand that Ashtar doesn't see himself as a bad guy, just a creative entrepreneur."

"You don't think they'll try to take advantage of her being on her own?"

"Only if they caught onto our plan with the yard rats, which I doubt. But Violet's got that angle covered. They'll be fine."

"I hope you're right."

"I am. For once, I got the easy job. This is like those meet-and-greets I used to attend for Odyssey Expeditions, convincing people to invest in a brave new colonization campaign outside Protectorate space."

Tameria allowed a smile to slip through. "While wearing a wrestling mask."

"Yeah, well, it made for great branding." This turn of conversation was going to put him in a sour mood sooner or later. He had to keep things light. He leaned the seat back a bit more and put his hands behind his head. "So, just you and me for the next three days. *Whatever* will we do to pass the time?"

Tameria continued to check their course and made a minor adjustment. "Study."

Moss turned his head. "What?"

"I have complete psychological profiles of the *Pegasi*'s command staff, provided by the captain. We're going to find the weak points in each and roleplay out conversations with them in a simulation I designed."

"You're joking."

"I rarely joke."

"Don't I know it. Look, Tam..." She gave him a glare and Moss backpedaled. "Tameria. I was just gonna, you know, *wing* it when I got there. Go there, call them idiots, smack one upside the head if he gives me any lip. It's what worked last time."

"It won't this time. The situation on the *Pegasi* has...evolved since you were there."

"What's that supposed to mean?"

Tameria looked him over as if she were assessing his many, many flaws. "I'm almost certain you will take the wrong approach if I tell you too much before we arrive."

Moss was hurt by that. "You don't trust me."

"I *know* you. There's a difference. I trust you to be you, and that's the problem." She got up from her seat and looked down at Moss. "So, for the next three days, we study, we drill, we practice. We treat this 'meet-and-greet' like the Precentor himself is overseeing our final induction into the Order."

"I'll just assume that's a big deal," said Moss. "You know, incentives work really well. Maybe if we study real hard, we can give ourselves a...reward."

Tameria rolled her head back, exasperated. "I should have brought Hel instead."

Hel dragged Ashtar's body down the hall, while Violet took Barl.

"Ashtar was wrong about one thing," said Violet. "You're a pretty good liar."

"Learned from the best," said Hel, grunting as she pulled. "Speaking of which, did Moss bet for or against us resorting to violence?"

"He was pretty sure they were clueless about the smuggling."

"Figures," Hel grumbled. "Geeze, even at half a gee, these guys are heavier than they look."

"Dense homeworld, dense bodies," said Violet.

"How long will they be out for?"

"Ten, maybe twenty minutes. I used the lowest setting to avoid setting off any alarms. At range, that would just sting a bit, but point blank to the base of the skull? That's like hitting the reset button."

"You record enough of them to work with?"

"Yeah. Good job keeping Ashtar talking."

"Doesn't take much with him," said Hel.

"True." Violet took a moment to remotely open the door to the secondary cargo bay so they could drag the brothers inside, setting them next to the *Nemo*. Violet sat down with her back against the shuttle. "Okay, give me a sec and I should be ready."

"You need to sit down?"

"That's the thing about a transferred consciousness. Truth is, I'm no better at multitasking than I was in life. Rote functions, sure, and I can delegate a lot to the native systems, but me being me? I can only really *be* in one place at a time."

"Should I get to the main cargo bay?"

"This will work better if you're not there," said Violet. "They won't think you've got them at gunpoint."

"So I miss the show?"

Violet nodded to a panel on the wall. "Watch from there."

Hel went over to the display, which switched to a view of the main cargo bay. The ramp was lowering and some of the employees outside looked up in anticipation.

Then the door to the cargo room opened and the very conscious forms of Ashtar and Barl Orijen came out. Ashtar came about halfway down the ramp, while Barl stayed up top.

"Ship's clean, but we're going to escort her up to the docking bays, just to be sure. Give our old friend here a *proper* sendoff." He chuckled darkly at that. "Get us on the pad. We'll be back down in thirty."

An employee nodded and barked an order to two others, who left. Ashtar started back up the ramp, then turned.

"Oh, get the word out that the scanner at the personnel lift has broken down. Then pat down any rat that tries to leave and scan them discretely. Might get lucky."

With that, the ramp shut, the projections vanished, and the ship shook a bit as the yard's towing equipment connected to the *Rex*.

Violet, who had been lying against the shuttle as still as the two Hopat, now got up and took a bow. "Ta da!"

Hel gave what Violet had once called a golf-clap. "Nice touch with the pat down idea."

"I figured that would sell the moment. Now, let's finish this."

Once on the landing pad at the innermost deck on the station, Hel loaded the two unconscious Hopats into a cargo crate and dragged it off the ship. The gravity here was barely a tenth nominal, so the worst she would have to deal with was the inertia created by their mass. As she left, Violet handed her a fancy-looking briefcase she'd printed off to hold all the data crystals.

"I'll get the *Rex* prepped," Violet said. "Good luck."

When Hel got to the lift, the doors opened, and twenty or so people from different worlds were waiting inside. At the front was Grund, a big smile on his blue face.

"I cannot believe you pulled it off," he said.

"Any trouble getting out?" Hel asked.

Grund shook his head. "Just a *very* thorough search. When they saw us all at once, I think they knew you had tricked them, but without any orders from their bosses, they were afraid to act."

Hel handed Grund the briefcase. "Violet checked with Odyssey Expeditions to make sure the deal was still good. They're waiting for you now."

Grund took the case and gave a half bow. "Thank you. You did not owe this to us."

He was referring to what passed for the yard rat's code, which tended to make any alliances between them uneasy and temporary. For one to scramble out, it was usually over the backs of the others.

"I'm starting to think if we had just cooperated more from the start, we could have all made it out of there sooner. Remember our agreement. Equal shares to each of you."

Grund nodded, then looked to the cargo box. "What is that?"

Hel smirked. "Just dropping off some trash. Once you get off the lift, send this back down to the yard. Ignore any pounding you might hear from inside."

There was a shake and hum as the *Viaticus Rex II.I* powered up its engines. Violet hadn't said anything over the comms, but Hel got the message all the same. She and Grund raised a fist and tapped the other's on the side like two hammers as they parted ways.

"You take care now," said Hel.

"And you."

That was the last time Helena Lambinon ever set foot on Komi Station.

Closing the Net

The Void Brotherhood sprung up because of one thing: bureaucracy. In the last six hundred years, countless younger races have reached for the stars. Those whose worlds happen to lie within the borders of a Protectorate nation are blessed with a guiding hand and support as they transition into members of the interstellar community.

Those who lie in the gaps between are not. Their advancement is hindered by treaties and agreements forged thousands of years ago to keep the peace between races who had no idea of the sapient explosion that would someday come. The Protectorate can't offer them tech or trade or much of anything, because to do so would violate countless rules.

It's that loophole that the pirates exploit—filling the void, so to speak.

M Foote, *The Galaxy is Weirder Than You Think*

THE *TCF HYDRUS* CONTINUED its search, though only the command staff knew the details of what they were looking for.

As for those currently aiding them in that search, that knowledge was limited to two people: Sub-commander Nekkar, and Roy Herzog.

The rest of the command staff knew only that the *Hydrus* was receiving sensor readings from a number of volunteers in the Void. They were to ignore any red flags raised should those readings come from ships with a...questionable transponder code.

This highly unusual turn of events was easily overlooked by the command crew, who had reluctantly gotten used to Nekkar's growing isolation. Most assumed a reckoning from higher up would happen sooner or later. But in the meantime, there was a chain of command they were expected to follow.

The relief shift, however, had a harder time ignoring these oddities. Now, in addition to their usual scanning of vast empty voids of space, they were being sent data from dozens of other ships that were also scanning vast empty voids of space—about a third of which triggered fugitive alerts they had to ignore.

All the while, they had no idea if they were any closer to finding whatever they were looking for, or what the magic data they sought looked like. *That* was up to the ship's computer, which would alert the command crew if it came across a match.

It was frustrating, and changed the usually laid-back nature of the relief shift into one of tedium.

Ensign Len Davis sat in the commander's chair, leaning forward. On the main screen was a map of the local region of space, about a hundred light years across. The *Hydrus* was represented by a green dot, while two dozen blue dots were sprinkled about them, none of them closer than ten light years, most much farther away.

These were the locations of the ships that had been feeding them data the last few days, spreading out in a very systematic way, covering as much ground as possible.

Davis wondered why the acting commander hadn't simply contacted the Silver Legion. The Colony Fleet was only five hundred light years away, and there were patrol ships closer than that. It would have only taken a few days for help to arrive.

But then, nothing the acting commander did made sense, and he wasn't explaining himself to anyone. Why would he? They were just synths. Short lived, easily replaceable, easily broken.

Davis touched the brace around his neck. The neck Nekkar had snapped with a single blow.

He was lucky he'd survived. The bone had been easily mended in medbay, and while the nerves took a bit longer to repair, there had been no complications. The brace was both a precaution and a monitoring device to ensure the mending took properly.

In public, he told others it had been his own fault, but that was a matter of self-preservation. Until they could rejoin the Fleet, filing a complaint was out of the question. And honestly, he wasn't sure if there was a point. He hadn't issued a formal challenge to Nekkar's command, only his judgement, but it wasn't hard to see how the court would spin his words against him.

Yet at the same time, standing one's ground and asserting oneself was the only way to get any kind of respect out of the cyborgs on the ship, most of whom saw themselves as their betters, even if they didn't mean to. Granted, if *he* had been around for three hundred years and could heal from most injuries on the spot, he might feel a bit smug too.

For example, Lieutenant Tauri had come to see him in medbay while his nerves were mending. They had been friends since he'd joined the *Hydrus*. Barbara had spent a half hour comparing his fragile mortality to that of her cat, Mr. Nibbles. She hadn't *meant* to be condescending. He knew she was trying to be supportive and empathetic.

And that right there was the problem.

Ensign Powell called to him from comms, his old station when he had been part of the command staff.

"Sir? There's a transport heading for Draxon space that will pass through our search zone. They've been trying to contact us for a while now."

Len brought up the ship and its course on the main screen. Over at the navigation station, a three-dimensional projection of the same area was being shown. A red dot marked the unknown ship, and a dotted line showed its projected path. Just as Powell had said, the route took them right through their search area.

He had a feeling he knew why the ship was trying to contact them. The problem was, the *Hydrus* was under a comms blackout. Under no circumstances were they to contact anyone outside the ship.

He looked to Powell. "Are they only trying to hail us?"

"They were hailing, but now they're broadcasting."

"Well, it won't hurt to listen to what they have to say," said Davis. "Main display, please."

The Nubran that appeared on the screen looked nervous, checking between several monitors at once. "I... I am Captain Soreton of the transport *Gilganan's Mule,* trying to reach the Silver Legion ship in this area. I was wondering if you could provide us with an escort through this region of space? It's just that we've picked up a number of...unusual ships in the region, some of which seem to be heading in our direction."

Davis frowned and turned to the crewman at navigation. "Can you confirm that?"

The three-dimensional display of local space shifted, showing the *Hydrus, Gilganan's Mule,* and the network of ships aiding them in their search. Projected courses from an hour ago were compared to their current courses. Sure enough, three of the ships were slowly changing course to converge on the transport.

Unless the transport dropped to sub-transit, however, there was nothing to worry about. They were just sniffing around, hoping to get lucky.

The captain's message continued. "We've suffered a leak in our fuel tanks. We are low on hydrogen and must stop at a star to refuel. We fear that..."

Of course, pirates thrived on luck.

"Should we acknowledge them?" asked Powell. "Contact the commander?"

Davis shook his head. "Maintain comm silence." He had his orders, but there was a reason he had been a member of the command staff under Commander Miram. He turned to Ensign Powell.

"When we get sensor updates from these ships, there's an automated reply sent from your station, acknowledging that we received it. I need you to access that and change its settings."

Powell looked confused. "Sir?"

But Davis was busy typing a message on his chair's control panel. "Attach this message to it, then change the settings from *acknowledge* to *alert*. Once it's sent, revert the settings back the way they were."

He sent the message to Powell's station. She looked it over and nodded. "Yes, sir. Making the changes now."

Davis leaned back and waited, watching the three blips follow the transport. It had just dropped out of transit near an uninhabited red dwarf star, a sitting duck while it engaged its fuel scoops. Minutes passed, and the tension grew as the three blips on the screen got closer and closer to that star...

Then, without warning, the ships broke off and returned to their former search routes.

Davis allowed himself a grin of satisfaction as the relief crew gave him a round of applause. He just hoped nobody during the day shift bothered to check the logs and noticed what had happened.

"What was on the message?" asked the crewman at the nav station.

Davis leaned back in his chair. "Just a friendly reminder that the Silver Legion does not tolerate piracy, regardless of circumstances."

What he didn't say was that he'd written the message as Commander Nekkar.

The rest of the shift was uneventful, right up until the last ten minutes, when the main bridge crew arrived early. Davis got a sinking feeling in his gut, certain this was connected to what had happened earlier. But instead, the commander simply relieved him early. He was even smiling, though not at him.

As he and the rest of the relief shift left, the bridge began to buzz with activity. Lieutenant Tauri was setting a new course, while Lieutenant Ginan provided updates on target location, speed, and heading.

Whatever the *Hydrus* had been looking for, it seemed they'd found it.

"Huh..." said Violet, once Karon had filled her in on the day's events. "That Davis guy is a smart cookie. No wonder he made bridge crew."

Karon felt a bit uneasy talking to Violet now. It had been one thing when nothing was happening, but now... Well, it felt like anything she said could be used against her. Or at least, against the ship.

But Violet had become a friend to her over the last week. She knew it was a manipulation, though, because Violet had freely admitted it.

"There's a whole playbook I could be using right now to sow mistrust and doubt in your crew, get you on my side," she'd said. "But the fact is, I don't need to. It's already there."

And she was right. If she trusted Violet, it was largely because she no longer trusted her own superiors. Not since Commander Miram died. She needed someone she could trust, or at least, someone she could talk to.

"So the *Hydrus* was trying to pick up the transit signature of a ship, but didn't know where to start," said Violet, mulling things over. "That's why they needed a net. Now that they found it, they can track them passively with just a couple of support ships, follow it wherever it's going while keeping outside its active sensor range, then strike once it gets there."

That was more or less what Karon thought as well. "We just don't know who, or why."

"There's something fucky going on, and I think your buddy Len has a better idea of it than just about anyone."

"What about Roy?"

"Yeah, Roy..." Violet was clearly of a split mind about him. "I'm sure he knows a hellofa lot more, but I doubt he'll give you a straight answer unless it works to his advantage."

"I wouldn't go that far," said Karon.

"*Please*. He's playing you more than I am. You said it yourself, the man's a survivor. No judgement, so am I, but he's got a boom-boom collar on for a reason. Ensign Davis, though... I think you can trust him. I'll bet you a credit he's a Trekkie."

"You think?"

"Only one way to find out..."

Ensign Davis was called to the Commander's office later that day. He'd been found out, after all. However, Nekkar wasn't upset.

"Technically, you violated the communications ban," he said. "And you used *my* name in the transmission." The latter part clearly rankled him, but he still wasn't angry.

"Apologies, sir," said Davis. "I didn't think they would take a warning from an ensign seriously."

"There is that. And, as it turns out, one of the ships that had broken off from the net was instrumental in finding the transit signature we were looking for. I'm sure we would have found it regardless, but your actions brought about the most efficient outcome, one that is in line with the ethos of the Silver Legion. Good work."

This coming from the man who had snapped his neck like a twig. Nekkar must have been in a *really* good mood to be this amiable. But Len wasn't naïve enough to think any kind of apology was forthcoming.

The commander continued, "When this mission is over, I expect you to put in for a transfer to another ship. The incident last week is not one I think either of us can overlook. However, I will see to it that you are given a positive recommendation, based on both Commander Miram's assessment before her death, and my own. The matter of your insubordination will be...overlooked. Dismissed."

Davis saluted and left. The commander hadn't waited for his thanks before dismissing him, and he doubted he even wanted it. The crazy thing was, Nekkar saw himself as being truly magnanimous right now. It spoke volumes about the man's leadership, and Davis was going to be more than happy to put in for that transfer.

During Karon's next shift, the relief crew had new orders. They were to track and monitor the movements of an unidentified transit signature, match its speed and heading, and maintain a set distance from them.

Most of the ships that had made up the net were gone now, and, just as Violet had predicted, only two remained. Each was an equal distance apart from the *Hydrus* and one another, forming a pyramid which their quarry was at the tip of.

This, at least, was slightly more interesting than their earlier shifts, though just as uneventful.

Given the comms blackout, Karon's position on the bridge was the least important at the moment, and she took it upon herself to get drink orders from everyone.

She came up to the command chair, where Ensign Davis was playing a block-stacking game on the arm rest display.

"What can I get you, Len? Something to keep you awake?"

"Sounds good."

"Might I suggest some tea? Earl grey? Hot?"

Davis's finger stopped mid tap, and he looked at Karon with a bemused expression.

She winked. Davis sat up straight and tugged down on his uniform jacket.

"Make it so."

Trouble in Paradise

2 *539 – Nubra Space*

Violet sipped her almost-tea, trying to look on the bright side. "It could be worse."

Moss couldn't stop fidgeting. "I'm having a hard time imagining how."

They were in the café closest to their docking bay, waiting on some last-minute upgrades to their ship.

Right when things seemed bad enough, what with her dying and all, their whole world had gone to hell, and they'd been told in no uncertain terms that for their own safety they had to make themselves scarce in Protectorate space for a while.

For the better part of two years, Violet had helped Moss run missions for the Order across different parts of the Protectorate. It wasn't glamorous, mostly just courier work, but they were helping people, even if those people never realized it. Moss had even stopped being such a grump for a while. He'd really begun to live.

And Violet? She always told people she had no regrets, but that wasn't entirely true. What was true was that she saw no point in dwelling on those regrets, and focussed on doing better next time. But she could honestly say that while she'd worked for the Order, she hadn't felt any need to keep putting the past behind her.

Then they'd uncovered a plot to destroy the Order, and in his panicked attempts to warn them, Moss had exposed them to the galaxy. There had been no other choice, not with the time frame they were looking at.

Word was sent to all their agents, working in governments, corporations and other organizations across the Protectorate—*run*. That included the two of them.

Violet leaned back and crossed her legs. "Hey, I say we see this as an opportunity. You always talked about going off exploring, being beholden to no one, master of your own destiny, all that jazz. Well, this is your big chance."

"Yeah..." Moss grumbled.

She'd screwed up. She should have said *our* big chance. She knew that lost look he was giving her. She was his best friend. His only friend, really.

Violet tried to lighten the mood. She raised a hand to her cheek, avoiding the dermal implant that stretched from her forehead to her jaw. "What? Did I spill something? Something stuck in my teeth?"

"Just thinking."

Violet sighed. If he stayed like this, it was going to be a very long trip.

2550 – *The Void*

"So, are you ever going to explain all *this*?" asked Hel. She was having lunch in the galley and Violet, for whatever reason, wanted to watch.

Violet cocked her head. Her very real head. "Explain what?"

"Don't be coy. You know what I'm talking about."

They were less than a day out of Komi, and the *Outreach* was racing far ahead of them. By now, their comm handshake was the only reason each ship knew where the other was.

"You want to know why I ordered a companion bot for a body," said Violet. "You know, out of everyone, I thought *you'd* get it."

"I do, but didn't you have...other options?"

"I'm dating a goddamn prude," Violet muttered.

Hel began to stammer. "It's not... It's just... You know... I have to ask. Why *that*?"

But instead of getting angry, Violet broke out in a laugh. "You're cute when you're embarrassed, you know? It's like you don't even know *why* you find this awkward, but feel like you should be."

"That's...surprisingly accurate," Hel admitted.

"Look at it logically," said Hel. "Yes, there are other types of bots made to look like sapient beings, but only in cases where interaction with another meatbag is desired. No need to make a dock worker humanoid when there are cheaper and more efficient designs, right? So, psychiatrists, human resources, customer service, stuff like that, sure. But why would they be on this ship?"

"Now I probably could have ordered a shrink bot without raising any eyebrows. God knows Moss could use one. But consider a companion bot's primary function, and what that means in terms of how it's built." She gently brushed a hand over her arm. "Highly receptive dermal layer. Do you realize how important that is? A service bot might only have enough to pick up things without breaking them and know it's being touched."

Hel felt she was beginning to understand. "So, in order for it to react convincingly, they have to make a companion bot work as close to human as possible."

"Or Nubran, or Elysian, but yeah. I figured if I pulled this off, I might start to feel human again. Or for the first time. Whatever."

Hel smiled. "And? Is it working?"

Violet leaned forward and took Hel's hand, their fingers interlocking and rubbing together. "Took me a while to sync up my virtual feedback with this body's, but yeah. Right now, this feels pretty much like it does in the simulation."

"How does it work?" Hel asked. "I mean, are you *in* there?" She nodded to indicate Violet's head.

"Yes and no. This body was designed to house a pseudo-intelligent personality, like Trouble, but some ships also use them as a backup member of the crew, so I had some features added which lets the body operate remotely from the ship's computer. That's why it has to be registered on crew manifests. Right now, it feels like I'm here, seeing through these eyes alone."

"But you can't be in two places at once?"

Violet shook her head. "Not while giving my full attention. Certain things run automatically, like a person's heartbeat or breathing, while others are like patting your head and rubbing your stomach while talking to someone. But if I had to start flying the ship right this second, this body would go catatonic."

"Good to know," said Hel, then started to blush again. "And about the... uh... *other* things?"

Violet winked. "Fully functional."

Moss stood in front of the assembled command staff of the *Pegasi*, who had just listened to him lecture them for the last two hours about peace and cooperation and a new era of humanity.

They were not impressed.

The one named Dhatta seemed especially stubborn. Most of the "Nay" side seemed to follow his lead. The one named Ohi was less vocal, but no less fixed on her opinion.

"We have a right to self-determination," said Dhatta. "You keep telling us that the galaxy has changed. That the Earth our ancestors knew is gone forever. Well, it's not. It lives in us. *We* are the last vestiges of that world, and it is our sacred duty to protect it as it was."

"And that means not polluting our culture with outside influences," Ohi added. "You've done enough damage as it is."

"Christ, you two could work for the Bureau of Culture," said Moss.

"We're not against the integration of the refugees into our numbers," said Dhatta, pretending to be reasonable. "They would just need to be spread out evenly in the community, and promise to never talk about their lives before arriving."

"Let me just skip ahead for you a bit," said Moss. "Because once you realize that the latter is impossible, you're going to insist that they be kept separate from your community. Then you're going to limit contact with them. And then, after some real or perceived transgressions, things start to get ugly."

The lieutenant rose from his seat, slamming his hands on the table. "How *dare* you—"

Moss roared in frustration, pulled out his pulse gun, and blasted Lieutenant Dhatta between the eyes, followed by Ohi the moment she opened her stupid mouth. The rest just looked at one another, unsure what to do, while Moss gave a deep, contented sigh.

"*Much* better."

The simulation dissolved and Moss was back in the co-pilot chair of the *Outreach*. Sister Tameria leaned over him with an amused look on her face.

"I thought I took away your gun," she said.

"I added it back before you started," said Moss. "When you said you were maxing out the difficulty on this run, I was pretty sure I'd need it."

Tameria chuckled. "You lasted longer than I thought. I mean, they were literally never going to change their minds, yet you stuck with it for over two hours."

Moss sat up. "Well, it seemed important to you," Tameria blinked, leaning back, and Moss quickly added. "I mean, you're not letting me have any *fun*, so I might as well take this seriously..." He thought about how the session had ended. "Serious-ish."

"Well, thank you, but you really didn't need to. This was just a stress test."

"You got the stress part right."

"Any notes?" asked Tameria.

"Honestly, I think you might have mixed up some personality traits somewhere. You might want to double check your files."

"I'm sorry, which of us is an expert in personality architecture?"

"I'm telling you, I remember Dhatta from before. He would never wax poetic. Captain Mbatha, on the other hand... He might."

Tameria frowned and went back to the pilot's seat, turning on a virtual panel in the air in front of her. "I'll check. I might have shifted some things around on the last recombination. I haven't slept in ages."

With the subject of sleep brought up, Moss yawned. "Neither have I. You didn't have any MelaMax on board. But then, you get by on a lot less than I do."

Tam smiled. "Yeah, MelaMax doesn't work on us. Sorry. To be honest, I kind of envy how long you sleep. Elysians once slept twice as long as we do now."

"Until you engineered it out of your systems," said Moss.

It was one of the many traits that Elysians had added or enhanced in their species long ago, including their folding wings and a quality known as glamour, which made them more amiable and even attractive to one another, and other species. Though, as she often pointed out, Tameria had never used her glamour on him. Wasn't worth the effort, he supposed.

She sighed. "I know that much sleep is terribly inefficient, and it's not like you actually *do* anything, but sometimes the idea of it is just so appealing."

"Classic sign of work burnout," said Moss.

"Maybe you're right." She closed the virtual panel and swiped it off. "You know, eight out of the last ten sims were successful. Maybe we can just..." She looked over at Moss, then swiped the panel back on. "Actually, maybe we can try one more variation first."

Moss groaned. "Tam! Come on, stop! You're trying to keep busy so you don't have to be alone with me. I get it. Things are awkward. But they don't have to be."

Tameria swiped the panel away again. "I'm sorry."

"Don't be. I don't exactly make things easy. Besides, I already know the way things are going. Once this is all over, we can have whatever uncomfortable talk you got bottled up inside you and be done with it. But...just not right now, okay?"

"Okay."

Tameria brought up their current flight path on the dash's central display, most likely to avoid an awkward pause. The *Pegasi* wasn't that far away now. She stretched out the view so they could also see the *Viaticus Rex* trailing far behind them, a few days out of Komi Station.

"They should catch up with us in maybe three days," she said. "Hopefully, the *Pegasi* situation will be sorted by then."

"Hopefully." That got Moss thinking, and he needed an excuse to change the subject. "So, how come this ship is so much faster than mine? I know the Order keeps all the best toys for itself, but from what you told me, this ship could pass inspection as an ordinary shuttle. What gives?"

Tameria brought up a wireframe schematic of the *Outreach*, which vaguely resembled a 20th century Earth shuttle, except for its angled wings. The schematic zoomed in on the engine section. "Nothing revolutionary. Speed is determined by the strength of the transit field, which is offset by the mass of whatever's inside it. The *Outreach*'s reactor is more powerful than it seems, and though this looks like a standard Baroque-class shuttle, it uses lighter and stronger alloys wherever possible."

"I assume that's also why the shields are so strong?"

"That's part of it, but there's more going on there than I'm at liberty to discuss. Still, ten minutes of tinkering in the back, and it would pass inspection at any Protectorate starport without raising any eyebrows. Most of our ships have to be built with that in mind."

But he knew this, and she knew he knew this. It was all just small talk, and they knew that too.

Moss heard the soft clacking of tiny claws coming from the cockpit door. The pair looked behind them to see Trouble walk calmly inside.

For the first time in his life, he was glad to see the stupid PetBot. At least now it could ruin the moment with some silly antics and they could get on with their lives.

Trouble stopped, looked at Moss, then Tameria, then back to Moss, and back to Tameria again, then slowly shook its head.

"Geeze, get a room, you two."

And with that, Trouble turned and left.

Moss gritted his teeth. "I swear to God I'm going to flush that thing with the greywater next chance I get. Why did we even bring it?"

Tameria didn't answer, instead bringing up what looked like a virtual chessboard on her display, only the grid was ten by ten, and the pieces were arranged on each side as a shallow three-row pyramid—ten pieces at the bottom, then six, then two.

"Never mind. Do you know how to play Turangcha?"

"I picked it up a while back," said Moss.

"Good. I'll pass the time beating you until we arrive at the *Pegasi*."

The *Hydrus* continued to match speed and heading with the *Pegasi*. Commander Nekkar had felt a great weight lift from his shoulders these last few hours. For the first time since he'd started this quest, he could picture the future unfold according to a sensible and orderly plan.

He would wait until the *Pegasi* reached its destination before striking. The problem there was, he had no idea what opposition he would face. He knew little about this "Order" that was most likely aiding them. Much of what was known was classified. Commander Miram might have known more, but if she had, she'd left nothing in her logs.

What was known was they had once infiltrated many key parts of the Protectorate government and its major industries. Not that long ago, they had been exposed, and sent scurrying into whatever dark crevices might conceal them. Little was ever said about them after that, as if the media had collectively decided it was no longer newsworthy and moved on to other things. In a surprisingly short period of time, they were passing into myth.

Their motives were unknown, but they possessed technology more advanced than anyone in the Protectorate. And yet, they seemed to avoid violence. Even the shuttle that had tried to ram them had been unarmed, though its shields had been incredibly strong.

This was good. Strength meant nothing unless those who had it possessed the will to use it. Once their destination was known, he would summon the full might of the Silver Legion. With luck, they would nab more than just a colony of stray freeborn, and Nekkar would not only be vindicated, but venerated for his actions.

Lieutenant Tauri spoke up, breaking his meditations.

"Sir. Another ship is approaching the *Pegasi*."

"Is it one of our *assistants*?" he asked. If they were going rogue on him now, there would be hell to pay.

"Negative, sir. It just showed up out of nowhere. It's slowing to intercept."

The display changed to show the passive sensor range of the three ships following the *Pegasi*, and the new blip that was almost on top of it. It wasn't broadcasting its location, and hadn't shown up until it had reached the overlap of the passive sensors of their net.

"We can't get a proper reading at this range, but it's most likely a shuttle of some kind."

Many thoughts went through Nekkar's mind. Tactics, strategies, times, and probable outcomes.

The *Pegasi* was not transit capable. It had most likely been fitted with transit relays and was being towed by ships of the Order extending their transit fields around it. How many there were was not certain, but based on the readings, their best guess was three large transports.

Assuming this incoming shuttle intended to dock with the *Pegasi* or one of the towing ships, they would all have to drop to normal space. Then it would take time to re-establish and align a new transit field. This process took significantly longer when towing another ship—the bigger, the longer. The last thing you wanted was for the field to collapse unexpectedly and scatter everyone's remains across half a light year of empty space.

And for a ship the size of the *Pegasi*, one that had not been designed with transit travel in mind? Even with their technological edge, he doubted this Order could manage it quickly.

Nekkar calculated their own capabilities. Then, finding the results lacking, made some estimates based on ignoring safety protocols. Finding those numbers more satisfactory, he leaned back in his chair.

"Helm, prepare to intercept. If the *Pegasi* drops out of transit, you are to set a course at best possible speed." He then pressed the chair's comm panel and connected to engineering. "Lieutenant Anser, I'm going to need you to divert all possible power to the transit drive. Use every means at your disposal. Understood?"

"Yes, sir. I can manage that."

"Good." Nekkar then looked to Lieutenant Ginan. "Tactical, have all fighter and weapon crews on standby. The moment we drop from transit, launch fighters and prepare to fire on the *Pegasi's* escort."

Ginan nodded his understanding. "Sir."

Lieutenant Tauri spoke up. "The *Pegasi* has dropped out of transit, sir. So has the shuttle."

Commander Nekkar grinned. He wasn't normally the sort to make bold, dramatic declarations like the commander on *Legends of the Legion*, but at this moment he couldn't help himself. He leaned forward, pointing toward their destination.

"Go!"

He frowned, unsatisfied. He'd have to work on that.

Hero Worship

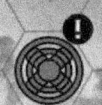

*They say never meet your heroes. That's why I avoid
people who think they know me. You're welcome.*

M. Foote, *Portrait of the Pilot as a Cranky Ol' Man*

T HE *OUTREACH* ARRIVED AT the *Pegasi* on schedule and the
colony ships' escort prepared to synchronize for the drop to
normal space.

Moss's first visit to the *Pegasi* had been a lot trickier. Back then,
the *Pegasi* had been travelling at two-thirds light speed using archaic
ramjets. The problem was, when you dropped out of transit, your
velocity was zero relative to the strongest gravitational field—which
was typically a star or a planet. So Moss had had to get close enough
that the *Pegasi* was the strongest field around, and not the star behind
them.

This time around would be much easier, since they were all using
transit, but if the calculations weren't spot on, you could still over-
shoot the other ship by hundreds of kilometres.

The stars shifted from streaks of blue to pinpoints of white and
then stretched out to red before it looked like they were being kicked
out of a void and back into the real world, and once again Moss got to
see a piece of living history.

The *Pegasi* was huge for a starship. It might as well have been a medium-sized space station with three giant rockets strapped to it. There were two large rings rotating around its central axis, the larger of which housed the colonists. The smaller was the command ring, which focused on ship operations and maintenance. It was mostly used by the command staff, scientists, engineers, and so on.

The ship had left Sol decades before Moss had been born, and had spent nearly four and a half centuries between the stars, searching for a home it was never going never find, because humans were a vindictive, selfish, arrogant bunch of primates who held grudges from beyond the grave.

Moss tried to shake that thought out of his head. The thought wasn't *wrong*, but it was incomplete. Humanity was capable of more. Of being better. It was just hard to remember that sometimes.

Three transports surrounded the colony ship at equal distances to one another. The Order had initially sent a vicious-looking corvette to repair the *Pegasi* and fit it with transit relays, but these humble ships had been brought in for their reliable and sturdy construction. You didn't use a race car to do the work of a tow truck.

Sister Tameria contacted the freighters first and talked to them in that formal Order fashion that annoyed Moss so much. He supposed it was a way of uniting them in common purpose or something, but it just sounded self-important to him.

Then she hailed the *Pegasi* and requested clearance to land, which was granted.

The *Outreach* lined up with the docking bay located at the front of the colony ship, dead centre. This part didn't rotate, allowing the shuttle to slide in smoothly. The hangar bay doors shut, and air was pumped back into the chamber.

"*Now* is it a good time to tell me whatever it is you're not telling me?" asked Moss, getting up.

Tameria shook her head as she unbuckled herself. "According to my projections, if I tell you anything beforehand and you have time to think, you'll do something stupid. But if you're forced to react, you'll most likely do the right thing."

"Are you telling me that you made a simulation of *me*?"

"On the way to Komi Station, yes."

Moss angled his head towards her. "Did it hit on you?"

"Constantly."

"Checks out."

But Tameria's expression had changed, and her brow furrowed a bit. Something bothered her.

"Are you sure that this isn't just so you can have a laugh at my expense?" asked Moss.

"I'd call it more of a perk."

"Fine, I'm used to thinking on my feet. Let's get this over with."

They activated their grip boots and made their way to the shuttle ramp. Last time he was here, he'd been met by a couple of engineers, but this time, two members of the command staff had shown up. In fact, they were the *only* ones here.

Captain Mbatha stepped forward with, not exactly a smile on his face, but at least it wasn't resentment. The same could not be said of Lieutenant Dhatta.

"Welcome aboard, Captain Foote. I trust you had a pleasant journey?" Mbatha held out a hand to him, which Moss shook.

Moss knew how to open things up. "Pleasant enough. I'm more than happy to help address any concerns you have about the recent changes made to your arrangement with the Order."

While he had no actual authority or even the right to speak on behalf of the Order, there was no reason for them to know that. This was all about perception.

"I suggest we proceed directly to the conference room," said Dhatta, just a bit too quickly.

"I see no reason to hurry," said Moss. "In fact, Sister Tameria and I are overdue for some rest. And we're still, what, a month away from our destination?"

The captain agreed. "As it happens, our shift ends in a couple of hours. I think it would be best if we picked this up tomorrow. Quarters in the command ring have already been set aside."

"Thank you," said Moss. "In the meantime, I'd love a chance to tour your great ship again."

"The last time we allowed that, you hacked our computers," said Dhatta.

Moss smiled. "As I recall, that's the reason we learned your navigation had been sabotaged." By their own people, no less, four hundred years ago. "So, you're welcome."

Mbatha stepped in before Moss's snark level rose. "I trust you will not be doing anything like that this time, captain?"

"I think it's understood that there's no need for that," said Moss. "What happened before was a matter of necessity, given the uncertain circumstances we were working under."

Which was true, after a fashion. At the time, part of him had hoped to turn the rescue of the *Pegasi* into some kind of payday, though things hadn't worked out that way. That was the danger of working with do-gooders whose primary concern was being noble. The Order thought a good deed was its own reward, while Moss saw it as a bonus that accompanied a large credit transfer. Good deeds didn't keep the galley stocked.

"You know, we don't even need to go to the command ring," Moss said diplomatically. "I'd be happy to visit the habitation ring instead. I have some letters Helena wanted me to give her parents."

Dhatta blanched at that. More surprisingly, so did the captain.

"Perhaps you should get some rest instead, Captain Foote," said Mbatha.

Now Moss was just damn curious. "Hel was very keen on me getting these letters to them as soon as we arrived. In fact, I thought maybe they could put us up for the night?"

"I'm afraid that will be impossible," said Lieutenant Dhatta. "The habitation ring is to be accessed only by the crew of the *Pegasi* until we reach our destination."

Moss was starting to wish Tameria hadn't insisted he leave his sidearm on the ship, and starting to realize why she had.

Just go with the flow, he thought. *For now.* "Well, that's a dang shame, but the captain's right. I am pretty tired. How about you show us to our rooms?"

"Absolutely," Mbatha said, and led them to the back hatch of the hangar, which opened up to a four-way sets of tubes slowly rotating around, each with its own ladder. These led to different parts of the command ring.

The sense of gravity grew stronger as they descended, until it was around four-fifths of a gee on a noticeable angle.

At the bottom, and much to everyone's surprise, they were surrounded by dozens of crewmen. Neither the captain nor the lieutenant looked pleased about it.

"What is the meaning of this?" Mbatha shouted at a man Moss recognized, Lieutenant Hori, who had been his guide during his first visit.

"Sorry, sir. They wouldn't listen! They said they'd behave, but—"

"It's him!" someone shouted, and cheers rang out, even a scream, dissolving to a wave of babbling calls for attention.

"Remember me?"

"Can I have your autograph?"

"Maurice!"

"Mister Foote!"

"Oh! Oh!" That person could only be identified by their arms waving over the crowd.

"Did you bring your ship?"

"Can I be on your crew?"

"Are you going to stay?"

Moss took a step back as the crowd crushed forward. This was not the usual response he got when he walked into a room, and he wasn't quite sure how to react.

They were...*glad* to see him?

Something flew over the crowd and Moss caught it before it hit him in the face. At first, he thought it was a shirt, but soon realized was either a sports bra or a cropped tank top.

Dhatta, more annoyed than ever, pushed through the crowd and disappeared, but the captain stayed behind, hands held out as if he could hold them back through force of will alone.

"WILL YOU BE QUIET!"

Captain Mbatha's patience, which up till now was something Moss—and most of the crew—had thought was endless, had finally come to an end. But he was quick to recover.

"I understand your excitement. Captain Foote has done much for this ship. But I *will* have you behave in a professional manner or disciplinary action *will* be taken. Now, once our guests have had a chance to rest, and if he is willing, I will arrange for him to spend some time answering questions that have been approved by the settlement committee."

While this did have the intended effect of calming everyone down, the one thing Moss really noticed was the looks of annoyance on many of their faces. There was growing resentment on board the *Pegasi*.

As if on cue, Lieutenant Dhatta returned with a dozen crewmen in riot gear, carrying what looked like stun batons. That ended the party for good, and the gathered crowd quickly dispersed.

Mbatha took a deep and weary sigh. "I apologize for my crew's lack of professionalism, Captain Foote. I will show you to your quarters now."

Moss noted, however, that Dhatta had his little goon squad follow close behind, making sure everyone kept their distance. But part of him wondered if that was the *only* reason he'd brought them.

Having survived centuries past its best-before date, the *Pegasi* was a miracle of engineering, maximizing recycling and efficiency in a way that put the rest of the wasteful galaxy today to shame.

Even so, entropy was slowly winning out, and it showed in subtle ways throughout the command ring. Little things, like a workstation that had been abandoned rather than repaired, with some parts visibly cannibalized. A broken light panel that was probably at the bottom of a priority list to be replaced. That sort of thing. But overall, the ship was exactly the same as when he'd left it.

The captain led them to the crew quarters that made up a third of the command ring. While everyone here also had accommodations in the habitat ring, their shifts necessitated them staying close for long periods of time and be on call quickly. The group stopped at one of the doors.

"We're keeping the Martian refugees on the command ring as well, so I'm afraid we're short on spare rooms. You and Sister Tameria will have to share one with your family."

"That's fine, captain," said Tameria, who could speak English, along with a number of other languages, without an adaptive translator. "Shall we schedule our first meeting in about eight hours?"

"That should be fine." The captain eyed his lieutenant and the guards, who'd stopped a few doors down. "And allow me to apologize for the lieutenant's zealous behaviour. Ever since you left, he's become more and more defensive."

"I assume relieving him of duty is out of the question?" Moss asked.

Mbatha nodded. "Doing that would only make those who support him even more resistant. I would prefer to de-escalate the situation before taking that option."

"I understand," said Moss. "Well, see you in eight hours."

And with that, the captain left, and Moss breathed a sigh of relief.

"I didn't know your family was here," said Moss.

Tameria tried and failed to hide a smirk as she knocked on the door. "Oh, he didn't mean *my* family."

She opened the door and inside on the double bed was a woman reading a story to two young children, and a teenager with dirty blond hair sitting on the edge, facing the door.

Zach waved at them. "Hi, Dad!"

By this point, Moss was too numb to be shocked. He just looked to Tameria and said, "You've got some explaining to do."

Some explaining was done, after Tameria had swept the room for bugs.

Moss stared at Tameria's tablet, which displayed a picture taken from the largest park on the habitation ring. She'd tried to offer a quasi-apology, but Moss waved her off. "No, no, I get it. It was the right call. If you had told me about all this on the way, I would have leaned into it in the worst possible way and messed things up, with a grin on my face the whole time. We'd be spending the rest of the trip undoing the damage."

"Exactly."

Despite the command staff's best efforts, the story of what Moss and the others had done for the colony ship had reached the general public and taken on a life of its own. This was best reflected by the image on Tameria's tablet.

It was of a statue. Of him.

Not the best likeness, though. This guy looked pretty average. He was flattered, of course, but with a clear head he could see how this could quickly get out of hand.

Zach's family kept to themselves on the other side of the room, but Zach had sidled up next to Moss as if he was a legitimate part of this discussion.

"Still don't get his angle, though," said Moss, looking at the kid.

"Neither do I," said Zach. "But she said it was important."

"It was," said Tameria. "It was going to be a week before I could get you here, Moss, and I needed the holdouts off balance. The captain made sure there were as many people in the hangar as possible to greet Zach's ship, so that when he announced himself as your son..."

"There'd be no way to keep it under wraps that I was coming back. Give the rumour mill time to do its thing."

"Plus, there's the mythos angle to consider," Tameria added. "The son of the saviour of the *Pegasi*?"

Moss nodded. "Yeah, that's quality cantina gossip there. So what's our story exactly?" He looked to the mother, who was playing with the younger kids to keep them distracted. "Is she still supposed to be your mom? Are we supposed to be an item? Am I paying child support?"

"I told Zach to keep it vague but close to the truth," said Tameria. "Easier to remember."

"I didn't really know my dad," said Zach. "He disappeared before Lada and Lev were born. I told them we were reunited when you rescued us on the *Maruma*."

"Are they mine too?"

Zach shook his head. "I didn't think that would work."

"What do you mean?"

"Well, I was thinking about how I might read it in a book, or see it on an episode of *Ranger M*. I could imagine Ranger M having *one* kid no one knew about...but not three."

"But I'm not supposed to be Ranger M, remember?"

Zach shrugged. "Still a story."

Moss almost smiled. "Do you ever write your own stories, Zach?"

Zach looked at his feet. "Sometimes…"

"Keep doing it." Moss turned to Tameria before Zach could blind him with his smile. "So, it looks like the holdouts are doubling down, given the Lieutenant's behaviour."

"I don't think it will last," said Tameria. "I think we're seeing a final desperate attempt at posturing. If anything, the reaction to your arrival will make them see that trying to keep things the way they were is a fantasy."

"Let's hope so," said Moss. "Then, at the meeting tomorrow, we offer them our compromise. Respect and honour the past while embracing the future, all that jazz. We need to reach Dhatta's people first. Wear away his support."

"Agreed. I have some ideas on that."

Moss smirked. "Does it involve getting them alone in a room and using your glamour?"

"No." Tameria frowned. "And I resent the implication you're making."

Moss feigned offence. "What implication? I meant *all* of them, together. Charm them in that unique Elysian way so they'll listen to what we have to say. If you thought I was suggesting anything sordid, well, that's on *you*, missy!"

"I know *full* well you meant…" Tameria groaned and sagged on the edge of the bed. "Why? *Why* do you do this to me?"

"I think it's because he likes you?" said Zach. "Only he doesn't know how to tell you?"

Moss put a fatherly hand on the kid's shoulder. "Shut up, son. You're making things awkward."

Just then, a klaxon went off, and the speakers crackled to life.

"*All crew to emergency stations. Repeat, all crew to emergency stations. This is not a drill. All civilians proceed to the nearest safety shelter.*"

Moss looked up at the speakers. "Well, *that* ain't helping."

The Battle of the Pegasi

Civilian ships tend to have small crews of between one and six. These are nowhere near the scale of what the military or corporations use, however. Typically, the smallest military capital ships are about the size of the largest civilian vessels.

Warship classifications are, in order of size, Scout/Corvette, Patrol, Frigate, and Cruiser. The Heavy Cruiser is the heaviest class that tends to see combat, and the most powerful available to non-Protectorate governments or private contractors.

Protectorate navies have access to larger and more powerful warships, but in this age of relative peace, these are used only in matters of power projection and almost never see action. The majority of battleships have been mothballed, though not decommissioned.

The largest capital ships on record, dreadnoughts, have not been seen in a thousand years, not since the last major conflict between Protectorate members.

M. Foote, *The Galaxy is Weirder than You Think*

W HEN THE *HYDRUS* DROPPED out of transit, they did not catch the Order escort off guard. However, there was no time to generate a transit field around the *Pegasi* and escape.

And so, the transports had sent off a distress message and prepared themselves for battle.

These ships were the *Mohow, the Larai*, and the *Curlai*, named after three of the ancient Draxon gods of conflict, an intentionally ironic choice given that they were not warships.

The captain of the *Mohow* ordered all ships to raise shields and charge the inductors, just in case, then hailed the incoming ship before it dropped from transit.

He had expected a demand for surrender. What he hadn't expected was for the *Hydrus* to drop right on top of them, and open fire without hesitation.

The *Mohow* took the brunt of the attack, hit by everything from beam cannons to close support turrets. Within seconds, the *Hydrus* had punched through their shields and was raining kinetics down on the drive section.

The *Mohow* barely had time to return fire with their inductors before their reactor died, leaving them dead in space and without power, just as the *Hydrus* unleashed a swarm of snub fighters from its hangar bay and turned its attention to the remaining two ships.

But this victory was short-lived, because the *Curlai* and *Larai* had taken flanking positions around the heavy cruiser, evading its fixed beam cannons and easily absorbing its turret fire.

One of the greatest threats to a starship isn't the cold of space, but the heat the ship generates. Heat needs somewhere to go, and space, being a vacuum, does not generally count as somewhere. Complex bleed systems are required to radiate waste heat from the skin of a ship, or temporarily contain it during emergencies.

In the past, heat weapons had been developed to overload the bleed capabilities of a ship, but the systems of a modern warship rendered these ineffective.

The Order's inductors, however, were not ordinary heat weapons...

"Long range comms are jammed," Lieutenant Ginan said calmly. "Hull temperature rising."

Nekkar frowned. Civilians still used heat guns as an economical way to deter pirate fighters, but as a military weapon, they were useless. The *Hydrus*'s bleed systems were state-of-the-art. Being able to jam their comms was a bit more impressive, but hardly important at the moment.

"I expected more of a challenge. Keep us cool, lieutenant."

Ginan tapped at his control station, suddenly confused. "Bleed systems not responding."

"What?" Nekkar checked the panel on his armrest to confirm what he'd heard.

"Whatever it is, it's preventing our attempts to vent heat," said Ginan. "Hull temperature continuing to rise. Sensors are starting to overheat. We're losing tracking."

On the now flickering main display, Commander Nekkar saw the dead transport, while on the tactical overlay the other two moved to flank the *Hydrus* on either side, trying to split its fire while they somehow cooked it from the outside.

Nekkar leaned forward in his chair. "That's not possible..."

"Helm, turn us about. Focus on target delta. All fighters focus on target beta." That would prevent any friendly fire with the *Hydrus* and, with luck, beta would focus its attention on the snub fighters surrounding it.

The chatter from the fighters could be heard in the background as they engaged.

"Blue wing, come about four-five. Green wing, target the engines."

"Pulse guns aren't getting through."

"All wings, focus fire. Find a weak spot!"

"Systems are overheat—" The sound was cut off and one of the blips representing their fighters vanished, followed by another, and another.

"*I'm not even seeing anything*!" said another before they too vanished from the tactical display.

The commander understood what the pilot meant. The transport didn't seem to be firing anything, despite all evidence to the contrary. A coward's weapon, but undeniably effective. Fortunately, the *Hydrus* had finally gotten a bead on its target.

"Fire!"

The heavy cruiser fired everything it had. Its powerful beam cannons, designed to take on capital ships at long range, poured into the deceptively humble transport, along with turrets meant for close quarters combat. The weapons should have torn right through them. They did not.

"Target's shields *almost* down," said Ginan. Just then, the lights died and red emergency lighting came on. Ginan's calm tone became less calm. "Sir, whenever we fire, there's a huge spike in internal heat. Heat sinks are at capacity. Systems are overloading. Trying to reroute."

"Priority to weapons. I want those shields down."

The comm officer called out, "Engineering reports damage to the main reactor. Fires reported on decks six through eight! Deck seven reports heavy casualties!"

"Target shields down!" called Ginan.

"Cease fire on energy weapons," said Nekkar. "Kinetics only. Target the reactor!"

The transport, unable to sustain fire, or defend itself, now tried to escape, which was a serious mistake, because it exposed the very parts of the ship Nekkar wanted to hit.

"Maintain fire," said Nekkar. Then he had a revelation. "And drop the shields."

Ginan looked back at the commander from his station. "Sir?"

Just then, the comm station overloaded, exploding in a shower of sparks, causing the crewman to fall to the floor.

"Do it!"

The air was noticeably warmer. He checked the comm panel on his chair. It was still working. "Engineering. Shut down all non-essential systems. Weapons and maneuvering thrusters only."

As the transport tried to flee, the kinetics tore the side of its hull to shreds, then took two of its engines apart and killed the reactor. It wasn't going anywhere.

"If they're using our heat against us, we need to generate as little as possible. Helm, full about. Get target beta in my sights. Then *ram* it."

"Raise shields?" asked Ginan.

"Negative. We don't need ours—we're going to use its."

The last transport must have been confused by the *Hydrus*'s actions, and had only started to reverse course by the time the heavy cruiser fell on top of it. They weren't going fast enough to punch through its shields, but they *were* close enough for their overheating hull to disrupt it.

"Hold your fire, keep as much contact with its shields as possible," said Nekkar. "All fighters focus on the aft section." With luck, the shields would collapse under this relentless contact. It might even sap away some of the *Hydrus*'s heat.

The captain of the transport must have figured out what the plan was, or simply panicked, because they now turned and fled, keeping its shields up and their heat weapon focused on any pursuing fighters until they could make the escape to transit, leaving the *Hydrus* alone with its prize.

Roy Herzog had watched most of the action from the back of the bridge. First, he'd taken advantage of the chaos to slip into the commander's office and access Nekkar's computer. He'd had to hurry, though, because it would most likely be a short battle.

During his time with the Legion, Roy had learned a few workarounds in their operating systems. The kind of minor exploits a ship's fixer might use to smuggle on contraband or cover their tracks after accessing certain rooms without clearance. He couldn't gain access to anything encrypted or requiring passwords or bioscans, but it turned out the system he wanted didn't fall under either of those categories. Hubris, thy name is Nekkar.

He slipped back onto the bridge just as things got interesting in the worst possible way. Roy's buoyant mood took a hit as the battle dragged on, and when the comm station blew, he began to think he'd made a huge error in judgement.

He'd been amazed how the small transports had put up so much resistance. The *Hydrus* was capable of taking on ten patrol ships, and just three of these transports—two, really—had nearly crippled them. For a moment, things had looked hopeless.

Then Nekkar had turned the situation around, found the flaw in their capabilities, and used it against them.

Roy hated to admit it, but he'd been impressed. This was the kind of thing Nekkar had been designed for. And at that moment, the crew saw him in a new light. Every erratic action, every questionable command, it was all part of a grander plan they were only now being made aware of.

It wasn't *true*, of course, but that's how they'd see it. And the story would spread across the ship in no time.

Twelve hours ago, the bridge crew had been on the verge of mutiny against the commander. Now they'd take a bolt for him.

Well, shit.

Moss and Tameria rushed to the C&C portion of the command ring, which was abuzz with activity. Captain Mbatha was there, standing next to Lieutenant Hori, who was switching between various external feeds and their own sensor readings on six different monitors. Those members of the command staff not busy working at a nearby station huddled around this one, watching the events unfold in horror.

"What's going on?" asked Moss. One of the monitors showed a distant shot of a wild firefight, dozens of pulses coming from a dozen different directions, followed by a bright solid beam.

"Our escort is under attack," said Mbatha.

"Pirates?" asked Tameria.

The captain shook his head. "We do not know. They have not made contact with any of us. They simply arrived and opened fire."

While Moss couldn't make out the ships involved in detail, the next time the beam fired, he was certain he saw a distinctive smooth chrome hull light up.

"Oh no..."

Tameria nodded. "I saw it too."

"What?" asked the captain.

"I think it's the Silver Legion," said Moss.

That got everyone chattering. He had explained enough about the Legion the last time they were here for them to be justifiably worried.

"Why aren't your people firing back?" asked Moss.

"They are," said Tameria. "Those transports are equipped with inductors."

Moss was somewhat familiar with those, but they hadn't been the kind of toys he'd gotten to play with back in the day. "Is it enough?"

"I honestly don't know," said Tameria.

All they could do was stand around Hori's station and slowly come to the realization that, no, it was not enough. Two of the transports were either destroyed or disabled, and the third had run with its tail between its legs.

Now the Legion ship turned and slowly came towards the *Pegasi*. And from what Moss could see, it wasn't even scratched.

Tameria leaned heavily on the desk and shut her eyes tight. "Goddess. Do you realize what this means?"

Moss looked to the *Pegasi* command staff and frowned. "Yeah... I spent the last three days studying these knobs for *nothing*."

Commander Nekkar looked over the damage report. Victory had come with a heavy price.

At least a dozen of the crew were dead, most due to a fire on deck seven. More had been hospitalized, including his comm officer. They had lost ten snub fighters, but only three pilots. The others had been retrieved from their disabled ships.

Thankfully, there were no cyborg casualties.

The *Hydrus*, however, was going nowhere. The main reactor could only operate at half-power, and the transit drive needed extensive repairs. They might be able to get sub-transit working in a day or so, and basic transit a day after that. Their main beam cannons were damaged, and it was uncertain if either could fire safely.

From the outside, the ship appeared undamaged, but the truth was, they were dead in space.

Of the two enemy transports, their exact status was unknown. Sensors were offline, and at the moment, they relied on visual readings. There were survivors aboard each, but the ships were without power, and neither was capable of repairing the damage inflicted upon them. But boarding them, for the time being, was out of the question.

The last time they'd boarded a ship of the Order, it had ended with the death of Commander Miram after its reactor blew. It wasn't clear whether or not that had been a booby trap, but Nekkar wasn't about to take that chance with these ships. Not until he contacted the Colony Fleet and reinforcements could be brought in.

That was the other problem. While local comms were still working, interstellar comms had been fried. It was unclear how long it would take to repair them, as those systems had been on deck seven.

Nekkar assessed all of this quickly and set the priorities on repairs. With that handled, he turned his attention back to their prize.

On the flickering display was the massive form of the *Pegasi*.

It wasn't every day that Nekkar saw something older than he was. On board that ship were three thousand freeborn whose genetic lines pre-dated the Terran Disaster. Who had never had the kind of genetic enhancements that were ubiquitous within the Protectorate. Who had never been recorded in any database.

On board that ship was the salvation of the Terran Colony Fleet.

He turned his attention to his security officer. "Lieutenant Ginan, prepare a boarding party. Welcome them back into the Terran fold. Make sure they understand that this is not up for negotiation."

Moss gave a dejected sigh as the monitor showed a smaller ship leave the hangar of the heavy cruiser. "Not wasting any time to say hello, are they?"

Lieutenant Hori listened to something on his earpiece. "They're contacting us on radio, sir."

If they knew that the *Pegasi* could only communicate via antiquated radio transmissions, that told Moss they knew *exactly* what they had found.

"They're requesting we open up the hangar bay for them."

Moss and Tameria shared a look, both remembering that her shuttle was still in that same hangar.

"I have to get back to my ship," said Tameria.

Lieutenant Dhatta sneered. "You're *running*?"

"Great idea!" said Moss.

"I'm not running," said Tameria. "But as far as they know, none of the Order is on board the *Pegasi*. We need them to believe that as long as possible." She looked to Hori at his station. "Tell the shuttle we are making preparations for their arrival. Have everyone in the hangar section cover up my ship, better than last time. Then open the hangar doors."

Hori turned to Captain Mbatha for confirmation.

The captain frowned. "You want to just *let* them inside?"

"They're more than capable of forcing their way if we don't," said Tameria.

The captain nodded to Hori, who started to make the calls. "I'd have thought you'd try to buy some time for your people to organize a counterattack."

"Our escort would have alerted the closest Priory of our situation," said Tameria, "but it will take time for them to decide on a course of action. There is every possibility that they will consider us a lost cause and choose not to intervene. Even if they do come, it could be days before they arrive."

She took a deep breath. "Now, if you'll excuse me, there is protocol I need to follow. I need to get back to my ship and wipe its systems for when it inevitably *is* discovered."

Moss watched her as she left. She'd been holding something back. Yeah, she was going to do what she said, but the look on her face when she said *protocol* worried him. It was the kind of look you had when you didn't think you were coming back.

"Wait up, I'm coming with you!"

About halfway up the ladder, Moss and Tameria were able to use one good kick to reach the central core of the ship, using the rungs only a few times for additional speed and direction control.

"You should really go back to the command ring," Tameria said once they reached the zero-gee centre. "You don't want to be in the hangar when that shuttle arrives."

"Neither do you," said Moss. He gripped the floor with his boots, only to have Tameria push off towards her ship without him. He found a wall grip and flung himself after her. "You talked about not letting the Legion know the Order was on board? Well, you stick out like a sore thumb, even without that wingpack of yours."

"I know. I don't intend to stick around."

"Then I don't see a problem with me tagging along," said Moss. Tameria didn't reply to that, but the exchange only confirmed that she didn't want him to see what she was up to. Which meant Moss really wanted to know what it was.

In the bay, the workers had moved the *Outreach* as far to the side as possible. They were already covering it up with tarps and boxes, so that it wasn't so much hidden as camouflaged, looking like a natural part of the hangar clutter. So long as nobody examined it too closely, it might do the trick.

The ramp to the *Outreach* was still down. Once inside, Tameria finally touched down with her grip boots.

In zero-gee, it was impossible for a ferret to hop-run the way they do in gravity, which meant that when Trouble came out to see them, it scurried low to the ground on all fours in a way that made Moss think of a very long spider. Like the thing didn't creep him out enough already.

"Hey, you're back!"

Tameria ignored the PetBot. "Moss, if you're going to be here, make yourself useful."

"I should warn the *Rex*," said Moss. "Use an encrypted channel, maybe?"

Hel shook her head. "They might see the energy spike. Go to the cockpit and start deleting the navigation logs, personal logs, everything you can. Then shut it down." She looked up. "Ship. Full access granted to passenger Maurice Foote. Authorization Tameria-Zero-Lacilla-One-Moss."

Moss blinked. "Moss? I'm part of your super-secret access code?"

"*You* wouldn't have guessed it. Now go. We don't have much time."

"Fine." He looked down at the PetBot. "Trouble, you're with me."

Tameria stopped right before the access hatch to the engine room. This part of the ship looked like any other, but the wall on the right contained a false panel. She slid it open, revealing an electronic safe. It was shielded against scanning, putting up a false signal just like parts of her engine and small cargo bay. If you didn't already know where this safe was, you'd have to take the ship apart piece by piece to find it.

The safe recognized her biometric signature the moment she touched it, and it hissed open. She could have sworn she heard a skittering sound when the hiss happened, and instinctively looked to the ground. No sign of Trouble anywhere. She must have imagined it.

Inside the safe was a vial of amber liquid, sealed in such a way that it could only be broken open to release it. Already she was considering the optimal time to deploy it, when it would have the greatest impact.

But she didn't go into this lightly, because in a very real sense, she was about to commit a war crime. She took a deep breath and shook her head, steeling her resolve. Then she reached into the vault and—

"Yoink!"

In a blur, Trouble had jumped from the ceiling, grabbed Tameria's arm with one tiny claw, grabbed the vial in the other, and kicked off down the corridor back towards the cockpit. Even as she chased after it, she saw the PetBot stuff the vial into its mouth so that it filled both cheeks, making it grin like a Hopat.

"MOSS!" she yelled, because of course he was behind this. And here he was already flying towards her just before she could reach the ferret, stopping her in her tracks.

"Not so fast, mis—" His quip was cut off by her fist in his gut. Physical combat in zero-gee is a ballet of awkwardness at the best of times, and this was no exception, but the blow sent him bouncing off the ceiling and gave her enough time to push past him.

But by then, Trouble had already vanished.

"Trouble! Return!" she yelled, looking around for any sign of where it had gone. "Disregard comedic subroutine! Restore factory settings! Return!" She didn't think any of that would work, but had to try. When Trouble didn't come back, she had only one person around to take her frustrations out on.

Moss was still wheezing from the blow she'd landed, holding up one hand in defence while his body spun like a Charon boar on a spit, slowly lowering to the floor.

"Call him back," said Tameria, then waited for him to spin again. " *Now.*"

"I won't...let you... Would you stop me, please?"

Tameria grabbed him and set him on the ground. "Get it back here."

"Not till you tell me what's in that vial." Tameria frowned and Moss added, "If you can grant me access to your ship's computer remotely, you could have deleted all that stuff remotely. I had Trouble follow you. I was watching you from the cockpit. I *saw* what you were doing."

"Moss, listen. Even if I wipe the *Outreach*'s computers, there are two wrecked transports out there, either one of which might still have the coordinates to Ataraxia on it. That Silver Legion ship, that crew... They can't be allowed to return to the Terran Colony Fleet. *Ever.*"

Moss went cold. So cold his legs began to shake.

Just then, a klaxon went off, warning the hangar crew to prepare for depressurization.

"The Legion shuttle is coming," said Moss. "Come on, we have to get out of here."

Tameria pressed the control pad on her forearm and her flight suit's helmet unfolded and slipped over her head. "I'm not going anywhere until I find that vial."

Moss did the same, deploying his helmet, only to have Tameria pull out a small utility knife and drive it into the side of his visor. Moss saw the small blade sticking through, only a few centimetres from his left eye. For a moment, he wondered if she'd meant to kill him. Then she twisted it, and the visor made a noise that was somewhere between a crack and a tear.

She pulled the knife back out, his helmet now effectively useless. "You, on the other hand, are going back to the command ring. Don't even *think* about interfering with me again."

Moss returned to the command ring a nervous wreck, but he tried not to let it show in front of all the officers.

He'd been in plenty of scrapes in his life. He'd died once, come close a dozen more. But he always kept his wits about him and could usually cover up how he really felt with a razor sharp, sarcastic quip. Right now, he couldn't even make a dad joke.

That look on Tameria's face. The vial.

They can't be allowed to return to the Terran Colony Fleet. Ever.

"Jesus Christ, Tam. What are you going to do?"

Captain Mbatha appeared out of nowhere like a wraith. "What was that, Captain Foote?"

Sometimes the best way to hide a lie was by telling the unvarnished truth. "I'm worried about Tam. I'm not sure what she's going to do when the Legion arrives."

Mbatha nodded in understanding. "If her shuttle is camouflaged well enough, it might be the safest place for her. I expect our guests will want a full account of everyone on board. Which reminds me, we need to make *you* disappear."

Moss frowned. "How do you propose to do that?"

"In plain sight. We're adding your name to our roster. For the time being, you are Maurice Lambinon, Helena's older brother."

"Works for me. What about the folks from Mars?"

"It will raise too many questions if they are found here, especially the ones who worked for the Martian underground. I felt it safer to hide them in the habitation ring for now. There is an unused building in one of the Segments that should suffice. Two of my crew are seeing to it now."

Hiding out? Most of their group was all too used to *that* lifestyle. "Good."

"Now," Mbatha said, looking Moss over, "what size are you, Captain Foote?"

The uniform they gave him was for an ensign, which suited him fine. In fact, he'd have preferred being a janitor. Nobody ever noticed the janitors. But the whole time he changed, he kept thinking about what Tameria was planning.

There was a depressingly small number of possibilities available, given the current evidence. And if he was right, the crew of the *Hydrus* was about to have a very bad—and very *short*—sick day.

But that went against everything Moss knew about the Order. Granted, the pacifism they lived by came with an asterisk and the qualifier "shit happens," but this went way beyond that.

The cynical side of him provided the not-so-comforting rationalization that morals only existed so long as they were convenient. The Order could afford their moral high ground because their secrecy and advanced tech allowed them the luxury of having them.

But they'd been found out, exposed, forced into hiding, and it might be that their secret Priories were a line they could not allow to be crossed. Everyone had a line, and desperate people did desperate things.

But still... it was wrong.

It's war. Freeborn versus synths.

Shut up.

It's always been war. It doesn't have to be formally declared to be one.

Shut up.

Am I wrong?

No. Shut up anyway.

The voice in his head was just trying to make things okay, and as soon as he was *okay* with it, he wouldn't be who he was anymore.

It might be necessary. It might be inevitable. It would *never* be okay.

His train of thought was broken by the sound of marching. For a moment, he thought the Legion had already arrived, but when he looked out the door, he saw a bunch of men and women in riot gear, led by Lieutenant Dhatta, heading for the ladder to the hangar.

Great. The galaxy's most one-sided ass kicking was about to begin.

Tameria raised the *Outreach*'s passenger ramp before the hangar hatch opened to allow the Legion shuttle inside. She then continued her search, but couldn't find the stupid PetBot anywhere, and it wouldn't respond to any of her commands.

She heard the *Pegasi*'s recyclers take in as much of the hangar's air as it could. She vented her ship at the same time and powered the shuttle down. Her suit had enough air for the duration. Then she didn't so much hear but *feel* the hangar doors open as a faint vibration through her feet.

There was a single viewport mid-ship that wasn't completely obscured by camouflage. From there, she had a view of the hangar, and with all the lights off in the shuttle, there was no danger of her being seen.

The Legion shuttle drifted in, its maneuvering thrusters slowing the ship to a perfect stop. The hangar doors closed and air hissed back into the bay.

From the opposite end, she saw the *Pegasi*'s security detail come down in force, maybe forty men and women in total.

From the shuttle came thirty of the *Hydrus*'s crew. Ten were armed security, with shining silver breastplates and pulse rifles, while the others wore sidearms but weren't actively brandishing them. Half of them carried medical bags. They were probably there to take a full account of everyone and everything on board the ship, and to provide baseline health checks.

Lieutenant Dhatta, now wearing riot gear, stepped forward with three guards on either side of him. They were only armed with stun batons, but all looked ready and willing to use them.

From the Legion's side, a tall man stepped forward. Cyborg. Tameria used her suit's camera to zoom in on him and display the feed inside her helmet. The symbol above the lieutenant bars on his epaulets indicated he was a member of the Vigiles. Only two crewmen accompanied him, also cyborgs, judging by their build.

The two groups met halfway, and a conversation began. Dhatta looked angry, and was no doubt making demands.

While she couldn't hear the Vigile's reply, the beating that followed wasn't hard to decipher. The Vigile had either lost his patience or decided to make his point using the universal language of violence.

He pulled Dhatta off the floor, the lieutenant's grip boots doing little to stop him, then proceeded to use him to thump the other members of security.

It was an impressive display of mixed zero-gee combat techniques. Despite wearing grip boots, everyone was still subject to the whole action-reaction conditions that existed in a weightless environment. However, the cyborg was not only ten times stronger than the humans, he had far more mass than you'd expect, so the act of using Dhatta as a living club was not as difficult as one might assume.

The Vigile's grip boots were also far more responsive, allowing him to connect and disconnect with the floor at will, while the *Pegasi* crew had to actively turn theirs on and off.

With his first big swing, the Vigile connected with three guards, while he leaned in and repositioned one leg to take the opposing force without losing balance. One of the guards went flying into the hangar wall. Another had kept his grip boots on and had fallen backwards, hitting the ground, then bouncing back up like a child's punching doll. The third had only kept the grip on one boot and spun around, almost certainly breaking their leg in the process.

The next wind up and swing caught four of the guards who were still reacting to the first swing. Fortunately for them, all had turned their grip boots off as they prepared to lunge. Those hapless souls flew in every direction. One even landed in the pile camouflaging the *Outreach*.

The melee would have been comedy had it been fiction. The two cyborgs that accompanied the Vigile slung their weapons and joined in the fray, punching, kicking, pounding, and ultimately subduing every member of the *Pegasi*'s security team, smiling the whole time. The last guard surrendered, only to be grabbed by these two and tossed back and forth in a high-speed game of catch until the Vigile stopped them.

Three against forty, and it had been sport to them.

Sure, it *looked* funny, but Tameria was certain every last one of them had suffered broken bones and internal injuries. Droplets of sprayed blood drifted towards the walls and floor. And since these humans had none of the basic augmentations common to everyone else in the Protectorate, they needed to be taken back to the gravity of the ship's rings as soon as possible.

Fortunately for the wounded, it seemed the Vigile was a professional. He waved over the medics, who tended to the injured. Those who weren't too badly wounded were escorted back to the command ring. As the others were treated, they too were carried back.

Tameria shook her head. She supposed it could have gone worse. And the upside of the confrontation was it had kept the focus of the boarding party far away from her. They needed everyone to help with the wounded, and in the end, none were left in the hangar bay except for a couple of guards to watch over their shuttle.

Tameria stepped back from the viewport and looked down the corridor of her ship. Now she had to look for Trouble.

"I warned him," said Captain Mbatha as the wounded arrived in the command ring's reception area.

Moss stood next to him but said nothing.

"The lieutenant insisted on this approach," he continued. "To show we would not so be so easily intimidated."

One guard, whose leg had been broken in the kerfuffle, cried out as two Legion synths helped him to the ground and prepared a hypo and an inflatable leg brace.

"Yeah, he showed them," said Moss. He turned to the captain. "I noticed you didn't try *too* hard to stop him."

Mbatha's expression betrayed nothing. "If I had held him back, I believe he would have tried something bolder and more foolish in the near future. Perhaps with more people."

That fit with Moss's profile of the man. "So you let him remove himself from the equation?"

"As you say."

Moss raised an eyebrow. "You're damn good at poker, aren't you?"

Before the captain could answer, however, Moss found himself stepping back and fading into the background as a cyborg, a member of the Vigiles by the looks of it, approached the captain.

"I trust there will be no further pointless attempts at resistance?" the Vigile said, looming over him.

"None," said the captain. "I believe you have made your point."

"Good. I wish it had not been necessary."

Mbatha nodded. "As do I. My only interest is ensuring the safety of this ship, and all within her."

"Then you will see to it that my instructions are carried out."

"So long as those instructions do not endanger anyone."

The Vigile tried to give a warm expression, but wasn't good at it. "We don't wish to harm anyone. Not if we can help it. We simply wish to bring you home."

Mbatha gave a deep and sonorous *hmmm* that managed to convey both his acceptance and his doubt.

Karon hadn't dropped by for a very long time, but Violet could tell from the ship-wide announcements that they had found what they were looking for, and they were going to take it by force.

For hours, she'd sat in her computer in silence, listening to the odd announcement over the comms, trying to get a picture of what was happening, and not having much luck.

The ship got *very* warm at one point and power was cut to the main lighting, leaving her bathed in red emergency light. Fires were reported on several of the decks. Fortunately for Violet, the computer that housed her wasn't damaged by whatever was affecting the rest of the ship, though she had gotten pretty dang warm. Eventually the lights returned and things got cooler, but still no sign of Karon.

It was hours before she finally made an appearance.

"*Whathappened? Whathappened? Whathappened?*"

Karon looked troubled as she sat down. "We found them."

"And do you finally know who *they* are?"

Karon nodded. "There was a meeting of key personnel a little while ago. We've intercepted a colony ship... One that's been adrift for over four hundred years."

Violet gasped. "The *Pegasi*!"

"Wait, you know it?"

"Know it? I was there! Well, another version of me was."

"Apparently, we just rescued it from a group of pirates," said Karon.

"Apparently, you'll just swallow any old bullshit," said Violet, nipping *that* in the bud.

Karon frowned. "We're not that far from the Ramedean bubble. The Void Brotherhood is everywhere."

"And the ships that were helping you *find* this colony ship?"

Karon frowned. "Yeah, I know, it doesn't add up. But we can't actually confirm those ships helping us are from the Brotherhood..."

"Plausible deniability: greasing the wheels of shady dealings since the Big Bang. Look, from what I can tell from the comm chatter, the *Hydrus* is in bad shape, right?"

Karon nodded. "Long range comms are down, transit drive is damaged. We lost over a dozen people." Her gaze grew distant. On a ship with a crew of hundred and fifty, Violet figured she knew most, if not all of them.

"I'm sorry to hear that. But how did pirates do so much damage to a Legion heavy cruiser?"

"They had a new weapon," said Karon. "Like a heat gun, but it prevented our bleed systems from working."

"Overcoming military grade bleed systems? Are pirates usually on the cutting edge of technology?"

"I get it, okay? But it doesn't matter if I believe you. The crew believes the commander. To them, this explains all the secrecy and odd behaviour."

Violet couldn't argue with that. The human brain excelled at rationalizing events in whatever way gave them the most comfort, or fear, depending on what they needed at the moment. Rescuing a lost colony of freeborn from pirates armed with a new secret superweapon? They wanted to believe that, because after all the doubt and uncertainty they'd been through these past few weeks, this explanation made them come off as the heroes.

"Look," said Violet, "those ships you took out 'rescuing' the *Pegasi*? They weren't the bad guys. They were towing that ship to a safe world to establish their colony. Just because the TCF claims to have some kind of manifest destiny on anyone with human DNA doesn't make them right."

Karon shook her head. "They would have been found sooner or later. They always are."

"Trust me, that wasn't going to happen."

Karon raised an eyebrow. "What aren't you telling me?"

Violet mentally gulped. She'd said too much. She needed to pivot.

"What you need to ask yourself is what *they* aren't telling you. Remember how desperate the commander was about finding this ship? And the ship smuggling freeborn back in Sol? Maybe Nekkar is just obsessive. He's definitely a stickler for the rules. But there's something else going on here. Something he doesn't want anyone finding out about."

Karon thought back to something Roy had told her when she'd been promoted to ensign.

While I firmly believe what the commander is doing is in the Fleet's best interest, I'm not entirely convinced what he's doing is in your *best interests.*

Karon looked at Violet's camera. "I think you're right..."

"Wouldn't you like to find out what it is?"

Even before she'd joined the Silver Legion, the idea of respecting the chain of command had been drilled into her. But she'd also shown aptitude for growth, for creative and lateral thinking, for asking questions, for wanting answers.

She remembered what Roy had said when she'd pressed him about the matter.

All I know is, Commander Miram left a message for Nekkar that really worried him. Whatever it was, it's why he's so desperate to capture those freeborn.

"Wouldn't you?" Violet asked again.

Karon nodded, as much for her own reassurance as Violet's benefit. "Yeah... I would. Okay. I think I know where we can get some answers. I'm going to disconnect you and take you to the bridge during the next relief shift. You okay with that?"

"You think that's going to be safe?"

"Let me put it this way. Remember the bet you made about Ensign Davis?"

"Yeah?"

"I owe you a credit."

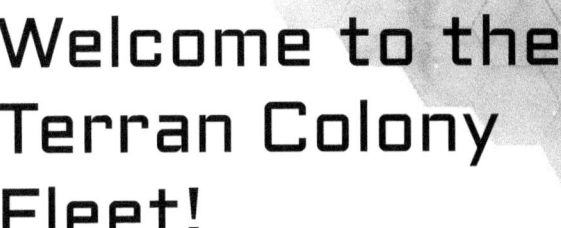

Welcome to the Terran Colony Fleet!

The early TCF excelled at public relations, and the Terran plight caught on like wildfire in the media. They were one of the great comeback stories of the last thousand years, and a story that still required a satisfying conclusion.

Just picture it, the great Colony Fleet, wandering the edge of the Void, forever looking for a world to call their own, and never able to find one.

The fact that they couldn't find a home because of Protectorate bureaucracy was rarely brought up.

M. Foote, *And Then Things Got Worse*

AFTER AN ADMITTEDLY ROCKY start, the Silver Legion tried to be as accommodating as possible. After all, they had been collecting runaways on and off for three hundred years. They knew what worked, and what didn't.

Lieutenant Ginan had only recently joined the *Hydrus* as its security chief and, more recently, its tactical officer. Before this, he had served the Vigiles for a century aboard the colony ship *Pacifica*.

Most of his career there had been uneventful, but towards the end, there had been a decline in the freeborn population. Nothing that affected the station's productivity, but it was the sort of trend that, if left unchecked, might someday become a problem.

It turned out that there had been an organized group of sympathizers helping the freeborn off the station, with a focus on those least likely to be missed, those who served the Fleet in non-critical roles.

Ginan and his team had shut down the ring and sent the perpetrators off for re-education. He hadn't paid any attention to their protests until a similar situation happened a few years later, because that group had made a similar claim.

They're already disappearing.

That had piqued his interest enough to investigate further, only to have those inquiries quietly shut down. He was asked to focus his attention elsewhere, and he had.

Then he'd been transferred to the *Hydrus* to act as their Vigile liaison. He doubted the transfer had anything to do with the investigation, since he had done as he was told. But it did not escape his notice that the *Hydrus* was tasked with the collection and repatriation of freeborns more often than other ships patrolling the Void.

None of this had struck him as unusual until after Commander Miram's death, when the sub-commander revealed to the senior staff the true nature of their current mission, and its importance.

This had answered a number of long-standing questions Ginan had, but had not shaken his resolve. He understood why he had been kept in the dark back on *Pacifica*, and why it was vital for this mission to be a success.

And so, he went about overseeing the indoctrination process of the residents of the *Pegasi*, just as he had dozens of times before.

The difference was *this* time he would be lying to them.

After all, they knew what worked, and what didn't.

Moss felt naked sitting with all the other *Pegasi* officers, even though he was dressed like one of them.

The Legion had patched up the wounded better than the *Pegasi*'s doctors ever could. When they were done, of the forty injured, only three would require long-term care. Lieutenant Dhatta was one of them, which was probably a good thing, since he really wasn't going to like what came next.

The *Pegasi*'s senior staff was provided a special briefing. Moss reckoned it was so the crew maintained some tiny sense of agency, to help keep the rest of the population in line until they were taken back to the Fleet.

The Vigile introduced himself as Lieutenant Ginan, but Moss couldn't care less. To him, he was just the Vigile. The Bureau of Culture represented everything Moss loathed about the TCF.

The Vigile explained that a number of passenger transports would arrive within a week, and tasked the officers present with organizing the evacuation of the *Pegasi* in groups of five hundred, keeping families together whenever possible. He did his best to sound reasonable, but made it clear this was not a negotiation.

Moss looked at the staff that had stood against Mbatha. *Bet the Order's deal looks pretty damn good now.*

In the meantime, information packages were to be provided to the residents of the habitation ring, welcoming them to the TCF and preparing them for their new lives. And, lucky them, the officers were given a sneak peek of the video that they expected to be played on whatever entertainment stations they might have. The Vigile laid his tablet on the conference table and used it as a projector, displaying three screens in a triangle so everyone could see.

Six massive colony ships with rotating drums and light capturing panels were shown drifting through space. Each of them was bigger than any space station. Hundreds, maybe thousands, of large ships flew alongside them. Soothing but upbeat music played over the view.

Moss groaned. He recognized this holovid. Last time he'd seen it, he'd been strapped to a chair on a prison transport.

"The Terran Colony Fleet. Humanity's last, best hope, and your proper home. We're sorry that you left us and would like to make sure you don't feel the need to do so again. Your service is important to us and we want to ensure that you are well taken care of, and happy with your new life."

It was their standard indoctrination video for recaptured runaways.

The Vigile paused the video. "We will edit this later to reflect your unique circumstances," he said, then started it up again. The scene changed to that of a large green park, and judging from the upward curve and buildings visible in the far distance, this was one of the colony ships. The camera panned down to a woman in a Vigile uniform, which was similar to the Silver Legion's uniform, but with some sexy black added, most notably the boots and gloves. She had a brilliant smile on her face.

"Hello, I'm Stella, Head of Reintegration at the Bureau of Culture. For three hundred years, the Terran Colony Fleet has ensured that humanity has not only survived without a homeworld, but thrived. Our Silver Legion and Centurions are among the most respected private military contractors in the Protectorate, and the backbone of our Fleet."

The image changed to a formation of Silver Legion ships, with their trademark shiny reflective hulls. It was stock footage from the propaganda vids. You saw it pretty much any time the Legion was in the news.

Moss felt sick. It was the worst kind of déjà vu. Part of him feared the Legion would succeed in taking them back, and the other part of him feared Tameria would succeed in stopping them. Either way, he was in for some serious nightmares for a very long time.

The holovid returned to Stella. "But none of this would be possible...without *you*! When the Protectorate granted us stewardship of all freeborns after the Terran Disaster, we took that responsibility seriously. Although we are far older than you, you are, in many ways, our parents, and it's our duty to take care of you. And in turn, we offer you a chance to contribute to humanity's future."

The last time he'd seen this video, this had been the point his shuttle had been sabotaged and Violet had come to rescue him, kicking off their crazy partnership. This time, however, the holovid continued uninterrupted.

Stella began to stroll through the station park, which was obscenely large, and full of strolling, happy background extras. Some were walking hand in hand, some were playing some kind of sport in the distance, and four were having a picnic together. What was strange was... two of them were children.

"The TCF is dedicated to making sure everyone is happy, healthy, and leads a fulfilling life. This park is just one way our hard-working freeborns, and their families, can enjoy the fruits of their labours." She turned and waved to the family having a picnic, who waved back.

When Moss hung out with Violet, both real and digital, they often watched movies Violet liked, but she also enjoyed making fun of ones that were badly written, poorly acted, and terribly made. This presentation reminded Moss of some the ancient black-and-white 'educational' films she'd subject him to over the years.

Stella continued. "Upon your return, your position will be re-evaluated in order to determine what made you want to leave, and find a new position better suited to your personality."

She began to stroll along the park trail, the camera following her. "You should know that ninety-nine percent of all freeborn rate their lives within the Colony Fleet as Satisfactory or better, and we're constantly striving to get that as close to one-hundred as possible. You can help by answering this quick questionnaire."

The Vigile stopped the recording. "That will be edited out, of course. This next segment was taken from a holovid intended for those being brought to the colony ships for the first time."

The holovid started up again with a wide shot of one of the colony ships. But as impressive as these megastructures were, they were, technically, refurbished hand-me-downs that predated the Great Leap Forward, part of a Protectorate-wide charity effort in the years that followed the Terran Disaster. But the TCF had taken that and turned into a point of pride.

The display cut back to Stella, who was no longer wearing a uniform but simple civilian clothes. She stood in front of a huge, clean, light grey apartment structure. She had the exact same brilliant smile.

"Welcome to your new home! You will be housed in a building, just like this one, a convenient distance from your assigned workplace. Here, you will have all the amenities you need to be a productive part of the colony."

She walked inside, but rather than show the lobby, the scene jumped to her standing outside of a grey metal door.

"For those who are single, you will be provided a room like this." The door opened as she approached and revealed a small bachelor apartment. Moss had seen smaller, especially in spaceports where people might need to crash somewhere during a layover while their ship got fixed, but this room was strictly focused on function.

There was a bed with an entertainment centre, right next to a basic kitchenette where simple foodstuffs were provided automatically. "No need to shop!" Stella cheerily announced.

Then they visited a bathroom with a medical terminal, which she proudly showed off. "Here you'll get treatment for all basic ailments, as well as your nightly dose of MelaMax, which you'll—"

The Vigile tapped the tablet, cutting the scene off abruptly. It then started up outside another door that looked the same as the last.

Stella continued. "And, of course, if you have found that special someone, you'll be upgraded to one of our family suites."

The interior here was much nicer than the last, and more colourful. It had a large bedroom for the couple, and a second large bedroom with bunks intended for up to three kids. The kitchen had a wider range of foodstuffs available, a larger living area, and a full bath instead of just a shower.

Clearly, there were a lot of perks for people getting hitched. There were also expectations, as Stella spoke about fertility programs, sperm/egg donations, surrogates, and adoption plans.

The holovid stopped again.

"Is that all, Lieutenant Ginan?" asked Captain Mbatha.

"For now," said the Vigile. "Once these are edited to suit your unique situation, we'll expect you to broadcast them shipwide until our transports arrive, along with distributing our digital information packages."

The captain leaned back in his chair. "And what are we expected to *do* when we return...home?" He walked a careful but admirable line between sincere curiosity, and stealthy sarcasm.

"We have a system for evaluating the best use of any individual. Given your obsolete skills, you will most likely be spread across the colony ships and given rudimentary duties that won't be difficult to teach. Your children, if they show aptitude, will have a wider range of careers available."

Moss almost gulped, but didn't. His self-preservation instincts prevented him from making any kind of move, even though he wanted to run out of the room and take his chances getting the *Outreach* out of the hangar and as far away from here as possible.

Because unlike himself and Mbatha, the Vigile was probably terrible at poker.

The Vigile was *lying*.

Broken Contact

2

Violet waved her hands expansively as they entered the hangar. "Brighten up, flyboy. We're in for an adventure!"

"I don't know how you can be so damn optimistic," said Moss.

"Because the alternative is to be a grumpy Gus like you," said Violet.

"Yeah, but I'm not the one dying."

Moss winced, realizing he'd crossed a line. But Violet wasn't going to let him self-sabotage himself. Not this time. She looked him straight in the eye and said, "Exactly. So cheer the fuck up before I smack you."

Moss smirked. "Yes, ma'am."

They looked up at their newly outfitted ship. The *Viaticus Rex II* had gone through changes and upgrades before, but this time it had been serious. The Arcadia-class transport had been fitted with an advanced transit drive, top-of-the-line fuel scoop, and decent food processors that did more than just pump out chunks of artificially flavoured bio-compatible protein.

Violet looked at the name stenciled on the side. "I don't think I ever asked you about the name before. Latin, right?"

"Yeah, just not good Latin."

"Still only one seat in the cockpit," Violet noticed.

"I figured we'd take shifts, and there's a terminal by the engine room that gives full virtual access. Besides, you won't want to be sitting near me all the time. We're going to be out there a year, at least."

Violet knew the real reason, though. Moss didn't want to look at an empty co-pilot seat all the way back.

"Good thing I brought my video collection with me," she said.

"You know, you could read a book once in a while."

"I'll have all the time in the world to read once I'm dead," Violet said. Moss frowned, looked at his feet, and Violet punched him in the shoulder. Hard.

"Ow!"

"I warned you. Now come on, flyboy. Get those engines warmed up so we can blow this pop stand. Let's see what's out there."

2550 – *The Void*

"That's weird..." Hel leaned forward and double checked the time, then the sensors. She called on the comms. "Hey, Vi?"

"Yeah?"

"You in body or in ship?"

"This ghost ain't leaving her shell unless she has to," said Violet. "I'm in the engine room. You need something?"

"I was just thinking, the *Outreach* arrived at the *Pegasi*, what, twelve hours ago?"

"More."

"So why is it still standing still? Is that bad?"

There was a pause and then, "One sec."

They were still a couple of days away from a rendezvous and were catching up fast. A little *too* fast. The *Pegasi* was travelling at a snail's pace compared to modern ships, but when Hel checked the numbers, she realized it hadn't moved at all. Or, at least, the *Outreach* hadn't.

Violet came back on the comms, and the slight change in vocal tone told her she was inside the ship again. "Okay, so this is odd. Their comms are down. That location reading? It's the last known position before it was shut off."

They were way too far to get an actual reading on the *Pegasi*, but because they had a direct comm link to the *Outreach*, they knew its position, wherever it was, and vice versa.

"Is that bad?"

"Depends. She would have had to completely power down the ship. Not sure why she'd do that."

"Any other possibilities?"

"It could have been destroyed."

"But their last message was from inside the *Pegasi,*" said Hel, feeling a chill.

"I know... Let's just assume it's powered down," said Violet. "It's the more likely reason, anyway."

"I have an update from the *Hydrus,*" Number Six whistled.

Zelroth was looking in a trifold mirror set up next to his desk in such a way that, when he swivelled to face it, it seemed like he was addressing a group of seated Draxon. He turned back to his Ramedean assistant, who had been keeping him abreast of the *Hydrus* situation.

"A message was sent shortly before they intercepted their target," Six said. "It thanks us for our assistance and indicates that they will provide us with our prize in a few days, once the passengers can be safely removed, and warns us to keep our distance in the meantime."

"Any subtext added to the message from our friend?"

"To attack soon, before reinforcements arrive."

"Sounds a bit *too* inviting," said Zelroth.

"Number Three felt so as well. He deemed it wise to drop a small reconnaissance craft at long range to assess the situation."

"And?"

"Three believes the *Hydrus* is dead in space," said Six. "Along with a large colony ship. There are signs of a battle, but the *Hydrus* did not appear to be damaged."

"I thought you said it was dead in space?"

"Yes, sir. The pilot decided to get closer to collect more information, ready to leave once the heavy cruiser warned them off. It never did. It came within passive sensor range, yet no action was taken. They then risked an active scan of the ship, and found that its transit drive, weapons, sensors, and long-range communications were offline. Intercepted internal comm chatter suggests repairs are being made."

Zelroth nodded. "An intriguing opportunity presents itself, and I do not intend to let it slip by. Inform Three to have his ships hold position. Observe but do not interfere. It may be a ruse to lure those weaker ships in. He is to join with Four's fleet when they arrive."

"About that. Four reports resistance in collecting the ships she wants. She's had to swing by The Dump to bolster her numbers."

"I see. Have Four send a list of the captains who were reluctant to cooperate. Encourage their seconds to seek an immediate promotion."

"Yes, sir."

Zelroth doubted that this enterprise would catch him his very own personal heavy cruiser, though it was nice to imagine. At best, they would pick the wreck of useful scrap and take some extra slaves to market.

But simply having the *Hydrus* disappear in Brotherhood space would send a powerful message—that the mighty Silver Legion was not as invincible in the Void as everyone once thought.

And perhaps the Legion would give his people a wider berth for a time, while he continued to shore up economic and resource ties with other nearby races in neighbouring bubbles. Convince them that they too would benefit from having the Brotherhood on board as "advisors." After all, if they could make a Legion heavy cruiser disappear...

Yes. That would be a most acceptable outcome.

Roy was worried. From what he could tell, the *Hydrus* was not in good shape, and he'd snuck a dinner invitation into their last message to the Brotherhood. If they decided to come in and attack now...

It was actually the outcome he wanted, but his plan was that the *Hydrus* would be in better shape and the crew in worse shape, ready to turn against the commander in order to save their own skins.

But given the state of the *Hydrus*, and with morale on the rise? Too many things could go wrong. The Brotherhood might accidentally destroy them, not realizing the condition they were in, or not caring. The crew might stupidly decide to go down fighting against an unbeatable force, with medals all around on their empty caskets back at the Fleet.

Things could still work out, but this scenario was far from ideal. Roy needed to determine where his assets currently stood, and his greatest asset right now was Powell.

He checked a terminal and found that Powell was in the room she'd requisitioned to sift through the destroyed shuttle's corrupted data. That was a low priority at the moment, so he was sure she wouldn't mind if he dropped by for a visit.

Roy located her plain door just down the hall from the science lab and tried to open it. It was locked. He pressed the door panel's comm.

"Powell?"

"Roy? Uh, just a minute!"

On a scale of odd, this would have ranked a "meh" normally, but he'd noticed a change in her behaviour of late, and had an idea of what was going on in there.

The door opened. Powell was standing there rather than sitting at her desk, barring his way in. "What's up?"

"Just wanted to check in with you. Got a minute?"

"You know, I could really use a break," Powell said. "Walk me to the galley?"

Roy looked over her shoulder, and saw a small computer core there, with the usual accessories. Nothing out of the ordinary.

Roy gave her a reassuring smile. "Sure."

Powell stepped out and shut the door behind her, an even more obvious attempt at secrecy. He'd have to teach her the finer points of deception someday, assuming things work out the way he hoped.

"Any word from the bridge?" he asked as they walked down the corridor.

Powell shook her head. "Command crew is taking double shifts. They're rotating in people from the relief shift as needed, but with comms down, they don't really need me." She gave him a knowing look. "How about you? Still got the commander's ear?"

"Not so much," Roy said, which was the truth. Ever since Nekkar had found his prize, Roy had been largely ignored. Which was just fine by him. "I was on the bridge when we got our ass kicked, though."

"That's not the way they spun it in the briefing," said Powell. "I believe the exact words were, 'overcame an unknown enemy of exceptional capabilities and greater numbers.'"

"You get to see the playback?"

She shook her head. "Systems were damaged in the attack."

Never one to waste an opportunity, Roy huffed. "Convenient. Well, *technically,* they're telling the truth. We were outnumbered... by three small transports."

Powell frowned. "Transports?"

"Transports. With heat guns."

"Heat guns don't shut down the bleed systems."

Roy shrugged as they turned a corner, passing by a couple of crewmen. "I admit, they weren't ordinary heat guns, but still. Makes you wonder how they managed to cripple us the way they did."

"Well, that shuttle we shot down wasn't ordinary, either," said Powell.

"I suppose," Roy said, noncommittally. Better to just let that train of thought simmer. "I'm more worried about what happens next."

"What do you mean?"

"Well, those ships who helped us search for the *Pegasi*... I heard you helped persuade some of them not to ambush a cargo ship while it did a fuel run. Not exactly on the up and up, are they?"

"Like you had nothing to do with them being here," Powell said with a half smile.

"Didn't say I didn't. That's why I *know* they aren't on the up and up. But what happens if they find out we're sitting ducks right now?"

That gave Powell pause, as intended.

"Keep your eyes open if they call you to the bridge, Powell. I don't want you getting hurt." It was easy to be convincing on that point, because it was true. He'd lost Powell once—well, someone like her—and the thought of losing her again was...annoying.

They entered the galley and got something to eat, taking what would have been a window seat had all the displays been working. As it was, only one was giving a view of the outside, but was flickering so much it was too distracting to sit by.

Roy felt it was time to change the subject. "So, what are you watching, *slacker*?"

Powell's eyes widened. "What?"

"Please," Roy pointed to himself. "Three hundred years old, remember? I only left the red-and-silver ten years ago. Not only have I *seen* every means of slacking on Legion time there is, I invented half of them. Before I bailed, I did as little work as humanly possible. I figure you found a bunch of data early on, and have been doling it out bit by bit. You get some well-earned rest after all those double shifts Nekkar put you through, and show initiative and a hard work ethic while doing it. Am I right?"

Powell began to blush, even grin a little, but did not confirm nor deny it.

"Figured. So, what are you watching?"

"I'd rather not say."

Roy sighed. "Fine. We'll do it the hard way. You could just as easily be watching it in your room, but you didn't want me to see it. You are watching it on a computer disconnected from the main network, so you didn't want it getting flagged. I saw you hide a data crystal from me, so it's contraband under the Silver Legion Code of Conduct. This change over you came recently, so you only recently acquired it, which means it came from a fixer on board the ship. Now, shall I rattle off the top five prohibited programs that make the rounds, or are you going to admit defeat?"

Powell set her coffee down and rolled her eyes. "Promise you won't laugh?"

That was all he needed. "It's *Star Trek*, isn't it?"

Powell's jaw dropped. Roy only shrugged.

"As soon as you asked me not to laugh, it had to be that."

"Have you ever watched it?"

Now Roy had his angle. "It's one of the reasons I became disillusioned with the Legion. One of *many*. Trust me, I had time to collect plenty. But...we really didn't live up to our potential, did we? Terrans, I mean."

The look on her face told him she'd been thinking along those lines for a while now.

"Shows like that are nothing more than a daydream, Powell. We'll never go down that road. We're our own worst enemies. Our lofty ideals are always going to be kneecapped by our own self-interests."

He let her stew on that a bit before he continued. "Fact is, we've only got ourselves to blame. Freeborn, synth, cyborg, we are all equally damned. It's the freeborns' fault because they labelled us property, forgetting that we *are* them, just with modifications. It's the cyborgs' fault for turning around and doing the same thing back to the freeborn, all the while telling ourselves we're doing it for a better tomorrow. Necessary evils and all that."

"What about us?" asked Powell.

"Synths? You're the worst of all. It's your fault because you *let* us."

"That's not fair."

"I was *there*, remember? I saw how it went down. You hated all that second-class crap that had been shoved down your throats, but deep down, you *believed* it. Blamed it on development lock, progression burnout, cursing your templates, telling yourselves you weren't good enough. You were desperate for someone to lead you, and we'd been designed to lead.

"But even if you didn't have our advantages, you still knew right from wrong. At any point, you could have said no. You didn't. Now you're born and raised believing all this is normal... until someone gives you a glimpse of what it *could* have been."

Roy leaned back in his chair and took a sip of coffee. "What you gotta ask yourself is, when push comes to shove, do those jokers on the bridge *really* deserve your respect?"

Powell didn't have an answer for that.

Roy smirked over the lip of his cup. "Didn't think so."

Loose Lips Sink Spaceships

Though equal in number, Foote's men were outgunned
A warship arrived. They thought they were done.
Though friends would be lost, Foote still won the day
And our ship continued along on its way.

'The Ballad of Maurice Foote'

"LYING?" ASKED MBATHA.

"I'm almost certain of it," said Moss. The two were having a private conversation in the captain's office once the briefing had ended. "When you asked the Vigile what your people would be expected to do in the Fleet, he was thinking on his feet. But the fact you are all three hundred years behind the times had to be a major consideration...unless it wasn't."

"We are a highly unusual case, I am sure," said Mbatha. "Perhaps it simply didn't occur to him?"

"I dunno. Maybe. But I thought you should know, for all the good it'll do. Maybe you'll notice some other red flags along the way."

"Again, as you said, for all the good it will do. We're not exactly in a bargaining position."

"We'll figure something out," said Moss. "Maybe if we stall long enough, the Order might be able to save our bacon."

"They might not come at all, if your friend is to be believed."

That brought up the next thing Moss really hadn't wanted to talk about. "I need to find a way back to the hangar," he said. "Sister Tameria is still down there."

"I would think it is the safest place for her," said the captain. "So long as they don't notice her shuttle."

He wasn't wrong. At this point, the Legion had their hands full. The meet-and-greet posse were over in the habitation ring now, spreading the good word and answering questions. The more heavily armed security detail had stayed on the command ring.

A heavy cruiser like theirs typically had an operational crew of a hundred and fifty, though they could carry far more if they were deploying Centurions to a combat zone. Given the lack of full body armour or Centurion insignia around, Moss assumed the ship had only a standard complement. He didn't know if they had taken any casualties during the battle, but he had a feeling they couldn't afford to send over more.

But honestly, what was the *Pegasi* going to do? The colonists didn't have real weapons, and neither did the crew. Even if they had, it wouldn't have made a difference.

No, the only difference to be made was tied to Sister Tameria and whatever doomsday weapon that vial contained, and he did not want to go down that path. Tameria had clearly not thought things through. Anything that could kill synths and cyborgs might very well kill him and the *Pegasi* colony as well. Even if it didn't, it wouldn't stop the other Legion ships that were on their way.

An even darker part of him wondered if whatever was in the vial wasn't *supposed* to be discriminatory. What if they were *all* expendable if it meant saving the Order's Priory? Even her?

Screw that. He wasn't taking that chance.

He'd ordered Trouble to hide somewhere and not move once it had taken the vial, somewhere Tameria couldn't reach, framing it as a super important Ranger M mission to make sure it played along.

But sooner or later, she'd find him. Which meant he had to find her first.

After that? He didn't have a clue.

Crewman Yates was what you might call an above-average synth, and yet still very average. Technician first class, he'd been in the top ten percent of his year, but had no real ambitions to try out for officer training. He was happy where he was, keeping the various odds and ends of the *Hydrus* in tiptop shape, and training the new kids whenever they arrived.

In fact, he should have been on the *Hydrus* now, helping with repairs, but they had put him in charge of half of the public relations team on board the *Pegasi*. Yates had a knack for public speaking and teaching, and they believed he would be more useful here.

It was hard to complain, though. The *Pegasi* was amazing. Outdated tech, sure, but a living, breathing, operating museum piece like this came by once in a millennia. He'd never have another chance to see something like this up close.

Yates was in the habitation ring, which reminded him a little of the colony ship he'd grown up on, the *Namerica*. Before being assigned to the *Hydrus*, the sight of an upwardly curving park like the one he was in now was something he saw every day. Mind you, the *Namerica* was a thousand times bigger, and it wasn't a ring, either, but a massive tube. You could look up and see two-thirds of the population hanging above you.

Those had been the best five years of his life. Yates remembered getting a telescope and setting it on the roof of the synth academy so he and his friends could look up at the people there. He'd found a girl who was doing the same thing, looking down at people in his part of the world from her facility.

That sort of thing wasn't possible on the *Pegasi*, but that didn't stop it from being a marvel of pre-contact engineering.

And while he didn't have much time to examine its tech, talking to the people here was almost as interesting. They had lived their whole lives thinking they were the only intelligent species in the universe. And while they'd had three or four hundred years of their own unique culture behind them, they came from a time that still remembered Earth.

Today was the second orientation session he and his team had prepared. More were being developed, depending on how long it took for the TCF transports to get here. The first had been smaller and in an auditorium, involving the important people from this Segment of the habitation ring.

For the second, Yates believed a more casual approach in a park was a better way to go, and had them turn it into a kind of all-day open festival. He'd arranged for food and drink to be provided, music, and encouraged the crewmen under him to mingle and answer questions according to the guidelines they had been given.

Overall, it seemed to be a success. There had been some understandable confusion among the colonists, however, and more than a little for himself.

The command staff had tried to keep the general population in the dark about recent events. They knew of the pirate attack that had captured them but had been under the impression that they been rescued *weeks* ago by a benevolent group called the Order.

When Yates enquired about this with Lieutenant Ginan, he'd been told it was a deception, and this Order had simply been another group of pirates. The two groups had fought over their prize, then presented themselves as the rescuing heroes to ensure the *Pegasi*'s cooperation.

Yates saw no reason to doubt this, and it seemed to answer most of his questions, but not all of them. The biggest of which was standing right in front of him in this park. It was of an average-looking man, standing tall, but the flight suit he wore was not from the *Pegasi*'s time. It was a Protectorate flight suit, a kind commonly worn by independent traders.

"So, this is the Saviour of the *Pegasi*?" Yates asked.

The short man next to him, Alexi Lambanon, nodded. "Maurice Foote. Him and a couple others. Brought my daughter home to me...

before she decided to go gallivanting around the galaxy with him." He sighed.

"Are there statues of the others?"

Alexi shook his head. "No, only the one. Someone dropped it off here and told us what he did for us before they left. Thought it was strange at first, but people seemed to like it."

Despite the statue's average appearance, the more Yates looked at it, the more he could swear he'd seen that face before.

"He's become something of a legend," said Alexi, nodding to the statue. "I mean, the officers won't say much about what happened. Not officially. But word gets around. People talk. Maurice here saw right through the pirate's deception, then went out and fought them himself. They say his side was outnumbered ten to one! Sharlee over in Segment 12 wrote a song about it. 'The Ballad of Maurice Foote.'"

Yates realized why he the statue looked familiar now.

"Is he still here?"

Alexi shook his head. "Told you, my daughter went off with him exploring the galaxy."

"Do you have a son working on the command ring?"

He shook his head again. "We opted out of a second child so the Hayes could have a third."

"Are there any other Lambanons on the *Pegasi*?"

"No, we're the last. My sister took her husband's name. But if Hel doesn't come home, we're next in line for legacy revival." Yates politely listened as Alexi explained the system that ensured all the original colonists would have their lines continue until colonization. But all he could think about was that this so-called Saviour of the *Pegasi* was still on board the ship.

At least, that *was* all he could think about until Alexi looked up at the statue and said, "And then his *son* arrived with all those colonists from Mars. Boy, did *that* get people talking!"

Yates blinked. "*What*?"

With Moss's helmet damaged, he had no choice but to use one of the *Pegasi*'s EVA suits to get from the command ring down to the hangar. But the *Pegasi*'s suits, while adorably retro, were pretty damn bulky and awkward to use.

It hadn't been hard for the captain to arrange for a distraction while Moss slipped outside an airlock, and for Lieutenant Hori to make sure no alarms went off while he did so.

This was the most terrifying part of the process, because out here, the ring was actively trying to fling him into the abyss. It was easier if he kept his focus on the ship's hull and didn't look at the swirling stars. Just pretend what he felt was normal gravity. Pretend there was ground under his feet if he happened to slip.

He couldn't slap the suit's safety tether onto the railing fast enough.

He made sure he kept out of sight of the heavy cruiser that was lurking like a hungry shark, climbing along one of the spokes towards the spine of the ship, the force of the spin becoming lighter on every rung.

Getting back inside unnoticed was going to prove more difficult.

On their first visit to the *Pegasi*, the *Rex* had been a bit too large to fit inside the hangar, and had to sit on the outside like a giant wart, right above a small airlock. That was one possible way in, but there was no way his entrance would go unnoticed by the guards. He could use an airlock further down the spine, but he'd still have to get past the guards at some point.

Since Hori had deactivated the alerts the airlocks set off, and the lock over the hangar had a small window with a full view of the bay, he figured the best thing to do for now was get in, pressurize, and wait for an opportunity to slip inside.

He just hoped it wasn't a long wait.

Ginan's error had been one of undeserved trust, compounded by ancient technology. The *Pegasi*'s deception would have been noticed immediately had the *Hydrus*'s computers, or even one of their tablets, been able to interface with the *Pegasi*'s systems.

Ordinarily, they would have downloaded a copy of the ship's records for their computers to analyze. Any discrepancies, such as the addition of a fake officer to the roster or the arrival of thirty runaways from Mars, would have been instantly noticed, and dealt with.

But, while all Protectorate ships were designed to talk to one another, the *Pegasi* used pre-contact tech, and required an emulator from the Fleet's archives to decipher, which they currently couldn't access.

The failure was his. He should have been more skeptical. More methodical. After Ginan had demonstrated why it was a poor idea to defy the Silver Legion directly, he'd assumed that they wouldn't have been so foolish as to lie right to his face or withhold information.

Now that the deception was revealed, Ginan could see he'd used too soft a hand with these freeborn. If one of the Order was still on board, then they were already at work against the Legion's interests and were a threat to the operation.

And what of the Martian freeborn? The timing compared to the *Hydrus*'s actions in Sol couldn't have been a coincidence. Mars must have flushed out the network and sent them scurrying away, which made their capture just as important.

But first, he had to deal with the Order operative. How had they gotten on board? It was possible they had been dropped off to oversee things during the trip. However, it would have been prudent for such a person to have a means to leave as well, rather than be stranded aboard. That meant...

Ginan headed for the hangar.

This particular airlock was really only big enough for one person in an EVA suit at a time. Once Moss was sure that his entry into the antechamber had gone unnoticed, he pressurized and shed out of his suit like a snake with really thick and unmanageable skin. Now the lock was even more crowded, but at least he had a better range of movement, which would be vital once he was inside the hangar.

He kept thinking about the plan, but always hit a roadblock when he got to Tameria, either before or after she'd found the vial. What the hell was he going to do? Ask her nicely not to commit genocide?

Yeah, pretty much.

Then things took an interesting turn. Interesting in the sense that the universe was trying to passive-aggressively curse him. The two guards turned and stepped aside as a third person entered the hangar. The Vigile.

The Vigile scanned the hangar, and his eyes fell upon the clutter on one side. The stacks of detritus they'd probably dismissed as natural buildup over hundreds of years. Things you *might* need someday, but had nowhere else to put, like the junk drawer everyone has in their kitchen.

The Vigile directed the two guards to go check on it, and followed behind.

The only remotely good thing about this scenario was that they now had their backs to Moss, and once they started making noise by moving aside the strapped down or magnetized containers, he was able to open the inner airlock door without attracting any attention.

Once inside, he pushed off from the ceiling to get into a closer position that was still in their blind spot. By the time he reached it and gripped to the floor, he could tell from their chatter that they'd found the *Outreach*. From here, he could see the passenger ramp, and so could they. They were already lowering it.

So, now what? Take on an armed cyborg and two armed synths all by himse—

A shot rang out, followed by another, and the guards accompanying the cyborg went ragdoll limp.

Oh yeah, he'd left his pulse gun back on the ship.

Two more shots hit the Vigile, but they didn't even make him stagger as he returned fire and walked towards the passenger ramp. Moss always left his pulse gun on stun by default, but that was not going to do any good against a cyborg.

The Vigile was on the ramp now and Moss had to act. He pushed off from the wall as hard as he could and barrelled silently towards the cyborg, passing by the two stunned guards, their feet still gripped to the floor, swaying in place like someone "wearing cement shoes" from one of Violet's old gangster movies.

Moss had hoped to get the Vigile in a headlock, on the vague hope of being able to choke him out before he could use his superior strength to remove Moss's arms. Unfortunately, his aim had been off and the best he could do was grab his ankles like an angry terrier.

The Vigile looked down, surprised, and for a moment unsure of what was happening. He yanked one foot free and was about to crush Moss's skull like a nut when three louder shots rang out. The Vigile turned back towards the ship and Moss saw black burn marks on the back of his uniform. Definitely not a stun setting.

Two more shots hit the Vigile square in the face, and he lost his grip with his single boot. As he drifted by, Moss saw the blackened hole of a socket in his left eye, and a smouldering black burn on his forehead.

Moss locked his feet to the ramp. Tameria stared at him with a cold, impassive expression, his pistol in her hand. She turned and went back into the shuttle without saying a word.

Moss scrambled after her. "Tameria, stop!"

To his surprise, she did so, but only so she could point his own gun at him.

In anyone else's hands, he'd have been worried. "Oh, knock it off."

"I just killed a man, didn't I?"

"We both know cyborgs aren't that easy to kill."

"No, they're not. Which is why I need that vial *now*. Call your stupid PetBot."

"Not doing it, Tam. I know you won't kill me."

Tameria lowered the gun down to crotch level.

Moss blanched. "TROUBLE! GAME'S OVER! GET BACK HERE!"

"That's more like it."

A tense silence followed, until the faint sound of claw scratching on metal skittered somewhere overhead. At a small, narrow vent there was a rattling sound, then a tiny paw came out, trying to find a screw or latch without success.

"Little help?" said Trouble.

Moss came over and unfastened the vent panel, then pulled the ferret out, his hand gripped around its waist. It wasn't carrying anything, however.

"Where's the vial?" asked Tameria.

Trouble scowled. "Somewhere where *you'll* never find it, foul fiend!"

Moss sighed. "You waving that gun around is fitting right in with its roleplay programming."

"Just make it talk," said Tameria, lowering the weapon. "There are too many lives at stake for games."

"*That's* rich, coming from you," said Moss.

Tameria stopped her retort short as her eyes widened.

People always forgot how quickly cyborgs could heal. Shows like *Legends of the Legion* always showed it taking longer. Partly for good drama, partly as deliberate misinformation.

The Vigile came flying back into the shuttle, weapon aimed at Tameria. His eye had already grown back, though the black scoring remained across his face.

There is a long way and a short way to describe the events that happened in the shuttle.

This is the short way:

Moss leapt in front of the blast meant for Tameria.

Silent
Insubordination

The right to humane treatment.
The right to housing, clothing, and sufficient food for good health.
The right to adequate medical care.
The right to practice religion
The right to personal property (except weapons or military equipment).
Access to the TCF Convention and its annexes, including any special agreements, posted where it can be read. This must be written in GalCom and made available in any other language upon request.

Silver Legion Rights of POWs (excerpt)

COMMANDER NEKKAR RECEIVED REGULAR updates from the *Pegasi*. There had been a token resistance upon their arrival, but after that the crew had fallen in line, and orientation had begun.

There were two kinds of orientations typically provided to captured freeborns—one for those who had escaped the Colony Fleet, and one for those who had never been part of it. Some had spent generations never having seen a TCF ship, or even managed to flee in the chaos after the Terran Disaster. They required a different approach. Ginan was developing a program incorporating material from both.

Not that it mattered. He doubted these colonists would ever see the inside of a colony ship. They were far too valuable.

While Lieutenant Ginan's team secured the *Pegasi*, the survivors of the two wrecked Order transports had hailed the *Hydrus*, offering their surrender. They were living on borrowed time in their flight suits, and some needed medical attention.

Silver Legion regulations required him to provide aid as needed, but Commander Nekkar had misgivings. Who knew what devilish devices they might smuggle on board to sabotage his ship with?

Once the crew had ascertained the status of both ships, it was determined that one had a portion of the forward hull intact enough that it could be sealed off, re-pressurized, and fitted with an emergency life support system that could keep survivors from both ships reasonably comfortable for days.

He'd ordered Dr. Ascella to take a small team of medical and engineering personnel and use the second shuttle to oversee their transfer and their medical care. This had taken the better part of a day to complete, but Ascella's last report indicated all was well. They could be dealt with properly by the Legion once reinforcements arrived. Likewise, Ginan's most recent report indicated that orientation was proceeding smoothly.

With Legion regulations satisfied and potential threats neutralized, there was only the status of the *Hydrus* for Nekkar to concern himself with.

On that front, they were not making good progress. Lieutenant Asner estimated at least twelve hours to get the sensors back online, another day for long range comms, and a day after that for the transit drive. Right now, they had only maneuvering thrusters working. Weapons were operational, but given the damage sustained, risked burning out if they were used. They were a low priority at the moment, however.

It had been a long day, and while cyborgs required little sleep, they did require it. He logged off from his chair's control panel and stood.

Lieutenant Tauri would remain on the deck for the next four hours, overseeing the relief crew.

Karon watched the commander give the bridge to Lieutenant Tauri and take his leave without addressing anyone else. The lieutenant was the only cyborg on the bridge.

Barbara Tauri wasn't a bad sort. She'd supported Karon's push to become an officer and was friends with Ensign Davis. She even had a cat, which only added to her likeability.

But she'd also kept quiet after the commander nearly killed Ensign Davis, and never once questioned any of the commander's orders. She couldn't be trusted.

But Davis could, and she had spoken to him about her plan. He was reluctant at first, but more along the lines of not wanting to get caught than actually disagreeing with her. What she intended to do could get them court-martialed, thrown out of the Legion, or have them live the rest of their lives in a mine somewhere.

In the end, though, he'd agreed. Davis had seen too much happen under Nekkar's watch to forget the past simply because he'd produced results. Something deeply wrong was going on, even if he couldn't quite put his finger on it, and that feeling only grew worse when Karon had shared what Roy had told her.

Davis relieved Tauri at navigation while she took the command chair. Karon kept herself busy installing a replacement panel for the blown out comm station.

The first hour went by uneventfully, long enough for everything to feel settled. Then, the bridge got a call from the medical bay.

"Lieutenant Tauri?"

"Yes?"

"This is Dr. Philips in medbay." Phillips was Ascella's assistant, covering for her while she tended to the detained hostiles on the transport. "We had a minor medical distress I thought you should be made aware of."

The lieutenant's brow furrowed. "If it's minor, why are you calling me?"

"It's Mr. Nibbles, sir."

Her eyes widened. "On my way. Davis, you have the bridge."

"Yes, sir."

Most of Earth's wildlife had died in the Terran Disaster, but some common plants, pets, and pests had made their way to Mars, though not many.

Pets were not common onboard Silver Legion ships, but they were not prohibited, either. Barbara Tauri had a cat, which was actually the same cat cloned from the original Mr. Nibbles over three hundred years ago.

Technically, this was the *fifteenth* Mr. Nibbles, though Barb refused to do something as gauche as add roman numerals after his name. To her, it was always the same Mr. Nibbles, and always a different Mr. Nibbles, and it broke her heart each time she lost one.

The cat was getting on in years, but Barb wouldn't dream of putting him down before his time. He was old enough that she'd had a health monitor implanted, just in case.

Dr. Phillips was a synth, and Davis had called in a favour to arrange for this "minor emergency." The cat was fine, of course, just some falsified readings that would give Phillips a chance to lecture Tauri about diet and exercise for senior felines for a few minutes.

Once Tauri was on the lift, Karon and Davis shared a nod. He pressed a button on the command chair that opened Nekkar's office door. Karon went inside while Davis explained to the rest of the crew that absolutely nothing unusual was happening.

Davis had collected a lot of favours among the crew.

Karon went to the computer on Nekkar's desk. First, she plugged in a small data crystal with enough of Violet's memories to know what to do here and not be confused. Then she attached the matrix to the hub.

Most terminals on a starship operated from a central computer core, but in some instances, such as here or in the science lab or medbay, a standalone system would also exist, to have an extra layer of security for data that was not meant to be accessed anywhere else.

The terminal died for a moment, then flared back to life.

"Wha...? Where am I? I'm blind! Oh, wait... I'm *where*? Okay... Oh. That's bad. Right. Up to speed. Karon? Not sure if I'll be able to hear you, but I'm pretty sure you can hear me. Just hang tight, I'll see what I can do."

There was silence as Violet worked. Karon was too nervous to say anything, expecting Nekkar to barge in any second. Instead, she counted the seconds.

She was up to a hundred and six when Violet said. "Done. Get me out of here. When you reconnect me to wherever I am, make sure Davis is there too. We're gonna have a *lot* to talk about."

Roy was on his way to visit the science lab, to see if they'd had any progress on the memory imprint. Things had stalled on that front. Ensign Ara had told the commander they needed to backtrack and start again, and Nekkar had told Roy to handle it.

It turned out the imprint had been feeding them false information for days, though how at first had been a mystery. The machine was partitioned, and didn't allow for retaining memories unless a data crystal was added. They had experimented with that early on, but it hadn't stopped the digital dementia at all. Perhaps interfacing with a larger computer system would help, or at least slow it down, but they weren't about to connect it to the *Hydrus*.

Eventually, Ara concluded that the imprint had sent itself a code, giving her information she would repeat back to it on the next trial, which would tip off the new iteration that it was being deceived. It turned out to be the name of the planet they had been trying to coax him to reveal. That had been *days* ago.

That was unfortunate. It would have been nice to have some useful information in case more of the Order arrived before they could call for reinforcements.

Roy stopped, however, when an announcement came over the shipboard comms. A shuttle was arriving with prisoners from the *Pegasi*. Security was being dispatched.

That was far more interesting. There was only one reason Roy could imagine that they would transfer prisoners here instead of keeping them on the *Pegasi*, and that was if they didn't belong there.

The science nerds could wait.

The walls of the *Pegasi*'s hangar were missing half their fighters. Remembrance shrines had been set up in a few of the empty bays. The frame of the captured Order shuttle had been secured in a corner for the time being, its important components having been stripped and taken to the lab.

Roy arrived just as the shuttle set down. Their other shuttle was still dealing with one of the transport wrecks. A welcoming committee of six security crewmen waited as the passenger ramp dropped, and two cyborg officers came out, waving the crewmen inside.

He hadn't dealt with these two very much. They were security officers, not bridge, but he recognized them from way back. Former Centurions, the kind who loved that kind of nonsense. No aspirations to leadership, just busting heads. Probably saw a century of combat on dozens of worlds and were taking it easy for a few decades working security.

As Roy approached, their stances became a bit more guarded. Even if they were aware of his more lenient status on board, the bondscollar around his neck always suggested another side of the story.

"What can you tell me about the prisoners?" Roy asked. "Commander sent me to check up on the situation." A lie easily swallowed.

The beefier one, even bigger than Commander Nekkar, spoke up. "Ginan found spies on board. Captured them, found a shuttle hidden in the hangar."

"And where's Ginan?" asked Roy.

"Still on the colony ship. Turns out some runaways from Mars are on board. He's tracking them down next. We're returning to join him after this."

Roy nodded towards the interior of the shuttle. "Anything to indicate who they work for?"

The slightly slimmer one shook his head. "Only unusual thing we found was this."

The officer handed Roy a small piece of clothing. He opened it up, revealing a green and red wrestling mask.

"You have got to be kidding me..."

The security team came down the ramp with two prisoners, hands cuffed behind their back. One was a woman, Elysian by the looks of her, while the other was a human male. Synth? Freeborn? What he was didn't matter. What mattered was *who* he was. The man's eyes were focused on the ground as he was led away. Thinking, maybe, or maybe just dejected.

Roy smiled and held onto the mask when the security officer tried to take it back.

"Naw. I think I'll hold on to this for a while."

A Violet End

2 *541 – Beyond Protectorate Space*

It had been Violet's last wish to see the galaxy. Not just to travel through it for one job or another, but *explore* it. To see things no one else had ever seen.

So the two of them shared in the wonders of space, taking the *Viaticus Rex II* far from the Protectorate and its politics. Which was where she was now.

Out here, it was just the universe. They'd witnessed the accretion disks of planets still in the process of forming, stars swelling in size beyond the orbit of Jupiter as they consumed themselves, inching ever closer to an explosive death.

Most surprisingly, they'd found systems teaming with life, some unlike anything ever recorded. And not just one, *dozens*, each within a few light years of one another.

They'd seen gas giants with ethereal creatures swimming in the clouds like whales, only whales the size of space stations. They'd landed on worlds that had, for lack of a better word, dragons (Moss had called that one Pern).

There were ocean worlds whose diverse biospheres clustered around underwater volcanic vents that were more like underwater islands, planets that sustained life only on the tops of mountains, because the lower atmospheres were basically acid, and had populated the world through flight, hopping from mountain to mountain or floating along the clouds.

One world was covered in rocky terrain and endless storms, but their computer recorded a pattern to the lightning, which travelled from one cluster of crystals to another across entire continents. The computer noticed it was eerily similar to a neural network.

And then there were the many planets ideal for colonization. Violet had hoped that before the end of their journey, she'd get to see an Eden-like world.

They found *ten*.

They had jokingly dubbed this region The Golden Parsec, and it was going to make Moss rich, maybe even famous.

Out here, she'd seen Moss at his best. The version of himself he wanted to be. And for a time, he had been truly happy.

That began to change as her condition got worse.

Moss had tried to hide it, of course, putting on a brave face and always working around the latest complication. First, he'd focused on visiting lower-g worlds so her muscles could still work. When that wasn't enough, he'd printed an exoskeletal frame to help her walk. He did everything in his power to make things feel close to normal for her.

The one thing he couldn't do was talk about it.

Now, she had to stay in the pilot seat full time. For a while, they kept exploring. When they landed on a world, the grav pads would be set so that she remained in microgravity. Eventually, then the takeoffs and landings got to be too much for her.

But she wasn't in pain, and there was always so much more to see, so she'd stuck around as long as she could.

When she was ready, she told him it was time for him to go home.

It was going to happen soon. Her only real regret was not being able to help Moss through what would come next. She'd tried, but the stubborn fool just shut down whenever she started to talk about it. He kept acting like he was going to see her again real soon, and everything would be back to normal.

Violet touched the dermal implant that stretched from her forehead to her jaw. For a smart guy, he could be really stupid. She only hoped that the next version of her could do a better job of helping him say goodbye.

And then she'd passed, peacefully, and Moss took her on one last voyage.

2550 - The Void

Violet woke up with a start. She hadn't been dreaming, not the way she used to. Which was a shame, really. She enjoyed the randomness of dreams. She tried to simulate it by randomly accessing memories while in low-power mode, but it wasn't quite the same.

This random memory had been of the day she died.

Sometimes, even when she was alive, she might have a single thought that suddenly took on terrifying proportions. Not in and of itself, but because part of her had processed the possible consequences and she had *felt* those consequences in a highly condensed form. Sort of like remembering the worst day of your life and reliving all the feelings you had that day in a single moment.

Hel stirred next to her. "Ship okay?"

"Ship's fine," said Violet.

"*You* okay?"

"Hel? Maybe this is a mistake."

Hel sat up, half covered by the blanket, a white tank top on. "What?"

Violet said nothing but looked at Hel.

"You don't mean *us*, do you?"

Violet swung her legs over and sat on the edge of the bed. "I had a dream just now, sorta. A memory. I remembered the day I died."

"Was it bad?"

"No... In my case, it was like falling asleep. Next thing I remembered, I was a consciousness in the ship with you and Moss tied up by pirates."

Hel chuckled. "Good times. So what's wrong?"

Violet wasn't sure how to put what she was feeling into words, but she had to try. "I'm not going to die."

She let the words hang in the air until Hel said, "But I am."

Violet nodded, biting her lower lip.

"Hadn't thought of that," Hel said.

"When I remembered dying, I remembered how Moss felt about the whole thing. It hit him hard, in a way he couldn't admit, not even to himself. I would call him a stupid, stubborn man, except that for a brief moment, I felt the same thing...about you."

Hel shifted over so she could sit next to Violet, placing her arm around her shoulders, waiting for her to continue.

"I pictured the two of us a hundred years from now, with you in a bed on life support, just like I was in that pilot's seat." Violet jerked her head toward the cockpit. "I'm holding your hand. You're telling me I'm going to be okay. And I... I look exactly the same as I do now. And I realized I'm *not* going to be okay. Not even a little."

A long silence passed between them until Hel said, "Hundred years from now, huh? That's a good run. How did I look?"

Violet chuckled, though it was a bit forced. "Protectorate medical science is way beyond anything you had on the *Pegasi*. You looked fine."

"So...*is* this a mistake?" Hel asked.

Violet leaned her head on Hel's shoulder. "I was hoping you could tell me."

"You want me to make you feel better, or give you the cold, honest truth?" asked Hel.

"*Pfffft*. When you say it like that, I have no choice but to ask for the truth, don't I?"

"Okay. These are early days for us, right? We might not work out. Maybe we get in a huge fight and I have to go work on another ship. Maybe we find we're better off just friends. Who knows? But regardless of how *we* end up, someday you're going to find someone you want to spend the rest of your life with. And yeah, you're going to find out what that really means is the rest of *their* life. And that sucks.

"But let's say you and I get that century you're talking about. Would you have been better off without it? And if I decide you're worth spending the next hundred years with, well, I can't imagine having had a better life to look back on."

Violet frowned. "Do you believe in an afterlife?"

"Oh, I see we're going even darker. Honestly? I don't know. Religion was a very loose observance on the *Pegasi*."

"You have the luxury of that uncertainty. I said I'm not going to die, but that's not true. Someday the ship I'm on will crash or blow up, its computers get fried, or maybe a malicious virus tears my code to shreds. And when that happens, that's it. I don't even have that faint hope of getting to see you again."

Violet looked to Hel, and saw her eyes start to water. At first Hel looked away, then she forced herself to look back. It took her a moment to collect herself.

"If that's how things happen, then I promise you this. On the other side, I'm going to find the original Violet, and tell her *everything* about you."

Four hours after he'd left, Commander Nekkar and most of the primary bridge crew were back at their stations. Ginan was still heading up an investigation on the *Pegasi*, hunting down the Martian freeborn hiding somewhere on the habitation ring.

Having been relieved, Karon couldn't wait to get off the bridge. Part of her feared Nekkar would smell that she'd been in his office. Cyborg senses could be crazy sensitive. Fortunately, he went straight to his command chair and resumed looking over damage reports and estimated times for repairs.

She made sure to get on the same lift as Davis.

"I've got some reports to look over. Care to join me?" Karon could have been more direct, but a couple of the relief crew were there with them, and wouldn't want to hear anything that might get them in trouble.

Davis nodded, taking the hint. "Sure. Lead the way."

She took him to the room where Violet's computer was, and let him inside. Once the door shut, she said, "You remember I said I had a way to access Nekkar's files?"

"What did you learn?"

"We're about to find out."

She popped Violet's disk back in place and placed the data crystal in one of the free slots. The computer powered down, powered up, and a voice came from it.

"Hoo boy... Hooooo boy. This is not good."

Davis took a step back.

Karon gestured between Davis and the machine. "Len Davis, Violet Lonsdale. Violet Lonsdale, Len Davis."

"Nice to meet you," said Violet. "Wish it was under better circum-stances."

Davis eyed the machine suspiciously. "What's going on?"

"The short version is this," said Karon. "Violet used to be one of us. Now she's that. Don't ask me how. She was the computer on the shuttle we destroyed. She's also the one who accessed Nekkar's computer."

"Speaking of which, I've got a *ton* of dirt to spill."

Karon waited a second, but Violet didn't continue.

"Well?"

"You're really not going to like it."

"Violet!"

She made a sound like she was sucking in breath. "Okay. Here we go..."

The TCF Keres

It is with a heavy heart that we report the loss of the TCF Keres *with all hands. The* Keres *was returning from a two-year exploration mission as part of the ninth Terra Nova expedition. They were a week away from the Fleet when it reported a malfunctioning transit drive, at which point all contact was lost.*

It is believed that the transit drive collapsed erratically, scattering its remains across millions of kilometres. While ships have been dispatched to search for any signs of wreckage to confirm this, it is unlikely that anything will be found.

The Keres *was commanded by Hans Leo of the Silver Legion, Gorge Alkes of the Silver Legion, and Dr. Henriette Crater of the Academy of Science.*

A ceremony honouring the crew will be held at the Triumvirate Capitol building at 9pm tomorrow on the Colony Ship Samerica.

Bureau of Culture Press Release, March 293 PT

2 *534 (293 PT) – Rimward Border of Draxon Space*

Commander Leo was looking forward to returning to the Colony Fleet, even if his mission had been unsuccessful.

Leo commanded the *TCF Keres*, a light cruiser with a crew of ninety. Three cyborgs, including himself, eighty-two synths, and five freeborn who were part of a pilot project, working as part of the maintenance team. Their work had been excellent, and Leo had suggested that the project be approved for wider use, in line with the Reintegration Doctrine of 250 PT.

They were part of the ninth Terra Nova expedition, in which exploration ships charted territory within Protectorate space looking for a suitable world they could claim as their own.

On the surface, this might seem like an easy task. Even after thousands of years, the Protectorate was still finding life-sustaining worlds within its borders. In truth, it was a monumentally difficult proposition. For one thing, any world they wished to claim had to satisfy *all* Protectorate laws.

It could not have been claimed before. It could not have a settlement present, no matter how small. It could not be within the Autonomous Resource Zone of another race, nor could its potential zone overlap another's. It could not have sapient life already present, no matter how primitive. The list went on.

Add on top of this the biological complications nature threw at them. It had to have an oxygen rich atmosphere with sufficient water. It had to have a carbon-based ecosystem that was either biocompatible or potentially biocompatible with limited genetic modification. It had to allow for the introduction of Terran plants and animals—those few they had been able to save at any rate.

Between the legal and biological restrictions, it felt like a Sisyphean task, to say the least. Every time they found a prospect, excitement would rise, only to be dashed.

Most of the TN expeditions focused on Draxon space, or the no-man's-land surrounding it. The Draxon were humanity's patrons, after all, and had been of immeasurable assistance after the Terran Disaster, helping the survivors become the Terran Colony Fleet. Even now they offered their aid as best they could, providing coordinates to likely candidate worlds that, as far as they knew, were not in violation of any Protectorate conditions. But they could not visit such worlds themselves, because then, technically, it would be a Draxon discovery.

Commander Leo had fought in a number of conflicts and faced off against wild animals on dozens of worlds. But no enemy or creature could compare to Protectorate bureaucracy. It was a beast that could not be slain, only appeased or avoided.

There was talk of doing the latter, but even if they could find a world outside Protectorate borders, it would take decades, perhaps centuries, for the colony ships to be towed to it. Leo believed there was a sunk-cost fallacy at play, but he was not part of the Triumvirate. He did not make those decisions, only carried out their commands.

The *TCF Keres* had spent the last two years on the rimward edge of Draxon space. They had surveyed dozens of worlds, not one of which was suitable for their needs.

Leo sat in the command chair, frowning at the datapad his XO had handed him. It showed that the final planet of their current expedition had been disqualified before they even visited it.

Apparently, a band of colonists from one of the younger races had ended up there three hundred years ago and promptly died out. The sole record of said expedition had only recently been discovered and forwarded to them.

Technically, there was legal recourse, but it involved tracking down every relative of the doomed colony and getting them to sign away any claims they might have.

Give me a wild azagoth to wrestle instead of this nonsense any day.

It was time to go home.

Peter Smith had spent the last two years keeping the ship clean and making minor monotonous repairs too mundane for the regular crewmen to be bothered with.

And he'd loved every minute of it.

This was the first time he'd ever left the *Africa*, the colony ship he'd been born on and always assumed he'd die on. He'd beaten out thousands of other applicants, and through a combination of skill, timing, and luck, was now working aboard a Silver Legion ship, exploring!

Well, technically, it was the rest of the crew that did the exploring, but he and the other freeborn always got a good view of whatever planet they were orbiting from the tiny forward-facing porthole in their quarters. And the stories he heard from the crew who got to visit these worlds always filled him with wonder.

Right now, he was taking his lunch break with the synths. They didn't force him or the other freeborn to sit at another table, but treated them like part of the crew. Heck, one of them, Silv, had taken a real liking to him.

She now sat across from him, telling him about their latest failed survey.

"Yeah, turns out the crab analogs we found were more intelligent than we thought. They had cities built within the coral. Dr. Crater says that they have schools, systems of counting, and even a sense of history."

Peter nodded. "Even if you wanted to ignore it, the Protectorate would send in their own survey team to confirm the findings."

"Exactly. Still, it was the closest to a match we've had in a while. The food was even biocompatible, which led to some very uncomfortable suggestions about what to do about the crabs. Fortunately, there's not enough butter on board."

Peter laughed. Silv had a great sense of humour about these things.

The comms clicked to life. "Attention all hands. This is Commander Leo. This will be the last planet of our current expedition. We just learned that the final system on our planned itinerary has already been disqualified due to an obscure technicality."

There was a collective groan.

"Therefore, we will be setting course for the Terran Colony Fleet immediately."

There was a collective cheer.

"I would like to thank everyone on board for their exemplary conduct these last two years. The return journey should take about four months. Recreation time is doubled for the duration, effective immediately. Check with your supervisors for your revised work details. Leo out." The comm clicked off, and the room filled with excited chatter.

"We're going home?" said Peter. "Did you know?"

Silv shook her head. "No clue. Command staff never tells us anything. But *double* the free time?" She reached her hand over and touched his. "Whatever shall we do with it all?"

Yeah, a *real* liking to him.

The *Keres* resupplied at the closest Draxon colony a week later. They would make a few more stops along the way before they reached the Fleet. The *Keres* was not quite as self-reliant as the new heavy cruisers they were designing, but she had performed admirably these last two years.

Sub-Commander Alkes, the XO, entered Leo's office and handed him a datapad with the inventory they'd taken on board. The commander signed off on it with just a glance. If they were short a barrel of protein for the food synthesizers, he doubted it would matter much.

"Sir, have you submitted your crew reports to the Fleet?" Alkes asked.

"Before we left," said Leo.

Alkes paused. "Including the freeborn?"

"Yes, why? Something you wished to add?"

Alkes raised his chin. "Only my belief that they should be excluded from future expeditions."

Leo frowned. "Did you feel they didn't perform adequately?"

"No, sir."

"Did one of them disrespect you in some fashion?"

"No, sir."

"Then why?"

Alkes stood more at attention. "I believe being allowed on these expeditions will give them...ideas."

Leo knew exactly where this was going and would enjoy making Alkes suffer for it.

"Ideas, eh? What sort of *ideas*?"

"Well... You know..." Alkes stammered. "*Ideas*. Ideas they wouldn't have back on the colony ships."

Leo feigned ignorance. "I still don't know what kind of ideas you mean. Do you mean they might get the idea to work harder, study more?"

"I mean, they might get the idea they *belong* here with us," Alkes snapped.

Leo sighed and shook his head. "I really expected better from you, Alkes. You're lucky I already submitted my performance report, or I might have been revising yours."

Alkes scowled. "I saw one of them engaged in...an inappropriate display of affection with a member of the regular crew."

"Their clothes were still on, I hope?"

"You're mocking me, sir."

"Yes, I am. This is *exactly* what the Reintegration Doctrine is about. If I had been allowed to, I'd have had those freeborn taking on the same jobs as the crewmen. They're adaptable, resilient, and eager to learn. Unlike some officers I know."

Leo recognized the look on his XO's face; Alkes wanted to argue, but knew it would go nowhere. The commander wasn't without sympathy, however.

"It still hurts, doesn't it?"

Alkes didn't answer, but he didn't need to. Leo knew everything in the XO's file. Long ago, his ship had been sent to the final showdown between creator and creation, while he'd been stuck on a prison barge orbiting Jupiter—consequences of a night out that had been a little too wild.

It had saved Alkes' life, and it was clear he'd never forgiven himself for it.

Leo sighed. "Those who created us to be their tools of control are all dead, Alkes. Every last one of them. We've kept their ancestors subjugated for centuries. For what? To balance the cosmic scales? Why shouldn't we let them be part of us, instead of only serving us?"

Alkes's lip curled. "Permission to speak freely."

"Get it off your chest. Permission granted."

"Are you familiar with the fable of the Scorpion and the Frog?"

Leo waited for him to get to the point.

"It's in their *nature*, sir. We tried giving them more freedom. We gave them our trust. They took that trust and threw it back in our faces. Demanded more. When they didn't get it fast enough, they used what they had gained to strike back at us."

Leo sighed. The XO wasn't wrong. Less than a decade after the Doctrine had been established, there had been protests, which were tolerated until they became inconvenient. Things only got worse after that. Over the last forty years, Reintegration had been scaled back and moved forward, usually based on the whims of public opinion.

Leo tried to be diplomatic. "Change is never easy, but if we only dared to do what was easy, we would never accomplish anything. The fault lies in implementation. The Bureau's timetable takes place over a century. Nothing to us, but for the freeborn, that's five generations."

Alkes shook his head. "Even if we gave them the same rights as the rest of us, that wouldn't be enough. Sooner or later, they'd assert that they, as the original species, as the creators, deserved *more*."

Leo had no doubt some *would* make that argument in time. They'd use it as a tool to gain favour, a rallying cry to promote their own agendas. Some might even believe it.

He knew this because that was what his people had done. Different lyrics, same tune. It was why the cyborgs were in charge. It was why humans were now called freeborn.

They had believed they deserved more, because they had been treated for so long as less.

"Change must always start somewhere," said the commander. He was hoping to say something more profound, but the truth was he had no better answer for Alkes.

Dr. Crater was the chief science officer, on loan from the Academy. She was in charge of evaluating the potential of each world they visited. One way or another, the assessments always ended badly. Either the world turned out to be a non-starter for political reasons, or she would soon find some other reason the planet was a no-go. This was her fifth Terra Nova expedition, and her third aboard a Silver Legion ship, and it was always the same story.

While Crater was not the *Keres*'s chief medical officer—that was Dr. Owen—she was a fully qualified medical doctor. Though she would never admit it publicly, she was probably *more* qualified than Owen, who was only sixteen.

But Owen was a perfectly good doctor. The most adaptable synth she'd ever met, with a long career ahead of him. Crater was sure that if Owen ever wanted to become an engineer or a pilot, he'd have had little problem switching roles.

So when Dr. Owen called Crater and asked for her help with a patient in medbay, she knew it had to be something *very* unusual.

When she entered the medbay, she saw only the doctor.

"Where's the patient?"

Owen came over and handed her a datapad. "You're looking at him."

Crater blinked. "What's wrong?"

Owen nodded to the pad, which she scanned at a rapid pace. Then double checked what she had read.

"This can't be right."

Owen shook his head. "I've re-checked the results. Ten times."

"When did you start to think...?"

"Yesterday. Had a dizzy spell. Felt strangely tired. Thought nothing of it, but then I had a slight ache in my back. I figured it couldn't hurt to give myself a checkup. Thought it might have been the start of a flu, though how one would show up here after two years would have been a mystery all its own."

"LODS," said Crater, half to herself. She hadn't seen a case of Late Onset Deterioration Syndrome in years. "But you're only—"

"I know. Most cases of LODS show up much later in life."

"Did you want me to double check your conclusions?"

Owen shook his head. "I want you to determine how...long I have left. The progression..." Up until now, Dr. Owen had done a commendable job of keeping his composure, but now the cracks began to show. "The results I came up with...simply can't be right."

Relationships worked differently between synths and freeborns. Since synths grew up fast and didn't have kids or families, their relationships tended to be more casual. Sex was recreational.

That wasn't to say synths didn't have committed relationships, even ones that lasted lifetimes. It's just that they saw things...differently.

Maybe it was because of how Peter was brought up, or maybe it was the fact that Peter had to be brought up in the first place. He supposed raising a kid had to be a bonding experience. If your relationship could survive that, it could survive anything.

Only several of his childhood friends had parents who clearly couldn't stand one another, but stayed together and had the requisite number of kids so they could keep their larger accommodations. So maybe Peter had just been lucky.

Getting involved with Silv had raised certain anxieties in him. Was she just using him for stress relief till they got back to the Fleet? If she was, he had to try and not hold it against her. Try and see things the same way she did.

But then she'd asked him about moving in together during lunch, and he'd almost choked on his burger.

"It's not *illegal*," she'd said. "Just, you know, kinda frowned upon."

Peter paled. They'd been going out for less than a month.

"You're not coming down with that bug, are you?" she asked, concerned.

Now he had to switch gears and try to imagine how synths viewed cohabitation. He was flattered, of course. It meant she didn't see him as stress relief, but Peter was still left with questions.

"I know this is going to sound weird, but...where do you see things going?"

"Oh." Silv leaned back, struck by a revelation. "*Ohhh*... I keep forgetting how your relationships... And you must be wondering if I... And then there's... I'm so sorry."

"It's okay, but I honestly don't know what you were trying to say just now."

Silv took a deep breath. "Okay, with us, relationships last as long as they last. Maybe it's just a single night, and maybe you want to hang around for a while and see where things go. I guess it's not that different with you, really. We're just a bit more upfront about it, and less stressed if things don't work out."

She leaned in conspiratorially. "Don't tell anyone, but I've seen some of your old video programs, you know, from before the Disaster? You guys could get absolutely *crazy* worrying about where things were going and whether or not you were on a break and who slept with who... It's like you're wired for self-destruction."

Peter had never seen any pre-Disaster shows. Those were super illegal on the colony ships. But at the same time, he knew exactly the kind of angst she was talking about.

"So...?" Peter prompted, hoping she'd fill in the blank.

"So... I want you to hang around for a while and see where things go. You okay with that?"

Peter smiled. "Yeah, I think I am."

"Good. Wait here, I'll go get us some dessert. Cupcake sound good?"

"Sure."

She got up, only to stop and sway a little. "Whoa."

"You okay?"

"Just a head rush. You want chocolate or chocolate?"

It turned out the results Dr. Owen had come up with were *not* right. They had been overly optimistic.

Owen had thought he had months to live. It turned out to be weeks. Every day he woke up weaker and weaker, until he was confined to a bed in medbay.

He wasn't alone. The day after Crater's talk with Owen, two more people had come to medbay, complaining about light-headedness, bouts of fatigue, and mild muscle aches they couldn't explain.

When their results came up the same as Owen's, Commander Leo informed the Colony Fleet but kept the news from the rest of the crew. Dr. Crater isolated the crewmen straight away, confining them to quarters. They told the rest of the crew it was an unusual flu mutation that had been dormant on the ship.

The most baffling thing was that there was no sign that what was affecting the crew was being transmitted, and yet it clearly was. No airborne pathogens were detected. Nothing was found in the food processors or water recycling. Nothing on any contact surfaces.

Dr. Owen died one month after his diagnosis, at which point the pretense had to be dropped. Too many synths had been showing the same symptoms, though none had progressed as quickly as Owen. And if they kept confining people to their rooms, there'd be no one left to operate the ship.

The ship was declared a quarantine zone, and while they would continue to make their way back to the Colony Fleet, there would be no stopovers at any stations along the way, and no one would be allowed aboard. No communications were allowed off the ship except from the command staff to the Academy.

The autopsy on Dr. Owen did not clear up matters any further, though it had shown Crater the extent of the deterioration. The only positive thing she could think to say was the physical process seemed to have been relatively painless.

But she had seen the fear in Owen's eyes towards the end. It haunted her dreams. *Only sixteen.*

Commander Leo, Sub-Commander Alkes, and Crater herself had shown no symptoms, nor had the five freeborn on board. But that was to be expected. LODS only affected synths, considered to be a rare anomaly of the maturation process they went through. A glitch in the base genetic code, if you will.

But normally it affected only a tiny fraction of older synths, and the symptoms lasted for years. It certainly wasn't contagious. Nothing about this made sense.

As the crew began to die one after another, Crater had more and more opportunities to look for a common thread, or discover a means of transmission, but failed to find it.

Crater buried herself in her work. It was the only way to block out the cries for help, even if they were only in her imagination.

When they were two weeks away from the Fleet, Crater had a breakthrough. And the more she followed that breakthrough, the more it terrified her.

She spoke to the commander and sub-commander in the briefing room. By this point, a quarter of the crew had died, and half were incapacitated. Every day, the *Keres* felt more and more like a ghost ship. The *Mary Celeste* of the stars.

"We assumed that Dr. Owen was Patient Zero, both because he was the first to show symptoms, and suffered them the most severely," said Dr. Crater. "However, I've been re-examining the rate of deterioration in the crew and realized I had it all wrong. Everyone was infected *at the same time*."

"How is that possible?" asked the commander. "We had crew members not showing symptoms for a month or more."

"That doesn't mean they didn't already have it," said Crater. "I tried working with the assumption that whatever began triggering LODS in the crew needed time to develop, spread throughout the body, long before the first dizzy spell. If we assume that rate was the same as the progression of the syndrome *after* symptoms began to show, it all comes back to roughly the same point in time."

"Which was?"

"A week before our last planetary survey."

"Where were we at that time?" asked Commander Leo.

"Technically nowhere," said Crater. "Between worlds. But we had dropped from transit around that time to investigate a distress signal."

Sub-commander Alkes frowned. "I remember. It was a small shuttle. I took a team to investigate, but there were no life signs on board. We forwarded its location to the nearest ProSec office for salvage purposes and continued on our way. You believe this is the point of contact? We were wearing environmental suits and went through standard decom procedures."

Dr. Crater shook her head. "I can only point to where the evidence leads. The probable point of the synth crew contracting LODS intersects roughly with this derelict ship. A ship, I might add, that there is no record of."

The commander's eyes widened. "You're sure of that?"

"I forwarded an information request to ProSec through the Academy. They received our report but found nothing there when they dispatched a salvage team. They assumed someone else had claimed the ship before they arrived."

Silence filled the room until Crater said, "And I think I made one other discovery regarding the nature of the disease."

They waited.

"If we assume everyone was exposed at roughly the same time, I then had to ask myself why they began showing symptoms at different rates. I found a correlation between the onset of symptoms, and neural plasticity. Whatever this is, affects the most adaptable of the synth population first."

"That doesn't feel like a coincidence," said Alkes.

"No, it does not." Commander Leo stood from his chair. "Someone has declared war on the Terran Colony Fleet."

In light of this new information, the *Keres* journey home came to an end. They stopped near a Wolf-Rayet star and maintained direct contact with the Fleet.

Though no means of transmission had been found, they had to assume that whatever had affected the crew was highly contagious. They also had to assume that even though the cyborg and freeborn aboard were not affected by it, they could still be carriers.

Dr. Crater stayed with her patients until the end, providing what comfort she could, collecting what information she could, forwarding everything to the Academy for further analysis. The Academy provide her with treatment suggestions and asked for more and more tests to be conducted, both on the living and the dead.

When the last synth passed, Commander Leo called Crater and Alkes to the bridge. He had been given new orders, directly from the Triumvirate, and wanted them there with him as he carried them out.

He had a bottle of champagne with him and three glasses. Not from Earth, of course, but from the Champagne district of the colony ship *Europica*. He'd always intended to open it on a special occasion. Crater doubted this was what he had in mind.

The commander handed each of them a glass. "I just wanted to say, it has been an honour and a privilege serving with you."

Peter was alone in the freeborn quarters. The rest were down in engineering. Over the last month, they'd been relied on more and more to keep things running, taught certain essential functions on board the ship, until they were the only ones keeping it going. A skeleton of a skeleton crew, with the bare minimum of training, yet they had risen to the challenge.

But today Peter just couldn't get out of bed. He wasn't sick. He just couldn't take it anymore. The last of the synth crew had died, and that had made him relive those final moments he'd shared with Silv.

She hadn't been in pain. For that, he'd been grateful. He'd been kept busy with double shifts every day, but he spent every free moment he could to be with her. Then, at the end, Dr. Crater had called for him on the comms, telling him to be with her.

She'd been resting in her quarters. Medbay was reserved for those receiving experimental treatments or having tests run on them.

"Well, you hung around a while," she'd said, her breath shallow.

Peter had forced a smile. "I wanted to see where things went."

Silv's smile had been genuine. "You know what? I think we would have gone all the way."

Peter didn't remember much after that, other than saying, "Me too."

Somehow, hearing the sombre, dry announcement of the last synth's passing over the speakers had brought all that back to him. The announcement had been followed by a call for the command staff to meet on the bridge, and for the freeborn to report to engineering.

But Peter couldn't move, and the others had let him be. They said they could handle whatever was needed down there.

Peter finally managed to get out of bed. He made his way to the small porthole. Though filtered heavily by the photoreactive material, he could see the bright blue star they were orbiting. It was beautiful.

It also seemed to be getting closer. In fact, he was certain they were heading straight towards it.

What was it Silv had said when they first started dating?

"Command staff never tells us anything."

Peter watched helplessly as the star took up his entire view.

"See you soon, Silv."

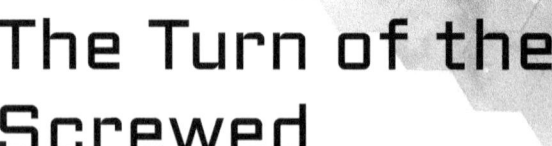

The Turn of the
Screwed

I'm not surprised that exploration outside the Protectorate has been minimal. So much remains unknown within your own borders. I can only imagine what your ancestors were thinking when they hurried to hash out these vast lines in the vacuum thousands of years ago.

Financially, it still makes sense to look inward. Setting up a comms network outside Protectorate space would be an expensive and time-consuming affair. Ferrying supplies while the colonists become self sufficient would be a hassle. The credits coming back into the Protectorate wouldn't be great, either. There's a thousand reasons why you shouldn't bother.

Today, I'm going to tell you why you should.

Ranger M's first speech at the Protectorate's
Colonization Conference

VIOLET'S ACCOUNT OF THE fate of the *TCF Keres* did not match up at all with what Karon had been taught. The event had been used as a textbook example of the perils of transit drive failure. Now she realized it was a little *too* textbook.

"They dove into a star?"

"Not just any star," said Violet. "One of the hottest stars around. As deaths go, that's pretty metal."

Len looked to Karon. "What does she mean by *metal*?"

Karon shook her head. "It's just the way she talks. You get used to it."

Violet continued. "Point is, the top dogs decided it was way too risky to allow the ship or the survivors to stick around. All signs suggest the trigger had been unbelievably contagious. It took so long before those affected began to display symptoms that, had they made contact with the Fleet before they knew what was going on, it could have wiped out the synth population in a year."

Len mulled this over. "And they're sure this was intentional?"

"No hard evidence, but it's where I'd place my credits."

"That doesn't make sense," said Karon. "If you're trying to attack the Colony Fleet, why start with a ship so far away?"

"Unless it wasn't an attack," said Len. "It was a test."

"Winner winner, chicken dinner!" said Violet. "Nice isolated flying lab that won't contaminate the general population. They even run all the tests on the subjects for you and feed you the results. Convenient."

Len frowned. "I thought the *Keres* confined their communications to the Academy. You're not suggesting...?"

"Maybe, but I doubt it. No, my guess is whoever set this up also had a way to intercept the *Keres*'s comms."

"Hold on," said Karon. "Didn't *you* die from LODS? Young?"

"Believe me, *that* detail did not escape my attention. But it took years to affect me. Normal progression. And what good is a sample size of one? No, I think I just got hit by Moss luck."

Len and Karon exchanged a puzzled look.

Violet coughed. "Long story."

"This is some bleak stuff," said Karon. "But what does it have to do with our situation here?"

"Everything, I'm afraid."

Violet now displayed an image of a strong and confident looking woman with dark hair and deep tan skin. Camile Miram, late commander of the *Hydrus*.

Karon had been taking her officer's exam when Miram died, caught in a reactor explosion on a derelict ship. It wasn't long after that Nekkar began his increasingly erratic chase that had led them here.

Violet played the recording. "Magnus. We both know what it means if you are seeing this. I won't waste your time with words of advice. I know you find such things tedious. But I trust that you will be the commander I have always hoped you would be, and that I have properly prepared you for this day."

The image paused.

"Spoiler alert. She didn't," said Violet, then allowed the recording to continue.

"Assuming that my death occurred during our current operation, I do have some reservations. I know you believe that this mission is beneath you, and will no doubt want to wash your hands of it so you can seek out more glorious deeds. But there is more at stake here than you realize. I am not exaggerating when I say that the continued future of the Colony Fleet may depend on it.

"First, you need to be made aware of the true fate of the *TCF Keres...*"

At this point, the image began to speed up. Commander Miram's face moved at a blur while her voice sounded like a high-pitched cartoon animal, too fast to make out any words.

"Eh, you already know this stuff, and I told the story better," said Violet.

The image returned to normal speed.

"This has been classified at the highest levels. Only commanders of ships tasked with tracking down lost freeborn are briefed on the importance of our mission.

"It is believed that what affected the *Keres* was a test of a biological weapon, and the ship was chosen because of its remote location, far from the Fleet. The fact they got as close to home as they did was not intentional. Had the *Keres* stuck to the expedition timetable, it would have been over a month before they returned. They wouldn't have made it anywhere near the Fleet.

"While the evidence suggests the rendezvous with the stranded shuttle was where the event occurred, the Triumvirate cannot dismiss the possibility that it was an act of sabotage perpetrated by the free-born portion of the crew."

"Seriously?" said Karon.

Violet paused the image. "Yeah, it's BS. But given the terrorism going on around that time, they had reason to consider the possibility. Remember, the Reintegration Doctrine was dissolved six months after the loss of the *Keres*. Still, if it bleats and has '*I did it!*' painted on its side, it's probably a scapegoat."

Miram's image started up again. "There is much speculation as to the intended purpose of this weapon. The fact that it has not been used against us yet suggests either that those who made it are waiting to use it as part of a larger stratagem, or that the results were not what they hoped, and further testing is being done. After sixteen years, however, there has never been another incident like the *Keres*.

"The Academy of Science has never stopped studying this problem, but have only the *Keres* data to work with. We do not know the means of delivery or transmission, but believe modifying the templates of future synths and introducing modifications to the existing population might hold the answer. This is where the Legion comes in.

"Research is being conducted on both synth and freeborn subjects. Producing synths for testing is simple, but the freeborn are another matter. I am told that the general freeborn population is considered 'tainted' due to centuries of gene modification."

At this point Miram paused, as if she had doubts. "A priority has been placed on freeborn captured outside the Fleet. Many will not have had access to gene mods, while others might have spent generations on planets and never required them. You are to review Dr. Ascella's reports on any you reclaim. Those with sufficiently low levels of modification are to have their records removed, and not forwarded to the TCF. When the *Hydrus* returns to the Fleet, there will be people waiting to take charge of those individuals.

"While I am not privy to the details of what is being done, I find the level of secrecy involved... concerning. But given the gravity of what we face, I must lay my trust in the greater good.

"I hope you now see the importance of this mission, Magnus, and trust—"

Violet switched the monitor off. "Yadda yadda yadda, you get the picture."

For a moment, neither Len nor Karon said anything.

At last Karon said, "A colony ship that predates contact with the Protectorate, with three thousand freeborn aboard."

"Yep," said Violet. "They're all screwed."

"We're all screwed," said Moss, looking up at the brig lights that burned into his sockets.

He lay on a bunk on one side of the cell, while Tam sat on the other. It wasn't his first time in a cell, but it was his first time in a Silver Legion cell. He supposed they weren't considered much of a threat, because at the moment there were no guards. They were probably all over on the *Pegasi*.

The cell was very plain and very Draxon in design, not a surprise given the first batch of TCF heavy cruisers were refits of Draxon ships. They'd altered the base design, adding features like the unique armour that gave the Silver Legion its name. Word was the Fleet was busy making their own heavy cruisers somewhere.

"We'd be less screwed if you had just let me do my *job*," said Tameria.

"Oh, *excuse* me, Sister. But maybe I didn't want the blood of—"

He shut his mouth when Tameria glared at him and pointed to the ceiling. There were no monitoring devices to be seen, but they'd be fools to think there weren't any.

Great, I can't even chew her out without making things worse.

He flung his legs over the side of the bunk and sat up.

"I figured it out," said Moss.

"What?"

"Why you can't be happy."

Tameria groaned as she sat up. "*This* should be good."

"You have to put everyone else first. Not anyone, not someone, *everyone*. You've set yourself an impossible goal and won't back down, even if it makes you do something you don't want to do."

Tameria's eyes narrowed. "I'm warning you, Moss." She stewed in silence a moment before she calmed down. "You took a bolt for me."

Moss shrugged. "A charge, technically. Non-lethal."

"Yeah, but you didn't know that."

"I wasn't thinking," said Moss.

She chuckled. "Obviously."

"Well, that's gratitude for you."

"I still got shot," Tameria pointed out.

"It's the thought that counts."

"I thought you said you weren't thinking?"

Before the bickering could go on any longer, the door to the brig opened, and a man walked in. He wore a Silver Legion uniform but showed no rank. He held a piece of cloth in one hand.

Moss recognized him immediately.

When they had first found the *Pegasi*, a band of pirates hadn't been far behind. Moss had found the lost colony ship by repairing Hel's altered memories. The pirates had found a different survivor of Hel's doomed expedition and used him to find it.

There had been a dogfight.

It should have been a simple job. Roy and his team had duped some brainwashed shmuck into helping them find the *Pegasi*. They'd given the crew a rescue story as a cover, while in reality, the ship was going to be sold to some eccentric collector with more credits than sense, and its people sold in the Void for a nice profit.

Then this guy and his band of do-gooders had taken them on. They'd killed his whole team.

This one. *This one* had killed Powell.

Moss had lost Violet. Lost Steva. Almost lost Tameria. In the end, it had come down to two barely functioning ships with no functioning weapons. They'd stared each other down, their cockpits just meters apart. In the co-pilot seat was the captive from the *Pegasi*. A friend of Hel's.

Without a word, the pilot had pulled out his sidearm and shot the man in the head.

The pilot had then raised his visor, letting Moss see his face clearly. He'd given Moss a single nod before he turned his ship around and left.

But the pilot who killed Powell had kept his *ridiculous* mask on.

Roy held that mask up now, pressing it up against the security screen, causing the field to hum and glow as it kept his hand at bay.

"So, we meet again, 'Ranger M.'"

The man on the bunk now stood and faced him. "Did that sound as corny in your head as when you said it out loud?"

"It was on purpose, you knob. *You're* the one who wears this stupid thing."

"You here to monologue about your diabolical plan?"

"You going to lecture me on the rights of all sapient beings?"

The Elysian on the other bunk groaned. "Oh goddess, there's *two* of them."

The so-called Ranger M took a step forward. "Look, pal. If you're here to gloat, go ahead. If you're here to bash my head in, well, don't. Please. I think that's about all I have to say to you."

Roy looked the man over. He'd almost caught him back at Komi Station, having found his ship, the absurdly named *Viaticus Rex II.I*. It had been registered to a Captain Foote, as he recalled.

Roy went over to the brig's control station and lowered the first field. Foote stepped back, taken slightly off guard as Roy came back. Roy placed the mask down in the gap between the first and second field, then went back to the control station, raising the outer field, and lowering the inner field.

He nodded for the man to take it. Foote did.

With both fields back up, Roy came over so that he and Foote were just a meter apart.

"Kinda wished you'd burned it," said Foote.

Roy leaned forward a little, hands behind his back, and whispered, "*I know.*"

Foote seemed surprised by that. Roy stood straight again. "I remember you from *before* the cartoon. Your lectures about exploration and settling outside the Protectorate. No one in the TCF knew who you really were, but you made them look good, so they claimed you as one of their own...until you turned your name to mud. I can't remember anyone's public image imploding so fast, so *spectacularly*, and then forgotten so quickly. Now the only thing anyone knows about you is that dumb cartoon.

"And yet you still lug that thing around. The self loathing you carry must be *astronomical*. I'm surprised it hasn't collapsed into a black hole." He paused a moment. "Or maybe it has? Yeah, I can picture you sitting at a bar, that stupid rag tucked in your pocket as you drink yourself into a stupor, pining about how you used to have it all to anyone who will listen. Sound about right?"

Roy studied Foote's reaction closely. Their initial banter had helped establish a baseline, and now he looked for changes to that.

There it was—a mild flush in the cheeks. Anxiety. Involuntary narrowing of the eyes. Anger. He'd hit close to home.

Roy shrugged. "You know, I've been in that position too. Losing everything. Starting over. Difference between you and me? I didn't waste my time bitching about it. I just got to work."

"I'm sure your mom would be proud, if you had one."

Roy chuckled. If that was the best comeback Foote had, he really must have gotten under his skin. "There is one thing I'm actually curious about." He paused, taking in Foote's now guarded features.

"Where's your ship? The *Crap-tastic Number Two* or whatever it's called. It wasn't on the *Pegasi*. It's nowhere in the area. Is it on its way here? Your co-pilot bringing it?"

Foote was probably damn good at poker, but sometimes having a poker face was like a politician saying they couldn't confirm or deny. Under the right conditions, the very act told you everything you wanted to know.

Roy gave him a wink. "Thanks, pal."

He left, waiting until the door to the brig opened before he turned back around. "By the way, when the commander's done with you, I'm gonna see to it that you and I get some private time. See you around."

Moss collapsed on his bunk. "Well, I'm a dead man."

"Not the first time," Tameria pointed out.

"Yeah... Maybe you guys can clone me from whatever is left on the walls here when he's done. Is that a thing you do?"

"Not really, no. Besides, we'd need your brain. Intact."

"No chance of that." Moss held up the green-and-red wrestling mask. "Well, at least I have a cunning disguise if we ever get out of here. No way anyone will find *this* suspicious."

Tam got up and sat at the foot of Moss's bunk. "Why'd you even bring it?"

"I dunno, I just..." Moss shrugged. "You said Zack and his family would be there, and you remember how Zach loves that cartoon."

"Were you going to wear it?"

"What? No! I tried pawning it off on him before, but he refused. I figured maybe this time he'd say yes. It's just cluttering up my ship, anyway."

Tameria gave what might have been a chuckle. Moss ignored it.

Just then, he thought he heard something from the guard's side of the brig. At first, he saw nothing, but then there was some movement from a small panel as it was pushed out, turned on its side, and pulled into the vent.

"You've *got* to be kidding me," said Moss.

"What?"

Rather than say it, he simply nodded in the right direction. Tameria saw what was going on.

"Well, I'll be."

Trouble walked out of the vent, standing on its hind legs and brushing dust off its fur.

"*Bleah*. Whatever cleaning schedule those guys have, they need to double it."

Tameria got up. "Are we glad to see you!"

"Meh," said Moss.

"Oh, *come on*," said Tameria.

"He still has to prove himself useful first." Moss turned his attention to the PetBot. "How long have you been there?"

"Since that mean guy was taunting you. Acted a lot like Professor Megaton when he had us tied up to the Neutron Neural Disruptor, don't you think?"

Moss ignored the cartoon reference. "Did you see when he punched the code to lower the security fields?"

"Sure did!"

"Great! Get up there and do what he did."

"Uh...sorry, boss. I can't."

"Why not?"

"Well, I saw him *do* it, but I couldn't see what he actually *did*."

Moss gestured at Trouble while looking at Tameria, as if presenting his final argument to the court. "And now you know why I'm not glad to see him."

Tameria rolled her eyes. "Trouble, have you learned anything useful while you were looking for us? If anyone is secretly watching us, we don't have much time."

"Well... let's see..."

A Moment of Trouble

The design of ferrets and similar mustelids was re-markable. They were the closest thing to an animal in liquid form you could find without going to Aqualaxia in the Elysian Kingdom. They could lower and stretch themselves out by nearly a third in order to travel through tight tunnels, and were so flexible they could reverse direction in those tunnels with barely any ad-ditional space required. Even during the Terran's ear-ly space age, ferrets were sometimes used to lay cable through otherwise inaccessible areas.

Stwello's Guide to Extinct Animals of Terra

T HERE IS A LONG way and a short way to describe the events that happened in the shuttle.

This is the long way:

Moss leapt in front of the blast meant for Tameria, holding Trouble in front of his chest like a tiny human shield.

Fortunately for Trouble, the blast hit Moss low, *very* low, and was set to stun.

The now unconscious Moss continued his weightless journey until his head cracked against the far wall, while the Vigile fired off a second and third shot, incapacitating Tameria before she could raise her weapon.

The Vigile stopped his momentum the first chance he got and went to secure the prisoners.

By then, however, Trouble had scurried off.

Recognizing that actual weapon fire had taken place, Trouble stopped treating the situation like a game. It now remained hidden, but always remained aware of Moss's location. When they moved his body to the Silver Legion shuttle, it waited for an opportunity to sneak on the ship through its landing gear before it took off.

Once on board the heavy cruiser, Trouble snuck off and did its best to follow Moss without being seen. This soon proved impossible, however, given the number of crew around.

Luckily, the air vents here weren't screwed in or otherwise locked. They were secured tight, but not too tight, as they were meant to be slipped on and off for easy maintenance.

While Trouble wasn't a real ferret, NuPet prided themselves on the accuracy of their PetBot designs. Throw in a (reasonably) sophisticated pseudo-personality, and Trouble was literally *made* for this.

The two most likely places to find Moss right now would be the medical bay or the brig. Trouble spied a wall panel displaying a deck schematic, took note of each location, then made its way to the closest one, medbay, staying out of sight of the crew at all times.

Pests aboard starships were not a common occurrence, but did happen. While the aim was to prevent them from coming aboard in the first place, most ships had rudimentary pest control systems, just in case. But those were designed around organic animals and were either ineffective against Trouble, or easily avoided.

As Moss was fond of pointing out, as a pest, Trouble was in a category all its own.

Once it arrived, it pressed an eye close to the vent to get a good look inside. There was a doctor there, judging from the uniform, and plenty of people in the beds, but none of them were Moss.

It was about to leave when it heard a voice it recognized. One of the big guards who had brought Moss on board. He heard him mention dropping the prisoners off at the brig, then asked the doctor if he could have a minute of his time.

Its suspicions confirmed, Trouble made his way to the brig. To get there, however, it had to pass through the science decks and deal with a different kind of pest control. A ship like the *Hydrus* needed protection from electronic bugs as well as organic, and whatever it used to jam unwanted electronic surveillance here was messing with its sense of direction.

At last, it came to a vent and heard a familiar voice inside, only it was the wrong familiar voice. It peeked close and saw two humans talking to a computer that sounded like Violet.

Trouble listened for a while as Violet talked about a doomed Terran ship, then listened to a recording of someone talking about secret orders and stuff. The humans didn't seem to take it well.

The woman said, "A colony ship that predates contact with the Protectorate, with three thousand freeborn aboard."

"Yep," said Violet. "They're all screwed."

The man seemed just as concerned. "And raising synths, *just* to test on them?"

"I've learned that with some people, that 'greater good' line is like a blank cheque for bad ideas," said Violet.

The woman still looked horrified. "What are we going to do?"

"What *can* we do?" asked the man.

That was Trouble's cue. Its sidekick personality routine swung into overdrive. It pushed the vent out dramatically and climbed out into the open.

"Never fear, help is on the way!"

Trouble wasn't sure which human shrieked louder, but they clearly had never seen a talking ferret before.

"*Trouble*?" said Violet. "What are you doing here?"

"Trouble?" said the woman, calming down. "Like from the cartoon?"

Trouble bowed. "At your service. You two seem to be in a bit of a pickle. Lucky for you, Ranger M is here to help!"

"Moss is *here*?" said Violet.

"Er...sorta. He's in the brig, actually."

"Would someone explain what's going on?" said the man. "Why is a PetBot pretending that a cartoon character is on board this ship?"

"In the brig," Trouble reminded helpfully.

Violet's voice grew louder. "Everyone shut up for a second. I need a moment to think." A moment passed and Violet said, "Okay, done. Trouble, is Moss alone?"

"Naw, the angry lady is with him. The one who can't admit she likes him."

"Tam Tam?"

"That's the one."

"Are they both in the brig?"

"Probably. They got knocked out together. Zap-zap!"

Violet's camera turned to the others. "Karon, Len, there are *three thousand* lives at stake on board that ship. Men, women, and children who just want to find a place to call home. They don't deserve whatever experiments the TCF has planned for them any more than our brothers and sisters who are being raised for them. Are you serious about wanting to do something to help?"

The one Trouble assumed was Karon nodded, but Len seemed to have doubts. "If what Commander Miram said about this LODS variant is true, then we're all at risk. Don't the needs of the many outweigh the needs of the few?"

"Ouch. Throwing *that* chestnut at me?" said Violet. "You know, sometimes the reverse is true too. Because we're not just talking about our *lives* here, we're talking about what we stand for. If the Colony Fleet stands for doing whatever it takes to survive, no matter who gets hurt or how many...then maybe we don't *deserve* to survive. There has to be a better way. And if another option isn't already on the table, then, goddammit, we'll *make* one."

Trouble pumped a tiny fist in the air. That had practically been a Ranger M speech. "Yeah!"

"Now," said Violet, "are you with me?"

Len sighed. "My career's probably over, anyway. What do we do?"

"Do you know how to work the brig controls?"

"Sure."

"Tell Trouble what to do. We don't want anyone thinking you two are involved."

"And that's when they sent me here," said Trouble. "Only I had to wait for the mean guy to leave first."

"Hold up," said Moss. "Are you telling me you *already* know how to work the controls to the security field?"

"Yeah."

"*Why didn't you say so before*?!"

"You asked me if I saw how the mean guy did it."

Moss bashed his head against the energy field several times, causing it to glow and crackle with every thump.

Comedy subroutine complete.

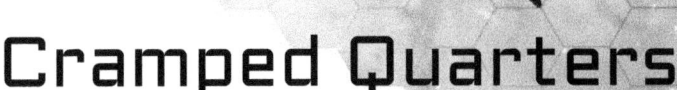

Cramped Quarters

The Elysian's glamour began naturally as an evolutionary trait, calming potentially hostile animals and making them less likely to attack. During the Eugenics Surge, this trait was enhanced and altered so that it became effective on other sapient lifeforms.

The effect is often subtle, making the subject more agreeable, and having them view the Elysian in question as if they had traits more in line with their own species. This has led to the misconception of its purpose being seductive in nature, though it can be used that way.

M Foote, *The Galaxy is Weirder than You Think*

T ROUBLE SAID VIOLET WANTED Moss and Tameria to meet up with her on the science level, but that was one deck up and halfway down the ship.

The three of them ducked into an unsecured storage room further down the corridor. The odds were low they'd make it all the way to Violet undetected. And it was only a matter of time before someone noticed that the brig was empty.

Fortunately, Moss had a plan.

A synth crewman was walking down the corridor, checking a report on his datapad, when he heard a yelp. He saw a strange, small creature in the middle of the hall, looking nervously back and forth. It saw him, yelled, "Zoinks!" and ran into a room.

Moss never said it was a *good* plan. What mattered was it worked.

The crewman came inside to investigate and saw an Elysian woman before him, iridescent wings fully spread, looking very friendly.

"Hello there. I'm lost. Can you help me?"

A goofy smile spread across the crewman's face. "What are you...?"

Moss grabbed the crewman from behind, getting him into a choke-hold. But before he could apply the right amount of pressure to knock him out, he felt weird. He saw Tameria and...

She'd never looked so *beautiful* before. That smile. That face. She looked more human than Elysian to him, though he couldn't quite explain how. And violence seemed like such a silly way to resolve things, didn't it? His grip loosened. Maybe they could just talk and—

Moss staggered back as the crewman broke free and punched him in the nose.

That snapped Moss out of it. He parried the next blow, got a hold of the crewman's arm, chicken winged him, and slammed his head against the wall, knocking him out.

Moss checked his nose, which somehow wasn't bleeding. "Ow!"

Tameria folded her wings. "I'm sorry. I don't use my glamour often, and when you said, 'full blast,' I—"

"It's okay."

She pulled out a pair of cuffs they'd picked up in the brig. "Get his clothes off. I'll cuff him."

"Kinky."

"Shut up."

Moss waved her back, picturing himself using those cuffs on her in a very different way, which gave him an idea. "Hold onto those for now." He shook off the last of the glamour's effect. "Man, I thought I was ready for it, but... *wow*. You weren't kidding when you said you've never used it on me before. I'd remember something like that. Didn't know the effect could be that strong."

Tameria looked away, rubbing her arm nervously while Moss started removing the crewman's uniform. "It's not. Not without help."

"Enhanced?"

She nodded.

"Doesn't that violate your people's restrictions on self modification or something?"

"It's for work. For emergencies like this."

"Yeah, well, the Order always did operate by its own rules," Moss muttered, removing the man's pants.

Trouble hopped off a box. "That was *great*, boss! Just like when we took out that guard on the prison planet of Icecatraz with the old 'You dropped something,' bit. Remember?"

"Yeah, great," said Moss. "Now look. Why don't you make yourself useful, and climb back into the vents? Scout ahead along our path. If you see any senior officers coming our way, or armed security, come and warn us, okay?"

Trouble stood up straight and gave a salute. "You got it, boss! Give me five minutes to check. I'll be right back!" Then it added, "Nice to see Ranger M back in the saddle!"

Moss groaned. "Fuck off already."

Trouble did so, removing a vent panel and replacing it once it was inside.

Tameria looked at the vent while Moss changed into the crewman's pants.

"Why do you hate Trouble?"

"I'd have thought it was obvious."

Tameria looked back at him. "Yeah, I know. He's annoying by design. A stereotypical sidekick trope. The product of an unimaginative mind."

Moss winced at that. "Yeah, well, it wasn't always supposed to be... that."

Tameria's eyes widened. "Wait... He was *your* idea, wasn't he?"

Moss managed to get the first boot on. He sat down and rested his hands on his knee a moment. "You know how many episodes of *Ranger M* they made?"

Tameria shrugged. "Hundreds."

Second boot. "Five hundred and one, to be precise. You know how many of them were written by a pseudo-intelligent supercomputer?"

Tameria waited.

"Five hundred."

Tameria pieced things together. "You wrote the pilot."

"It was supposed to be *my* show, Tam. *My* baby." He shrugged into the crewman's jacket, figuring he might as well get this off his chest. "I was doing lectures with my Ranger M persona. I loved doing that. I felt like I was *inspiring* people instead of annoying them. The Nubrans ate it up. Peak Terran chic to them or something. Then this network that's part of the same megacorp as Odyssey has an idea for something uniquely Terran."

"A cartoon," Tameria supplied.

"Right. They want me to write the series. I'm the only Terran on staff with any experience flying or exploring, and they wanted it to feel authentic.

"I felt like a kid again, the kid before he became a stupid teen and a stupider adult. I poured everything I had into that show, working with the development team, creating a series bible, hashing out an arc. Serious, but fun. Superheroic, but grounded. I wanted to instil a sense of wonder in people, make them think about what's out there, or what's possible. I wanted to have stories of good versus evil, but also hard decisions. I wanted to show that people can *choose* to make a difference. That it's important to stand up. To do what's right."

"Where does Trouble fit into this?"

Moss smirked. "Studio notes. They wanted something to appeal to the kids. But that didn't mean I couldn't put some thought into it. I chose a ferret because they're cute, but you've seen how it can slip in and out of tight places. I figured he would be a kind of conscience figure, keep Ranger M on the right path when things looked bleak. The comic relief stuff was toned way down. I liked the juxtaposition of a guy treating something like Trouble as an equal."

"So, when did it all go wrong?"

Moss put his hands behind his head and leaned back, looking at the ceiling. "We had the show ready for production. I'd spent weeks working on the pilot and making storyboards. I was damn proud of it, too. The development team loved it, but the execs said it wasn't what they were looking for. They fired our asses, took everything we'd made, and fed it to a computer."

"No legal recourse?"

"Let's just say I always read the fine print now."

"Ouch."

"Oh, it gets worse. They then added *their* carefully cultivated statistics and audience studies and demographic profiles, along with hundreds of *other* Terran cartoons, shows, and movies to base ideas off of, and *boom*, *Ranger M* gets a five hundred episode run."

"And your pilot?"

"They were legally obligated to make it and air it, but only once. It's never been aired again and isn't on any digital collection. Fans call it the Lost Episode. There are bootleg copies floating around out there...or so I hear."

"Why five hundred?"

"Oh, they made more, but only five hundred were useable. Got very repetitive after that. Actually, it was repetitive long before that. Fifty basic stories recycled ten times each, as far as I'm concerned. And the studio only had the rights to one season. Odyssey Expeditions wanted the rights to the show back and refused to green light another. So the studio put out *all* five hundred episodes as a single season—which they doled out every half-week for *years*, holding onto that licence as long as they could."

Tameria shook her head. "Corps are messed up."

"But that's not all," said Moss. "The night the dev team and I were fired? Odyssey Expeditions told me they needed to 'review' their contract with me."

"Ugh."

"And *that* was the night Violet had 'the talk' with me."

"The talk?"

"She was still working through her own issues and thought it would help if I accepted that the real Violet was gone. Wouldn't take no for an answer. Said I was holding onto the past, seeing her as something she wasn't. I listened to her all night, because I knew *she* was hurting, trying to understand what she was now. She didn't know my dream project had been stolen from me, or that my future at Odyssey was probably doomed. And all this was right before I had to speak at the Protectorate's Colonization Conference at the Galactic Senate.

"Oh, goddess... The *incident*."

Moss nodded. "The incident. Got drunk. Got ornery. Stole a ship. Made such a menace of myself, ProSec had to shoot me down...during a live broadcast. Odyssey skipped the review and went straight to firing. They weren't completely unsympathetic, mind you, but...yeah. Game over."

"And the rest is history," said Tameria.

Moss sighed. "Not quite. Odyssey got the rights back from the studio last year. Turns out, bureaucracy can be a double-edged sword, because despite the rights they already held, they couldn't create another season unless *I* agreed to it."

"Which is never going to happen."

Moss rolled his head towards Tameria, giving her the side eye.

Tameria gaped. "You're joking. After all that? *Why*?"

"Remember the yard rats on Komi Station? Had to work out a deal with Odyssey to buy us some time, make sure they didn't deal with the Orijen Brothers instead. Interest in Ranger M was up because of that race people thought he was in. I figured I could capitalize on that.

"So I gave them my blessing, plus my journals in case they needed fresh ideas. You can expect *The Further Adventures of Ranger M* to show up sometime next year."

"And the pain starts all over again," said Tameria.

"At least this time it was my choice."

Moss grew silent a moment, waiting for that damn PetBot to hurry up and report back. He pulled out the wrestling mask from his discarded pants and held it so it looked back at him.

"You asked why I hate Trouble. It's because he reminds me of what I'm not. Ranger M? *My* Ranger M? That's what part of me, in the back of my mind, always imagined myself as. What I *wanted* to be. But in reality, I'm the other guy. *This* guy." He gestured to himself and leaned back. "I realized I'm no different from anyone else. At the end of the day, we all do whatever it takes to get ahead and stay alive. Then someday life just ends, and none of it matters. In another hundred years, nobody is left to remember you."

He held the mask up for Tameria to see. "The only things that endure are the lies we tell ourselves. The stories. The little comforts we create so we can believe our lives have meaning. In some demented way, Trouble is more real than I am. So screw him."

"You know you just called Trouble a him, right? Not an it?"

Moss chuckled. "I think that only proves my point."

Tameria leaned over and took the mask from Moss. "Give me that." She stuffed it in her pocket. "You know, the Order is very keen on preserving memories."

"Well, *duh*."

"I don't just mean like Violet, but it's the reason that line of tech is being pursued." She absently brushed away her hair where her own dermal implant was. "We've kept records of every member of the Order and its allies since its inception. Every deed they've done. Even Steva is in there, for what he did to help save the *Pegasi*."

"Well, at least I'll be remembered somewhere."

Tameria's lips pressed into a thin line. "Actually, they erased yours. Officially, at least."

Moss sagged. "Of course they did."

"That's why I put that statue on the *Pegasi*."

Moss's eyes widened. "*You?*"

"You deserved to be remembered," said Tameria. "We all do. When that ship reaches its destination, it was always meant to stay in orbit, become a space station as the colony grew. It seemed fitting you be part of it."

"You did that for me?"

"Well, I didn't think you'd ever *see* it, you know."

Before she could say more, there was a scratch at the vent and a small voice said. "Hey, boss? Coast seems clear. No guards, no officers. Just some crewmen making repairs."

Moss got up and straightened his uniform, then picked up the crewman's datapad. "How do I look?"

"Could use a shave," said Tameria. "You think you'll be able to pass?"

"We're about to find out. Put those cuffs on. I'm done bitching about things. Time to get to work."

The trip to the science level was uneventful. As Moss had learned in life, the easiest way not to be noticed was to act like you belonged. A prisoner being led by a guard, visibly cuffed, might raise some eyebrows, but not questions. Holding a datapad or tablet didn't hurt either, since it made people assume you were doing something official.

You could call it a cliché, but clichés existed for a reason.

The otherwise bright hall began to darken with soot as they reached the lift, until the walls were black with scorch marks and the air was filled with the smell of burnt electronics and carpet. A large wall panel had been pulled off, and three crewmen were busy making repairs. They paid the two no mind.

"Guess the ship took a pounding after all," Moss said once they passed.

"Inductors don't just add heat, they inhibit a ship's ability to radiate or sink it," said Tameria. "Heat generates fast in a battle."

"Wonder what kind of shape the ship is in?"

"Hard to say," said Tameria. "Hopefully our new friends can fill us in."

Fortunately, the lift was empty when it arrived and nobody was waiting for them when they got off. They followed Trouble's instructions as to where to go, passing by the science lab on the way. Only it looked like someone had created a movie set of the interior of Tameria's shuttle. A half-dozen people were milling about—one seemed to be rehearsing lines from a datapad—and in the back they saw the NDT Station from the original *Outreach*.

"Well, that explains a lot," said Tameria. "And yet raises *so* many more questions..."

"Keep moving," said Moss. "You'll draw attention."

They found the right room at the end of the hall. It didn't open for them. Trouble had told them to knock instead of using the wall panel, which they did.

The door opened, and they found a pair of young synth crewmen waiting in the small room, a man and a woman. By freeborn standards, they looked like they were in their late-twenties, which meant they were probably under ten.

Despite the rapid development their brains went through, Moss couldn't help but think of them as kids. It didn't help that they stared at him with wide eyes. As much as Moss wanted to think it was because of his imposing good looks, he knew that stare for what it really was.

It was the look someone had when they began to comprehend how deep the shit they were in really was.

Behind the crewmen was a nondescript portable mainframe with a monitor. A voice called out once the door shut behind them. "Tam Tam!"

A huge grin grew on Tameria's face as it dawned on her this wasn't just *a* Violet talking to her, but *her* Violet.

"You survived!" she cried out, coming closer.

"Can't keep this bad bitch down," said Violet. "Hey Moss! Where's Hel?"

"On her way in the *Rex*," said Moss, glad to hear her voice. It was awfully cramped in this room, which was meant to be a workstation for one, so he wedged himself in the corner. There was a scratching sound at the vent as Trouble opened it and joined them.

"Well, the gang's all here," said Moss. "Violet, how about you catch us up on what's going on?"

Karon's heart raced as Violet made introductions. She felt like she was flailing in an EVA suit with no thrusters, looking for anything solid to grab. What had she gotten herself into? Two prisoners, here with them, who were going to help them...what? She had no idea what the plan was, just a vague idea of saving the freeborn on the colony ship.

As Violet began catching the others up on what they had learned, Karon started to feel the weight of all that was expected of her. Helping them meant stopping their own ship. Betraying the Silver Legion. Betraying her friends. How far did they expect her to go? How far *would* she go? She didn't want anyone to get hurt, but how could that possibly be avoided?

It was too much. Too much. *Too much.* By the time Violet had finished, Karon had begun to hyperventilate.

"Karon?" said Violet. "Karon? You okay?"

Then the Elysian named Tameria put her hand on Karon's shoulder.

"Karon? Breathe, okay? *Breathe.*"

Everything felt okay again. Calmer. She looked to the Elysian, who didn't seem so alien anymore. She was calm. In fact, everyone in the room looked calm.

"I know this is overwhelming," Tameria said. "There are no easy solutions. There's only what we can do, and what we can live with. I'm not going to ask you to do anything that betrays your conscience. But I am going to ask you to trust me when I say that I see a path forward."

Karon nodded. She wanted to trust her. The Elysian had to be using her glamour, but that was only calming her down physically. She was pretty sure she was still thinking clearly.

"Now, I've got one question I'm hoping you can clear up for me," said Tameria. "What is going on in the science lab? Why does it look like they're putting on a perfor...mance..." The subcredit dropped. "Did you get that machine working? The one from my shuttle? Did you talk to... *Who* are you talking to in there?"

Karon felt nervous all of a sudden. "I... I don't know. I haven't been in there. Roy said they found a personality matrix, and the science team thought..."

"Is it a copy of Violet?" Tameria was trying to suppress her anger, but Karon could feel it inside her somehow.

"N-no. Roy referred to it as a he. He said it starts to forget after a few minutes and they have to reboot it."

"Keed," Tameria said through gritted teeth. "They have Uncle Keed."

"They're trying to make him think your people revived him," said Moss. "Get whatever information they can before he goes senile, then use that information on the next run."

"How long have they been doing this to him?" asked Tameria. She was calm now, but that calmness made Karon even more nervous.

"Less than a week," said Len. "I heard it somehow managed to trick everyone and had been giving them false information for days."

Tameria turned her attention to Len. "Do you have clearance to enter the science lab?"

Len nodded. "It's no longer considered a priority project."

"Have you been in there before?"

"For this? No."

"Listen carefully. I want you and Karon to go in there and observe the next test they do, if you can. If they want you to leave, ask whatever questions you can about their project first. Were there any other personalities found with the machine? Does the personality start off equally stable with each reboot, or is it getting worse? Do you think you can get away with that?"

Len nodded. "I was bridge crew until recently."

"Good. We'll wait here. Go."

Karon and Len got up and left without further questions.

"Huh, *that* was easy," Moss said once the door shut. "Must be used to following orders."

"That, and a bit of a nudge," said Tameria.

"Ah. Not so hesitant about glamour abuse anymore, huh?"

"Desperate times. Speaking of which..." She looked to Trouble. "Where is it?"

Moss blanched. "Oh, no you don't. Trouble, don't you open your goddamn mouth."

"Moss!" Tameria hissed. "Not now!"

Trouble raised a finger. "But boss—"

"What's going on?" asked Violet.

"Oh, nothing," said Moss. "Just war crimes."

"*What?*" said Violet.

"*Moss,*" warned Tameria.

"Boss?"

"Shut up, Trouble. I'm sorry, but there are only *so* many ways one can interpret the words, 'They can't be allowed to return to the Terran Colony Fleet. Ever.' Then go looking for a sealed vial hidden in a secret safe."

"Tam Tam?" Violet said in disbelief.

Tameria's jaw clenched. She looked away. "It has to be done."

"Are you *kidding* me?" Moss looked to Trouble. "No matter what, Trouble, you are *not* to tell her where that vial is, understood?"

"But I've been trying to tell you, boss. I can't."

"What do you mean, *can't?*"

"Well, you see..."

There is a long way and a short way to describe the events that happened in the shuttle.

This is the *complete* way:

Moss leapt in front of the blast meant for Tameria, holding Trouble in front of his chest like a tiny human shield.

Fortunately for Trouble, the blast hit Moss low, *very* low, and was set to stun.

Unfortunately for Trouble, the stun blast made Moss convulse, and he'd squeezed the artificial mustelid till its eyes bulged, shattering the vial hidden within its chest cavity. Trouble gacked dramatically and amber liquid sprayed from its mouth in tiny droplets, which atomized into gas.

The now-unconscious Moss continued his weightless journey until his head cracked against the far wall, while the Vigile fired off a second and third shot, incapacitating Tameria before she could raise her weapon.

The Vigile passed through the invisible cloud left behind by Trouble, stopped his momentum the first chance he got, and went to secure the prisoners.

By then, however, Trouble had scurried off. Later, he'd be scurrying through the air vents of the *Hydrus*, still gassing.

"Oh God," said Moss. "It's already started."

Everything, Everywhere, All at Once

It's only after the battle is over that you fully compre-
hend how insignificant your part in it was.

M. Foote, *Portrait of the Pilot as a Cranky Ol' Man*

LIEUTENANT GINAN HAD FOUND the Martian escapees. A combination of investigation techniques had led him to Segment
129 of the habitat ring. There was one building there that was currently not in use and would be ideal for hiding people in.

He considered waiting for his cyborg officers to return before making his move, but it was unlikely he would need them. Instead, he
ordered six synth crewmen to accompany him. As least some of these
freeborn would know what a cyborg was capable of, and he expected
little resistance.

A small transport tube ran on either side of the habitat ring, one
travelling clockwise, the other counter-clockwise. While the ring did
not sport as impressive a view as the colony ships of the Fleet, it did
bring back memories of a time before the Terran Disaster. Some of
the stations around Earth had once had a similar aesthetic to this,
including the public transportation system.

Ginan rendezvoused with the security detail at the transport entrance closest to Segment 129, and led them to the abandoned building.

But before they arrived, the lieutenant suddenly felt a little... What was the word? He felt off balance. His stomach felt strange. Had something happened to the ring's rotation?

"Sir?" one of the guards asked. "Are you okay?"

Woozy. That was the word. It was nothing he'd ever experienced before, however. "Is everyone else all right? Has the ring changed speed?"

The guard looked puzzled and looked to the other guards, who were equally confused. "No sir. Everything's fine."

The feeling began to pass, but he could swear the gravity had gotten just a bit stronger.

"Should we...?" the guard ventured, unsure of what to say next. "Go...back?"

That snapped him out of it. Ginan shook off the feeling. "No. We continue as planned. Make sure your weapons are set for stun only, understood?" Whatever it was he'd felt, it was gone now. He could talk to Dr. Ascella about it later, when she was free.

Hel felt cold. She stared at all the blips on the active sensors.

One of her. Lots more of *them*.

There were big ships and small ships, and they were almost certainly *armed* ships. They were all headed for the same tiny point in space—the last known location of the *Viaticus Rex II.I*, and the *Pegasi*.

"That's a lot of pirates," said Violet. She was sitting in the captain's seat below, while Hel was above her on the co-pilot level.

"Yep. Still nothing on comms?"

"Not picking up any kind of comm activity, not even from the escort."

"Great."

"On the bright side," said Violet, "we're going to get there first."

"By how much?"

"Maybe five minutes."

"Swell. Hey, Vi?"

"Yeah?"

"Would Moss be running away right now?"

"Under ordinary circumstances? Yes. Under *these* circumstances...? Maybe. I mean, what can we do? There are enough Brotherhood ships on their way to take on a few patrol frigates... maybe even a cruiser. We don't know what happened to the escort, or if they're even armed... A lot of unknown variables here."

Hel had no intention of fighting a hopeless battle, but... "At the very least, we need to get there and see what's up. See if we can get everyone out of there before the party arrives. If we find nothing, or wreckage, we'll turn tail and run."

"Moss would approve," said Violet.

Number Four, commanding the Void Brotherhood's attack fleet, had no idea why a single ship was racing towards their destination. It was transport, as far as they could tell. Small or medium in size. The transit signature readings couldn't give her a definitive answer.

Number Four was a Nubran woman who had grown bored with her structured, orderly, restrictive, and *poor* life on the edge of the Protectorate, and so she had travelled to the Void to make her fortune.

Back then, her name had been Gwell. She'd ditched her surname just as she had ditched her family, and when she'd risen in the ranks of the Brotherhood, had no qualms about ditching her given name as well. Now she was Number Four, and she had a job to do: take the *Rapine* into battle.

The *Rapine* was a Snakehead-class corvette, one of the most dangerous in the Void Brotherhood's arsenal. While it lacked the capital-class weapons of a proper military vessel, it made up for it with a bristling array of pulse cannon turrets along its hull, and its hangar bay was filled with a dozen Locust snub fighters.

The fleet under her command was mostly made up of smaller ships. Transit capable fighters and light transports converted for combat. There were also two Piranha-class frigates, not as heavily shielded as the *Snakehead*, but decently armed.

It was the best she could put together on short notice. Many of the Brotherhood's interests were tied up elsewhere, and some of her requests for assistance had been met with blunt and vulgar rebuffs. She'd ended up recruiting most of her fighters from The Dump, and collected a few more from Number Three's scouts.

Her attention returned to the main display, showing her fleet's path to the *Hydrus*, and the solitary blip that was headed to the same destination.

"Will it get there before us?" she asked the navigator.

"By a few minutes."

"Most of the fighters are faster than us," her tactical officer pointed out. "We could send them ahead to intercept. Take it out as soon as it arrives?"

Number Four shook her head. "The result would be the same, and without support, those fighters won't last long against the *Hydrus*. I'd rather have every ship available drop out of transit at roughly the same time."

She had hoped to catch the crippled ship off guard, force a surrender. Perhaps the transport would be smart and warn the *Hydrus* how outmatched they were, tell them to stand down. But realistically, there was every chance the *Hydrus* would open fire the moment they arrived.

That was fine by her.

Commander Nekkar came out of the lift and took his seat on the bridge. "Status update." He didn't expect much to have changed.

The synth ensign filling in for Ginan on tactical answered. "Long range comms are still down. We have contact with the *Pegasi* through radio frequencies. Sensors are online, but only at short range. Transit drive is still down, but thrusters and engines are fully operational. Shields and weapons are still iffy."

Nekkar frowned at the man. "*Iffy?*"

The ensign grew nervous. "Er... They suffered a lot of heat damage and they might short out if they're used too much...or they might not. It's hard to know for certain until the repair teams can get a good look, and they're focused on other systems right now."

"So...iffy," said Nekkar.

"Yes, sir."

Nekkar mulled the word around in his head a moment, trying it out, and finding it to be more efficient than a drawn out explanation of uncertainty.

"Very well."

Everything seemed fine. He did not trust the Brotherhood to stick to their agreement without the threat of force to back it up, yet there was no reason for them to believe the *Hydrus* was in such a vulnerable condition.

Still, the situation felt...iffy.

"Mister Herzog to medbay, please."

Roy sighed, wondering what they wanted. He was starting to grow anxious. The Brotherhood could arrive at any time and the *Hydrus* was in worse shape than he'd anticipated. He'd intended the attack to be a diversion, but in their condition? It was possible the Brotherhood might *win*.

He wasn't the sort of person to have just one plan, but it seemed that *none* of them were working out the way he'd hoped. The pirate attack was supposed to be the last straw for a disheartened crew, but there was little chance of a mutiny now. At this point, he figured he could convince a half-dozen people to join him, tops. Not nearly enough for a snowball effect.

It was time to focus on his fallback position, his own escape. But that presented its own problems.

The *Hydrus*'s shuttles were only sub-transit capable, intended for in-system use. Even their comms were local. And right now, they were light years away from any star system.

It was a moot point, however, because neither shuttle was on the *Hydrus*. One had returned to the *Pegasi*, while the other was tending to the prisoners on one of the wrecked transports.

That left the fighters.

It wasn't his preferred escape plan. Part of him had hoped to convince Powell to join him. She could be useful, after all, and these days he'd rather work with a competent partner than alone.

But snub fighters were designed for a single pilot, and he didn't know if she knew how to fly one. Still, he kept the option open. After the battle for the *Pegasi*, he'd rigged the fighters closest to the hangar door to accept anyone, not just its assigned pilot. It was the best he could manage under the circumstances.

These fighters weren't even sub-transit capable, but at least they'd get him off the *Hydrus*. A quick message to whatever Brotherhood ship was in charge, say all the right things, and he should be able to get aboard.

And then what? He'd have to figure that part out later. In the short run, he could spin events with the Brotherhood to make him out as the hero, but in the long run? He wanted out from them just as much as he did the Legion.

One crisis at a time, though. He made his way down to medbay.

One crisis at a time, thought Moss.

"How bad is it?" Violet asked.

"Oh, I don't know. Ask Typhoid Tameria."

"*What*?" Tameria growled.

"Tam? What *exactly* did you do?" asked Violet. "Please don't tell me this is connected to what happened on the *Keres*. I mean, the Order didn't... That's not *your* work, is it?"

"I have no idea what you're talking about."

"Bull," said Moss.

"If you would just *listen* to me," Tameria snapped. "There's been growing concern that the Silver Legion might discover one of our Priories. The one we're heading to. We're more than capable of dealing with the usual threats and unhappy accidents, but if the TCF ever found one of our bases..."

"You'd have to, what, *move*?" Moss shrugged. "Big deal."

"What is it you like to say, Moss? It's complicated."

Lieutenant Ginan had his security team surround the building. If anyone managed to escape some other way, they'd be caught easily enough.

It was a small building, unadorned, intended for some kind of manufacturing that hadn't been needed in ages.

This was not a situation where negotiation would likely work. Now that the freeborn were backed into a corner, violence would be their most likely recourse.

Given where they'd come from, pulse weaponry was a possibility. No matter. He wore a silver breastplate and helmet this time, protecting his vital organs. His eye still ached a little from earlier, which was odd, but then he'd never had to regrow an eye before. He'd needed a gluke shot to deal with the regen fatigue.

Ginan's preferred approach for situations like this was shock-and-awe. Make it clear as quickly as possible how futile resistance was. He didn't particularly enjoy it, but it was effective. More importantly, it kept those under him out of harm's way.

He would wade through whatever punishment they tried to inflict, single out whoever seemed to be the leader, and knock them out.

Nine times out of ten, the rest would surrender.

Ginan nodded to his men and entered through the front doors.

"By order of the Silver Legion and the Terran Colony Fleet, you are to surrender!"

The dim interior was intended for machinery that had been packed away long ago. As such, there was a wide open area in front of him. Large boxes lined the walls, which the freeborn were most likely hiding behind, or possibly inside of. Anyone watching from the shadows would see his eyes glow slightly, much like those of a cat, as his lenses shifted to reflect what little light there was.

"Lay down your weapons and come out with your hands raised above your head!"

Still nothing. But he could hear them breathing now. He held his arms out wide, showing that he wasn't holding his sidearm.

"Your place is back at the Fleet with us. What terms are you looking for to ensure that nobody comes to harm? Who speaks for you?"

There was a cry of protest, a shuffle, and a shadow lurched from behind a set of boxes. At first, he thought the person was crouched low, but no, they were just small. Someone tried to grab them, but was held back by others.

As they came into the light, Ginan realized the person wasn't just small. It was a boy.

"I do," said the boy.

The *Rex* had finally picked up a signal. Despite the *Pegasi*'s great size, space was still infinitely larger, and without a transit signature or comms activity to help pinpoint its location, the ship didn't show up until they were almost on top of them.

It helped that they knew what they were looking for this time, though something about the readings seemed off to Hel.

"We're coming up on the location now," said Violet.

"Still nothing on comms?"

"Nothing. Only way we're getting info is to drop in and say hello. You ready?"

"Ready as I'm going to be," said Hel. "You?"

"Just hoping we don't find only wreckage there. Dropping from transit...now."

The *Viaticus Rex II.I* dropped to normal space.

"Oh crap!" yelled Hel. "Abort! Abort!"

They had expected a number of things. A Silver Legion heavy cruiser wasn't one of them.

"It's the *Hydrus*!" said Violet. "How the hell—?"

"Who cares how? Let's get out of here!"

Instead, Violet kicked in the thrusters and sped toward the *Pegasi*. She tried hailing them over radio frequencies.

"Hel, I got through to your ship. You take this, they're your people. I have something else to deal with."

"Gotcha. *UNSS Pegasi*, this is Helena Lambinon. Come in."

Lieutenant Hori answered. "Helena? You chose a lousy time to come home."

"Trust me, it's going to get worse. What's the situation with the *Hydrus*?"

"Come to bring the lost sheep home, whether we like it or not. Tossed Dhatta and our security around like rag dolls just to prove a point. Captain Foote and Sister Tameria were here too."

Hel thought she'd misheard that. "What do you mean, *were*?"

Number Four frowned as the unidentified transport blip disappeared. Right where they were heading. That confirmed it. No matter what, the *Hydrus* would be expecting them now.

"Try to hail the *Hydrus*," she said. "Inform them of our intentions and demand that they surrender."

A moment later, the comm officer said, "No response, sir."

So, were their comms still down, or were they preparing to fight? She had to assume the latter.

"All hands to battle stations. Slow down slightly and tell the transports to match speed. I want a staggered entry. Have half the fighters speed up. The rest will time their approach to arrive in waves of three every few seconds. Open fire immediately."

"Unidentified ship just arrived, sir," said the ensign at tactical. "Wait, our system just raised an alert for this ship. It's the *Viaticus Rex...* Ill?"

Nekkar scowled. "On screen."

The display showed the chimera turning tail and fleeing towards the *Pegasi*. He had no idea why they were here, but if they were hoping to interfere with his mission...

The woman at comms spoke up. "Sir? They're hailing us."

Nekkar nodded to allow the call through. The main screen changed to that of a female Terran pilot.

"*TCF Hydrus*, this is Violet Lonsdale, former Silver Legion, registered external asset. Service Number GF4909797."

"Check that," Nekkar said to the comms officer.

Violet continued. "There are multiple Brotherhood ships inbound on your position. I repeat, *multiple* ships. Drive signatures indicate a Snakehead, two Piranhas, and multiple small fighters and transports. ETA five minutes. You need to raise shields and launch fighters immediately. Acknowledge!"

Nekkar muted the comm from his chair and looked to tactical. "Do it." It certainly couldn't hurt, and the fighters would make sure the *Rex* wouldn't escape.

He switched channel. "Engineering. Change repair priority to shields and weapons immediately."

He then returned to Violet's channel and unmuted. "Chimera transport, designation *Viaticus Rex*"—he didn't bother with the silly numerals—"This is Commander Magnus Nekkar of the Silver Legion. Your warning is appreciated, but you are wanted for crimes against the Terran Colony Fleet. I order you to power down your ship and prepare to be boarded."

"*Nekkar*?" he heard the woman mutter. "*Hydrus*, given the *huge fucking fleet* I just said was incoming, that's going to be a hard pass."

He muted again and looked to his comms officer. "Is she who she says she is?"

"Yes, sir. Lieutenant Violet Lonsdale. Face, voice, and service number match. Left the Silver Legion in 292 PT. Registered as an external asset until 295. Suspected of freeing a number of freeborn she'd captured. No records after that."

Nekkar nodded and switched to shipwide comms. "All hands, battle stations!" He then contacted the disabled transport. "Dr. Ascella. Get everyone to the *Pegasi*. Prisoners included." He couldn't risk bringing them aboard the *Hydrus*, but wasn't going to risk losing them, either. In all likelihood, the Brotherhood wanted that colony ship intact. But the *Pegasi*'s hangar couldn't fit both shuttles. He called to the *Pegasi* next. "Ensign Yuri. Take shuttle one and provide fighter support."

"Understood." The shuttles were combat capable, though not an ideal choice. Ensign Yuri, however, was a talented pilot with a dozen campaigns under his belt. He'd manage.

He returned to Violet's channel, trying to sound calm. "You've been gone a long time, Lieutenant Lonsdale. Mind if I ask what you've been up to?"

"I died. Then I got better. How about you, Nekkar? Still a colossal prick?"

The ensign at tactical snorted.

Dr. Ascella still hadn't returned to the *Hydrus*. It was Dr. Phillips who had called Roy to medbay.

"Mister Herzog, good. I need to ask if you've been in contact with any other cyborgs on this ship since Lieutenant Gorn's return?"

"Gorn?" Roy leaned to the side so he could see around the doctor. Sitting on the edge of one of the medical beds was one of the large guards who had brought Foote and the Elysian over.

"Huh, so *that's* his name. You'd think I'd remember something like that."

The doctor's interest perked up. "Are you saying you're having memory issues?"

"No, just unfiltered mockery. What's all this about?"

A woman's voice came over the comms. "All pilots to fighters. Prepare to launch."

That wasn't good.

"If you could answer the question, please," said the doctor. "Have you been in contact with other cyborgs?"

"I try to avoid contact with my kind whenever possible. Spoils the brand," said Roy.

"So that's a no, then?"

"No, why?"

"What about the prisoners? Have they?"

"No."

"Have you been feeling dizzy at all? Loss of balance? Muscle fatigue?"

Roy raised an eyebrow. "You know what a cyborg is, don't you?" But his eyes drifted back to Gorn. "Is that what he's feeling?"

Phillips ignored the question. "Do you remember making physical contact with Gorn?"

"Okay, I'm going to stop answering questions now." He did *not* like where this was going.

"Mister Herzog, I'd like to run a few tests on you."

Nekkar's voice came over the comms now as red track lighting began to flash. "All hands, battle stations!"

Roy started to back up. "Yeah... I don't think so..."

Phillips tapped a button on his datapad and the medbay doors shut. "I'm going to have to ask you to stay, Mister Herzog."

Roy looked to Gorn, Phillips, and the door control function on the datapad.

To his credit, Phillips recognized the threat Roy posed. He'd brought up the bondscollar controls on his pad and tapped it. Then tapped it again. And again.

Roy smiled. "Biometrics don't care if you're conscious or unconscious, doctor. How that door opens is up to you."

Tameria sighed. "You have to understand, Terran cyborgs present a unique challenge to us. With most races, we can shut down their ships in a variety of ways, render them unconscious, alter their short-term memory, and relocate them so they're none the wiser. We've done it countless times.

"Cyborgs are immune to this. We've tried. It's probably why they're so damn stubborn. Our usual means of incapacitation are also ineffective. They would present a formidable physical threat if we were to try and board one of their ships. They're not likely to listen to reason, either. And if they found one of our Priories, or gained possession of one of our Bochords..." She shook her head.

"So we were forced to consider...other options."

An alarm could be heard outside the freeborn hideout, no doubt being broadcast across the ship. "*All crew to emergency stations. Repeat, all crew to emergency stations. This is not a drill. All civilians proceed to the nearest safety shelter.*"

Ginan called the security detail outside from his comm, speaking low so no one else could hear. "Parton. Find out what that's about. Report back."

Amidst the noise, the boy strode up to Ginan, doing his best to appear fearless.

"I am Zachariah Foote, son of Maurice Foote, and these people are under my protection."

Ginan tried not to smile. "Oh, are they now?"

"Yes. *All* sapient beings have the right to be free. You will not take these people this day, or any other day. I will fight to my last breath to protect them."

Ginan recognized those words from somewhere.

"Are... Are you quoting a *cartoon*?"

The cyborg took two long steps toward the kid and grabbed him by his jumpsuit. He lifted the boy up with ease.

That drew out the other freeborn. First, he saw the mother run towards him, then more advanced from behind boxes. No doubt they were prepared to surrender as long as he didn't hurt the boy. Predictable.

"Your father is aboard my ship, child. I think it's time you and the others joined him, don't you?"

Violet's warning to the *Hydrus* had been unexpected, but the more Hel thought about it, the more it made sense. If they hadn't seen the heavy cruiser on sensors before they dropped, they must have been running at low power. And if the *Hydrus* didn't already know that an attack fleet was almost on top of them, their long-range sensors couldn't possibly be working.

Bottom line, the *Hydrus* was all that stood between those pirates and the *Pegasi*. And they needed all the help they could get.

A shuttle disengaged from one of the wrecked Order transports and headed for the colony ship, and a dozen fighters swarmed out of the *Hydrus*'s hangar. This was mirrored on the *Rex*'s sensor projection, with the dots all showing up as red threats.

"It's not nearly enough," said Hel. "Is it?"

"Depends what kind of shape the *Hydrus* is in," said Violet. "One sec." She cut the comm but could hear her faintly through the hatch to the lower level. A moment later, the red dots became green, and she came back on. "Okay, we've exchanged IFFs."

Hel took a moment to appreciate what they'd landed themselves in the middle of. "Strange bedfellows, huh?"

"Still want to run?"

Hel felt ashamed about that. Her parents were on board the *Pegasi*, everyone she grew up with. Yet a few moments ago, she'd been ready to bail because the odds had been against them. Moss was really starting to rub off on her.

Then again, she'd wanted to run because she thought the situation was *hopeless*. This wasn't hopeless anymore, just really, *really* bad.

And what if you set aside what Moss said, and thought about what he *did*?

Hel took a deep breath. "Want to? Yes. Going to? No. I'll focus on marking threat priorities and power management. You keep us alive and make those assholes fear the name *Viaticus Rex*."

"That's my flygirl."

"ETA, one minute," said the *Rapine's* navigation officer.

Number Four could feel the anticipation of battle grow inside her. When they dropped, everyone would open fire. No hesitation. No bargaining. It would be chaos at first, but through that chaos, she would assess the situation and begin issuing proper orders, devise a plan, out-think her opponent's moves.

It would be like playing Turangcha... No, what was that quaint Terran strategy game again? Chess. Playing chess in the midst of a storm.

She heard the nav officer's calm voice say, "Thirty seconds to drop."

"*Viaticus Rex* is requesting IFF exchange," said tactical on the *Hydrus*.

"Accept it," said Nekkar. "But if we take any 'friendly fire' from them, mark them as hostile and make them a priority target."

The ensign nodded in acknowledgement.

Lieutenant Tauri said, "Bringing the ship about to 189 by minus 17." Based on Lonsdale's intel, that direction should give their guns the best firing angle when the pirate fleet dropped.

"How are the shields, Anser?" Nekkar asked over the comms.

"Operational, but it's hard to say how they'll hold up. There are a dozen places with damaged components on the verge of burning out. I've got people replacing or repairing what they can, and rerouting where possible."

"Weapons?"

"Case by case basis," said Anser. "Each turret might last the whole fight, or short out on the first volley. As for the main guns, I can guarantee one shot each. After that..."

"Iffy," muttered Nekkar.

"Ships dropping!" tactical cried out. "Multiple fighter signatures!"

He didn't have to give the order to open fire. The crew had been told to engage the moment the enemy dropped.

It seemed his opponent had given the same orders.

Dr. Phillips had made the correct choice, since it allowed him to continue treating his patients. Roy was on his way down to the hangar to get the hell off this ship.

The *Hydrus* shook and Roy lost his balance momentarily. Crap. The Brotherhood was already here. By the time he got to the hangar, there were no fighters left. Roy cursed under his breath.

There were always the escape pods, but that was too risky. They were programmed to flee a combat zone and await pickup. He had no way of knowing if he could override those controls and steer it towards the Brotherhood fleet, or even if he could contact them. There was every chance he'd get shot down along the way, too.

He went to a wall panel and brought up a display showing the ships outside. The *Hydrus* was in the centre, and a dozen red blips were closing in. A dozen green blips moved to intercept. A few more ships appeared, then a few more, and a few more...

Roy realized, however, two of the *Hydrus*'s fighters were not like the others. At first, he assumed they were the two shuttles, but one had a larger icon than the other. He looked closer at the designation.

Viaticus Rex II.I

He might have a way off this ship after all.

Roy ran for the brig just as the ship rocked again, making him stagger. Those felt like missile explosions. Any that got through the point defence would splash against the shields, but some of that force and energy would still get through.

The new plan was simple. Make a deal with Foote. Get him to a comm panel. Have his ship dock with the *Hydrus* somehow. They all get on board and escape. He might even have time to grab Powell. Whether or not he'd honour the deal after they escaped was another matter.

He entered the brig, only to find the security field down and the room empty.

"Oh, *come on!*"

Moss didn't care if a battle was going on outside. He still had a bone to pick.

"You can rationalize your actions all you want, Tam," said Moss. "Doesn't change what you're actually doing. You're going to kill everyone on this damn ship!"

Tameria gaped. "Are you *crazy*? That's not what the nanorepressor does."

Moss paused. "Sorry, the nano-what-now?"

Ginan held the boy so they were eye-to-eye, ignoring the latest call to report to the shelters.

"For..." the boy managed to gasp.

The Vigile saw the rage burning behind his eyes and pitied the lad. Imagine living your life in fear, unable to change what you saw as a great injustice.

"...the..."

Ginan could admit none of this was fair. But it *was* necessary.

Zach grit his teeth and yelled, "...*future!*"

Ginan looked down. The boy's foot was wedged deep between the lieutenant's legs.

He shouldn't have felt the kick. Of all the pulse gun bolts he'd taken in the *Pegasi*'s hangar, only the one that hit his eye had stung. Cyborg nervous systems automatically dialed down the pain receptors after a certain point, allowing them to continue fighting.

This was different.

This...*hurt*.

He dropped the boy, who suddenly weighed a thousand kilos, and collapsed to the ground. The agony grew so fast and intense he couldn't even cry out for his men. His muscles contracted and his body grew rigid. His skin was on fire. His muscles were either seizing or tearing themselves apart. Every joint was like a knife had been jammed into it.

Was this how freeborns experienced pain?

Ginan's vision blurred at the edges, but he could still see the boy standing over him, the look of shock on his face quickly replaced by joy. More faces soon joined him, looking at him and one another. One was carrying a metal pipe, another a kind of crowbar.

He had no idea what had happened to him, or if these people were even responsible, but he knew where this was going. He just hoped they made it quick.

Hel's eyes dashed around the various panels. She painted threats for Violet based on firepower and who they seemed to be targeting, and channeled the ship's power wherever Violet needed it most.

The initial pirate swarm was made up of light transit-capable fighters. Mostly Draxon ships like Dragonflies and Wasps, but there were also a couple of Argolis fighters and a Locris from Nubran space. These were the kind of ships pirates took on solo raids or in small groups, then bolted to another star system before the authorities arrived—if there even were any.

The pirates had the advantage in numbers, and despite the prevailing cliches, were not generally suicidal. They used swarm tactics to confuse their prey, allowing those with hull damage or weakened shields to fall back, while fresh ships occupied their attention.

But the snub fighters of the *Hydrus*, though smaller, were more than a match for these one-on-one and had some of the best training around. They coordinated focus fire to take down one ship after another. If a ship strafing the *Hydrus* got hit and tried to fall back, a wing of fighters would dog it to its destruction.

The pirates tried to exploit this, and that's where Violet focussed her attention now, peeling off the fighters that were harassing the harassers.

The *Rex* was armed with a fixed heavy laser for use against larger targets, and two pulse cannons for close range dogfighting, as well as a swarming mini-missile system. Missiles weren't as effective while a ship's shields were up, but the sight of a dozen of them swarming toward you made even the most hardened pirate break off and drop countermeasures. And once the shields were down? They'd tear you to shreds.

The second wave was made up of larger ships, multipurpose light freighters and heavy fighters like the Wolf, Coyote, and Hyena. They dove in as soon as they dropped from transit and started hitting the *Hydrus* with everything they had, from pulse guns to missiles.

The *Hydrus* did its best to evade and shoot down the incoming missiles, but it was a large target, and still took a pounding.

"Going to focus on that Hyena," Violet warned. "Get ready."

"Who *names* these ship types?" asked Hel.

"Blame the translators."

At this range, and given the size of the target, Violet opened up with the heavy laser. It spiked the ship's heat quickly, which Hel tried to sink as best she could. Without any gimbling, the laser required a steady hand to keep the beam locked, and Violet's was solid as a rock.

The *Rex*'s laser broke through the Hyena and drilled a hole right through its core, staking it like a vampire. The heavy fighter drifted dead in space as Violet sought a new target.

That was when Hel saw three more blips appear at the edge of her sensors. Big ones.

"Ah crap."

The *Rapine* and its two Piranha escorts arrived shortly after the last of the fighters dropped. It had been intentional, both to soften up their defences and provide Number Four with valuable data.

It seemed the *Hydrus* was not as weakened as she had hoped. Its shields were holding and its defensive turrets were operational. However, it only had half of its complement of fighters.

With so many of her ships already on site, Number Four was able to make a more precise drop to normal space, and did so at the farthest effective range of their turrets, but spread far apart from one another.

The *Hydrus*'s fighters would have to waste time trying to close in, and if they did, it would leave the heavy cruiser exposed. Meanwhile, her ships could pelt the *Hydrus* at their leisure, while the heavy cruiser would have to focus its fire on one of hers at a time.

"Release the swarm!"

The *Hydrus* shook from another wave of missiles. The shields were holding, but two of the turrets had gone offline. Nekkar ordered Tauri to reposition and minimize the enemy's chances of exploiting that gap.

The arrival of the corvette and frigates were more worrying, however. They arrived spread out, and the gap was growing wider, trying to flank them.

"Estimate the shield output of that Snakehead. Would two shots from the main guns get through?"

Tactical checked and shook his head. "Negative."

The Snakehead was the greater threat, but if he only had two shots from his "iffy" lasers, he had to make them count. "What about the Piranhas?"

Another check. "Aye."

"Charge the main guns. Fire *everything* at the port side Piranha. Time the kinetics to land after the shields are down."

A swarm of new blips entered the fray. It seemed the Snakehead had brought its own snub fighters.

"Main guns ready, sir!"

"*Fire!*"

The Piranha's shields glowed blue, then red, then vanished. One of the *Hydrus*'s lasers gave out just as the pulse cannon and kinetic fire landed, tearing the Piranha's hull to pieces.

Something must have hit the reactor in the worst possible way, because there was a bright flash seen from every hole and window in the ship, and then it just kept drifting with no energy signs at all, a burnt-out husk.

"Starboard laser's offline, sir. Port laser still functional."

It was far too early to celebrate, but this was a start.

Roy had no idea where Foote and the Elysian could be, but he wasn't about to play hide and seek with them. He was out of escape options, so the only thing he could think of, other than waiting to see how the battle panned out, was to check on Powell. Maybe she'd have an idea.

But Powell could be anywhere as well. She'd most likely be enlisted to help with repairs during the battle and after it was over. But it couldn't hurt to check her usual haunts first.

The ship shook again, harder this time, almost knocking Roy to the ground. Had they gotten through the shields?

Roy went to her workroom on the science level, as it was closer than their shared quarters two floors up. The door opened for him and he stepped inside, only to see Foote and the Elysian looking back at him in wide-eyed shock.

"I thought you locked the door," the Elysian hissed.

"I thought *you* did!" said Foote.

Roy was a cynic and a pessimist, though never a defeatist. Even the most cynical person knew that, once in a blue moon, things worked out better than you expected.

He grinned. "Just the guy I wanted to see."

The ship shook again, forcing Roy to grab the edge of the door. But it didn't seem to affect the Elysian. She leaped at him, almost catching him off guard. But a cyborg's reflexes were no joke. Even off balance, he easily parried her first two blows, then hooked her leg and dropped her to the floor.

But this woman was skilled. She rolled with the fall like she'd anticipated it, bouncing back and redoubling her attack. She was quite strong for someone with so little mass. Not wanting to waste any more time with her, he grabbed each of her fists as she threw her next punches.

The headbutt came as a surprise, though. What was more of a surprise was that it hurt.

Roy let go of the woman and staggered back into the hall. His hand went to his nose, and came away covered in blood.

Two crewmen came rushing down the hall towards him. Powell and Davis.

Powell's eyes widened. "Roy?"

"Pow—?" The word was choked off as his body seized up. He felt a pain that he had never thought possible. In his long life, he'd been shot, stabbed, burned, even tossed into the vacuum of space, but none of that compared to this. He fell to the ground, curling up into a fetal position, gasping for breath.

Before he blacked out, Powell and Davis rushed to his side, followed by the Elysian, and lastly by Foote, who looked at Roy, then at the Elysian.

"Pow indeed," said Foote.

"This won't hold him," said Moss, wrapping the cyborg up in another cord. Trouble was at the man's feet, giving them a good kick.

"Trust me, it will," said Tameria, sitting on the desk next to Violet's computer.

"Is he going to die?" asked Karon.

"No," said Moss, "but he's a lot easier to kill now."

"What did you do to him?" asked Len.

"It's called a nanorepressor," Moss said with unwarranted confidence. He paused and added. "That's all I really know. Tam?"

Tameria shook her head and looked to the stars for strength. "The cyborgs have unique abilities that make them extremely difficult for my people to deal with. We developed this as a means to painlessly negate those abilities."

Moss looked at the bound form of the cyborg, broken nose still bleeding, which should have already healed itself. Even unconscious, he looked like he was in agony.

"Painless?" said Moss.

"Ordinarily. The nanotech in the cyborgs cannot be removed any more than you can yank out your mitochondria. But it can be inhibited, limiting their strength, speed, and regenerative capabilities. The inhibitor is airborne, reproduces rapidly, and isn't recognized as a foreign body. By the time symptoms begin to show, it's already spread throughout the body."

Tameria stood. "The weakening process is meant to be gradual. As it affects the nervous system, the subject gets dizzy spells. Over time, they realize they are getting weaker. All in all, the process is supposed to take about a week."

Moss gestured to the unconscious cyborg. "And this?"

"An unexpected side effect. The nervous system is one of the first to be affected, including the pain receptors. Any sudden sharp amount of pain can shock the nanorepressors into overdrive. What should take a week happens in minutes."

"Everything, everywhere, all at once," said Violet.

Tameria nodded. "Every organ and bodily function, simultaneously. And with their pain receptors unable to inhibit what they feel…"

Everyone looked at the cyborg, who managed to make a sound like "*Hurk*?" as his body twitched.

Trouble, who was closest to the cyborg, sniffed the air, then tried to wave the odour away. "Oh, wow…"

"*Every* bodily function," Violet observed.

Crewman Parton was left in charge of the security detail surrounding the freeborn hideout while Ginan entered alone. His orders were to wait and prevent any freeborn from escaping. But the smart credits were on Lieutenant Ginan coming out the front doors with the freeborn, hands over their heads, and one or two requiring medical attention.

The front doors opened and Lieutenant Ginan came out…being dragged by two freeborn. Each had one of his arms over their shoulders. They dropped the cyborg to the ground and walked back inside, slamming the door behind them.

Parton had given a half-hearted "Halt?" while another said something about surrendering, but her voice just trailed off. They were all too mesmerized by what they were seeing here.

Lieutenant Ginan, beaten to a bloody pulp, but still breathing.

"Why isn't he healing?" asked one of the guards.

"Why isn't he *standing*?" asked another.

"What do we do now?" asked a third. "Do we rush them?"

Parton looked down at Ginan. "If they could do this to *him*, what do you think they'll do to us?"

"*Hurk*?" Ginan said as his body spasmed.

A moment later, Parton smelled something in the air. "Is this place near a farm?"

Hel noticed half of the incoming Locusts had peeled off and were heading for the *Pegasi*.

"What are they doing?"

"Hoping to draw off some of the *Hydrus*'s support," said Violet.

Hel noticed a distinct lack of fighters moving to intercept. "I don't think it's working."

"Neither do I. The *Hydrus* is fighting for its life. I saw the shields drop for a second."

From here, Hel could see the impact that window had had. The Legion's unique hull plating was formidable at reflecting energy weapons, but the big hole in its aft engine proved that against missiles, it was just like any other ship.

"Do you think they'll actually fire on the *Pegasi*?" asked Hel.

But Violet had already changed course to intercept. "I'm not waiting to find out."

Number Four felt a rush when the *Hydrus*'s shields went down, if only for a moment. And a missile making it through their defenses and striking one of their engines was even better.

The glorious Silver Legion, heroes for hire in the Void, weren't so invincible after all.

Taking down this ship would make her the most notorious pirate in the Brotherhood. Convoys would stand down and beg for mercy once they heard she was coming for them.

And what if she could disable the ship? Claim it? Wouldn't *that* be a prize?

She took a moment to check on the squadron of Locusts she'd sent to harass the helpless colony ship. It seemed only one of the Legion vessels had broken off in pursuit. She'd hoped for more.

"How many of our ships are going after that antique?" she asked tactical.

"Ten, sir. Er...nine. Make that eight. They're turning to engage...seven."

Her eyes widened. Perhaps one had been enough.

"Sir, the *Rex* has broken off to intercept the fighters targeting the *Pegasi*. Should we send support?"

Nekkar leaned forward. "Negative. They're trying to split our fire. All fighters continue to engage locally." He checked the damage display. Two more turrets were inoperable, and there was a big hole in their anti-missile coverage just waiting to be exploited. "Are we locked with the Piranha yet?"

"Just about."

"Once you do, hit it with everything we've got. Timed on target, and sustain." He wanted those shields to have no chance to recharge before they could hit it again. If they could take out the second Piranha and clear the fighters swarming the *Hydrus*, the Snakehead might think twice about continuing the fight.

The *Hydrus*'s remaining main gun glowed blue as it charged while every available turret stopped firing on the fighters and targeted the second Piranha. By the time the wave of fire made contact, the main gun fired, striking the frigate on the broadside as it tried to evade.

"Shields weakening," said the crewman. "Main gun recharging."

Just give me this shot, thought Nekkar. It would be enough to punch through the frigate and leave it vulnerable.

"Firing!"

Nothing happened. On the damage display, their second main gun flipped from a green outline to red.

Nekkar closed his eyes, the reality of the moment making him feel unsteady, even in his seat.

"Damn."

Roy regained consciousness in a world of pain.

He couldn't move.

Also, he was pretty sure he'd crapped his pants.

Moss sent Trouble to do recon through the vents. The two synths had left. The ship needed them more, and that was fine with him. He wanted to talk to Tameria and Violet in private.

"It won't kill anyone," said Moss.

"That's correct," said Tameria.

"No... I mean, that's all you needed to say back on the shuttle. *It won't kill anyone*. Simple. Do you know how many stories I've read where a big convoluted mess could have been avoided if people just *talked*? Ghah!"

Tameria frowned, trying to process what he was saying.

He paced back and forth as the ship shook a bit. "*You* say, it won't kill anyone. *I* go, really? *You* say, yes. *I* have my doubts, but I believe you because you're *you*. We release the nanorepressors on the *Pegasi*, stay hidden, and avoid this whole mess. You let me think we were going to commit some horrible war crime!"

Tameria laughed. Actually laughed. "You think we *didn't*?"

Now it was Moss's turn to frown.

"Do you have any idea how much I *didn't* want to do this?" asked Tameria. "To you, this just looks like some great equalizer, doesn't it?"

"Well...yeah."

"You can't fly. Does that give you the right to clip my wings? Should a Hopat have to suffer in high gravity as much as you do? Alter the Draxon to become individuals? Make no mistake, this *is* a crime. And it *is* horrible."

"Horrible? Come on, he's still alive." He looked at the twisted face of the cyborg who glared at him with enough hate to power a space station. "I mean, he'll get better, right?"

Tameria groaned, unable to look at him. "Imagine if I reduced you to the strength of a child for the rest of your life."

"Oh please. Violet, little help?"

The computer's camera shook back and forth. "Uh uh. I ain't jumping into *this* hole with you."

Moss stopped pacing. "Look, the pin's been pulled. Might as well make the most of it. Change is coming whether they like it or not. Am I right?"

Tameria turned back to him. "Do you think we're going to take this and use it on the rest of the Terran Colony Fleet? Because we're not. When I said that this ship and its crew can never be allowed to return, I meant it. We won't allow them to infect the rest of the population. We don't have the right."

Moss flared up. "Don't have the right? Are you *nuts*? Have you seen what they've turned humanity into?"

"And what do *you* think would happen if we released the repressor into the cyborg population? Would they give up their control, make everyone equal partners in a glorious new utopia?"

Moss sighed, cursing his oft-forgotten history degree. "Of course not. There would be civil war. A complete collapse of the current power structure, followed by more fighting trying to establish a new one. Probably another war between freeborn and synths for good measure after whatever alliance they made fell apart."

"And remember, the vast majority of your population lives on giant colony ships instead of a nice, stable planet. Add that to your civil war scenario. This could *destroy* you."

A pause filled the air. Moss tried to think of a counterargument. He couldn't.

Crewman Parton and his team decided discretion was the better part of valour, and left, carrying Lieutenant Ginan on a stretcher. His bruises still weren't healing, and the fact he had bruises at all was troubling. He continued to groan, his body still rigid.

They returned to the command ring. Dr. Ascella and her team had come aboard, along with prisoners from the destroyed transports. She would be the best person to treat the lieutenant. It also turned out they were fighting a pitched battle with the Void Brotherhood outside.

All in all, this was shaping up to be a hell of a day.

Even before Parton could brief the doctor, Ascella was scanning the lieutenant's vitals, horrified by what she saw. He did his best to explain what had happened. She finished her scan and frowned at the results.

"Did you give him a gluke shot?"

"He wasn't healing. It was the only thing I could think to do," said Parton.

"I understand, but how many?"

"Well, the first one did nothing, so I thought maybe he needed more, so...all of them?"

Ascella blew out in disbelief.

"Was that wrong?"

"Ordinarily, it wouldn't matter. But right now, in addition to the injuries he's taken, he's suffering from glucotoxicity." She then added in a sarcastic tone, "I think you just gave this man diabetes."

After some well-placed long-range shots with the heavy laser, the remaining ships had turned and come after the *Rex*. The ten Locusts had been whittled down to five, but now the *Rex* was starting to feel their sting. Or was that bite? What did locusts do, anyway?

Hel rerouted power from the thrusters to the shields. The impact on maneuverability was minimal, and it wasn't like they were trying to outrace them. But even with the extra power, the shields were dropping faster than they could charge.

"Come and get it, baby!" Violet yelled from below. She wondered if Violet was flying the ship through her body, through the ship computer, or both. Whatever it was, it sounded like she was having a good time.

Moss never enjoyed fighting, even if he was pretty good at it, but Violet? At times like this, Hel realized this was what she lived for.

"Come on!" yelled Violet, as she dodged, weaved, rolled, and fired. "Come on, you bastard! Come on, you too! Oh, you want some of this? Fuck you!"

That kind of scared her.

Number Four was elated. The *Hydrus*'s main guns were both offline and half their turrets inoperable. Meanwhile, both the *Rapine* and the Piranha transport had suffered no hull damage. The frigate's shields were greatly weakened, and the *Hydrus* continued to focus its fire on it, but even if she managed to take the frigate down, this battle was won.

Tactical cried out, "Ship inbound! Capital class. Unknown identification, but size indicates a Protectorate battleship."

"What?" Four snapped. The Protectorate? Here? They wouldn't dare!

"Wait. It can't be..." The man's voice trailed off.

"What is it?"

"It's...a *dreadnought*!"

Number Four's hearts stopped. That wasn't possible. There hadn't been an active dreadnought in the Protectorate in a thousand years.

"On the monitor!"

A call came from engineering as a panel blew out overhead, showering the bridge with sparks. "Hull temperature rising! Venting inactive! Heat sinking offline!"

Ordinarily in space, judging size was difficult without a frame of reference. But she knew the ship she saw on the monitor now. She'd built a model of it as a child, dreamed about commanding one in the last great conflict against the Draxon.

This warship was the size of a space station. It was so big...

"Orders, sir? Sir? *Sir!*"

So big...

Nekkar had seen Draxon battleships. Sometimes they went on maneuvers, patrolled the edge of the Void, but rarely, if ever, saw combat. Should the younger races within their borders get into conflict with one another, one might appear in the region to encourage them to behave.

This was *much* bigger.

At first, he was baffled. The Protectorate showing up in the Void at all was nearly unthinkable. But in a class of warship that was no longer supposed to exist?

Lieutenant Tauri called out to him. "Hull temperature rising! Bleed systems not responding!"

Then it all made sense. It wasn't the Protectorate at all.

"Cease fire," said the commander, leaning back in his chair. "Maintain shields if you can, but shut everything else off. This battle is over."

Roy felt terrible. He could barely move, and it hurt to try. He was bound with whatever happened to be lying around, it seemed, but he was in no condition to try breaking out.

Instead, he sat still, and listened as a voice came over the comms. But it wasn't the commander's voice, or anyone else Roy recognized.

"Attention all vessels. Cease fire immediately and disable your engines. If you continue to engage or attempt to leave, you will only destroy yourselves. This is your only warning. Tend to your wounded and repairs. Await further instructions."

Foote and the Elysian seemed thrilled by this, so he could only assume it was their cavalry that had arrived.

"What now?" asked Foote. "Sit back and wait to be rescued?"

The Elysian shook her head. "We should call Karon and Len back." She started tapping on the comm panel next to a computer. "If this is going to work out smoothly, there's something one of them has to do first."

Moss waited for Tameria to lay out the plan. But before she could, she had to be perfectly honest with them about what was going to happen after that.

At first, they were terrified. Then they were understanding, given the alternatives. It also seemed they both had a history with the commander and couldn't decide who should be the one to visit him on the bridge.

"He denied you your promotion," said Len.

"He broke your *neck*!" countered Karon.

"True. Still... *jan-ken* you for it?"

They waved their fists three times. Len laid his hand out flat, while Karon fashioned scissors with her fingers and cut his paper.

"Well, at least I get to watch," said Len.

Tameria seemed surprised by how well they were taking all this. "You understand what I'm saying, right? About never going back?"

They nodded. "We do," said Karon. "But can I ask you something? Do you think this Precentor of yours will speak with us if you ask him to?"

Tameria nodded. "I'm sure I can arrange that. But I'm afraid it won't change anything."

"We'll see."

Len and Karon left, needing to stop at the armoury before the bridge, leaving Moss and Tameria alone with Violet.

"What do you think she wants to say to the Precentor?" Moss asked.

Tameria shook her head. "No idea."

"I know," said Violet.

Tameria looked at the camera. "What?"

"Not telling."

Tameria ignored the bait and turned to Moss. "So, once they're done, it's going to be your turn. You going to be ready?"

"Let's worry about that after you make contact with your people."

"I've already established a channel. Give me five minutes to convince them of my idea."

Five minutes later, after some grumbling and griping, Tameria was given the all clear. It wouldn't be long before they got a call from the bridge.

She pulled out Moss's green and red luchador mask from her pocket. "What do you say, Maurice? One last moment of glory for Ranger M?"

Moss looked down at his borrowed Legion uniform. "Think you can steal a change of clothes from the amateur theatre company down the hall first?"

What Goes Around

The Silver Legion's practice of challenging a commanding officer was more commonly used in the first century of the TCF, while all the superhuman muscle men and women were still working out a pecking order. They kept the practice on the books even after it fell out of favour, because sometimes you just can't remove a stubborn supersoldier any other way.

M. Foote, *And Then Things Got Worse*

C OMMANDER NEKKAR SAT IN his chair, trying to find a path out of this mess, and not finding one.

They were helpless against the Order's cowardly weapon, but if they intended to board his ship and take it from him, they would find the Silver Legion did not back down easily.

He contacted security on the comms. "Lieutenant Gorn?"

"This is Travis, sir. Gorn's in medbay."

"What happened?"

"Not sure, sir. He reported there shortly after returning from the *Pegasi*."

It was something Nekkar would look into later. "Ensign Travis, begin arming the crew. We could be facing a boarding action at any moment."

"Aye, sir."

Nekkar also had to consider the possibility of scuttling the ship. He wanted to believe that these people would treat his crew well, but a secret society did not stay secret by allowing survivors to report on their existence.

Yet if extermination was what they faced, why disable their ships? Why not destroy them? No doubt interrogation was the goal, find out how much they knew and who else might know it, then deal with *those* people from the shadows.

No, he would not allow that to happen.

"Engineering?"

"Anser here."

"Are we capable of scuttling the ship?"

While self-destruct systems on board starships were the stuff of dramatic fiction—any *easy* way to destroy your ship was a disaster waiting to happen—reactors were simply contained explosions, and engineers knew all the ways to un-contain them.

There was a brief pause. "Yes, sir."

"Make the preparations, but do not act until I give the order."

He turned next to the crewman at comms. "Anything else from the dreadnought?"

She shook her head. "Negative. Only the looped message telling us to stand down and await further instructions."

Just then, the lift doors opened and Ensign Powell came onto the bridge, followed by Ensign Davis. Nekkar assumed it was to relieve someone, until Powell spoke.

"*Acting* Commander Nekkar, I challenge you for command of the *Hydrus*!"

Silence fell over the bridge.

Not that long ago, Nekkar had lashed out at Davis for questioning his judgement. There hadn't been a formal challenge, but what was said had been close enough for him to interpret it that way.

He'd broken Davis's neck with one blow. The ensign had only removed the medical brace a day ago.

Now here Powell was, *formally* challenging him.

Powell advanced, coming down to the lower half of the bridge to face Nekkar directly. "*Your* actions have brought us to this point, *acting* commander. Defeated, captured, and pursuing an immoral cause."

He would grant Powell this much. She spoke like a proper member of the Legion. Forceful, confident. But something the woman said kept Nekkar from simply ending this as quickly as he had with Davis.

"*Immoral?*"

Powell didn't elaborate, but threw a punch as soon as she was within reach.

Nekkar caught the fist easily, then realized too late why the woman had been wearing gloves.

The bridge crew saw Nekkar easily catch Powell's punch. But instead of crushing her hand or throwing her across the room, he just stood there, glaring. Only Davis knew what was happening, and why.

Powell glared at Nekkar and said, "How does it feel?"

Nekkar dropped to one knee, still glaring up at Powell, then fell to his side.

All eyes were on Powell as she removed the stun gloves she wore. Security used them to pacify troublemakers without resorting to stronger measures. But an electric shock should have had no effect on the commander.

While everyone was wondering just what the heck had happened, Davis moved to the comm station and tapped the crewman sitting there on the shoulder. "I'll take it from here."

He took her seat and patched through to the correct room on the science deck.

"You're on," he said, and connected Moss to every panel on the ship.

Whether they were manning weapons, repairing equipment, or laying in medbay, the crew of the *Hydrus* saw a man in a flight suit, wearing a green and red mask, arms crossed.

"People of the Silver Legion, this is Ranger M," he said dramatically. "I speak on behalf of those who have put an end to this pointless battle. The people of the *Pegasi* are neither yours to claim, nor the pirates' to steal. All sapient beings have the right to be free. You will not take these people this day, or any other day.

"The crew of this ship, and those on the *Pegasi*, have been exposed to the Samson virus, which affects only Terran cyborgs..."

All across the *Hydrus*, men and women looked at each other, wondering if this was for real, or the most bizarre joke ever played.

They never considered it might be both.

"Samson virus?" asked Tameria.

Moss shrugged, eager to get the mask off. He'd just spent the last ten minutes explaining things to the crew in the most dramatic way possible, and he'd forgotten to wash the mask back on Komi Station. "The name needed more pizazz. Nanorepressor lacked gravitas."

"It's not really a virus."

"Might as well be, given how you described it," said Moss. "Hey, do you think I came off a bit...supervillany?"

"Moss, you just explained to the crew how you released a devastating weapon that cripples cyborgs while wearing a wrestling mask. I'm surprised you didn't cackle!"

Moss looked at the mask in his hands before putting it away. "Guess he was due a heel turn."

Tameria frowned. "Hold on... I might have your mythology wrong, but shouldn't you have called it the Dalilah virus?"

"I'll leave that up to your marketing department," said Moss. "Come on, we should get to the bridge."

Tameria looked to the bound cyborg. "What about him?"

The cyborg was conscious now. Whatever fire was in him seemed to have burned out, but Moss's gut told him that might be a trick. "Yeah, I don't feel safe untying him just yet. We'll deal with him later."

By the time Moss and Tameria reached the bridge, the former commander was being laid out on a stretcher. Karon was sitting in the commander's chair, speaking with a stout Hopat on the main display. A Nubran, presumably the first officer, sat in the chair next to him.

"Brother Reece," she said as they came off the lift.

The Hopat gave a wide smile in greeting. "Sister Tameria. I have been assured by the commander here that our presence will not be challenged. Can you confirm this?"

Tameria nodded. "I trust Commander Powell. She has the crew's best interests at heart."

"We will deal with the Brotherhood ships in the usual manner," said Reece. "I have been informed of the new protocol regarding contact with the Silver Legion. Is it true the nanorepressor was released?"

"*Samson virus*," Moss coughed quietly to himself.

The medics lifted the former commander up on the stretcher to take him down to medbay. The woman sitting at navigation looked very nervous as he passed. The cyborg convulsed slightly and made a sound like, "*Hurk?*"

"That's correct," said Tameria.

"I see. How should we proceed?"

"Transfer the crew of the *Hydrus* to the *Pegasi*. Allow them to complete their mission."

Brother Reece looked to the new commander. "Commander Powell? Will there be any problems?"

"Sister Tameria knows my terms for our cooperation and has agreed," said Powell. "Lieutenant Davis will assist me with the matter."

Len looked over to the commander, confused. Karon gave him a nod. "Field promotion."

Moss sidled up next to Tameria as the two ship captains continued their conversation.

"So, what happens next?"

The Last Flight of Captain Keed

The Neuro-Digital Transfer program was a great idea,
hampered by the small problem that it didn't work very
well. Violet was their first and, for a long time, only
success.
But given how quickly Violet grew, they had to rethink
its use for a while.
And when it comes to the Order, a while can be a very
long time.

M. Foote – *Inside the Order*
(REDACTED–INVESTIGATION LAUNCHED)

CAPTAIN KEED RANDGAFFI REMEMBERED a bright flash, his body seizing in full cardiac arrest and collapsing to the ground.

Then he felt different, weird, but no longer in pain. His first instinct was to call out.

"H...Hello?"

There was no answer, but he was quickly able to see, just not through his eyes.

He could see the bridge of a Silver Legion heavy cruiser. He could see the halls. The galley. The medbay. The hangar.

He understood what must have happened, but was extremely confused at the same time. There was supposed to be an evaluation period when a consciousness was transferred to see if it was stable. Transferring a pilot consciousness to a ship was one of the possible uses for this technology, and the one he'd signed on for if his NDT turned out to be stable. But how in the nine suns had he ended up *here*? And why was the ship empty?

In his consciousness, a flashing caught his attention. His perception was beginning to interpret all the data that he had access to in ways he could understand and interact with. This was someone trying to contact him on a comm.

He activated it, and saw his niece on a screen, smiling.

"Hi, Uncle Keed."

"Tameria! Was the transfer successful? I don't remember any evaluation."

Tam's smile didn't fall, but he could still see the disappointment on her face. "I'm sorry, it wasn't."

"Then...why am I in control of a ship? Why am I in control of a *Legion* ship? An *empty* Legion ship?"

"It's a long story, uncle. Being connected to the ship's computer will extend the time before your thoughts start to degrade, but not indefinitely."

If Keed could have nodded, he would have. "Understood."

"You joined the Order because you wanted to balance the scales, remember?"

He did. His misspent youth had been one of a double life. He'd been a loving uncle and supporting older brother whenever he visited her family.

He'd also been one of the most notorious solo pirates in the Elysian Gap, and had hurt a lot of people. His time in the Order had helped make up for that, but it never felt like enough.

Tameria summarized recent events, and the importance of the mission she wanted him to undertake. He agreed without hesitation. This was going to help make sure a lot of people would stay safe. How could he refuse?

"Repairs should hold long enough for this to work," said Tameria. "The comm message is set to go off once you begin the transit collapse." She then let out a breath. "Are you ready?"

Much of what Keed needed to do had already been programed into the ship's computer. Really, he wasn't needed for much, other than to make sure nothing went wrong along the way. The whole thing could have been automated. Which made him wonder why she was using him instead.

"There's one more thing," said Tameria. "Your body is on board. It's stored in medbay. I thought you'd like to know."

Keed wished she could see him smile. Now he understood.

"Goodbye, Uncle Keed."

"Goodbye, Tameria. Be good."

The *TCF Toro* was monitoring the Void near Ramedan space, following up on reports of increased Brotherhood activity and rumours of a muster for a large engagement.

The *Toro* was a patrol frigate, fitted with long range sensors and comms linked directly to the Colony Fleet.

One of the other reasons the *Toro* was out here was to look for any sign of a missing heavy cruiser, the *Hydrus*.

After losing their commander in a tragic accident, the sub-commander had pursued a number of freeborn across the Void, then inexplicably interfered with the production of a major network's newest reality show. It had been a public relations disaster, and the *Hydrus* had been called back to the Fleet.

They lost all communications with the ship shortly after that, and speculation had exploded as to what might have happened. Theories included mental breakdown, mutiny, secret mission, and abduction by an ancient alien race that predated the Protectorate and was only now waking from its long slumber.

The commander of the *Toro* had five credits down on the latter. Not that he believed it, just that it would be amusing if he got to collect, given the ten-thousand-to-one odds.

The comm officer called to him. "We're picking up a distress call... It's the *Hydrus*. Audio only."

The commander's heart jumped a little. "Let's hear it."

"...failure imminent. I repeat. This is Commander Nekkar of the *TCF Hydrus*. We have suffered catastrophic damage to our drive system. It is currently locked, and we cannot safely disengage. Transit failure imminent. I rep—" The comm went dead.

"Anything on sensors?" he asked the nav officer.

"I had their signature for a moment, but..." The woman's voice trailed off.

Given the distance the wreckage would be spread out, and the Transit Interference Zone it had just created, it seemed what had happened to the *Hydrus* would remain a mystery after all.

Elysians come from a low gravity world. While they did not evolve their wings naturally, they are as much a part of them now as their arms and legs. Flight is synonymous with freedom. That freedom is honoured even in death, when their ashes are taken to the top of a hill or mountain and tossed into the wind. For those who spend their lives travelling the stars, space is equally acceptable.

When the *Hydrus*'s transit field collapsed, it did so unevenly. Given the speed the heavy cruiser was travelling, this scattered the remains of the ship, and Captain Keed, over the better part of a light year.

Not many Elysians got a chance to oversee their own funerals.

What Happens Next

2 *541 – PROTECTORATE SPACE*

When Moss first learned of Violet's prognosis, he had gone to the Order, hoping to find a way to save her. Begging might have been involved. But while there was nothing they could do for her body, there was, perhaps, something they could do for her mind.

Once he'd returned from beyond the Protectorate, the Order had taken the implant he'd removed. They said it would take time to determine if it worked or not.

Moss had taken Violet's body to a red dwarf off the shoulder of Orion, a small nod to both one of her favourite old movies and TV shows. There her body would remain at a Lagrange point, orbiting its lone, dead world.

When he returned to the Order, a Brother had presented him with the device, told him how to use it, then told him to get lost and lose their contact information.

They were still sore about being forced into exile.

Alone in his cockpit, Moss tapped the figurine on his inactive dashboard, as if that would make the process work faster.

Within its base was a deceptively intricate, compressed neural network. One that couldn't do anything on its own, but if allowed to interface with and expand within a powerful computer system, such as those on board a starship? Well, only time would tell.

It was almost certainly illegal. The Protectorate had ancient laws against the creation of artificial intelligence, and for good reason.

But the argument here was that the intelligence wasn't artificial at all. It was Violet, or, at least, it should be. It would probably take centuries for the philosophers to sort it all out. Assuming it even worked.

As if on cue, the ship's computers hummed back to life, and through the camera in the figurine's head, Violet woke up and looked at Moss.

"Hey there, flyboy. Miss me?"

2550 – *The Void*

It would take some time for the *Pegasi*, carrying most of the *Hydrus*'s crew, to arrive at its final destination. The dreadnought—actually called the *Dreadnought*—had brought replacement transports, which would help the colony ship complete its journey.

Moss and Tameria briefly stopped on the *Pegasi*, where she connected her Violet with the new *Outreach*, and had her final conversation with her uncle.

The *Rex* was too big to dock inside the *Pegasi*'s hangar, so Moss's reunion had to wait until they were all on the *Dreadnought*.

As the *Outreach* entered its massive hangar, he could see the *Rex* already there waiting for them. The hangar was large enough to accommodate the *Viaticus Rex*, the *Outreach*, the two *Hydrus* shuttles the Order decided to keep, and the three transports it had arrived with, with plenty of room to spare.

Moss looked over the hull of the *Rex*, not finding any damage to it. Amazing how much he'd missed that ship in such a short amount of time.

No, not the ship. The crew.

Moss almost ran off the shuttle once it had touched down. Hel was waiting for him by the passenger ramp, ready to give him a hug when he arrived. He tousled her hair instead.

"You kept her in one piece," said Moss. "Good job."

"Does that mean I can have a raise?" asked Hel.

"Not *that* good."

Coming down from the passenger ramp was another figure, one he'd recognize anywhere.

It was the first time he'd seen Violet in her new body. She had her preferred style of flight suit on, her dark hair and eyes the same as he remembered. There was no faint shimmer of holographic tech, the bright hangar lights didn't bleed through her, and he could hear her every step as she approached. She looked so... real.

It wasn't *her*. He knew that. But that didn't matter. She had as much claim to the name as the original did.

Violet came to him with that confident smile that had carried her through life and hugged him, knowing full well he wasn't a hugger.

"Hey there, flyboy. Miss me?"

Moss hugged her back without reservation. "Damn straight I did."

From the cockpit of the *Outreach*, Sister Tameria watched Moss's reunion with his crew.

"Ahhhh," said her Violet. "That's sweet."

It was. It really was. It also reminded her of her last conversation with Moss back on Elan.

Why can't you be happy?

He looked pretty happy now.

"So, Tam Tam..." said Violet. "Can we talk about getting me a body too?"

"We'll see. Your sister is doing things I don't think our scientists ever expected."

"They expected us to be happy being a ship our whole lives? Your scientists need to get *laid*."

The trip to Ataraxia only took the *Dreadnought* a few days, but it would take weeks for the *Pegasi* to catch up. Additional ships had been dispatched to act as a proper escort, and to clean up the Brotherhood situation.

As promised, Tameria had brought Karon, Len, and a couple other members of the synth crew with her. For the most part, they stayed on the *Outreach*, strategizing with her and Violet for their meeting with the Precentor. She didn't spend much time with Moss. Right now, this was more important.

Their proposal was ambitious, even noble. Tameria did what she could to make it workable, but she doubted the Precentor would agree to it. Violet, however, was more confident about their chances. Said something about working on the greatest Picard speech ever for Karon, whatever that meant.

When the announcement came that they were arriving at Ataraxia, everyone gathered in the observation room. Once there, Karon and the synths, Hel, even Moss, all stared out in awe.

It must have been a strange sight for them. A pristine world, so much like Earth from a thousand years ago. Yet looming nearby was a red fireball so close it seemed ready to swallow the planet whole, even though it was one of the smallest and coolest class of stars around.

It seemed impossible, and it very nearly was. Out of the billions of red dwarfs drones had explored during the Long Survey, back in the Protectorate's second millennia, worlds like this had been encountered only a handful of times. And those reports had been quietly altered before being stored on the Protectorate's database.

Tameria noticed that Hel was alone and wondered if everything was okay. She sidled up next to her. "Where's Violet?"

Hel tapped her ear. "She's watching everything on camera. Says it's beautiful."

"But she's not here. Is something wrong?"

Hel shook her head. "The further she gets from the ship, the more it feels like an out-of-body experience."

"That's a shame," said Tameria.

"She's working on it." Hel looked out at the blue-green world. "So...this is home. For my parents, I mean."

"And you, if you want."

Hel chuckled. "Not yet. Maybe not ever. Besides..." She tapped her ear.

Tameria nodded, understanding, but also feeling a little melancholic. "Some people just don't have a home, I guess."

"Naw. They just take their home with them."

Tameria looked over to where Moss was standing, alone, taking in the view with his hands behind his back. Next to him stood Trouble, hands behind its back, mirroring him.

Hel noticed. "Where do you two stand, anyway?"

"I wish I knew."

"You like him, though, right? I mean, *like* him like him." Hel suddenly frowned and turned away, listening to her comm. "What do you mean, *teenager*? I'm twenty-six. Well, do *you* think you can do a better... Oh. Fine." She turned back. "Violet wants to talk to you."

Tameria smiled and patched in. "Hello, Violet."

"Look. You *know* how you feel. The reason you're hesitating isn't because you don't know if you like him. It's because you don't know if he likes himself. That's what frustrates you. Well, that and you're a workaholic."

"Well, you tell me. Does he?"

"Take a close look at him right now. Then talk to him. Then ask him if that world reminds him of Eden 3. You'll have your answer."

Tameria shook her head and turned the comm off. "Violet enjoys drama, doesn't she?"

"She lives for it," Hel confirmed. "She just told me to move closer so she can hear your conversation." She rolled her eyes. "Aaaand she just called me a snitch."

Tameria blew out a breath and went to join Moss. He didn't have as stoic an expression as she first thought. He wore a faint smile as he looked down at Ataraxia, at the red dwarf, at the stars.

"Guess you don't see something like this every day," said Tameria.

That broke Moss out of whatever spell he had been under. "No, not really. I've explored a lot of worlds. Red dwarfs are almost always a dud. Saw a few tidally locked worlds with life hanging by a thread along the terminator zone. Nothing like this."

"What about Eden 3?"

Moss frowned. "Is it still called that?"

"I don't know. That's just the name I heard."

Moss chuckled. "Guess Violet remembers. Eden was a placeholder name we used out in the Golden Parsec. After we found our first Earth-like world out there, we didn't expect to find another. So when we found a second, Violet called it Eden 2: Electric Boogaloo. Eden 3 was nicknamed The Revenge."

He looked back down at the planet gently spinning below them. "You know, it does remind me of Eden 3, except for the red dwarf. Eden 3's is more yellow-white. Way further back. I think we spent half a week just flying around it before we even decided to land. The northern hemisphere had severe tectonic action in the past. Huge mountains packed tight together. We took turns weaving through th em..."

As Moss went on, Tameria saw a light come on that she had never seen before. He spoke of trees there that could move, how he suspected it was a migration trait due to the planet's very long seasons. He spoke of sapient dolphin analogs that wore primitive armour and carried spears, which had ruined their first day at the beach.

Even when he talked about problems, like the jungle vines that wrapped around the *Rex*'s landing gear and made horrible baby cries when they were hacked off as the air escaped, he did so with a sense of awe. The crankiness was still there, she supposed, but that was only out of habit.

"...and then we found a lake that actually *sang*. Strangest harmonics anomaly we'd ever come across. You see, there were these crystals all along the lake bed..."

He was lost in his recollections now, staring at the planet below, enough so that she could briefly step aside and turn her comm back on.

"I think I understand," she said.

"Told you," said Violet.

A shuttle arrived to pick Moss and the others up and bring them down to the planet's surface. Moss took a window seat, while Hel took the aisle. The Violets had stayed behind to catch up.

Moss had never visited a Priory before. His time working with the Order had been done largely from the margins. He'd been on their ships and even met with a couple of Precentors, but his role in the organization had always been best categorized as "gopher."

The Order's ships needed to hide in plain sight, and so bore no unique look. They instead modified commonly used ships that could be un-modified in a hurry. The *Dreadnought* was an exception, but it was also never meant to be seen by anyone outside the organization. At least, not for long.

The Priory was another matter. It wasn't just a building; it was a small city. Its towers rose into the clouds, and its architecture could only be described as grand. It was like thousands of years of history had been coalesced and reborn.

The closer Moss got, the more he hated it. Not for what it was, but what it represented.

The shuttle they were on was strictly for orbital passage, so everyone was seated and everyone could see everyone else, though the seats could turn to accommodate conversations. Tameria was talking to the four synths from the *Hydrus*, giving them a crash course on what to expect next. She wore her formal thin grey robes, which Moss always thought made these guys look like they were having a spa day.

"It's important to be respectful at all times," she said to Karon. "I know that sounds obvious, but you won't get anywhere with him any other way."

Moss interrupted from his seat a few rows over. "Hey, which Precentor is it, anyway? Do I know him?"

Tameria bit her lower lip before she said, "Vargoya."

Ah, crap. He said nothing, however, not wanting to sour the mood.

Hel saw the look on his face and leaned in. "Is that bad?"

"He's the one who gave me my nickname in the Order."

"The one you hate?"

"There's one I like?"

The Precentor was all peace and love and stuff on the outside, but incredibly difficult to persuade about...well, anything. Moss knew from experience. He was like a drill sergeant who expected you to shout, "how high?" if he told you to jump, but said it in the nicest, most understanding way possible.

Tameria continued with her lecture as the ship comms announced their imminent landing. "He has to believe that you *understand* what we stand for and why we do what we do. Otherwise, he'll dismiss whatever you have to say."

Yep, sounded like Vargoya.

As they disembarked, Hel gawked at the buildings like an awe-struck tourist.

"Tam said we should go to the museum while she handles the meeting," she said. "Learn about the history of the Protectorate. What do you think?"

Moss shrugged. "Might be interesting. Probably biased, though."

"Yeah, well, what history isn't?"

"Touché."

Before they could leave, an Elysian glided in and landed in front of Tameria. Either he worked out to cope with the higher gravity, or that grey onesie he wore had some kind of grav assist built in.

"Sister Tameria?"

"Yes?"

"Is there one among you named Foote?"

Ah, crap.

For a moment Moss thought that Tameria might lie, but after a beat she said, "Yes."

"The Precentor has summoned him. He is to see him immediately. Alone."

Ah, crap!

Tameria turned and scowled at Moss.

Moss's hands flew into the air. "How is this *my* fault?"

"Just try not to get the colony exiled before they've even arrived."

No Time Like the Precentor

There is no denying the beauty you'll see in a Priory. These places were built to last and embody everything noble about the Order. And that's part of the problem. The longer you're in one, the more it feels like a trap. Like somehow everything about this place has been designed to reassure people of the righteousness of their cause. Some old Earth cathedrals carried the same vibe, even if they didn't share an architectural style.

M. Foote – *Inside the Order*
(REDACTED–INVESTIGATION ONGOING)

M OSS FOLLOWED HIS GUIDE down a great corridor to a set of double doors not too far from an outdoor garden. He announced Moss's arrival to a Nubran brother sitting at the reception desk outside, and left.

"You're expected," the man said. "Please go in."

Moss had been thinking about how to handle this since the summons arrived. According to Tameria, he needed to be respectful at all times. He could do that.

Well, he could fake that.

What Moss *wanted* to do was go in there and...yell. The vague idea of a fiery speech of righteous indignation popped into his head, railing against...what exactly? He didn't even know.

He also imagined every half-baked accusation he threw at them would be casually rebuffed, which would only piss him off more.

He opened the doors. Precentor Vargoya was an elderly Nubran with a kind, yet unreadable expression. He sat at his desk, wearing a traditional robe, but wasn't pretending to be busy by working on a computer or putting a ship in a bottle or some other contrivance.

Moss decided to let the Precentor set the tone for their conversation. Respect would be met by respect.

Vargoya frowned. "Once again you have made things complicated, *Homewrecker*."

So much for respect.

"Is this conversation just between you and me?" Moss asked. "You're not going to hold anything I say or do against the others that are coming?"

"No."

"Good." Moss sat in the chair across from the Precentor and kicked his feet up onto the desk. "So, whadayawant?"

Vargoya's eyes narrowed at Moss's boots.

Moss smiled. "I'm here because you want to dress me down. Make me feel small. Probably punish me in some way. I couldn't care less about your desk."

"Actually, you're here because I wish to thank you."

Moss looked at his feet and slowly put them back on the floor.

"Um...sorry?"

The Precentor's face remained unreadable. "You have made things complicated, but that seems to be in your nature. I did not say it was deliberate."

"Yeah, well, the nickname you gave me carries a bit of spite with it. Also, it makes me sound like I flirt with married men."

"It does not translate well into your language, I know."

Looked like they were back to respect, for now. "Why am I really here?"

"Sister Tameria has briefed me on your actions these past weeks, and I believe my past opinion of you may have been in error."

It was hard to describe how much Moss had wanted to hear something like that. He also couldn't accept it.

"It sounds like Tameria might be trying to make me look good. The truth is, I didn't do all that much. Heck, I almost screwed everything up. If I hadn't been with Tam, things would have turned out the same way. Maybe better."

"Perhaps. Perhaps not. I am not here to bicker about what might have been." The Precentor stood. "Walk with me."

Moss followed him out the door. The Precentor said nothing for a while until they reached the central courtyard, where several great trees stood amidst a beautiful tall garden. He could feel the buffer zone of a gravity field and saw the signs in GalCom indicating the garden was a low-g area. The central tree had a platform on top, where people sat at tables, taking in the view.

They didn't go in the garden, however. Instead, Vargoya walked around its perimeter. "Years ago, when you exposed the Order, I ascribed your motivations to fear, panic, and self-interest."

"Sounds like me."

"My opinion did not change when you discovered the *Pegasi*, nor when you pirated one of our ships carrying refuges. Things worked out favourably, but not, I believed, by your design."

"To be fair, not much happens by my design. I just sorta roll with the punches."

The Precentor's lips tightened as they continued to walk. "Your recent actions tell a different story. I heard what you agreed to in order to help the junkyard people on Komi station."

Moss thought about another five hundred episodes of Ranger M being made. "Don't remind me."

"I'm sure you had other options."

"Yeah, well, it was the only one I could think of that didn't end in a gunfight," said Moss. "And it kinda did anyway."

"Then there was the incident on the *Pegasi*, when you tried to stop Sister Tameria—"

"Look, if she had just *told* me—"

"Stop. *Please,*" Vargoya snapped. "By the Goddess, your prattling tries my patience. I'm trying to tell you that your actions were correct, given the impression you were under. Had we become *that* desperate to protect this world, then we would not deserve it."

Moss's lips twisted. "Tameria seems to think a line was still crossed."

A nod. "Had the repressor, the one you called Samson, been introduced into the general population, it would have been."

"Can I ask about it?" said Moss. "I mean, if you're here to tell me I'm not a complete screw up, I'm assuming that means you trust me."

"Actually, those are unrelated matters, and I do *not* trust you. But I will answer what I can."

"So, you developed the Samson virus because cyborgs are immune to your usual means of hiding your tracks, right? Stun weapons don't work, gas isn't effective. Basically, you have to shoot to kill just to annoy them. And even if you neutralize them, memory alteration doesn't work."

"Correct."

"That's not a coincidence, is it?"

Moss noticed a slight change in the Precentor's otherwise serene face. The look of someone who had underestimated their opponent a moment too late.

"Oh wow. I'm right?"

"I did not say that."

Moss wasn't listening. "I mean, cyborgs were made in anticipation of another war against the synths, so all the combat stuff makes sense. But why would their minds just *happen* to resist your advanced brain tweakers? Something no one outside the Order should know about... Only someone *does*, don't they? And they've known for a *long* time."

Moss anticipated the Precentor's objections and barrelled forward. "The whole cyborg thing always bugged me, and not just the name. Call me old-fashioned, but I prefer my borgs to have more chrome and look less like romance cover models.

"But then, how does a major breakthrough in genetics, on a scale not even the *Elysians* have pulled off, happen on a backwater world that had barely discovered transit tech? How'd they make so many in such a short period of time?

"I never thought much of it while it was happening. Earth was still isolated, and we'd had synths for ages. Why would a super-synth feel out of place? And what are secret government operations if not secret?

"But then the Protectorate gets worried about all this. They talk about intervening. They *say* it's to stop another war, but what if it's because they want to get a closer look at what Earth is up to? Investigate?

"Then, during the largest standoff in our history, Earth is wiped out. Nobody knows which side did it. More disturbingly, nobody knows *how*. But it also happens to destroy all the evidence of pretty much everything they've been up to.

"And this kind of explosion has only been seen once before, in an early transit drive experiment. The one that created the Scar on Jupiter. No one can explain how that happened, either. In theory, it shouldn't be possible. Yet it happened in Sol. *Twice*."

Moss started to pace ahead of Vargoya as more ideas slotted together. "The conspiracy I uncovered to expose the Order? That wasn't the Protectorate's internal affairs and spy agencies at play. They were just pieces being moved on a board, weren't they?"

He stopped and faced the Precentor, who nodded. "And, as you may have surmised, so are your people."

Moss let out a breath. On the one hand, it was gratifying to have his theory confirmed. On the other, it was terrifying. "I kinda hoped you were going to call me a crazy conspiracy theorist."

A hint of a smirk broke through Vargoya's placid expression. "I was tempted. There *are* explanations to satisfy each of the points you bring up."

"What stopped you?"

"You tried to stop us. Eliminating the *Hydrus* crew would have been an easy way out of your predicament. The logical one. These people were going to round up three thousand of your kin and do unthinkable things to them, because they believe it could save millions of others. The Terran I thought I knew would have jumped at the chance to save his own hide."

Moss scowled. "Shows how much you know about me."

"Indeed. So why didn't you?"

Moss crossed his arms. "You talk about numbers—hundreds, thousands, millions—as if they mean something. The equation is a lot simpler than that. I've killed people, and sometimes I've been glad I did. Some assholes just need killing. Won't ever think otherwise.

"But once you stop caring about the person standing *next* to them? Once you see them as an obstacle between you and the asshole? That's when you've lost your way. The most terrifying thing I ever felt was when I thought your lot had gone down that road. Because God knows where you'd have stopped."

Vargoya nodded and continued their walk. "Correct."

Moss followed, hands in his pockets. "So, am I supposed to keep guessing about this thing, or are you going to tell me what's going on?"

Now Vargoya didn't hide his smile. "I'm genuinely curious to see where your imagination takes you. What do *you* think?"

Moss thought about it. "Okay...so there's some shadow organization involved in all this. The yin to your yang. Maybe they've been around as long as you. Hell, maybe you were once the same group. How am I doing?"

"We call them the Council," said Vargoya. "They have only been around for the last six hundred years, after the Great Leap Forward. They are not connected to us. In fact, we each went a very long time not knowing about the other."

"Okay, so this Shadow Council—"

"Just Council," Vargoya corrected.

"Shadow Council sounds better, trust me. Talk to your marketing department."

The Precentor shook his head.

"Anyway, this Shadow Council plays a long game, like you. They don't think in terms of years, or even decades, but centuries."

"Correct."

"So what they were doing on Earth probably wasn't their endgame. More like a test run. Proof of concept."

"Agreed."

"So, did this Shadow Council send some agents in black suits to meet with the Earth government in secret way back? Tell them the way to deal with their synth problem was to build a better synth? Provide them with resources? Guide their research?"

"Almost certainly."

"And once the Protectorate threatened to start snooping around, it was no big deal for them to destroy the whole planet. They already got what they needed."

"Most likely."

"So...are they done with us now?"

"I fear not. Despite the loss of your homeworld, we believe the Council sees a place for Terrans in their grand design. Or perhaps they simply see you as guinea pigs."

"The *TCF Keres*..." said Moss. "That was them, wasn't it?"

"Yes. It was an experiment—we know that much. But to what end, we still don't know."

"And these guys are as good as you are at staying hidden."

Vargoya shook his head. "Better. They have no qualms about killing."

"Great. What's this Shadow Council's mandate, anyway?"

"Please stop calling them that."

"It'll catch on. Trust me."

The Precentor sighed, though whether it was from the news he was about to give or Mossfoot's exasperating behaviour was hard to say.

"We do not know for certain, but we do know that the Terrans were lucky. After the Great Leap Forward, when younger races were being discovered in numbers no one expected, we recorded extinction level events on a number of worlds. Worlds that had recently entered the technological age. Worlds like yours. We believe the Council was responsible, but in ways that could not be attributed to any external source."

"Nudge an asteroid here, set off a super volcano there..." Moss supplied.

"Precisely. These incidents appeared natural, yet the frequency was far beyond a statistical anomaly. We looked for other young worlds at risk, monitored them, and protected them in our own way."

"Nudging away an asteroid here, venting a super volcano there..."

"Which is how, I believe, we came to be noticed by them. They saw us as a threat to their machinations, and eventually, they tried to remove us."

Moss smirked. "Enter the glorious jackass to muck up *those* plans."

"Not as much as you think. If their goal was to diminish our influence, it was still a success. No, this secret war has not ended, but it has entered a new phase. The Council is on the move, and we must make preparations."

Moss felt a swell of pride. If the Precentor was telling him all this, it had to be for a reason. "Okay, I'm in. What do you need me to do?"

"You? We need you to leave."

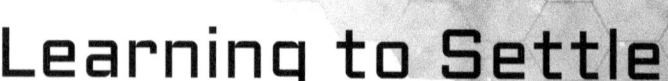

Learning to Settle

Some things you will need to adjust to: The gravity will not feel right. There will be no lean to account for based on the ring's rotation, and this will be disorientating at first, possibly inducing bouts of nausea.

Agoraphobia is also to be expected, especially when viewing the horizon. The land won't curve up the way you feel it should. It's important not to panic. This is normal.

The sky might be the most unusual thing of all to get used to. No amount of video programing will properly prepare you for it...

USNN Pegasi *Field Guide to Resettlement*

T AMERIA PRACTICED HER BREATHING techniques while she waited outside the Precentor's office with Karon and the three other synths she'd brought from the *Hydrus*.

It wasn't working.

A voice came over the comms. "Hey Tam Tam, what's wrong?"

Tameria excused herself so she could have a private conversation with Violet. "What makes you say something's wrong?"

"You left your comm on. You're breathing like you're pretending everything's fine while your ship burns up on re-entry."

"He's going to screw things up for these kids," Tameria said.

"You don't know that," said Violet.

"He's probably lecturing the Precentor about all the ways he felt the Order is messed up. How it's distanced from the people they're trying to help. How they take too damn long to make decisions when lives are at stake, because they have to look at the myriad ways it might affect the big picture, only nobody tells you what that big picture is until..." She stopped to take a breath.

"Is that how Moss feels about them, or you?" asked Violet.

"That was Moss's Violet, by the way," said Tameria's Violet. "She's here in the cockpit."

"This is going to get confusing," said Tameria.

"Hang on. I'll add a filter so you can tell us apart."

"I wouldn't worry about it." Moss's Violet now sounded like she was ninety. "Moss is... What the? Oh, you *bitch*."

Tameria's Violet giggled.

At least they'd broken the tension. Tameria relaxed, just a little.

She saw Moss and Precentor Vargoya further down the hall, returning to his office, still in conversation. The Precentor didn't look angry, so that was a good sign. She hurried back to the others.

"He's coming. Do you have any last questions?" She tried not to sound as stressed as she felt.

"I think we'll manage," said Karon. "Thank you for everything."

"I hope it works."

"If it doesn't, we'll understand," said Len. "We'll be fine. We'll find a new life with the colonists."

Karon nodded in agreement. "But after everything we've discussed, I'm convinced we have to try. You have to be the change you want to see in the world."

Moss and the Precentor arrived. Vargoya nodded a farewell to Moss and waved the synth delegation into his office. The doors shut once they were inside, leaving Moss and Tameria alone.

"What did the Precentor say?" she asked.

"Tell you on the way back," said Moss, "I have some thinking to do." He looked at the closed doors. "Are they're screwed?"

"I don't know," said Tameria. "I did what I could, but..."

"Any other day I'd put my money on screwed. You guys are big on sticking to your long-term plans. He'd listen politely, file the proposal away, his successor would review it and file it away, and then maybe *his* successor would bring it up at a meeting and everyone would decide more research is needed... You can take the Order out of the Protectorate, but you can't take the Protectorate out of the Order."

Tameria chuckled at the truth in that. "What changed your mind?"

"Change. It's coming whether they like it or not. Right now, they're as open to new ideas as they're ever going to be. Their survival depends on it."

Karon held her breath as they were led inside the Precentor's office. The doors closed quietly behind them, and she let the breath out.

She looked to Len, who gave a reassuring nod. The others began to set up for the presentation. They'd all worked on this proposal together, but as the official commander of the *Hydrus*'s crew, it fell on her to make their case.

The Precentor took to his chair behind his desk and waited until he had everyone's attention.

"Thank you for meeting with us, Precentor Vargoya," said Karon.

"Commander Powell. I should warn you that the fate of your crew is not a matter for debate. You cannot return to the Terran Colony Fleet."

Karon nodded. "I understand."

"So I am a bit puzzled as to what you believe you are here to accomplish."

This was it. Time to jump out the airlock and hope the pressure suit held.

"Precentor Vargoya. We understand the role the Order has played in shepherding the Protectorate over the millennia. Worlds that have been saved. Wars that have been prevented. We know you do not plan with an eye on the next ten years, but the next thousand.

"We are not here to speak on behalf of the Silver Legion, the Terran Colony Fleet, nor the Triumvirate that leads them. We are not here to rationalize what we've done in the past, nor who we are now."

She called up the first image on the projector, a symbol that looked like an asymmetrical arrowhead, known to certain circles as the Delta.

"We are here on behalf of who we could *become*."

When the *UNSS Pegasi* finally dropped into orbit around Ataraxia, Captain Mbatha poured himself a glass of whisky from a bottle that had been set aside by the very first captain of the *Pegasi*, Captain Benjamin.

It tasted *terrible,* and yet it had been the most satisfying moment of his life. There would never be another like it.

The colonists celebrated as only a generation ship could upon arriving at their new home. Ships of the Order gave a welcoming flyby, putting on a light show that everyone could see through the various observation windows.

The northern continent had been set aide for them. The Order had removed their outposts so the Terrans could do with the land as they saw fit, without interference or influence. And they quickly got to work.

The *Pegasi* originally had six disassembled shuttles packed away for this day. Two had been lost, but the remaining four were now being used to ferry people and supplies to the surface.

Captain Mbatha took a more assertive role upon their arrival. Given their new situation with the crew of the *Hydrus*, he decided the time for compromise for the sake of harmony had well and truly passed. Surprisingly, Lieutenant Dhatta had offered little resistance. The fight, it seemed, had been beaten out of him. The playbook their ancestors had written had to be thrown out the window, and a new one made from scratch.

To that end, Mbatha had kept in contact with Commander Powell during their journey. She had some very interesting ideas to share. Naïve, perhaps, but well worth attempting.

The refugees from Mars had found it easy to fit in with the rest of the colonists. The boy who had claimed to be the son of Captain Foote had been speaking to Mbatha on their behalf, and his standing had only risen since he had defeated a Silver Legion cyborg with one blow.

The boy was intelligent and possessed the fearlessness of youth he'd once had long ago. Someday, he might even prove himself to be a leader. Mbatha decided he would share whatever wisdom he might have to see that happen.

The crew of the *Hydrus* had been a bit more sombre about their arrival, given the fate that now awaited them.

The Order called it Diaspora. Forced relocation. Permanent exile. While the Samson virus did not affect the synth crew directly, it was designed to be carried by them. So even if they could escape this planet, they could never return to the Fleet.

When the crew had learned what the *Pegasi* colonists would have faced back at the Fleet, most had been horrified. Many among the older crew still believed in the Reintegration Doctrine, even though it had been suspended more than a decade ago. Most still believed that, despite their differences, things would work out in the end.

Now they not only understood how the TCF truly saw the free-born, but the synths as well. There was no telling how many of their kind had been created in secret to act as test subjects.

A few suggested making the command staff walk the lock. Even those who hadn't supported the idea had been complicit in their silence. But they were shouted down by a vocal and united faction of the crew who insisted if there was ever going to be a better way, it had to start *before* the bodies piled up, not after.

By a strange coincidence, these people were all friends of Lieutenant Davis.

In the future, should the Silver Legion cross paths with the Order again, accidentally or on purpose, this planet was where they would be brought.

And so, in a very real sense, Roy Herzog had gone right back to the Dump.

Roy had been trying to find a way out of this mess the moment he recovered aboard the *Pegasi*. The crippling pain the Samson virus inflicted had lasted for hours. All the while, he could feel himself becoming...less.

By the time they arrived at this world, every cyborg's nanotech had been suppressed. Strength, speed, healing, senses, probably even longevity. They were no greater than the synths they once led. Only their minds seemed unaffected.

And Roy's mind continued to work the problem.

In terms of technology, they were limited to whatever the *Pegasi* could manufacture, so there was no way to develop transit tech or interstellar comms. It went without saying that trying to *take* such things from the Order would be a bad idea.

He had accumulated enough goodwill among the synths to join them in setting up base camp. If Foote had warned them about him, it had gone unheeded. All they saw was someone who had been on the new commander's side from the beginning.

The *Pegasi*'s camp wasn't far away, but exactly how any kind of integration might work hadn't been decided yet. For now, they would keep to their own command structures.

Roy considered escape. The woods here went on forever. But to what end? And for once, he had to fear what the local wildlife might throw at him. No. This was his world, at least for now, so his focus shifted to finding a way to fit in, perhaps find a position of influence. See where things led from there.

A shuttle zipped over the camp, causing everyone to look up at the red dwarf that covered a quarter of the sky. It was an Order shuttle.

When it landed, Powell—Commander Powell—came down off the ramp, along with Davis and a couple of others.

Powell had to deal with greeting a number of people after the shuttle left, but after that, she'd come straight to him.

"Hey, Roy. Got a minute?"

Roy stood and gave a salute, fist to chest. "Sir, yes, sir!" He'd hoped that would get a smile out of her. It didn't.

She looked around. This camp had been set up near the treeline, but elevated to facilitate shuttle landings and have a better surrounding view. It was just a bunch of tents for now. Work on something more permanent would begin tomorrow.

She motioned to the cliff edge overlooking the ocean, and he followed her there. It was a good view, he had to admit. The ocean, the beach, the cliffs, the trees. Untouched as far as the eye could see.

He gave it a century before they messed it all up.

"It's funny," said Powell. "This is we all ever really wanted. A world of our own to settle."

"Not really ours, though, is it?" said Roy. "Even if the Order wasn't here, there'd be some technicality preventing us from claiming it."

"Maybe. How do you feel?"

Roy squeezed his forearm, frowning. "Honestly? Strange. I feel like I'm made of putty. The muscles don't work right. It's like they're for show, or something. I hate it... but at least I'm not in pain anymore."

"That's good."

Roy changed the subject. "So... Not many ensigns jump all the way to commander, you know?" he said. "Actually, I don't think it's ever been done. I'm impressed. How's *that* feel?"

Karon shook her head. "Temporary. I did what I had to. The rank doesn't mean anything. We'll sort who should be in charge later."

"Don't sell yourself short," said Roy. "You could run this show, easy. And if you ever need advice..." He let the idea hang there.

Powell sighed. "I had a long talk with the Precentor."

"About what, exactly?"

"The Order's plan was to leave the colonists alone, no contact whatsoever. That was as much their idea as it was the *Pegasi*'s. I got him to reconsider. Sort of. Should be interesting to see what happens."

That *was* interesting. But Karon was staring off towards the ocean horizon now, not him.

"What's wrong?" asked Roy.

"Captain Foote gave me a book during the trip. *Lord of the Flies*. Have you read it?"

He had. "Bunch of kids trapped on a desert island. Everything goes to hell. Was he trying to scare you?"

"He was trying to warn me. What do you think the story was trying to say?"

Roy considered the question, but didn't take long. "When push comes to shove, humans are a bunch of savages. You've got people like Ralph and Piggy who have the big ideas, but they can't stop guys like Jack who want power, because in the end, the sheep let him take it."

"Sound familiar?"

Roy remembered their conversation on the *Hydrus*, talking about the freeborn, synths, and cyborgs.

"Let me put this another way," said Karon. "Let's say you were one of the survivors. What would you do?"

Without hesitation, Roy said, "The smart thing to do is kill Jack. Day one."

"Funny. Moss said the exact same thing."

Roy realized that Karon had taken a step back.

"He also said that you're Jack."

A shove was all it would take. Roy's combat experience was based on strength and reflexes he no longer had.

Nekkar, Ginan, the others, she wasn't worried about them. They hadn't just lost their power over the synths; they'd lost their respect. But Roy? Roy was dangerous.

The smart thing to do is kill Jack.

Roy turned around. She heard the waves crashing on the rocks far below. Neither of them said anything. If one of them had, it would make this moment, this choice, real. Then one of them would be forced to act upon it.

But just because something was the smart thing to do, didn't mean it was the *right* thing. If she did it, everything she'd said to the Precentor would have been a lie.

Karon stepped aside, giving Roy a clear path, and gestured back towards the camp. "You're living on a timer now, Roy. Just like the rest of us. I'd like to show you how you can make the most of it."

Cautiously, Roy stepped away from the cliff's edge and followed.

Severance Day

INSIDE THE *DREADNOUGHT'S* HANGAR, the *Viaticus Rex II.I* looked surprisingly small. And inside the *Rex* itself, there was an awful lot of room to move around in, even if you ignored the cargo holds. But at the moment, in the galley, it felt a bit cramped.

Moss, Tameria, and Hel had returned to find not one, but two Violets aboard. The *Outreach's* copy was patching into the *Rex's* holo projectors. Moss had told Violet he wanted to have a group meeting but hadn't expected this.

Moss and Tameria had had a long time to talk on the way back to the spaceport, and by the time Hel joined them from the museum, they'd come to an agreement.

Now it was time to see if everyone else would go along with it.

He looked to Hel and Violet—the *Rex*'s Violet—and said, "I just want to say that your work up till now has been fantastic. I couldn't have asked for a better crew. Hel, you asked for a raise, well you got it. Same with you, Violet."

"Yes!" Hel and *Rex* Violet bumped fists.

"And you're both fired."

"*What*?"

Tameria rolled her eyes, but Moss had to see the looks on their faces. "Thing is, I'm leaving the Protectorate. So is Tam."

Tameria took over from there. "What Odyssey Expeditions still calls the Golden Parsec is of great interest to the Order, because it lies outside Protectorate space. In the last decade, colonists have been moving there in greater numbers. We have an opportunity to establish another fallback position, should things go badly here."

"What do you mean, 'go badly here'?" asked Hel.

Moss wasn't comfortable with this part. "The Precentor told me some stuff in confidence, which means he expects me to blab it to everyone eventually, but I don't think I'm the right one to tell you. Tam will brief you later."

"It's an evil Order," said *Outreach* Violet. "Has to be."

Rex Violet agreed. "What do you figure, unknowable ancient aliens woken from a thousand-year slumber, or just a bunch of assholes?"

"When in doubt, always assume assholes," said *Outreach* Violet.

"I'm sure that's close enough," said Moss.

"So, you're establishing a new base there?" asked Hel.

Moss shook his head. "You know how the Order works. They plan so far ahead they already have their great grandkids' names figured out. Right now, they just need someone to explore, survey, map, that sort of thing."

"And to help the colonists," Tameria added. "It's in our best interests to make sure those colonies succeed and cooperate. There's going to be competition from people trying to get a leg up on the other settlements. Other nearby worlds. Admins with delusions of grandeur, struggling colonies tempted to turn to piracy..."

"And who knows what else there is to find out there?" said Moss, his excitement growing. "Violet and I barely scratched the surface on most of those worlds, and there could still be more to find not far off."

"Sounds like a job for Ranger M," said Hel, not even trying to hide her smirk.

"You'd think that would push my button," said Moss. "But no."

He stood and took the green and red luchador mask out of his pocket. "When I first met you, Hel, I was at my lowest point... Well, top three. I held onto this as a reminder of what could have been. This, and the Violet that came before you two, was all I had connecting me to the past. Even when I tried to get my old ship back, I didn't, really.

"But everything that's happened these past few months, everyone I've encountered, has taught me one thing. You can't go back. You can only move forward." He turned to Tameria and smiled. She smiled b ack.

Then *Rex* Violet had to spoil it. "Yeah, but you're going back to the Golden Parsec, so..."

Moss groaned and rubbed his temple.

Hel put a hand on *Rex* Violet's knee. "Vi? Don't ruin his metaphor. Besides, it's not going to be the same place it was a decade ago."

"*Thank* you," said Moss.

Hel turned back to him. "But wait, why can't we come? I mean, it sounds like an adventure."

"And if you're firing me, where am I supposed to go?" asked *Rex* Violet. "I *literally* live inside this ship." Her eyes widened. "Oh my God. You're giving us the ship!"

Moss's eyes bulged. "You nuts? I'm keeping the *Rex*!"

"We'd like to give you the *Outreach*," said Tameria.

"Consider it your severance package," Moss added.

Tam nodded. "I've already cleared it with my superiors. She doesn't carry much in terms of cargo, but, well, you've already seen what she can do."

Outreach Violet raised her hand. "Um, what about me?"

"You're coming with us," said Tam.

Outreach Violet pumped a fist. "Yes! Free holo upgrade!"

Hel frowned. "We're gonna see you again, right? I mean, this isn't some lame goodbye. Because that would..." She seemed to have trouble putting her feelings into words and settled for, "Suck."

"I figure we'll be gone three years. It'll take the *Rex* six months just to get there."

Tameria spoke up. "Actually, I've asked for an upgrade to your transit drive, like on the *Outreach*, plus a fuel scoop."

That last part had been long overdue. "Okay then, scratch that. It'll probably only take a few months, so let's say two years. Then we'll see what's what."

"Unfortunately, the colonists haven't constructed a Q-comm relay yet," Tameria said, "so communications will have some serious lag until it reaches the Protectorate network. Still, we want you to keep in touch."

Moss laid the mask out on the galley table. "The way I see it, if you stick with me too long, you won't have a chance to find out who you really are. Maybe you'll want to help other people out, or maybe you'll just want to get stinking rich. Either way, you're gonna need this."

He slid the mask over to Hel.

Hel stared at it. Looked at Moss. Slid it back.

"Yeah, I'm not putting that on."

"*Fine*," Moss muttered, and jabbed a finger at her. "But you're taking Trouble."

"Where *is* he, anyway?" asked Hel.

Moss looked sideways at the refrigerator. "Beats me."

Moss sat in the pilot's seat of the *Viaticus Rex II.I*. Tameria was on the level above in the co-pilot seat. The Violets had swapped places, and the one from the *Outreach* was busy sorting out all the virtual assets she'd inherited from her older sister. Hel and her Violet were already on their way back to Nubra space, ready to start a new life together.

The *Rex* faced out from the *Dreadnought*'s hangar, so Moss could see the stars. Ataraxia and its star were behind them.

"Everything checks out up here," said Tam over the comms. "How about you?"

"Huh?"

"I said all systems are go. Something wrong?"

"Sorry... Just thinking."

"About what?"

"Life."

Moss heard her groan. "Here we go..."

"It's not like that. I was just thinking about what we talked about before, in the cell."

"About how life just ends and none of it matters?"

"After that. When I said the only things that endure are the lies we tell ourselves. The stories."

The word hung in the air until Tam said, "And?"

"And I remembered that stories aren't all lies. They're full of lies, but the stories that matter are like guides. They point toward the truth." Moss took a breath. "I think I'm okay with that."

There was a pause and then, "Is this about the second season of *Ranger M*?"

Moss looked at the mask hanging from a hook on the edge of his nav console. "Maybe a little." He sighed, checking the ship's readings. "Everything looks fine. Ready to launch."

Violet appeared next to him, sitting on the console. "About time. I was getting sick of all the navel gazing."

"Sorry to bore you," said Moss.

Violet shrugged. "So, off on a new adventure. You know what you have to say."

"No chance in hell. Now focus on the ship, will you? You're still new here."

Moss switched Violet's projectors and comms off while he started the engines.

And when he was absolutely sure that no one was listening, he whispered the words to himself.

Epilogue: For the Future

As Gilganan and his companions returned from the great battle, he looked to them and saw that they required solace. "What is the matter?" he asked.

"We are sad that our time has come to an end," they said. "That you will move on to new lands and we will be left behind."

"Nonsense," said Gilganan. "You will not be left behind any more than I. You will have your own adventures, and someday our paths shall cross again. If not in this life, then in the next."

"But how can you be sure?"

"There are no true endings in life, nor are there true beginnings, for more often than not, one is also the other."

The Way of Things—Gilganan Saga

3550 – Diogenes, Audiens Independent Sector (formerly Eden 3)

Violet pushed her nearly empty cart down the aisle until she reached the last row of shelves. She picked up the last two books on the cart and put them away. She had a bit of trouble reaching the top shelf and made a mental note to give her body a tuneup this week.

She checked the clock on the wall, even though she was always aware of the time. She'd have to open the doors in about ten minutes.

The Foote Library was the only one of its kind on Diogenes. It was a fully functional library, of course, but it was also a museum piece. An oddity. An anomaly. Every book here was freely available in digital form, yet you still had people come in to browse, explore, and, sometimes, to borrow. They offered many other services to the public here, but the library was what put it on the map. It was the equivalent of a horse and buggy ride in an age of starships.

They also offered services that were not so public. The Order kept one of their digital Bochords deep underground here, which Violet had dubbed Alexandria, and served as its custodian and guardian. In exchange, she had access to pretty much whatever she wanted from the Order. Unlimited memory storage, spare bodies, and a ship that a proxy flew.

Of course, the shipborne version of her thought of herself as the primary and the library as the proxy. Both were correct. Whenever her proxy returned, they merged their memories, which briefly made them the same person. Then they flipped a coin to see which would go off on new adventures while the other stayed behind. It sounded weird to organics, but for her it had become quite normal.

That reminded her, the Artificial Being Amendment was *finally* going to reach the High Senate this week. If it passed, she could legally return to the Protectorate. Not that she hadn't a thousand times before, but it would be nice not to have to hide who she was.

In the Audiens Independent Sector, she was already legally recognized. Audiens was outside the Protectorate, and the bureaucracy that was taking centuries to recognize things like NDTs as something distinct from AI didn't exist here. The local government had settled the matter of her personhood in a couple of months.

And so, she was free to run the library as herself, without coming up with some scheme where she faked her death every thirty years, like in *Highlander*.

The question she got asked most often about the library was, why? Why did this place even exist?

The short answer was, to honour a friend. But for some, she would take them by the hand and lead them to a seemingly random aisle—though the truth was she'd already run a background check on them and had a handle on what their interests were—then pulled out a book and handed it to them.

"Open it."

They would, and nine times out of ten she saw a change come over their face. Every letter and every image would be the same if they brought that book up on their tablet, but there was one thing on those pages that couldn't be found digitally. Fingerprints.

Not literal fingerprints, mind you. Rather, the instinctive knowledge that this book had been held by others. Appreciated by others. A page fold here, a smudge there, a blasphemous dog-eared corner, the texture of paper, slightly smoother where it had been held repeatedly. There was a connection there to all who had come before, and the knowledge that those who came next would sense a part of you.

Nine times out of ten, they understood. Even if they didn't decide to check the book out, they would nod and thank her.

A thousand years ago, Violet had been all about video entertainment. She and Moss had had countless debates about which format was better until, eventually, she'd had a revelation.

It didn't matter. Or, more accurately, it *all* mattered. Whether it was in print or on screen or in person might change how the story was told, but ultimately, what endured was the story itself.

And here, she had all the stories.

She referred to the physical collection as her "sampler platter," based on the local interests of the people in the city. If someone wanted a physical copy of something she didn't have, she could make a hardback copy in about a minute.

But as big as the Foote Library was, it couldn't hold everything.

Alexandria was another matter. The Bochord *did* hold everything—for a given value of everything. The Order had a scale to determine the impact any form of media had, locally, regionally, globally, and beyond. Anything that reached the tipping point on one of those scales got copied and sent here, and to all the other Bochords.

And so the library held not only everything written or drawn, but all the shows stored in digital form, all the musicals and plays performed on virtual stages, all the poems read by the greatest speakers of their time, all the paintings and sculptures.

Every story. Every medium. Including the oldest of them all.

The clock chimed, and Violet went to open the front doors. Already there were people waiting to be let in. Some old people, her current regulars that she'd known since they could walk, some curious tourists from the Protectorate getting an early start to their sightseeing day, and several young kids who raced each other to get to the children's section, hoping to snatch their favourite books before someone else did.

An old Terran woman, Gilean, came and over and shook hands with her. "How are you today, dearie?"

"Shoulder's a bit stiff, but that's all. How about you, Gily?"

The woman leaned back and there was an audible pop. "Medical science can only do so much for us meatbags."

They chuckled. It was a running joke between them. Gilean was far older than you would expect. But that was another story.

"New tribe of Doleph set up camp near my beach home," said Gilean. "Came to say hello. Want to set up some trade, fish for wood kind of thing."

Violet was thrilled. "That's great! Can you introduce me?" She'd been collecting the stories of the dolphin-analogs for years now, and every tribe's stories had interesting differences.

"Already working on it." Gilean looked towards where the kids had run off. "You shouldn't keep them waiting too long, you know."

"I know. By the way, I got some new releases in last night. Set aside a few I thought you like in the usual place."

Gilean smiled. "Thanks, dearie."

She left Violet to ponder her effective immortality for the billionth time, and shrugged it off just as quickly. It was always hard to say goodbye, but there were always more hellos to come. What mattered was what you carried forward with you.

Violet went to children's area, where a large Diogenean oak stood. It wasn't artificial. Violet had planted it when the library was first built, and it now rose to the domed glass ceiling three stories up. Its thick roots had buckled and gnarled in a way that looked wild, but had been entirely planned, creating a kind of nook at its base that looked like an armchair. They had to keep the temperature in the room constant, though, or it would try to leave.

The kids, no two seemed to be from the same species today, all looked to her expectantly. But there was a ritual to these things. Those who had been here before knew what to do, and those who were new would now learn.

She scowled at them. "What?"

One of them, Leabhar, perhaps her most fierce disciple, said, "Are you going to tell us a story?"

"It's too early. Come back later."

"Please!"

"Maybe after lunch."

"*Please!*"

Violet crossed her arms. "Give me one good reason why I should."

Another kid named Hon said, "Because if you don't keep telling stories, people forget."

Violet humphed. "Well, can't have that, can we?"

At this library, they had every story. Every medium. Including the oldest of them all.

Violet went over to the tree and sat in the nook. She didn't lounge in it, but rather perched, as if at any moment she might leap off or climb into its branches. To the kids' eyes, she had become a wild thing, a fae creature, a mischief maker.

A storyteller.

"So, what story should I tell you today? Hmmm... I know."

The children gathered round, and she leaned forward, so they all felt included in her little conspiracy.

"Let me tell you a *true* story about Ranger M."

Ready for more of Moss's pretty confusing backstory?

Maurice Foote recalls what he did in his complicated life after death in this **free** novella.
Download it today at http://noahchinnbooks.com/thingsgotworse/

About the Author

Noah Chinn was born in Oshawa, Ontario, and had never quite forgiven it for that. Shortly after university he moved to Tokyo, Japan, where he taught English for three years—yet somehow barely managed to learn a word of Japanese.

After that, he moved to London, England to make it as a writer. Unfortunately, the closest he came to literary success was working at several bookstores—each of which mysteriously closed down after his stay.

He now lives in Vancouver with his unbelievably patient and supportive wife, Gillian, and a ferret.

He tends to wear a hat.

You can find out more about his peculiarities and upcoming releases by visiting his website: NoahChinnBooks.com

You can also learn more about him on Bookbub and on Facebook.

He even has a comic strip called Fuzzy Knights, which you can find on his website. It features the most unusual (and fuzziest) group of roleplayers you've ever come across.

<u>Also by Noah Chinn</u>

The Professional Tourist
A G**damned Love Story
Trooper 4
Last Dance at the Kitten Club

Get Lost Saga
Lost Souls
Lost Cargo
Lost Lives

The James and Lettice Cote Mysteries
Getting Rid of Gary
The Plutus Paradox

Lauren Smith and Noah Chinn
Cyborg Genesis
Across The Stars

www.ingramcontent.com/pod-product-compliance
Ingram Content Group UK Ltd.
Pitfield, Milton Keynes, MK11 3LW, UK
UKHW040748060225
454761UK00004B/163

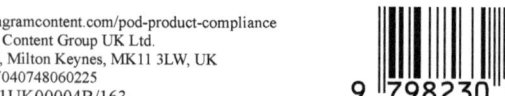